# BLOOD FEUD

## ANNA SMITH

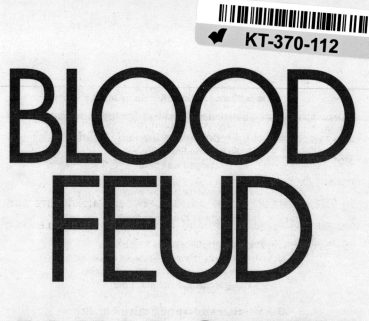

Quercus

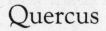

First published in Great Britain in 2018 by

Quercus Editions Ltd
Carmelite House
50 Victoria Embankment
London EC4Y 0DZ

An Hachette UK company

A CIP catalogue record for this book is available
from the British Library

PB ISBN 978 1 78648 652 3

10 9 8 7 6 5 4 3 2 1

Typeset by Jouve (UK), Milton Keynes

Printed and bound in Great Britain by Clays Ltd, St Ives plc

# BLOOD
# FEUD

Anna Smith has been a journalist for over twenty years and is a former chief reporter for the *Daily Record* in Glasgow. She has covered wars across the world as well as major investigations and news stories from Dunblane to Kosovo to 9/11. Anna spends her time between Lanarkshire and Dingle in the west of Ireland, as well as in Spain to escape the British weather.

Also by Anna Smith

*The Dead Won't Sleep*
*To Tell the Truth*
*Screams in the Dark*
*Betrayed*
*A Cold Killing*
*Rough Cut*
*Kill Me Twice*
*Death Trap*
*The Hit*

For Mags, Eileen and Ann Frances,
and some ridiculously good times.

'The most effective way to do it,
is to do it.' Amelia Earhart

# PROLOGUE

*Glasgow*

Mickey Casey wasn't even on edge. He was that cocky. Untouchable, he thought he was – always did, even when they were kids and he was up to his arse in trouble. Frankie Martin looked across the table at his oldest friend, watching the way he preened himself, pushing back his slicked dark mane even though there wasn't a single waxed-to-perfection hair out of place. That was Mickey – handsome bastard that he was. His impeccable midnight blue suit fitted his muscular frame like a second skin, the crisp white shirt and pale blue polka dot silk tie giving him the look of a successful city trader. Which in some ways he was, when you came to think of it. The markets went up, they went down, and if you were smart you could control whichever way they moved. Winner takes all. It didn't matter whether you were a trader shifting shares in oil, or a gangster moving cocaine or heroin. The stakes were as high for both, and those with the biggest balls never, ever lost. The shallow graves were littered with the failures. And Mickey Casey always vowed he would never be one of them. He glanced at his gold Rolex watch, beckoned the waiter across and ordered a glass of red wine. Frankie declined. Just coffee, he told him.

'What's with the fucking coffee? This is a celebration.'

'Too early yet for me, Mickey. I'll wait till they go.'

Frankie glanced over his shoulder through the window of the empty Italian restaurant in the West End of Glasgow, where the meet had been arranged. 'They'll be here shortly. I'm starving.'

He picked up the menu and scanned it, trying to look as though he was engrossed, even though his mind was elsewhere.

The waiter arrived and placed the glass of wine beside Mickey, who nodded thanks. He put the espresso next to Frankie, who looked up and blinked a thanks as the waiter backed away and disappeared into the kitchen. They sat for a moment saying nothing, listening to the rattle of pans in the kitchen as the staff prepared for the lunchtime rush of customers. The place felt gloomy with its empty tables and shadowy corners. Mickey looked relaxed. He'd told Frankie that this was a day they would talk about when they were old men – the day Knuckles Boyle, the cocaine and heroin king who controlled everything that moved from Manchester northwards, was coming to him to make a deal. To his turf, his town. That was how much clout Mickey had. That was how far they had come. Frankie knew different, but he hid his betrayal well. He'd always been good at that. But he wasn't comfortable in the long silence, and he was glad when Mickey raised his glass and spoke.

'To the Caseys,' he said. 'Top of the world. Nobody's going to stop us now, mate.'

Frankie clinked his coffee cup, and managed to pull a smile.

'Aye. We've come a long way, Mickey.'

Mickey's eyes shone.

'We have.' He gazed beyond Frankie. 'You know, Frankie, I've always felt that niggle of my da kind of watching me down the years since I took over. Like a ghost. Sometimes I could feel his anger, the way he tried to make me feel ashamed for going down this road. Know what I mean?'

'Yep,' Frankie said. 'It was a different world back then, Mickey. Your da couldn't see the long game.'

Mickey nodded, enthusiastic. 'That's what I mean. If we'd done things his way, we'd be rich all right. We'd have a few quid. But you have to speculate if you're going to build your own empire. If we hadn't started doing the coke and heroin, we'd have been steamrolled over by some of the other crews in Glasgow. We'd have been easy pickings – bounced right out of the game. My da just couldn't see that. He wasn't clever enough. I reckon now, if he'd lived to see this, if he could have seen how far I've taken us, that he would forgive me. He would understand.'

Frankie nodded in agreement. And he did agree. Mickey was right. His old man's ambition was to buy a few flats, maybe a string of pubs, and that would do them. But that would never be enough for Mickey. Money was power, and the more money you had the bigger you were. But Frankie knew that nothing would ever be enough for Mickey.

Mickey sipped his wine.

'You know, mate, the business we've done with Knuckles Boyle over the years is what really gave us the base to build on. I'll always be grateful to him for that – but we made him plenty of money too – let's not forget that. But Knuckles, well, he's just not top drawer, is he?'

'It's not how Knuckles would see it though.' Frankie allowed himself a slight grin.

'Of course not. Because he's not that fucking smart. That's why he knows the only thing to do is to come here and deal with me.' Mickey leaned across. 'Knuckles is coming here to me – to my turf – not me going to him, the way it used to be. He knows the score. And when he leaves here today, I want him to be happy and onside, but in no doubt that I'm the big player now and it's me he has to make deals with if he wants to survive. I have all the power now.'

Frankie nodded but said nothing. He felt the shudder of his mobile in his pocket and took it out. He glanced at the screen and put it back in his pocket.

'Who's that?' Mickey asked.

'Some bird. Meeting her later. Getting a bit too attached for my liking though.'

Frankie could feel a little sting of sweat under his armpits and he shuffled his feet, took out a pack of cigarettes. He knew it was time.

'I'm going out for a smoke, man, before they come. You coming out?'

Mickey got to his feet.

They went outside and stood in the doorway. He handed Mickey a cigarette and watched as he put it between his lips. Frankie held the lighter under it, glad there was no tremor in his hand, then lit his own. He took a long drag, holding the smoke in for a moment, his eyes scanning the street, watching for the car to arrive with Knuckles Boyle and his sidekicks. He wondered how many of them there would be. His mobile shuddered again in his jacket, but he didn't need to take it out this time, because now he saw the blacked-out Range Rover coming through the traffic lights.

'That'll be them,' Frankie said, jerking his head in the direction of the car. 'You want to go inside?'

Mickey shook his head, squared his shoulders.

'We'll wait here and meet them. This is my town.'

They watched as the car slowly came towards the restaurant, as though the driver was trying to check it was the right place. Then the window behind the passenger seat slowly lowered. Frankie saw the gun barrel first and took a step out of the doorway – and the firing line. He glanced at Mickey and saw the shock in his face. Or had he suddenly spotted the betrayal? Whatever, it was too late. By the time Mickey saw what was happening, he'd already been hit, straight through his forehead, and he was buckling to the ground, his hand attempting to go into his jacket for his gun but his brain already dead. Then, as he lay on the ground, two more bullets pumped into his body, making it jerk. A crimson pool seeped out of his chest and all around him. All Frankie could hear as he dived to the ground was the screech of the wheels as the car sped away, and people in the street screaming as they ran for cover. He crawled over and knelt beside his best friend. He bit back his emotion. This was not how it was meant to be when they started out, when they dreamed of being top dogs. Now, as he cradled Mickey's lifeless body, Frankie could hear the sirens in the distance. He should run, before the police came. But he couldn't bring himself to leave Mickey. He braced himself as the police car raced towards them. He had to get his story straight.

# CHAPTER ONE

*Six days later*

The funeral was going at full pelt, and the bulk of the mourners were three sheets to the wind. Kerry gazed around the pub, packed to the rafters, as her Uncle Danny led the sing-song, his eyes puffy from crying, his thick jowls crimson from years of boozing, but his velvet voice sweet as she remembered.

The room was silent as he sang about missing the hungry years, when people had nothing but each other, and how so much of that was lost along the way as they made their fortune.

Kerry closed her eyes for a moment and listened to the old Neil Sedaka song, her mind drifting back to the days when she'd sat as a kid at the top of the stairs in a relative's house, her knees hugged to her chest, while they belted out songs down in the living room. More often than not, there was a corpse in a coffin in the corner. They were second generation Irish, and they would sing about love and heartbreak, and missing the ould country, yearning to go home. Though none of them ever did.

She opened her eyes and swallowed hard as she looked across the table at her mother, Maggie, staring into space, her cheeks wet with tears as Danny sang. Kerry watched as her mother nudged her sister, Auntie Pat.

'I don't miss them, Pat. I don't miss the bloody hungry years. They were miserable as sin.'

Kerry reached over and clasped her mother's hand, feeling its warm softness as she held it tight. Maggie had buried her first-born child, Mickey, today, executed by rival gangs in some turf war she couldn't comprehend. All she knew was that they took her only son. Her once lovely face was now etched with the pain of loss and heartache that she would carry to her grave. Kerry knew that in her mother's heart she may not have missed the hungry years, the poverty, the struggling, but at least then they were all alive, her children around her, her husband by her side. The Caseys were top of the heap now, but they had paid a hefty price. I should have been here, Kerry said to herself. I should have been with you all these years, Mum. *I should have come home.*

But it had been her mother who'd sent her away at fourteen, when her father died suddenly of a heart attack. Get out of all this shite, her mother had told her as she gathered her cases and accompanied her to Spain, where she was being sent to live with her aunt and uncle. At the time, Kerry had been heartbroken and bewildered as to why her mother was sending her away, when she'd just lost the father she adored, her hero dad who had promised he would give her the world if he could. But she'd suspected it was because her brother Mickey was now going to be taking over the family, and from what she could gather in the snatches of whispered conversation she had picked up, things were going to be a lot different. Mickey would take them in another direction that would make them rich and powerful and feared. You're better than this, her mother had told Kerry as she'd wept on her shoulder when she'd left her that scorching morning on the Costa del Sol. It wasn't the first time Kerry had been told by her mother that she was so precious to her. Many times she had spoken of how she and her dad had almost given up hope of having another child, after three miscarriages. Then Kerry arrived, she'd said, like a gift from God. She was the golden child. Mickey was always going to take over from her father, but Kerry was going to be different. You'll make something of your life, she'd said. I know you will. And she had. Privately educated in an expensive English-speaking school, Kerry went on to study in London and gained a first class honours degree in law. The world where she'd grown up seemed a lifetime ago, and she would never be a part of that. She was home now, for her brother's funeral – but for her mother's sake, not Mickey's. Kerry had never forgiven Mickey for what he had done to ruin their father's dream of building a business where they would be respected and admired, instead of supping from the same trough as the drug-dealing filth he had despised and resisted. Kerry would be gone in the morning, and her mother knew that too.

'I wish you weren't going away tomorrow, Kerry,' her mother said. 'Could you not stay a while longer? We've hardly had any time together.'

Kerry could see the sadness in her mother's eyes. All those years they had spent apart while she lived in Spain, coming home only for school holidays or seeing her when she came to visit. So much time wasted. So often, Kerry had resented her mother for sending her away, even though she knew it was to keep her from what Mickey was doing to the organisation.

'I know, Mum,' she said. 'I'd love to stay, but I have to get back to the case I'm working on. Once that's finished, I promise I'll come back for at least a month and we'll do things together – you, me and Auntie Pat. We'll go up north, maybe, or down to Ayrshire for a break.' She squeezed her mother's hand. 'Remember when we used to go to Butlin's when I was a kid? The laughs we had?'

Her mother smiled for the first time today.

'Oh, aye. And your dad would come down at the weekend and take us all for a slap-up feed out of the camp. We felt we'd escaped. Jesus!' She sighed. 'You know, Kerry, I blame myself sometimes – for you being so distant.'

'I'm not distant, Mum. I just don't live here.'

'Oh, I know. But you're different. With your education and stuff, your life is different from ours. You're in a different world.'

'But I'm still the same person deep down.' Kerry glanced around. '*This* was my world. I loved Glasgow, my family and friends here. This is all I ever wanted. But it wasn't to be, and maybe it was for the best that you sent me away, because I've done all right. I like what I do in my job.'

'You know, if it hadn't been for Mickey – God forgive me – your father would have made something to hand over to you. Something respectable. Something you could build on in his memory, to make him proud. But this . . .' Maggie shook her head. 'This is not what he wanted. All this time, I've had to take a back seat and let Mickey get on with the business, because I wouldn't have known where to start. But he's gone now. I just don't know what will happen. I know I'm not up to it.'

'But you've got Danny, Mum, and Frankie and Marty. All of them. They're all loyal to you and to Dad.'

'Yes. They're loyal. But the Caseys are now a bunch of drug dealers. '

'I know, Mum.' Kerry didn't know what to say.

Her mum looked at her. 'What about you, Kerry? Would you ever think about coming into the business? I mean,

I know you have another life, and maybe I'm just being a sentimental old woman, but, could you ever come back? Not to this, but make something different?'

For the first time in her life, Kerry could see her mother vulnerable, weak, and it tore the heart from her. She was always so vibrant, so full of life and so driven, especially in the very early days when they had nothing, and her mother held it all together. But now she was getting older, reliant on others. Mickey would always have taken care of her, and she knew that, but with him gone now, there was no figurehead, no Casey to keep alive her father's dream. There never would be. Kerry didn't know what to say, because she couldn't lie to her and make any promises that she knew she couldn't keep even if she wanted to.

'Oh, Mum,' she eventually said. 'I wish it could be different.'

They were still holding hands when the music trailed off; with the noise of the crowd they hadn't heard the doors burst open and the first cracks of gunshot. For the first few seconds, Kerry was rooted to the fear in the eyes of her mother and Auntie Pat. Then everything happened in slow motion. People were screaming, and diving below tables as the burst of gunfire echoed round the room, glasses plinking as the gantry was peppered with shots. It sounded like machine-gun fire. Jesus Christ! There were three masked men shooting randomly around the room.

Then, suddenly, she saw her mother and aunt's shocked expressions, as they were hit.

'Oh, Christ! Oh, Christ, no, Mum!'

Maggie slumped off the chair and Kerry lunged across and caught her as she fell to the floor. She looked up and could see a bloodbath now, because the people she knew were family bodyguards were shooting back, and there were bodies everywhere. She watched in horror as blood spread on her mother's white satin blouse, the big collar saturated. Kerry clasped her hand as she heard sirens in the background.

'Oh, Kerry,' her mother muttered. 'Jesus, Mary and Joseph protect us.'

'It's okay, Mum. The ambulance will be here. Stay with me. You'll be okay.' Kerry could hear herself say it, but she was dazed with the carnage all around.

'Kerry! Don't leave me!' The colour was draining from her mother's face.

'I'll never leave you, Mum. Jesus! I never should have left you.'

'Kerry. I'll never, ever leave you . . . I'll always be on your shoulder.'

Blood pumped from her chest and through Kerry's fingers as she tried to stem the flow.

'Mum! No! Please, Mum!'

Kerry cradled her in her arms and pulled her close, but her head lolled to the side, and she looked up through tears to see Auntie Pat, weeping on her knees. She was clutching her arm and blood streamed through her fingers.

'Holy fucking Christ almighty! Aw, our Maggie. Aw, Jesus no!'

Kerry sat staring at her, tears streaming down her face. They had killed her mother, her beautiful, innocent, precious mother. They'd murdered the only constant in her life. She could see armed police and medics come in through the doors to what looked like a battlefield, with bodies all over the place. She stared into the mayhem, feeling sick and dizzy. Then she noticed blood dripping off her own chin and onto her blouse. She'd been hit and she hadn't even felt it. She'd been conscious of a stinging sensation, but nothing else. A bullet must have grazed her cheekbone. She touched her face and it felt tender. She looked up to see Uncle Danny, pushing his way through the upturned chairs and tables. He fell to his knees, crouched over his sister-in-law's body.

'Aw, Maggie! Aw, Christ, Maggie!' he murmured.

Kerry's chest felt like it was going to burst open and she could barely breathe. 'They killed my mother,' she muttered. 'They killed her.' She touched her mother's silver hair and smoothed it away with her bloodstained fingers. She knew there and then her life would never be the same. Whatever – whoever – she'd been before was over. She would find who did this, and make them pay, as long as there was breath in her body. Every fucking last one of them.

# CHAPTER TWO

From her bedroom in the big sandstone villa, Kerry stood gazing out of the bay window at the thin grey morning. She watched as, now and again, the men guarding the solid steel gates spoke on walkie-talkies, then the gates would slowly open. Car after car pulled off the main road into the driveway, making their way up the treelined path. There was the sound of gravel scrunching under the wheels of blacked-out Mercs, Jeeps and Jags. When she looked across the expanse of clipped garden and lush trees, she spotted at least two other men, bulked up with protective vests and clearly armed, patrolling the perimeter walls. Christ! It had been like a fortress when she arrived three days ago for Mickey's funeral, with all the security and CCTV cameras everywhere, but now it was as though they were under siege. And the fact was they were. She could hear the front door opening and closing and the soft tones of the men whispering downstairs. The atmosphere, the heavy silence was oppressive, and inside she was bursting to scream why it had come to this. Two other people had died, caught in the crossfire at the wake – one of them was a well known Glasgow jeweller-come-fence who had been close to the Casey family for as long as anyone could remember. The other was one of their bodyguards who had just got out of jail after a four year stretch. And there were seven people still in hospital with gunshot wounds, some of them serious. Kerry touched the wound on her cheek where the doctors had put three stitches in last night, and it was still tender. Every time she looked in the mirror for the rest of her life, she'd be reminded of yesterday, of the carnage. She didn't care that the high cheekbones admirers had always remarked on were now flawed. What kind of shit had led to killers coming into a funeral and spraying the place with bullets? Her mother was lying in the funeral parlour, and they would bring her body back to the house later today, when relatives and close friends would gather for the rosary around her coffin. Her coffin. The image brought a pain in Kerry's chest and she was dreading the moment the hearse would pull up outside, carrying her mother in a box. How had it come to this? Kerry never shed a tear over Mickey's death, other than the sadness for her mother whom she could see was heartbroken. Whatever Mickey was, to his mother he'd once been the little hungry kid she'd bounced on her knee, who she'd made the world safe for. But it was because of the direction he took the family in that her mother was now coming home in a coffin. And she could never forgive Mickey or any of the rest of his cohorts for that.

She saw Marty Kane arriving in his black Mercedes, and as he stepped out of the car in his navy cashmere coat, his breath steaming in the cold, she saw him look up through the rimless glasses that gave him the look of the distinguished professional he was. They exchanged glances, and he pulled his lips back a little in a sympathetic grimace. He was older now, much older, more like an ageing, loved great-uncle who had always been pragmatic and considerate. He had been her father's best friend, and the family lawyer for thirty years, and he was the most trusted of all. Marty had called her last night as she lay in her bedroom drifting in and out of consciousness, watching the day turn from light to dark. He had suggested for her to meet with him and a few of the men but first, he would see her privately. She would be glad to talk to him, because she had nobody to turn to right now while her Auntie Pat was still in hospital with a gunshot wound to her arm. Kerry had done all of her weeping alone, listening to the floorboards creak as someone patrolled the top landing of the house checking everything was secure. She closed the curtains, took off her clothes, then went into the shower. She stood under the warm spray, her eyes closed, wishing she could open them and find this had all been a terrible nightmare. She had never known she could feel this sad about anything. She'd been devastated when her father died, but this was like a sword slicing through her heart.

As Kerry came downstairs, she saw one of the men sitting on a chair in the hall. He stood up quickly, as though she was arriving royalty, and she looked at him curiously. She didn't know him, and he hadn't been there last night, but Marty had told her he was posting men all over the house, twenty-four seven. The guard was hard-looking, with thick black crew-cut hair and a broken nose. He nodded when she passed him.

'Where's Marty?' she asked.

'He's in the study.' He pointed to the closed door at the end of the hall.

Kerry walked down the wide hall. The study. She almost smiled to herself. She remembered the two-bedroom damp tenement the family had lived in until she was seven, and now this was where they lived, in this massive six-bedroom stone-built villa in the heart of one of north Glasgow's poshest areas, among the lawyers and the surgeons and the millionaire businessmen. But at what price? She pushed open the heavy oak door and Marty looked up from the long mahogany desk, immediately rising to his feet. He had been at the hospital yesterday in the mayhem, to console her and hug her and promise her everything would be fine. But it never would.

'Kerry, sweetheart!'

He opened his arms to her and she allowed him to

envelop her, holding her close, and she could feel herself fill up with tears again. She swallowed hard when they parted, and she could see the glistening in his eyes.

'Tough days, Kerry. Tough days. But you'll get through it.'

Kerry didn't say anything but sat down opposite him.

'Tea?' he said.

'Thanks.'

He poured a cup and handed it to her and she looked at the table, where his briefcase sat with papers and files stacked around it. He sat back for a moment, his cup in his hand, looking pensive. Kerry looked at him and waited for him to say something. Eventually he did.

'Kerry.' Marty took a breath. 'I know this is the most difficult moment of your life, and I want you to know that I will be here for you any day, any time. You know that, don't you? Always.'

'Yes. I do.'

'Your father and me, you know how far back we went. I knew him when I was a young duty lawyer and he was a bit of a rogue. Before he got involved in any serious crime. Even before his safe-cracking days. But you know something, Kerry? He was a villain, but he was never a bad man. I knew that straight away. Your father only wanted the best for his family. He wanted you to have everything he didn't. Him and your mother – they grew up with nothing.'

'I remember when we all had nothing.'

'I know you do. And now?' He waved his hand around

the vastness of the room. 'You have all this. More than your father ever dreamed of.'

Kerry shook her head.

'He'd have given it all up if he'd known my mother would be murdered like this at their own son's funeral.'

Marty nodded in agreement.

'I know. I know he would. He never wanted any of that crap Mickey got involved in. He would have been spinning in his grave these past sixteen years.'

'I know. And as you know, that's why Mum sent me away.' She shook her head. 'Christ, Marty! I was miserable over there. I hated Spain. I didn't belong there.' She sighed. 'But now? I don't know where I belong. I . . . I just feel . . . Aw . . . so angry! So angry! How could they do this to my mother, Marty? How? How did something like this happen?'

He took a sip of his tea and put down the cup.

'It's been a long road, Kerry. A long story of bad things and dark places Mickey took us.'

'Why couldn't you stop him?'

'I'm only the lawyer. I don't have the power to change things – especially not with Mickey. I didn't have the same closeness with him as I did with your dad. But I gave Mickey my best advice. I told him: stay clear of that shit, the drugs, the people-trafficking. It's all East European gangsters now, so different from when your father was a young man. But it was all about money and power with your brother. Mickey moved in with everyone – a finger in too many pies. It's a long story and complicated, but we'll talk about it. We're still trying to get to grips with why he was murdered, and by who, but information is coming in. It's hard to get to the truth.'

They sat for a moment in silence and Kerry watched as he shuffled papers.

'Listen, Kerry. You need to know the extent of the business. Everything. There's a lot of money. A fortune. Businesses everywhere. From here to the Cayman Islands. It's yours now. All of it. Your mother made a will. Everything was left to you. Mickey didn't even know that. He didn't leave a will, not that he owned anything on paper. Everything was in your mother's name.'

Kerry swallowed. She knew this was coming. She'd known it last night as she tossed and turned in her bed. She'd known the way everyone looked at her, from the men on the door to the people in the house. She was the head of the family now. Her life was going to change. The life that she'd led – the world she'd lived in since she was sent away from here, had not prepared her for a world of violence, where scores were settled at the end of a gun by people who know no other way to exist. And yet inside her right now was a feral anger that somehow made her feel more affinity with the armed hard-men surrounding her house than she did with all the sophisticated figures in the legal establishment where she had spent her past years. She was educated to react to violence and murder by bringing in the police, by letting them chase down the criminals, put them behind bars. But that was not how they did business in the world where she was now in charge. The thought that she might be capable of retribution both frightened and spurred her on.

She sighed and clasped her hands.

'You know, Marty, I could walk away and go back to Spain or London after my mother's funeral and never set foot in this place again. Leave this all to the police to sort out. I could do that. You know that, don't you?'

'Yes. I know.'

She waited for a moment.

'But I'm not going to. So talk to me.'

'Okay. It's going to take a lot of going through, but you're a lawyer so you'll understand and look closely at things in the coming days. It's not for now. Let's get your mum's funeral over with, give it the dignity she deserves, and have some time to grieve before we look at the business.'

Kerry felt that red mist coming up again. She took a breath then leaned forward, looking Marty square in the eye.

'I'm going to tell you something. And you need to listen and understand. You're telling me this is all mine now. I'm in charge, right?'

'Yes.'

'You think that makes me proud? In charge of a bunch of gangsters who sell heroin to kids in the street, who traffic women?'

He frowned. 'Kerry. Look. I know how you feel about that, and I'm the very same. So was your mother. That's why I want to talk to you about making changes. Your father wanted nothing more than to go into property, make everything legit. Your father was no angel. He was a criminal, a safe-cracker. He made money from armed robberies in the early days. But he resisted the moves Mickey was trying to push him into. He raged about it. I know he did.'

'I know that too, Marty,' she said. 'I was very young, but I remember overhearing a conversation between my father and some people Mickey had brought to the house to discuss some business opportunity. I remember there was Mickey and these two guys, well-heeled, powerful men. I don't know exactly what was said that night, but I remember later, my father was furious with Mickey and telling him that he'd humiliated him in front of these guys. My dad was nearly in tears, and Mickey just stood there, defiant as ever. I hated him from that moment. My father died a few months later. I think his heart was broken.'

Marty nodded. 'I remember that. This crap we're in now is all Mickey's doing. But we can make it different. *You* can make it different, in time.'

'Okay. And we can talk about that. But, right now, I only want to talk about one thing. And I need you to bring in here the people you know I can trust.' She paused. 'Somebody betrayed us yesterday and allowed this murdering orgy to take place. Someone betrayed my mother yesterday, and my father.' She shook her head. 'To hell with Mickey! Those're the kind of people our Mickey lived with. And you know what? God forgive me but he got the death he deserved for someone who sells junk to kids. But my mother?' She tightened her mouth to stop her lip quivering. 'This isn't over.'

Marty looked at her. 'I know you're burning with anger right now.'

Kerry put her hand up to stop him.

'Marty, I'll be burning with anger till the day I die. I'll see all this paperwork later. But listen now. Get me your most trusted guys in here: Danny, John, Jack – those guys. The old ones. The people I can trust. People in the know.'

'But why?'

'I told you. A turf war, the papers will be calling this. Well, this war isn't over. I don't know who these guys are who got people to come in and kill innocent mourners at my brother's funeral, but it doesn't end here. It's just beginning. It will end when every one of them is dead and their business ruined. That's all I'm going to do right now.'

'But, Kerry – you have lived a different life.'

'Well, I live this one now,' she snapped. 'I'm a quick learner. So bring me the people I can trust, and get me some intelligence on who I go for first. That's all I ask.'

'Who you go for? It's not a playground brawl, Kerry.'

'No. And I'm no kid, Marty. Just get me the people and we'll meet here later this afternoon. Before my mother comes home.' She could feel herself shaking, and her voice quivering a little. 'I want my revenge, Marty. Even if Mickey was an asshole who brought us all to this day. And if we can afford to live in the splendour we do now and have all the money you're going to tell me I have, then we can afford to find out exactly what happened. No matter what it takes, what it costs, I'm taking all of them down, one by one.'

Kerry stood up on shaky legs.

'We'll meet back here at three,' she said as she turned and left.

Marty stood up and she could feel him watching her all the way out of the room.

# CHAPTER THREE

There were five of them seated around the kitchen table when Kerry walked in. They got to their feet, and in turn came forward to embrace her. Uncle Danny was first, and as he hugged her close she could feel his pain next to hers. He said nothing, but his face had somehow lost that easy charm and twinkle he was famous for. She'd always known there was a darker side to Auntie Pat's husband. A brutal, angry side that he never displayed to his family or children, but her mother had told her it was there, and that he was not a good enemy to have. Next was John O'Driscoll. She remembered John from when she was a teenager and he was in his thirties, already moving up the ranks with his father. He had always been quiet, watchful, with the blackest eyes expressionless under dark heavy brows. He never had much to say about anyone or to anyone. There was something of the quiet danger about him. But he would do anything that was required of him by Tim Casey or anyone belonging to him.

'I'm so sorry for your loss, Kerry,' was all he said as he embraced her.

Jack Reilly stood with his hands in his pockets, waiting to greet Kerry. He must be in his forties now, she thought, a snapshot of him as a young man in the firm flashing up in her mind. She knew that her father trusted him as though he was his own son, and he was the favourite of all the crew. Jack, an ex boxer, was clever as well as handy on his feet and with his fists. As he came forward, part of her was almost overcome by the gentle, quiet respect of these men who she knew were hard, raw individuals whose loyalty was without question. None of what happened in the last few days, and especially yesterday, would break them. They were men of violence. But she could see they were shaken. They had all grown up together, their fathers villains through the years with her father, and the younger ones with Mickey. They all enjoyed the wealth that came to them from the firm, and they never flaunted it. But now, with the events of the past few days, they seemed to be on the losing side.

Frankie Martin stood behind them, his dark hair slicked back, shining in a charcoal-grey suit, ever the sharpest dresser on the block who had always looked like he spent more time at the mirror than anyone. He was Mickey's best friend and most trusted sidekick, who had more or less lived with them since he was twelve. Growing up, Kerry had been a little bit in love with him when she was thirteen, but he was twelve years older than her, and never saw her as anything other than an annoying little sister. Now he looked rich, prosperous, and he was. He took her in his arms.

'So sorry, Kerry. Your mother was a great lady. And Mickey . . .'

His voice trailed off as he broke away from her, and Kerry looked him in the eye. The uncomfortable truth was that he was part of the problem, because he was Mickey's closest associate. He must have been involved in everything Mickey was doing, so he was part of what had brought them all to this. He was with Mickey when he was murdered, but he had told everyone he had no idea who had shot him. It had been a routine business meeting, he said. Someone must have ordered the hit. They had plenty of enemies – it went with the territory. That was all Kerry was told by Danny, but her gut told her there was more to it. But she had asked Marty for the most trusted people, so here they were.

Marty remained seated at the table, and Kerry sat down next to him as they all took their places. She waited to see if Marty was going to speak, but he looked at her. She was in charge now, and all of the faces were waiting for her. She cleared her throat.

'Gents. Thanks for your condolences.' She self-consciously touched her face. 'These are hard days, the hardest of my life. But I know they're hard for all of us. I need everyone, now more than before, to be tighter than ever with each other, with everyone they work with. Do you understand what I mean?'

She glanced at each of them momentarily and they nodded in agreement. She turned to Marty.

'Marty and I had a talk this morning about the business, and I'm dealing with some things, looking over papers and stuff. As you know, I've been away.' She paused, knowing they were hanging on her every word. 'This was not my life. My mother sent me away because she didn't want this for me. I have lived a completely different life from all of you. That is not to say I don't respect you or understand what you have done over the years, for my father and my family and for the whole organisation.' She swallowed, took a sip of water. 'But I'm here now. And I'm here for good. You probably know I've been in London in recent years working in corporate law. But I've told the company that I'm not coming back, that I have family commitments. My life is here now. From here on in, everyone reports to me or to Marty, who will keep me informed on everything. Nothing moves unless I say so.' She waited for any response. None. They listened. 'But I'm telling you this: there are going to be some changes. I will discuss them when I'm ready, and I will expect the same loyalty from you that you have shown to my brother and father. Because that is what they would expect.'

'That should go without saying,' Danny said, his face like flint.

'I know, Danny. But I'm saying it anyway. I was young when I went away. I didn't know much about my father's business. They shielded me from it. But I know he was a crook, and I'm not ashamed of it.' She sat forward. 'But what I want to know is how it came to this. What has happened in the way we do business these days that people can walk into a funeral and murder people.'

'We live in violent times,' Frankie Martin piped up.

'I know we do. But we are supposed to be able to protect ourselves. Someone let us down yesterday. I need to know how that happened.' She looked directly at Frankie, who didn't flinch. 'Someone let Mickey down when he was gunned down five days ago. So I want to know what's going on.'

'We've been looking at what happened to Mickey, Kerry. We're trying to get to what's behind that,' Jack said.

'Good. Well, that's why we're here. I want to know all of that. And then I want to tell you something else. This doesn't end here. This is only the beginning.'

Silence.

'You mean you want to go after them?' Jack said.

Kerry looked at him but didn't answer, waited to see what else he said. He went on.

'There are some real crazy fuckers attached to the

Manchester mob, Kerry. That's who we think was behind Mickey, and yesterday's shit. We're working on it.'

'Who are these people?'

'They deal a lot with Eastern Europeans. Mickey was involved in that. We . . . well, he was always looking for other investments. Something went badly wrong. The gunmen got away yesterday – though two of them got hit, so that might throw up something of who exactly they are. But so far the word we're getting is pointing to the Manchester mob – to Joe "Knuckles" Boyle's gang.'

Kerry clasped her hands on the table as she looked around at everyone.

'They're going to have to pay for what happened.'

There was a silence and shuffling of feet. Eventually, it was Frankie who spoke.

'Kerry, with all due respect, I think you have to trust us to do this our way.'

'What's your way?' Kerry knew her voice had a snap to it.

'They will pay. In terms of business.'

'That's not how it's going to happen.'

He sat back, almost snarled, 'You talking more carnage here? It's getting like all-out war. I mean. You know nothing about this. It's business. People get killed. People get caught in the crossfire. Can I ask you something? And I'm not putting you down. You're in charge and you have our respect – of course. But have you ever even fired a gun? Have you ever even held one?'

Kerry glared at him, but didn't answer. There was a stony silence in the room, and somewhere she had a sense of the others' unease with the way Frankie was talking. It was as though he'd had some kind of clout around here because he was powerful as Mickey's sidekick. But Kerry had worked in corporate affairs for the past fifteen years, and she knew when someone across a desk from her was lying, or squirming, or hiding something. And she was thinking right now that Frankie was protesting too much. Eventually, Marty broke the silence.

'Okay. We have some things to get through here. Let's look at the Manchester connection.' He turned to O'Driscoll. 'John. What can you tell us? You were down there recently.'

O'Driscoll sat forward, rubbing his chin.

'What I found out from the people I talked to was that there's been some trouble between Knuckles Boyle's family and their rivals in Dublin, the Durkins. The Boyles, as we know, control everything that goes in and out of Manchester, and a lot of what comes up here. The Durkins were told they can shift some gear in Marbella, but everything has to go through Knuckles initially for discussion and agreement. But old man Durkin has retired, taken a back seat, and his son Pat Junior is running the show, and by all accounts he's just taking liberties. So that's when the rough stuff started. The Durkins have got some serious artillery on the go there. They do a hefty gun-running operation and deal with the London mob – the Hills. Mickey got us involved in that, and it spiralled from there.'

'We know a bit of that, John,' Marty said. 'But we still have to find out what pushed the button so that Mickey got taken out the way he did. Something must have happened. There was no warning came here; not to me, not to any of us.'

'And I was there, as you know,' Frankie said. 'It was a meeting that should have made us good money. I have no idea why it went down the way it did.'

Nobody spoke. Kerry let the silence hang, and studied the faces of everyone around her, not really sure what she was looking for, but knowing she would recognise it if there was even a flicker.

Then she saw it. It was in the face of Frankie Martin. She stared at him, willing him to look at her, but he didn't. None of the rest of the men around the table showed any real suspicion of him, or if they had, then they were hiding it from her. But from that moment, Kerry knew what she had to do next.

# CHAPTER FOUR

Sharon Potter was scheming. It occurred to her that she might have been scheming for a very long time, without being really aware of it. But it was only the last couple of days that it began to really grip her that she should start thinking about putting her plan into action, finding a way out. She lay next to Joe 'Knuckles' Boyle in their super-king size bed, far enough away from him that she didn't have to catch the stink of last night's stale booze wafting out of his gaping mouth. She watched his chest rise and fall as he breathed steadily in a deep, snoring sleep, his puffy man-boobs circled with spidery, greying curly hair. She felt a twinge of disgust, remembering last night, when she'd pre-tended to be asleep as he'd come in pissed, and she'd heard him stepping out of his clothes and padding barefoot on the marble floor across the room to slip in beside her. He hadn't even had the decency to take a shower, and she could smell the perfume on him as he flopped into bed and flaked out. Bastard. Sixteen years they'd been together. Sixteen bloody years, of lying for him when the heat came close, covering his tracks and watching his back, visiting him in jail when he was doing time. And now it came to this. A younger woman. She wouldn't have been the first by any stretch, and Sharon knew that. But this one seemed to have her nails dug deep into him. She hadn't even had the dignity to be discreet as she'd fawned all over him last night right in front of her nose.

Sharon slipped out of bed and pulled on her cobalt blue silk Chanel bath robe and walked out of the room. He would sleep till midday with the blackout blinds shielding him from the blinding Costa del Sol glare. It was already eight in the morning, and the sun was splitting the road, the heat rising in the distance as she went out to her terrace, where she stood surveying the blue of the ocean twinkling in the early morning sun. She picked up a packet of cigarettes from the table and sparked the lighter, then she drew deeply, feeling the tobacco sting all the way down to her lungs. She'd been trying to give up the fags, but the last two weeks she was back on twenty a day. She took a deep breath and let the smoke out. Then she opened her robe to let the sun warm her body, and stood that way for a few seconds, until she heard the click of the high steel gates open in the villa across the road. She pulled her robe over and tied it, then stepped back out of sight, so that she could see them but they couldn't see her. She watched as the women, five or six of them, young, Eastern European, traipsed silently down the stairs towards the waiting blacked-out cars. They were tall, skinny, typical Ukrainian or Russian girls, escort girls with faces and figures to die for, and all of them had that haunted, gaunt, sullen look. Probably been kept up all night on cocaine to keep the party going. She'd seen them arriving as she'd come home early, having had enough of the dinner-party-come-orgy round at Ted Massey's villa.

Sharon sat down at the white stone-topped patio table and drew on her cigarette, glancing down at her little paunch of a belly above her scrupulously waxed bikini line. No amount of ab exercises or spinning classes could ever turn that into a six pack. She liked her grub too much for that, though she did watch her diet and her drinking. At forty-three, Sharon knew she was no match for the parade of airhead birds who flocked around Joe Boyle like he was George fucking Clooney whenever he swanned into a bar or café in one of the fashionable spots on the Costa. Whether it was the smell of his money or the lure of feeling they were part of the edgy Costa crowd who hung around Joe and his entourage, she never quite knew. It was probably the cocaine more than anything. Most of them were coked out of their silicone tits half the time, and no party down in the port went without a blizzard of charlie racked up on every table. They didn't even bother to hide it. Sharon had been there and back with all that shit long before she even met Joe. She watched these women from the sidelines these days, with their puffed up, pouty mouths, and faces botoxed and frozen, and she didn't envy them one iota. Not their youth nor their figures, and certainly not their delusions that they were actually going somewhere in life. She knew that a few of them worked for Joe's organisation, some as arm candy for visiting gangsters he might be entertaining, others occasionally to accompany a dealer way down the food chain on a drop so that they would look like just another glam Costa couple out on the razzle. Sharon had copped on early that there was a lot more to be gained if she could hook Knuckles Boyle in and keep him. That was sixteen years ago, when he followed her around like a dog after a bitch on heat. He wasn't the big-time Charlie that he was now, and she'd been with him through leaner times, when he was making trips to Spain and Amsterdam to deliver money or pick up drugs. And she'd been with him when he did his time in jail, waiting for his release so he would make a step up, because he had kept his mouth firmly shut when the cops had promised him the good life if he grassed up his bosses. She'd given him a handsome son, Tony, thirteen, away at private school in the Scottish Borders, hopefully learning not to be a gangster like his dad. But the past three years had been tough on her. She always knew about the women, and stood by him nonetheless. She was part of his business, and over the years as he branched out and was given his own turf, she had become a key part of his growing empire. She knew and tracked every movement of his drug operation and bank accounts, and his money-laundering. She made herself crucial. But while Joe admired her and was impressed by her brightness and organisation, she could sense he was turning off from her, for younger women. It was hurtful, because she had loved him once, no doubt about that. Not any more. Or at least not blindly, like she had for a long time. The writing was on the wall, she knew that, and one of these days he'd tell her it was over. But she wouldn't be allowed just to leave – that wasn't how it would work with her. She knew too much. One of these days, she knew, she would be made to disappear. In fact, call it paranoia, but she didn't actually like the way Joe looked at her sometimes. As though he was plotting something. That's when she'd started planning her way out.

Sharon padded through the hall towards the massive kitchen feeling her feet cold on the marble floor, and went to the fridge. She took out the large jug of fresh orange juice she'd prepared yesterday and poured herself a tumbler, then spooned some peach yoghurt into a small bowl. She flicked on the kettle for some coffee, and as she stood listening to silence in the house and the kettle beginning to gurgle to life, her mind drifted back to last night at Ted's house. She'd had a few drinks herself and was enjoying the evening along with some of the other men's girlfriends and women she'd known over here for the past decade.

None of them were whiter than white, but most of them were good enough sticks to spend some time with. She began to rerun the part of the evening that had sparked her interest, and she could still see Joe's sneer on his face when he talked around the table to his mates. The women were at the other end of the table, mostly engaged in chat about TV soaps or clothes – all the usual shite – but Sharon was more interested in the chat at the other end.

'They say she's a bit of a cold fucker,' Knuckles said, looking across at Jimmy Hall. 'I hear she's laying down the law, telling the boys that everything has to go through her.' He sniggered. 'I know what she's needing. I'd go right through her, if you ask me. She's a bit of a darling too, by all accounts. A beauty. What else have you heard, Jimmy?'

Jimmy Hall swirled the big lumps of ice in his tumbler of Jack Daniel's and looked at Joe. 'Just that, really, Knuckles. It's early doors. She's only just stepped in after Mickey's untimely demise, so I guess she's trying to flex her muscles a bit. Her being a bird an' all that. She's going to have to do that to look the part in front of all the blokes, isn't she?'

Knuckles shrugged.

'Suppose so. But she can't be swanning around all over the shop thinking she has any clout outside of that fucking shithole in Glasgow. Mickey didn't run his own show up there, not by any stretch. He was up to his arse with all of the rest of the mob, working hand in hand. In bed with fucking Pat Durkin and his pikey mob, and Billy Hill. Fuck that for a game of soldiers. Not having those cunts muscling in on my turf. So Mickey had to go. The shit at the funeral – well, they had to get a message good and proper.' He sniffed. 'But it wasn't meant to end the way it did – with her ma getting fucking shot at her son's funeral. I mean, I feel bad about that. But they'll have to get over it, and this Kerry bird will have to understand that if she wants to work with the big boys, shit happens sometimes. We can't have her thinking she can move the goalposts. Someone needs to talk to that girl, make her understand how the world works.'

'I hear Frankie's already had a word.'

'Has he? And?'

'It didn't go down too well. She put him right back in his box, she did.'

'What, Frankie? And he took it just like that? Fuck me! He was Mickey's right-hand man. He knows the score. He'd have a bit more clout than that, you'd think. You'll need to get onto him, get him to talk to me. I need to know what's what with this bird. Maybe we should organise a meet with her. Make her get over all this and get back to doing business. What's past is past. But if the Caseys do any other fucking deals with the Durkins or the Hills, things are going to get a whole lot worse for her.'

'Yeah,' Jimmy said.

They were silent for a moment, then Del Brown, who'd

been sitting at the far end of the table, got up with a litre of whisky in his hand and went around the table filling up tumblers. Del was a few years older than Knuckles but they'd come up through the ranks in Manchester together, before fighting their way to the top and forming their own crew. People looked on Del as the brains behind a lot of deals and he was, but he also had a ruthless streak. Business was business, no matter who had to be removed and for whatever reason. If they weren't playing ball, they disappeared. Simple as that.

'Two things here, Knuckles. This Kerry bird. She's just got in from wherever it is – London or some fucking place; her brother's been bumped off, though I don't think there was a lot of love between them – probably disapproved of the way Mickey did business. She's an educated girl. Smart. A lawyer. But she was only back for the funeral. I mean, she wasn't going to have any part of running the family, as far as I know. It would have been down to Frankie or whoever to work things out. But with those fucking idiots bumping off her old ma by mistake, then everything changed. I mean, can you imagine it? Any of you? Your mum dying in your arms at your brother's funeral. That's enough to turn any mild-mannered punter's head. So maybe it's all knee-jerk. She'll want to take charge, but she'll see very quickly that this isn't her bag and she'll fade out the picture.' He glared down at Jack Turner. 'It's your fucking boys' fault, anyway, that she's now running things. I mean, what the fuck were they doing going in like that to the fucking funeral? It was fair game to take Mickey out, but turning up shooting people at a funeral?'

'It was meant to send a message, Del. You know that. It wasn't meant to end the way it did. We was supposed to be firing off a couple of rounds over people's heads. But suddenly these fuckers start shooting back and it's bodies everywhere.'

'What the fuck did you expect them to do? You've got three guys firing off rounds all over the fucking place. You didn't think they'd have bodyguards? Are your boys completely cunting clueless? Why the fuck did you not get the boys just to fire a few rounds at the building from the outside, or into the cars that were parked? Something that would send a message? Make a bit of noise but no bloodletting?'

Knuckles put his hand up. 'Enough of that business, lads. Not here. Not in front of the girls.' He jerked his head towards the women's side of the table. 'Anyway. Right now, they'll not be a hundred per cent sure who's behind it because Pat Durkin or that fucker Billy Hill are just as capable of stabbing the Caseys in the back while working with them. And also, the Caseys have enough on their plate as it is, because there's a turf war going on up in Glasgow between a couple of the poxy crews jostling for more power, so let them fight among themselves. She'll think it was one of that mob who did it.'

Nobody answered. A few nodded their heads in agreement, but Del Brown just sipped his whisky and looked at the table.

At the other end, Sharon heard everything that was said, and she'd remembered Joe had mentioned a few days ago about some sister of Mickey Casey's who'd taken over the firm back in Glasgow. She liked the idea of that straight away, and from what she'd heard here, she liked it even more. Kerry Casey. She was looking forward to meeting her some time.

The kettle pinged and Sharon finished making her coffee, then put it with the juice and bowl of yoghurt onto a tray and carried it out to the terrace. Kerry Casey sounded like a force to be reckoned with.

# CHAPTER FIVE

Kerry had gone over some of the papers Marty had given her, but she hadn't scrutinised them the way they needed to be scrutinised. They were definitely light in detail though, so anything she really wanted to know of the workings would have to come from someone as close to things as Mickey had been. Clearly, that was Frankie – he had been Mickey's right-hand man and would know everything and everyone involved in every operation. But she didn't trust him. Her gut had been screaming at her since three days ago around the table. She hadn't discussed her misgivings about him with Marty, and thought it best to keep them to herself. She had replayed the meeting over and over in her head. Was that really her who had told Marty that she wanted to take out every one of their enemies? Was she the one talking tough to the hard men sat opposite her, their faces managing to hide the shock they must have felt hearing this kind of talk from little

Kerry Casey? The words had come out of her mouth, but where they came from she still wasn't sure. The word would already be out in the city that she was in charge and things were going to be different. How different, she would only know once she got out there and saw the Casey business for herself. She'd decided not to tell Marty about that either. But a couple of the bits of paperwork she had been reading over had jumped out at her, and to find out what was going on, she'd have to go there and see for herself. She sat back in the leather chair in the study and finished her breakfast of coffee and poached eggs, then picked up the phone. She called Jack Reilly.

'Jack. It's Kerry. Where are you?'

'I'm out at the taxi office in the town. What's up?'

'Can you come back in here, get a driver and take me out to a couple of places?'

'Sure. Be there in fifteen.'

She knew Jack wouldn't ask where they were going, and she was sure he would also not tell anyone what he was doing, unless she asked. She'd agreed with Marty that under the circumstances, with not knowing if someone out there still wanted more victims, she should not leave the house without a bodyguard. An armed one. She didn't argue with that.

Kerry dressed casually, in black jeans, ankle boots, a blue cotton blouse and a black leather jacket. She checked herself in the mirror of her bedroom, made sure her make-up was minimal with a hint of lipstick. Then she messed up her auburn hair a little, bringing it over to cover the stitches in her cheek where the skin around it was still a little inflamed. Pale blue eyes stared back at her, and she took a deep breath. There was work to be done.

Downstairs, she got into the back seat of the Merc as Jack held the door open for her, then he got into the passenger seat. The driver, Eddie, had been her mother's chauffeur for the past fifteen years. He turned around and nodded.

'Where to, Kerry? Where do you want to go?'

'The Paradise Club.' Kerry waited for a response, but there was none. She saw Jack cast a sidewards glance at Eddie, who said nothing as he eased the car towards the metal gates.

'It's still quite early doors yet. Only half eleven,' Jack said. 'It won't be that busy.'

'That's okay. I just want to look. Who've we got running the place?'

'McCann.'

'What's he like?'

Jack swivelled his body around a little to face her, a half-smile playing on his lips.

'How can I put this, Kerry . . .'

'Whatever way you like, Jack.'

'Well. He's an arsehole.'

'In what way?'

'I'm sure you'll find out when you meet him – if he's

there at this time. McCann was left very much to his own devices to run the Paradise Club, and to be fair it brings in a lot of money. He takes a fair whack of it, but he pays his way.'

'But we own it, right? The building, I mean?'

'Yeah. Of course.'

'So if he's such an arsehole, why did Mickey and Frankie let him run it himself, as if it's his place?'

He sighed. 'Not sure. It's a place I never go into. So I've no idea really. I only see him from time to time if he's out and about in the town.'

Kerry didn't want to ask any more. She'd see for herself soon enough, now that the Mercedes was turning up the side road off Sauchiehall Street and into the area where the Paradise Club nestled between a bar and a row of shops. Kerry looked out of the window at the neon sign of bright yellow with a champagne cocktail glass with neon sparkles coming out. It couldn't really be much tackier.

'Let's go.'

Eddie and Jack exchanged glances again, as Kerry got out of the car.

Jack pressed the buzzer once on the side of the building and the main door clicked open. He walked in first, with Kerry behind him. Immediately, the smell hit her: perfume, the steamy smell of cigars and grubby couches. She could feel her feet sticking to the filthy carpet. They walked into the reception where a skinny girl sat behind a leopard-skin patterned Formica unit. Jack nodded to her. She glanced at Kerry but didn't say anything, and Kerry was hoping Jack didn't introduce them.

'McCann in?'

The girl's eyes darted nervously.

'Er . . . yes. He's in his office. Will I buzz him through? I . . . maybe I should buzz him.'

Jack put his hand up. 'No. Don't buzz him.'

Jack jerked his head for Kerry to follow him and they walked along a hallway. Glancing through an open door off the hall she could see some scantily clad women who at a glance looked Eastern European. Two of them were crying. Then, as they approached McCann's office at the end, they could hear a woman sobbing.

'No. Please, Mr McCann. I sorry.' Then a squeal and a thud.

Jack shook his head and blew out a frustrated sigh. 'Fuck!'

Kerry said nothing as he put his hand on the door and pushed it. She hoped her mouth hadn't dropped open when they stepped inside. She could see a man pistol-whipping a young woman on the head. Blood streamed out of her forehead and her eye was puffed up. A fat minder stood at the side with a shocked look on his face when he saw Jack.

'McCann!' Jack spat. 'What the fuck are you doing?'

McCann turned around, surprised, with the wild eyes of a man who'd had a recent coke hit.

'She's a fucking thief, Jack! Stole two hundred quid from a punter's wallet.'

'Fuck's sake! You don't do shit like that! You don't hit the birds!'

McCann looked at Kerry and she could see the colour drain from his face.

'You haven't met Kerry, have you?'

Kerry stared at him, her stomach sick with rage and anger at this piece of shit. She took a step forward and he stretched out his hand.

'Hello, Kerry. Sorry you had to see this . . . B-But—'

Kerry put her hand out. 'Give me the gun.'

McCann looked from her to Jack. The girl stood, before sliding down the wall, legs buckling. He handed Kerry the gun.

In one seamless movement, Kerry pistol-whipped him four times as hard as she could, the blood pumping from his shocked face. She had to stop herself hitting him another time because right now she wanted to beat the shit out of him until his face was a bloody pulp. She stood, her blood cold with an anger that she didn't until now even know she was capable of. She had never hit anyone in her life. Ever. McCann writhed in pain, crouched over his desk.

'Fuck's sake! Jack! What the fuck!'

Then Kerry found herself turning the gun and holding it to his head.

'You listen to me, you filthy parasite bastard. Get your fat arse out of here now. You're out. End of.'

McCann's lips quivered but nothing came out. Then he looked at Jack.

'Jack . . . Jack! Tell her, for fuck's sake!' He grabbed his phone from the desk. 'I need to phone Frankie! Fucking hell! What is this?'

Kerry knocked the phone out of his hand to the floor.

'Are you deaf as well as a complete prick? Get out of here now. While you still can . . .' She pointed the gun at him.

The girl on the floor looked up at Kerry but didn't move.

McCann grabbed his wallet from the desk and picked up his phone. He scurried to the door and disappeared.

Kerry turned to the fat boy. 'You. What's your name?'

He put his hands up. 'B-Brian. This is nothing do with me, miss. Honest. I only was asked to tell the girl to come in. I work the front door mostly.'

Kerry turned to Jack, who was looking at her with a shocked expression.

'Jack. Can you wait outside until I come out? This place is closed as of now. Tell the girl in the reception I want to know the names and nationalities of all those girls. Get her in here.'

Jack nodded slowly. He didn't ask any questions, but reached down a hand to the girl on the floor, helped her up and walked her out of the door, jerking his head to the fat guy to come with him.

Alone in the office, Kerry gazed around at the grubby

surroundings, the brown two-seater sofa that looked stained and filthy, the high-backed bamboo chairs against the wall. She went behind McCann's desk, cluttered with paper cups and dirty cutlery, papers and rubbish. She pulled open the top drawer and lifted out the pencil tray. Underneath were a few wraps of coke. She lifted one of them out, examined it, then put it back in. She looked closely at the desk and saw a CD, and on closer inspection she could see powdery remnants of a snorted line. Useless bastard, probably in here like some kind of king of the road, coked up, using and abusing the women. She hadn't even really examined the paperwork on the sauna and massage parlour, but on the surface it was making money. A lot of money. Whether it really was or not was a different story. It was all money-laundering. But she wanted to know if McCann had been using it for anything else – maybe he was bringing drugs in and dealing on his own. There was a gentle knock at the door.

'Come in, Jack,' she said.

The door opened and Jack came in, turning to the girl in the doorway and telling her to wait a moment.

'Kerry,' he lowered his voice, 'McCann is a vicious bastard, but he's also dangerous. He won't take this lying down. He'll already be out there trying to do damage.'

Kerry looked at him. 'Okay. Get someone on it, Jack. I want to know what he's up to, where he goes, who he talks to. If he's that dangerous, then we'll have to deal with him.'

Jack took his phone out of his pocket.

'But give it five minutes, till I talk to that girl. Bring her in.'

Jack opened the door and beckoned the ashen-faced receptionist in.

Kerry came out from behind the desk and stood in front of her. She could see the girl was terrified.

'What's your name?'

'Karen.' Her voice was a whimper.

'Karen who?'

'Karen Watson.'

'How old are you, Karen?'

'Twenty-three.'

Kerry watched as she sniffed and ran the back of her hand across her nose, which was a little red.

'Do you do coke?'

'Whit?'

'You heard me. Answer the question.'

The girl swallowed hard.

'No.' She sniffed. 'Well. I've done it a few times. But I've got the cold just now.'

Kerry looked at her, then at Jack, and sighed.

'Don't bullshit me, Karen. I'm really not in the mood.'

'I'm telling the truth. I smoke some weed. I've done coke. But not for ages. I've no money. And I don't like it much anyway. I just like weed.'

'How did you get a job in here?'

'I . . .' She hesitated. 'I used to be the cleaner. I did all the towels and the stuff like that – you know, from the punters. I did all that.'

The idea of piles of sweaty towels discarded by fat punters paying for sex disgusted her.

'And McCann made you the receptionist? Just like that?'

'I've only been looking after the reception for a month. I mean . . . I don't know anything that goes on. Honest. I just needed a job.' Her lip began to tremble. 'I've got two weans. The hours were all right. Mostly the afternoon. I . . . I needed a job.'

'How much did you get paid?'

'A hundred and fifty a week. Sometimes I got tips from the punters.'

'Did McCann ever ask you to do anything? I mean with the punters?'

She swallowed. 'Aye.' Her cheeks blushed.

Kerry waited a moment, watched her.

'And did you?'

Tears came to the girl's eyes and she looked up at Jack then at Karen.

'Aye. Twice.' She broke down. 'I . . . It was for my leccy bill. I only did it twice. I felt like shit after it. Look, I'm sorry. But I haven't done anything. Can I just go?'

'No. You can't. I want to ask you some more questions.'

'But I don't know anything.'

'Tell me this, Karen. And I mean honestly. Have you ever seen McCann beat any of the girls before this morning?'

Karen squirmed and wiped her nose.

'Have you?'

'Aye. He does it all the time. He's a bastard. The lassies are terrified of him.'

Kerry took a breath and let out a sigh. She glanced up at the greying ceiling and the bare light bulb. What a shit-hole of a place.

'These girls out there. Where are they from?'

'I don't know. Foreign. East European, I heard McCann say. They were brought up here from down south. It's nearly all East Europe girls. McCann got rid of the local girls. Said they were all on smack and he wanted to make the place a bit more glam with glam birds. The girls are beautiful.'

'Are they all using coke?'

She shrugged. 'I don't know. That's the truth. All I know is that they're terrified all the time.'

'Do you know where they stay when they're not working here?'

'Not really. The address might be somewhere in the reception desk. But I think they live in some place down by the Clyde. That new block of flats. Some of the girls work out of there. They belong to McCann too.'

'What? The flats belong to McCann?'

'Don't know about that. But the girls do.'

'How do you know that?'

'I was here when they were brought in. Couple of weeks ago. They came up from Manchester, I think.'

Kerry looked at Jack who shook his head. Enough said here.

'Where do you live, Karen?'

'Easterhouse.'

'Okay. Go home now. Tell Mr Reilly what your hours were this week and how much you're owed. Then give him your phone number. You've been helpful here. But you keep your mouth shut tight about this conversation. You hear me? As much for yourself as anything else. So keep it shut.'

'Is the place really going to close?'

'It's already closed.'

She stood up. 'Okay. I'll need to look for another job.'

Kerry looked at her, skinny, the tight T-shirt barely covering her midriff, the drainpipe jeans and worn trainers. She looked like she needed a good feed and a few nights' sleep. But she didn't know her, and couldn't trust her. How did she know she wouldn't walk out of here and phone McCann straight away?

'Listen, if you're smart you don't talk to McCann. And I mean ever again. Don't answer your phone to him, don't meet him. Just stay away from him.' She looked at Jack. 'Leave your phone number, and I'll see if we can find some other work for you. But you keep your mouth shut, because if you don't, I'll hear about it.' She leaned a little closer to her. 'Because, eventually, I get to hear everything that goes on in this city. You understand that? Are we clear here?'

'Aye. No problem. I'll no' speak to anybody. Honest. Nobody.'

Kerry nodded to Jack as he motioned her towards the door.

# CHAPTER SIX

Maria Ahern watched from the window of her sixth floor council flat as the metallic blue 4x4 pulled into the car park of the multistorey flats. Her stomach dropped. She didn't need to wait until the driver got out. She knew even before he looked up at her with his skinny rat face that he was coming for her. She was two days late with her loan payment – the second payment she'd missed – so the three hundred quid she'd borrowed was now eighteen hundred. She'd been well warned not to go near Tam Dolan, the loan shark who owned half the people in the scheme, but she'd been beyond desperate. It was either borrow the money or take her fifteen-year-old son Cal and go out and live on the streets. She was already working twelve hours a day cleaning offices in the city centre to pay off her daughter Jen's drug debts, but everywhere she turned, her world was falling down around her. She hadn't slept for days, knowing that her Jen was out there, somewhere, in some junkie den, or propped up in some shop doorway on the drag, touting for business from cruising cars. Any day now, Maria knew she would get the knock on the door that her daughter was just another statistic, found up some close with a needle in her arm. Everywhere she looked it was nothing but blackness. She stepped away from the window, feeling her bowels churn. She tiptoed into the bedroom where Cal slept peacefully huddled in a ball under the duvet. Everything she did now was for him. It broke her heart the way he looked at her, knowing he was feeling her pain, her helplessness. He'd taken a job in the car wash two evenings a week and at weekends to bring in some extra cash. That was the only thing that kept them in food and electricity. Everything Maria earned went towards the loan shark. Jen was a lost cause. Despite the drugs Maria had taken her back many times, but after Jen had stolen from her she couldn't have her in the house. She waited, sensitive to every sound. She stood at the hall door, barely breathing, as she heard the lift pinging on her floor. Then the footsteps. The knock at the door was loud, and she knew that all along the top hall, punters would recognise that knock; it would send a shiver through at least three or four of them up to their necks in hock, but they'd be glad it wasn't their door today. Maria braced herself and opened the door. Tam Dolan stood there, bomber jacket, dirty fingernails and hair, and eyes like black dots on a rat face. His shark-thin mouth stretched tight. He glanced her up and down, his tongue darting in and out.

'Tam . . . I-I'm—'

'Fuck up!'

He pushed past her into the hall, knocking some photos off the wall. They smashed to the floor, the glass shattering. Maria felt herself shivering.

'You're fucking late again, bitch. What do you think this is, the St Vincent de fucking Paul charity?'

'Tam . . . Listen . . . Just let me talk . . .'

But he was already pinning her against the wall, his rancid breath in her face, pushing himself against her, and his hand at her throat, pressing on her windpipe, as she struggled to breathe.

'T-Tam . . .'

He put his hand up her skirt and ripped her pants off, then unzipped his jeans. She knew there was no point in protesting. It was either let him do it, or get her ribs bruised.

'This doesn't mean you're paid, by the way. This is just because I can.'

He thrust himself inside her and pushed her against the wall. She stood as he thrust, groaning, and she could feel her eyes well up, thinking of Cal in bed, of her daughter somewhere out there. Christ! If she had a gun she could shoot this bastard right now. Hurry up and finish in case Cal hears you.

Afterwards, he pulled up his jeans.

'That was no' bad for an old bird. I'm going to let you pay

the eighteen hundred. But no more hanging back. I can get a shag anywhere. So you pay next week or it might be some-one else coming to beat the shit out of you. And by the way, they'll no' just be taking your telly. You pay up, or tell you what, that junkie hoor daughter of yours is over into the Clyde. You got that?'

She sniffed back tears, her legs shaking. He turned and walked out, slamming the door.

Cal lay in bed, curled up, his hands over his ears. He had heard it all. His entire body felt on fire with rage. He wanted to get up and knife the fucker in the back. But what then? Cops, jail, the whole fucking shooting match. Leaving his mother alone. Why was it like this for them, for him, for guys like him? There was a time when all he dreamed of was to study and get to university, find a good job. But it was so different now. That was never going to happen. There was fuck all for him in this place with this shit happening all around him. He adored his mum, his big sister was gone, and all he could do now to help was work as a runner for the drug dealers, dropping stuff off and taking their stinking money. His ma would go mental if she found out, but the money from the car wash where he worked four nights a week would barely feed them. Plus, if he stayed close to the scene, he could keep an eye on his sister.

*

Frankie Martin lay in the steam room, staring at the tiny eyelet lights on the ceiling as they changed colour every few seconds. He was knackered after a heavy workout at the Hilton hotel gym, where he'd spent the past hour, pounding the miles on the treadmill, then punching hell out of the heavy bag until his knuckles hurt under his boxing gloves. Hitting the bag helped get some of his aggro out, but his gut still burned. That conversation around the table with Kerry and the boys three days ago hacked him off – the way she'd slapped him down in front of everyone. That was bad enough, but worse still was the fact that none of the boys pitched in to defend what he was saying, even though the fuckers knew he was right. Cunts always resented him because Mickey chose him to be his right-hand man as opposed to the rest of them, who were second generation hands in the Casey empire. Some of the fuckers were only there because their das had been thick with old Casey before he popped his clogs. Sure, they were hard enough, but more was needed these days if the organisation was going to survive and grow. Cunts like Knuckles Boyle, as well as Billy Hill's and Pat Durkin's mobs, were on a different level when it came to success. If the Caseys didn't shape up to that then they were history. How the fuck could Kerry not see that? Frankie had asked as he'd punched the bag earlier. How can she not see? Because she's a fucking woman with a privileged life who didn't have a fucking clue. He was right and he knew it. The

Caseys could be anything they wanted. If they played their cards right, they could be bigger players than just Glasgow. That was the message that had been coming to him over the past few months, but it was made clear to him that Mickey was not the man to front the family. He was an asshole, a bullying fucker who didn't know how to schmooze with people like the Boyles and Durkins. You had to know how to do that, even if you were quietly planning to knife them in the back. That's why he'd had to get rid of Mickey. Frankie wasn't the kind of guy to be soul-searching, or feel guilty that he'd organised a hit on his best friend. Fair enough, they'd been like brothers growing up. He shouldn't have been capable of doing him in. But he had to. It was business. With Mickey gone, he was the natural heir – until Knuckles' crew fucked up at the funeral and bumped Mickey's old mum off in the crossfire. Jesus Christ! The old bird had loved Frankie to bits. She'd treated him like her second son, and she'd have been glad to see him taking over the reins for as long as she lived – even though she'd always made noises that one day the Caseys would be legit. She had been clueless as well. Mickey and Frankie had paid lip service to that shite, but they both knew it would never happen. Last week at Mickey's funeral, Frankie was genuinely choked, and he had to push away the image that kept coming back to him of the look on Mickey's face the moment he realised what was happening outside the restaurant. But he'd told himself it had to be done. Mickey had to go. Even though he'd talked of making the Caseys the biggest and most feared, the reality was that Mickey was hated by people like Knuckles Boyle, as well as the Durkins and Hills – and he was holding them back. It was Frankie who was continuously building bridges, cleaning up after Mickey had insulted someone or pushed things too far too fast. Mickey hadn't been trusted, yet his massive ego and bullishness hadn't allowed him to see that. It was Frankie who'd always had the easy charm about him, even when they were young guns. And more and more, it had been Frankie who had to step in and stop his best friend from screwing up. But in the long term, he was going nowhere, and sooner or later the rest of the mob, from Manchester to London to Spain, would pick them off. Frankie had needed to make his move. He knew he could handle the heat that came from the execution of a major gangland figure like Mickey Casey. He knew there would be the finger of suspicion because he was there, and yet survived the attack. But that was exactly how Frankie had organised it with Knuckles' mob. And so far, he was getting away with it – even if he did miss the part of Mickey that he'd grown to love like a brother.

As he had watched his best mate being lowered into the ground, Frankie had stood at the graveside with his mind on bigger things. But now, suddenly, he was being shoved to the side, frozen out by Kerry. Christ! He could remember when she was a teenager and used to swoon every time he walked into the room. Now she was strutting around the fucking place like she'd been doing this all her life. No wonder he was on edge. Not only that, he was having to deal with Knuckles Boyle asking questions he couldn't answer. And if he didn't get things back on track soon, the word would get out to the Durkins and Hills that Frankie was being kept on a tight leash. He could almost hear the fuckers chuckling. He sat up, wiped his face with his towel and examined his knuckles that were now as angry red as he was feeling inside. He needed a plan that would make him invaluable to Kerry – at least until he could make his move.

# CHAPTER SEVEN

For the first few minutes after they finally drove away from the Paradise Club, nobody spoke. Kerry couldn't believe what she had just done. It had been as though she was watching someone else pistol-whip McCann; like she'd been dealing out punishment beatings all her life. It went against everything she had ever known. She had never even seen anyone being hit other than what she'd seen in the movies, or scene-of-crime photographs she'd examined while she was studying law at university. But what niggled her more was that she didn't even regret it. She didn't like herself for doing it, but she didn't regret hitting him. He deserved it. What the hell was happening to her?

She lowered the window in the back, taking in a lungful of the damp November air. She should be sitting in some pavement café in Madrid or Valencia, or wherever her business took her, instead of here. They drove up onto Maryhill

Road past the rows of grim tenements under the leaden sky, and out towards the north side of Glasgow, heading back to her house. Eventually, she spoke.

'I feel as though I need a bloody bath after being in that place. What a dive! How in the name of Christ did we get involved in a place like that?'

Jack shifted his body a little, and pulled down the visor so he could see her in the mirror.

'It's just a business, Kerry – like a lot of the other places the firm owns. It's not something we really get involved in, but on paper it belongs to the firm. Other people run it for us, same as the others. It's how everything is – the taxi companies, the property company – all that stuff. Some good places too, but also some shitholes. There's a couple of bars up in Saracen you wouldn't be seen dead in, but it's all about spreading the business around. Frankie would be able to tell you more. And Marty, of course.'

'I have all the papers. I've been looking through them. But I just wanted to see for myself. I'm not impressed. Not at all.'

She was silent for a moment, recalling the encounter a few minutes ago with the East European women. She told Jack to give them whatever money they were due for today and got taxis to take them back to the flat they lived in. That would be closing down too, she decided. Jack had already called to get someone down there to look after things. Take care of the women. Make sure they didn't leave. That in itself was a dilemma for Kerry. She needed to find out in what circumstances these women were brought here. It seemed they were McCann's property, but she needed to know more.

'That girl Karen said McCann brought these women up. Was he allowed to run the place to the extent that he could buy women? Is that how this was?'

Jack was hesitant. 'Kerry, you'd need to talk to Frankie. He'll know more detail. It was all organised by Mickey and him.'

Kerry met his eyes in the rear-view mirror, then leaned forward and touched his shoulder.

'Jack. Listen to me. Right now, I'm not of the mind to ask Frankie anything. You know what I mean? Before I talk to Frankie in any detail, I want to know everything – not what he chooses to tell me. I need to know exactly what kind of shit he was involved in with Mickey that brings girls up from down south. What's going on? Tell me what you know. I'm not trusting everyone, but I trust you. We go back a long way. You were my dad's favourite. My mum loved you like her own.'

Jack's eyes softened. 'I know. I'll never forget those days. Your ma and da were legends. Especially your da.'

'So respect his memory. I'm running the show here. Not Frankie, not Marty, and certainly not anyone from Manchester or anywhere else. But before I make any real moves, I need to know some background.'

Jack sighed. 'I can tell you some things, Kerry, but I'm not a hundred per cent certain everything will be accurate.'

'Okay. We'll go back to the house and have a coffee and a chat. Have you got much on?'

'Just the bookies. I run two up in Maryhill. They're ours, and we've got managers in them, but I like to pop in now and again, make sure everything is going okay. But I'm clear for a while.'

'Fine. Let's have a chat.'

Jack's phone rang and he fished it out of his jacket pocket. Kerry listened as he spoke in one-word answers to whoever it was. Then he put it back in his pocket.

'That was one of my boys. They followed McCann to his house. He must have gone home to clean up, then come back out shortly afterwards. He's gone out to the East End now. To a bar.'

'Who's out there?'

'Pollock. That's Pollock's patch. So the wee weasel bastard is obviously scheming. I told you, Kerry. He won't take that slapping lying down.' He turned around, smiling. 'By the way, I didn't know you could slap people around like that.'

'Me neither,' Kerry said, straight-faced. 'And I'll be honest, I'm finding all of this hard to cope with, Jack. This is a whole new world for me. But I have to get used to it. So if McCann makes trouble we'll deal with him. I'm not having bastards like him anywhere around me.'

Jack nodded. 'Would be no loss to the world if he went missing, put it that way.'

Kerry didn't answer. She didn't know if she was expected to answer. The car pulled up to the house and she got out.

'Thanks, Eddie.'

'No problems, Kerry. If you need anything any time, you just let me know, sweetheart.'

Kerry smiled. He called her sweetheart. Old school. She was in charge of the organisation and the chauffeur was calling her sweetheart.

'You pistol-whipped McCann?' Marty looked slowly from Kerry to Jack, then pursed his lips. But somewhere beneath the disbelief on his face there was a wry smile dying to get out. 'Well . . . I don't quite know what to say to that. I'm sure the podgy little bastard deserved it, but I'm not sure it's what you should really be doing, Kerry. I mean, I know you're going to be hands-on . . . but this is taking it quite literally.' Now he did smile.

'It was a spur of the moment thing, Marty. Call it the red mist rising. I was so disgusted and angry at him beating that poor, defenceless girl. But I can't believe I did it.' Kerry shrugged, her face serious. 'I can't promise it won't happen again. Because if I see some little gobshite beating up on a defenceless individual, then something kind of snaps in me. Don't know where it comes from.'

Jack chimed in. 'To tell you the truth, Marty, Kerry just

got there in front of me. I was going to tell him to hand over the gun so I could batter the shite out of the wee prick, but . . .' he glanced at Kerry, 'I wasn't sure it was what you'd want me to do. So I held back.' A grin spread across his face. 'But I was well impressed, I can tell you that.'

Kerry took the compliment with something resembling a smile then leaned back in her chair, stretching her legs.

'Look, Marty, I don't want places like that or people like McCann being part of this organisation any more. So, talk to me about it.'

Marty waited a moment, then spread his hands.

'You're forgetting one thing. Who we are. The entire business is built by gangsters. We work with gangsters from other patches, here or down south, or wherever. I know you're not naive. There are killers, robbers, drug dealers in our everyday lives here, in every area of the business. That's why the Casey family is at the top of the heap. Places like the Paradise Club, or any other massage parlours, bring in money, are used to launder money, and are useful businesses to have. And on paper they are legit. If we close all ours down, punters will just go elsewhere. We can't afford to be seen to be out of the loop in any area. So you need to think about that. I'm only the lawyer here, and all I can do is tell you how to keep your organisation functioning at the top – while steering away from trouble.'

'The place stinks. It's the lowest of the low.'

'Then you should get it cleaned up a bit. My advice is to

keep it closed for a couple of weeks, get someone to have a look at the other places and make whatever changes of staff or decor you want. Anyway, by this time, the message will have reached the other sauna bosses that they'd better not be ill-treating the girls or you might go round there yourself and pistol-whip them.' Again the wry smile.

Kerry thought about it for a moment. She could see that even though Marty was shocked and was giving her sound advice, there was a part of him that admired her ballsy attitude. But she knew his job was to keep things running smoothly, so that nobody outside their organisation could see there were any weaknesses, especially now with Mickey gone and everyone appearing to be on the back foot. Kerry's way of doing things all her life was to march right in and do it. She had really no fear, when it came down to it. When she decided she wanted to study law – even though she knew her family were gangsters, she went right ahead and studied, and passed with flying colours. Perhaps it was being sent away at an early age to Spain that made her build a self-preservation wall around herself. She had hardened herself to the feelings of loss and homesickness, and she threw everything into her studies and making a success of her life. She knew she could make things happen. In her job as a lawyer she was highly respected, everything her father and mother would want her to be. But now, she was the same as the rest of them out there. A gangster. She didn't feel like it, but Marty was subtly pointing out that this was what she was. Fine. She was a gangster. But she was going to be different.

After a long silence, she spoke. 'Okay. I hear what you're saying. But I want someone to go to the three places, get me all the info on who's who and where the girls come from. I mean, what's that all about? Why are we taking East European girls up from down south?'

Marty said nothing, and they both looked at Jack.

'Mickey and Frankie ran all this, with some kind of swap or something or deal with the London mob – you know . . . the Hills? Billy Hill and his crew.'

Kerry looked at him.

'So tell me, Jack. What do you know? I need you to talk to me about it. Forget Frankie for the moment. Your loyalty is to me. What the Christ is going on? I'll be asking Frankie myself when I pull him in later, but, like I said, I need to know stuff before I do that. So I know if he's pulling the wool over my eyes.'

Jack nodded. 'Okay. Well, as you probably know, most of our drugs come up from Manchester. All agreed prices and all aspects done through the Boyles. Joe Knuckles Boyle. He's top dog down there. But Knuckles floats his prices around a lot. Sometimes he does a good deal – others it's not so good. But he controls nearly everything that comes into Scotland. But Mickey became close to the Hills after he got involved with Pat Durkin during some Marbella jaunt. When he came home, he decided to do things a bit different.'

'Like what?'

'Well, he seems to have done some kind of special deal with Billy Hill and his mob who move drugs through the Durkins – the Irish mob. The deal, as far as I know, is that he got a cheaper rate, but to get this it involved him buying their birds for our saunas and brothels. I don't know the exact set-up, or whatever else is involved. I mean, who knows? Maybe some of our boys get used for bringing drugs in as well. I honestly don't know. But what I do know is that Knuckles somehow got wind of this, and that's how the trouble started. He was raging that Mickey was dealing with the Durkins and Hills as well as him. He hates them and the feeling is mutual. That's what started all the killing – all the sending messages.'

'Why did Mickey change things? What did he stand to gain?'

Jack sighed, looked at Marty.

'Cheaper drugs for a start. But you know what Mickey was like. He got impressed by people like Pat Durkin. The big set-up he has in Marbella, the gun-running and all that. Mickey wanted us more involved in that. He felt there was a bigger slice of everything to be gained if he moved a bit closer to the Durkins and the Hills. And eventually froze the Boyles out.'

'And that pissed off Knuckles, no doubt.'

'Yep. That's putting it mildly.'

'It shouldn't have got so out of control.'

'Well it has.'

Kerry looked at Marty and shook her head.

'Well. If it was easy, everyone would be doing it,' she puffed.

A knock came at the door of the study and one of the bodyguards stuck his head in.

'The CID are at the door, Kerry. Two cops. Man and a woman. A Detective Inspector Burns. They want to talk to you about the shooting. They need a statement.'

Kerry looked at Marty.

'Oh,' she said. 'And there was me thinking that McCann had run to the cops already.'

Everyone chuckled, letting some of the tension out.

'You want me to stay, Kerry?'

'If you don't mind, Marty. That would be great.' She glanced at Jack who was on his feet. 'Thanks, Jack, for today. I really appreciate your help.'

'Always, Kerry. No worries.' He made his way to the door.

'Tell them to send the cops in. We might as well get this over with.'

A few seconds later, there was a knock on the door.

'Come in, please.'

The door opened and a stern-looking plain-clothes policewoman came in, wearing a dark jacket and trousers, looking every inch the store detective. Behind her a tall, handsome figure with close-cropped dark hair and a char-coal grey suit stepped in. He didn't even look at Marty, but his eyes locked with Kerry's, and for a moment she was startled by the flash of recognition.

'Morning, Kerry. Detective Inspector Vincent Burns.' He didn't quite smile.

Kerry stood up, taken aback.

'Vincent Burns? Vinny Burns? From . . . from . . .'

The DI nodded slowly, but it wasn't a great-to-see-you-after-all-these-years nod. His face was like flint but those eyes, piercing blue, softened a little.

'From St Aidan's. Third year. I remember you well, Kerry Casey.'

It was on the tip of her tongue to say *You could have fooled me, Vinny Burns. You broke my heart.* But that would have been ridiculous – it was all such a long time ago. They were kids. How could they be in love at fourteen years old? She pushed the thoughts away, surprised at how much they still stung.

'Christ almighty!' It was all Kerry could say as she stepped forward and shook his hand.

For a moment he said nothing, then Marty stepped forward, stretching out his hand.

'Marty Kane, Detective Inspector. I'm the family lawyer.'

The DI looked at him briefly.

'I know who you are, Mr Kane.' He took a breath, then turned to Kerry.

'I'd like to talk to you about a couple of matters, Kerry.' He turned to the woman detective. 'This is DC Jane Black.

Obviously you'll know we'll need your witness account of what you saw at the funeral, with the gunmen.' His expression did soften now. 'And ... I'm very sorry that you lost your mother in all of this ...'

Kerry waited, wondering if he was going to say 'tragedy', but he looked as though he was trying to find a word that didn't somehow give the gangland massacre any kind of tag of respectability.

'... in all this terrible business. But we want to gather everything we can to track these gunmen down.'

Kerry looked at him, but didn't say anything.

'Look, Kerry, I know how these things work, and your ... your organisation will perhaps be looking to make their own recriminations. But I'm trying to avoid a bloodbath here, and the best thing you can do right now is sit down with me and tell me everything that happened. Everything you know.'

He glanced at Marty who raised his eyebrows as though to say that was never going to happen.

'Well, I can only say what I saw, Vinn—' Kerry stopped mid sentence. 'Inspector. The gunmen were wearing ski masks so we have no way of knowing who they were.' She sat down, and motioned him and the DC to the table. 'I'm sure anyone who was in the room at the wake will tell you the same. Nobody knows who they were, or why they did it.'

DI Burns put a folder on the table and sat forward, looking from Marty to Kerry, a little frustrated.

'There's a couple of ways you can do this.' He looked at Kerry. 'You can say it was a random attack by masked gunmen at an innocent person's funeral, or you can sit down, and let's go over everything you know. I understand you have now taken over the Casey organisation. You are head of the empire, as it were.'

Kerry looked at him. 'As it were.' She repeated his words deadpan.

It wasn't lost on the DI, and she saw a slight flush on his neck, gratified that she'd hit the spot. He shifted in his seat a little.

'Kerry, listen to me. I'm not your enemy. I'm here to help. I've been brought up here from London to work on this, and a whole bigger picture outside of your organisation, which I'm sure you and ... Mr Kane here ... know all about. This is not going to get any better with some tit-for-tat killing spree – that has already been going on in the city with other turf wars. But what happened at your brother's funeral is bigger than this. It's bigger than you, Kerry, or your organisation. Trust me on that. I've been working on these people for a long time, and I know a lot about how they do business.' He paused. 'It's time to rein them in. I need your help to do that. The other way is to create a bloodbath of revenge. And who knows who'll get caught in the crossfire next time around. So, please. Just think about that for a moment.'

Kerry looked at Marty, but said nothing.

'Inspector Burns, I think my client has made clear what she saw at the funeral. She can make a statement about that, of course. But anything else you talk about – outside of this organisation, then I'm afraid there will be no discussion on that. My client knows nothing. Nobody knows anything.'

DI Burns shook his head. He glanced at the female cop who looked bored.

'Have it your way. Okay. So let's just go over step by step from the funeral to what happened in the bar that afternoon.' He nodded to the woman to take notes, then looked at Kerry.

She studied his face, remembered his broad grin, the handsome heart-throb of the third year, who was smart and could fight like a hard man. She recalled their first awkward kiss on the way home from the school dance, and how that summer they made promises to each other. Promises he never kept. But that had been a long time ago. Whatever Vinny Burns had been to her, he was now a hard-nosed cop, and there was nothing Kerry could talk to him about today, or any other day.

# CHAPTER EIGHT

Kerry mulled over documents and papers while she waited in the study for Uncle Danny. Since the Paradise Club incident two days ago, she'd been poring over all their business interests. She felt exhausted. The grief over her mother was crippling at times, and when she'd finally gone to bed at night, she'd collapsed with fatigue, only to waken a couple of hours later with nightmares, lying in bed, staring at the window waiting for the morning light to come. But there was no time for soul-searching or wallowing in self-pity. She was head of the family now, there was no going back. She'd come to the conclusion that she could rely on all of her closest men to have her back at all times, with the possible exception of Frankie. On the face of it, he looked like he was an integral part of the family, Mickey's closest aide, yet he had survived where Mickey had been murdered. There was nothing pointing the finger at him, but then Frankie would be too smart to let that happen.

The word was coming back through Jack and O'Driscoll that Knuckles Boyle's mob were behind Mickey's death and the shooting at the funeral. Now it was falling into place. Because Mickey had been double-dealing with the other mob – the Durkins and Hills – this was the message being sent, that he'd stepped out of line. Knuckles wanted a stranglehold on Scotland because heroin more than anything was big business up here, and heroin was a major part of Knuckles' operation. Mickey had assured him he had it, yet was working with the others behind his back. If Kerry stripped it down to purely business, then she could see Knuckles' point of view. Gangsters ordered hits on rivals, and she knew that if she wanted to be regarded as capable of running things, then she would have to be able to do that. Before she'd watched her mother die in her arms, she could never in a million years have imagined herself able to order the killing of another individual. It went against everything she was, everything she stood for as a lawyer. What she should be doing right now was sitting down with DI Vinny Burns and working with him to bring the killers to justice. *She* didn't live outside the law – her family did. She wasn't a gangster, and she had never wanted to be. She'd spent half of her life living down what her family did, how they made their fortune. Now that she was head of the organisation, she should be starting with a clean slate, bringing in the cops and working with them. But something inside her changed the day her mother died. She'd agonised over it, thought about finding another way to get revenge without more killings, but she could feel herself being driven in another direction. It wasn't just that her rivals would be watching to see her reaction, how she would deal with such a direct hit at her brother's funeral. That was only part of it. She *wanted* to hit back, the way they hit her, and that was what kept her awake at night. In her darkest moments she was beginning to feel that when she scratched the surface of who she'd been for the past fifteen years, deep down she was no different from the men of violence who surrounded her. Perhaps she had never been any different.

She'd instructed Danny to pull out all the stops, call in every favour, to get the names of the hitmen behind Mickey's murder and the gunmen at the funeral. It wasn't enough to know that it was Knuckles' men. She wanted to know who they were, because they had to be the first to go. In the middle of all this, there had been a call through to Frankie with some kind of olive branch being offered by Knuckles, asking if he could have a meeting with Kerry. In your dreams, Knuckles Boyle. When you see me, it will be the last time you see anything or anyone. But that was for another time. Now she would send the message right back by taking the gunmen out. And she wanted it done pronto, because if she spent any more time agonising over it, she would be seen as weak. Danny was bringing in Jake Cahill for the job.

There was a knock on the door.

'Come in,' Kerry said.

She looked up as Danny came in, with Jake Cahill at his back.

'Morning, sweetheart. How you doing?'

'Good, Danny. Getting on with things. You know how it is.'

'Day by day, Kerry. That's how you do it.'

'I know. I'm trying. How's Auntie Pat? I've not had a chance to see her since she got out of hospital. It's been like a hurricane every day. I'll call over tonight.'

'Ach. You can imagine. She's shattered. Your ma wasn't just her sister, she was her best friend. The two of them – some double act. Some pair. She'll get there, though.' Danny turned to Jake, who'd been standing at a respectful distance.

'You know Jake, of course.'

Kerry stood up. 'Of course. Hello, Jake. Thanks for coming. Good to see you. It's been such a long time.'

'Sorry for your loss,' he said. 'Your mother was a lovely woman. A real lady.'

The soft Irish lilt took her back a lifetime ago. She stepped forward to embrace him, and was surprised at the strong if fleeting hug he gave her. It brought a little catch to her throat. Her family and his had gone back such a long way. He'd been in his early twenties when her father died. To Kerry, he'd always seemed a bit of a cold fish, working in the background on some operation, like some kind of ghost. All she knew about the Cahills was that his father was a big friend of her dad back in Ireland, where he'd lived until they were teenagers. There were whispers that Jake's father was a high-ranking IRA man, but Kerry was too young to know anything about that by the time her father died and she was shipped off to Spain. Jake apparently still lived between somewhere in the south of Ireland and Spain. But nobody knew much about him. The only thing she'd been told years ago by Danny was that Jake had earned his stripes as a teenager, and he was only ever called in for one reason. He was the most reliable hitman anybody had. There were always plenty of men on hand to take people out, but to get a clean, efficient job done every time, you had to get Jake Cahill. From what Danny had hinted, his specialist skills were not only used by people like her family, but also by government spooks – or so went the folklore. Nobody knew for sure and nobody ever would. It was Danny who'd suggested bringing him in, now that he knew the faces involved in the killings last week. The hitmen Knuckles sent were just thugs from his crew, none of them with any notable reputation that made them stand out from any other thick bastard who would do their boss's bidding without question.

Kerry motioned them to sit down and poured tea into mugs for them. Jake sat, his hands clasped on the table, an air of quiet calm about him.

'We now know all the names,' Danny said. 'We know how they do business, their phone numbers and where they go on a daily basis. Jake's been on it twenty-four seven. So we're ready to go. He has a plan.'

Kerry glanced at Jake who gave the slightest nod, and for a second looked her squarely in the eye.

'Just say when, Kerry. I'm ready.'

'Thanks, Jake. Where are they? Are they all here? Or back down the road in Manchester? How many?'

He sipped from the mug and placed it back on the table, then looked beyond her.

'Four. Three of them from Manchester. One for Mickey and three for the funeral. Mickey's killer was living here for three weeks before the killing, and he's still here, lying low. Two travelled up after Mickey's hit, but are still holed up here – separately. And one is from Belfast. I know who he is. That'll be easy. But if it's okay with you, I'll do that one last. Once the others are done. It'll be on the same day though. Needs to be clean and quick. Don't worry.'

Instinctively, Kerry wanted to ask names, and other details about them. Even in the midst of her determination for revenge, part of her still saw them as people, not just hitmen. She wondered how old they were, did they have families, children, a mother who would weep for them, the way her mother wept for Mickey? Stupid irrational thoughts that she knew she had to push away if she was going to make any of this work. She glanced at Danny and had a feeling that he was reading her mind. He managed to convey with his eyes that in this kind of matter, it was

best to know as little as possible. Leave it to the professional. It was as good as done.

'Okay,' Kerry said, taking a breath and letting it out
slowly. 'The funeral is the day after tomorrow. I'd like it
done then.'

The words didn't choke her, but they rang in her ears,
and she knew that for the rest of her life she would never
be able to escape this moment. She knew that Jake and
Danny were studying her face for a flicker of emotion, but
she made sure there was none.

Jake nodded but said nothing. Danny looked at his watch.

'Kerry, if that's all you need right now, we're going to head
off. I've got a few things to do and so has Jake. So will we see
you tonight? Come over for dinner. Pat would love that.'

'I will,' Kerry said.

In the middle of all this, she craved the normality of a
dinner with two of her most favourite people in the world.
Jake was first to stand up, and Kerry followed, walking
them to the door.

Jake leaned in and hugged her again.

'You look after yourself now, Kerry. I'm there for you,
any time. I always will be. You understand that?'

Kerry nodded, but again felt the catch in her throat.
They left, and she closed the door, standing for a moment
with her back to it, gazing out at the steady drizzle weigh-
ing down the leaves on the sycamore tree.

*

Across the city, Cal Ahern stood outside the school gates, a cigarette held between his thumb and forefinger. He took a long puff and inhaled deeply. His thin bomber jacket did nothing to keep out the icy November wind, and he shivered. He watched as the last line of cars and school buses left, taking the noise and buzz of pupils with them. Now it was silent, and in the grey afternoon he felt more dismal by the minute. He glanced around and listened to the stillness, suddenly feeling alone and isolated. He wished they would hurry up and come so he could pick up the stuff and make the drop. His stomach was rumbling. If he made good time, then he could be home and buy a take-away for him and his mum as a surprise for tea. Cal didn't hate what he did, he didn't despise the drug dealers or the hard men around them who'd taken him on to do some running. It wasn't that he was comfortable with it, because he always dreaded that his mum would find out, or worse, that he'd make a mistake and maybe get picked up by drug squad cops or some bastard would rob him of the gear he was delivering. He was smart enough and cool enough to know that when an opportunity presented itself, even if it was on the wrong side of everything his mother had brought him up to be, then you had to grasp that chance. Living where he lived, being brought up in the scheme, many of his mates were already into drugs, lots of them smoking heroin. Two of the older guys in his block of flats were already hooked and living rough. He shook his head, and thought of his sister, Jen. The last time he'd seen her she was in a doorway up the drag with some pimp bastard in the background. When he'd stopped to talk to her after searching for her, she'd more or less pushed him away, telling him she was working. Then her pimp came out of the car nearby and told him to fuck off. Cal had stood his ground, and told him it was his sister and he was talking to her and he wouldn't stop him. Then he got a slap, and that's when he made his first move. He punched the guy flat out and he landed on the ground. He almost couldn't believe what he'd done, looked at Jen, as startled as him, then he did a runner. That was months ago. But it got him noticed, and within a week, while he was working at his job in the car wash, he was approached by two men. He could see the pimp with a plaster on his nose in the driving seat. The other men had got out and Cal had braced himself for a hiding. But the older man, well dressed, had simply asked him if he wanted to make some money. Cal had stood, arms folded, told him he already had a job. Call this a job? You want to double your money from time to time, earn more in an hour than you do in a week? Not all the time, just now and again? Cal knew what it would be, but he agreed nonetheless. And that was it. Since then, every two or three weeks, he got the call, meet outside the school gates and make a drop. Usually somewhere in the city, or near the train station someone was waiting. They'd hand over the holdall, and a wedge of cash for himself.

Or it seemed a wedge – but it was only two hundred quid a time. A fortune when you earned a fiver an hour among the immigrants and illegals freezing your tits off in the car wash. He looked up as he saw the car come over the brow of the hill and pull into the side of the road. They beckoned him over, and the back door was pushed open. He'd never been in the back of the car before and he was wary, watchful.

'Get in.'

'What's up?'

'Get in. Boss wants to talk to you.'

Cal stood.

'You're not in any trouble. Get in, for fuck's sake.'

Cal got into the back, the smell of leather and expensive aftershave hitting him square in the face. He glanced at the boss and nodded.

'You all right, son?'

'Aye.'

'Listen, son. The boys tell me you do a good job.'

Cal didn't answer.

'And we already know you can handle yourself.' The big man gave a wry smile and glanced at the back of the driver's head. Cal didn't move a muscle.

'So we've got a good wee job for you. It'll pay a bit more money. Might be a one-off, might be a bit more. You up for that?'

Cal shrugged. 'Depends.'

'What? You getting choosy?'

'I need to know what it is first.' Cal shifted a little in his seat. 'I don't want to end up in the pokey.'

The big man half smiled.

'Aye. Neither did any of us, pal. But you have to speculate to accumulate in this business. So you have to take the chance. You scared of that?'

Cal looked him in the eye.

'I'm already taking a chance every time I do a drop for you.'

The big man took a breath and let it out slowly. He looked impressed.

'Aye, fine. I like your balls, son. But you might want to watch that cheek or you might get your face wasted some day.' He watched and waited for Cal to answer, but he didn't. 'So here's the situation. You take the train to Manchester, make a pick-up, and bring it back.'

Cal was silent for a moment. Anything he'd done before was merely dropping off. He had never even opened the holdall. He didn't know if it was money or drugs or stolen jewellery. He suspected it was money for a drug deal, but he didn't need to know. He just did the job, took the money. This was a bit different.

'So I'm picking up a package?'

'Got it in one. You all right with that?'

Cal sat for a moment, looked at the seats and the clothes and the cashmere coat. The plush interior of the car. He wondered where guys like him ate, where they shopped, where they slept at night in their big fancy houses. They wouldn't be freezing in their beds or hungry, or worried about the loan shark coming up the stairs.

'Yeah. But why me? I mean, don't you have other people to do something like that? I mean a bit further up?'

'Christ, you ask a lot of fucking questions, son.'

'I'm just wondering.' Cal wasn't of a mind to apologise to this guy. He'd been nervous outside, but here, he wasn't scared at all which surprised him. He didn't like him but he wasn't afraid of him, even if he should be.

'Aye. It's a package. All right? We're asking you because you're a young lad and you'll be travelling with an older guy. Makes it look like a trip. Now are you clear?'

'Sure.'

'You'll get five hundred for the job. You take down a holdall, bring another one back. All right?'

'Sure. But I want six hundred.' Cal couldn't believe what he'd said, but he kept his face straight.

'You want a belt on the fucking jaw?'

Cal was silent, stared straight ahead, his stomach knotting. Then the guy shook his head and chortled.

'Right. Six hundred it is. And a hundred of that is for having the cheek to ask. You could go far in this business, son. Or you could get a knife in your back.'

Cal said nothing for a long moment.

'When is it?'

'Saturday morning. Eight o'clock train. Be at the Central Station.'

'Okay.'

The man went into his pocket and handed him two twenty-pound notes.

'Go and get yourself some dinner.'

Cal looked at the money briefly and stuck it into his trouser pocket.

'Off you go.'

He got out of the car and watched as the engine whispered its way down the hill and into the traffic beyond. Cal stuffed his hands in his pockets and felt the crispness of the banknotes. It was a good feeling, having money in your pocket. He ran his fingers over it. His mobile rang. It was his mum.

'Cal, where are you? I was going to get some dinner cooked.'

'I'm on my way, Mum. Don't cook. I'll get us a takeaway. Chinese okay?'

'What, you found a purse in the street or something?'

Cal chuckled. 'No, I got a tip from a guy at the car wash. I'm flush. I'll be home in twenty minutes.'

He hung up.

# CHAPTER NINE

Sharon lingered at the door of Joe's office, listening as hard as she could. She knew he was on his mobile to someone called Frankie, and she assumed it was this Frankie Martin character from Glasgow, who was Mickey Casey's sidekick. She'd met him a couple of times – once in Spain and twice in Manchester. Now that Mickey was dead, and his sister Kerry was running the show, she began to wonder just what role Frankie had played in Mickey's hit. If your best mate and partner in crime got offed by some mob out of your own turf, surely the last thing you'd be doing was chatting on the phone to the man most likely to be behind it. The only talking you'd be doing would be at the end of a gun. Unless, of course, she mused, you were part of the murder plot. She'd no idea why that would be the scenario and had no evidence about it, but she was suspicious by nature and as far as she was concerned it was all sorts of strange that they were even talking in the first place. She listened, pressing her ear to the door, barely breathing, watchful in case anyone came down the hall.

They were in their massive six-bed house in Manchester from where Knuckles ran his empire, after returning from the Costa del Sol a few days ago, and the two of them had barely spoken a word. Knuckles had been polite, but cold, and she had hardly seen him the two days before they left, as he'd stayed out both nights with his new bird. Sharon felt more frozen out than ever, and she wondered if he was waiting till they came home to drop the bombshell that she was getting the heave-ho. Christ. She'd even wondered how he would do it. He was an evil bastard when it came down to business like that, and he had people who could show the Nazis a thing or two about torture. But with her he might do the kind thing, and just put a bullet in her head. Either way, she sensed the end game was coming. She listened again, and heard a couple of snatches of what he was saying.

'What do you mean she hasn't talked to you yet, Frankie? You're the main fucking man there, are you not?'

She listened, wondering what Frankie was saying, but it wasn't looking like he was this Kerry Casey's golden boy.

'Okay. Well, we'll just have to wait and see. But somebody has to let her know that what happened the other day was business. There's no reason why we can't sit down, get over this, and make a promise not to do it again. No more killings. No more violence. Just the business, as it was. But she has to fucking quit dealing with the Durkins and the Hills. I won't have that.'

Sharon heard Knuckles slamming down his phone, and she scurried away and into the bedroom. She put on her jacket and boots and went back down the hall. As she was heading for the front door, she heard Joe coming out of his office.

'Where you off to, Shaz?'

'I've something to pick up from the dry-cleaners. I'll not be long. You hungry? What you want to eat tonight?'

'Oh, nothing for me. I'm going out. Got a business meeting up the city, and we'll probably grab something. Just you sort yourself.'

Sharon stood and looked at him, but he avoided her eyes.

'Joe, we haven't even eaten together since we got back from Spain. And we barely spent any time together there either. I . . . I mean . . . You were out every bloody night.'

Knuckles put his hand up.

'Look, darlin', don't give me that grief, will you? Please. Give me a break. You know what's going on. There's a lot on the go here. Problems all over the fucking shop with this mob in Glasgow.'

Sharon stood defiant. 'No, Joe. I don't know what's going on because you haven't sat down and told me anything. How am I supposed to know if we're still doing business with that crowd if you don't fill me in? What about the gear that's to go up there? You've told me nothing.'

'Look, don't worry. Just go and get your stuff from the cleaners. You don't need to get involved in all this. Just give me a bit of peace. I've a lot on my mind.'

She glared at him, and could see by the way he looked at her that he knew what she wanted to say. That she knew exactly what was on his mind, and that she knew he wasn't going to any business meeting tonight either. He would be with the slag who had her hooks well and truly into him. She thought of their son, Tony, in school, and how they'd break the news to him, because every single message she was getting here from the man she'd spent the last sixteen years with was that her time was up. She felt her bottom lip trembling and it took her by surprise. She turned away before he could say any more, opened the door and went out, tears of rage and resentment blinding her as she walked to her red Mercedes sport.

Sharon drove towards the town, her mind a blur as she tried to focus on her next move. She tried to tell herself that deep down she'd always known that one day it would come to this. She knew the kind of ruthless character Knuckles was when she met him. In fact, the clinical, decisive way he did things was part of the attraction. He was fearless, confident, striding his way through any deals he made; nothing fazed him even when the cops came calling and took him off in handcuffs because someone had grassed him up. He did his time, coldly, calculating his next move, while keeping tabs on the business, and when he came out, the traitor was dealt with publicly so that everyone in the organisation would know never to betray Knuckles Boyle. She'd become more and more involved since then as he'd had to take a backward step in how money was moved, and he trusted her implicitly. She thought this was her, set for the rest of her life. But she should have known. In the past year she'd realised he was tiring of her. That's when she decided to make her exit plan. She hoped it would never come to it, but she knew that it would.

She drove into the car park behind the bank and got out of the car, then went to the bank's reception. They showed her to the vault where the safety deposit boxes were, and once inside, the receptionist left her alone. She had three safety deposit box keys in her hand. She opened the first two boxes, checking the contents. Between the two there was a hundred grand in cash. It wasn't much, but it was readies, so that she'd have money on her when she left. Then, in the third box, she took out the small external hard drive. She had bought it months ago and didn't dare keep it in the house in case Knuckles asked what it was – even though it was unlikely that he would know what it could really do. He left all that stuff to her. She stood looking at it, knowing what she was doing. When Knuckles was out tonight, she would work quietly in the office, copying everything, all material, every damning bank account, every dirty money-laundering scheme, names of directors of companies started up and dissolved then restarted under a different name. Every single area of the business was there. She closed the boxes with the money, then went back out and into her car. Now that she had physically done the dry run, she was ready. But first, she had to make a phone call. In the car park, she sat in the driver's seat and scrolled down on her mobile until she found a number. It answered after two rings.

'Freddie,' she said. 'It's me.'

'All right, chuck, what's happening? How you doing?'

'I'm okay. Listen, I need to ask you a question.'

'Anything. You know that.'

'You know that Casey mob up in Glasgow?'

'Course I do.'

'Yeah, well you know it's all change at the helm now – with Mickey being taken out.'

'Yeah, that's right. He was a fucking idiot, that one. Well rid, I'd say.'

'You know the sister, this Kerry blade – she's head of the family now.'

'Yeah, I know. And by all accounts cracking the whip.'

She paused for a moment.

'Listen, Freddie. I want to talk to her. Totally, *totally* just between us. I mean nobody in the fucking world must ever know about it. But I want to talk to her – to meet her. Can you arrange it?'

Silence for a long moment and Sharon could hear him breathing.

'Sharon. Sweetheart. Are you all right? You know if I do this, and if you do it – I mean meet this girl – well, it's the end of the line. You know that, don't you?'

Sharon swallowed. 'It's already the end of the line, Freddie.'

'Christ, Sharon. I'm so sorry, darlin'.'

'Freddie. Can you do it?'

'Sure. I'll sort it. Go and get yourself another mobile, call me with the number. Don't use your normal mobile for the call. Understand?'

'Yeah.'

He hung up. Sharon sank back in her seat. There was no going back now.

It was nearly nine in the evening, and Sharon got up from the sofa and went down the hall and into the office. The house was deadly quiet. Knuckles didn't go out until after seven, so it would be unlikely that he'd be back before midnight – if he came home at all. She'd picked at her dinner which she'd eaten in front of the television, watching the screen, her mind a million miles away. She'd tried to push away the niggle of wondering where he was, what he was doing, who he was with. There was no point. She wouldn't be able to change things anyway. She had to go about this business in an organised, planned way, devoid of emotion. She took the external hard drive and pushed it into the USB port on the computer. It pinged up on the screen. Then she took a deep breath and began. Sharon had been very meticulous in how she stored accounts and documents. All under names that only she or Knuckles would understand. She used to have to write them down for him, because she knew he wouldn't remember, but she didn't need that. She called up the secret folder marked 'Out', and began. In the first one, she downloaded accounts and bank statements from one of their businesses, then moved onto the next. She kept going until all twelve files were on the drive. Then she opened them and checked they were there. Everything she needed to ruin him, all account details and passwords, encrypted. She ejected it, stood up, clutched it in the palm of her hand and went into the kitchen and poured herself a generous glass of red wine. Then she went into the living room, sat on an armchair and took out her new phone. She keyed in the number that Freddie had given her. He'd told her that he'd passed her number on so that when it came up, Kerry would know the caller. Sharon took a gulp of her wine. Once she hit the call button there was no going back. She didn't need to ask herself again. She was sure. She'd been sure for some time now. She pressed the call button. It answered after four rings, the voice soft.

'Kerry Casey?'

'Yes.'

'My name is Sharon Potter. Freddie—'

The woman cut in. 'I was expecting your call.'

The abrupt interruption threw Sharon a little, and she found herself on the back foot for a second. Then she recovered.

'Thanks for taking my call. I'd like to talk to you.'

'About what?'

'Knuckles Boyle. I have information you will want. A lot of information.'

'His men murdered my brother. Killed my mother.'

'I know. You want revenge.'

'I'll get my revenge.'

'Kerry. I can help you ruin him. Can we meet?'

Silence. It seemed to go on for an age.

'I'll meet you in Glasgow. Tomorrow night.'

Sharon swallowed, surprised. Glasgow. Her mind already working out how she could pass this off. Maybe she'd tell Knuckles she was flying back to Marbs for a few days, meet up with some friends.

'Fine.'

'I'll let you know the place and the time tomorrow.'

The line went dead.

# CHAPTER TEN

Kerry had been undecided whether or not to bring Marty into the meeting with Frankie. Over the years he'd been more aware of how Frankie operated than she could be. She'd also wanted to bring in Jack Reilly, because she'd been impressed by his honesty and loyalty when it came to giving her as much of the background to the saunas as he could. But she decided that to suddenly bring Jack in, as though he'd been given some elevated status, would put Frankie's nose out of joint. She needed Frankie onside, for the moment anyway. No doubt he'd already been told through the grapevine about the scene at the Paradise Club, and he might already be resentful that it was Jack she had called on to accompany her and not him. He would be on the back foot as it was, and more so if she brought Marty into the meeting as well as Jack. So, in the end, she decided to go it alone. She wanted to look into the whites of Frankie's eyes and ask him a few searching questions, but she had to be careful they weren't wild or naive questions, because he was no mug. He wouldn't go running off at the mouth. Kerry would put her corporate lawyer head on for this meeting. She would be cool, polite and friendly, and she was confident she could get the measure of him. But if Frankie thought they had a special bond because she'd had a crush on him as a hormonal teenager, then he would be wrong – even if he *was* more handsome now than he was back then.

She immediately banished any of those thoughts from her mind as she ruffled her hair a bit in the mirror while she waited for him. Kerry had always been aware of her beauty, but she never saw it as something to be used to her advantage. In fact, she sometimes thought it was a hindrance. It wouldn't be the first time she'd felt that, when she was talking to a client or a group of businessmen, they weren't hanging on her every word the way she'd have wanted. Often she'd catch them eyeing up her long slender legs, or her cleavage, or just staring fixedly at her face. She wasn't comfortable with her beauty, but she liked how she looked. Today, there were tiny dark smudges beneath her eyes from restless sleep and worry, and her eyes stung a little from crying so much over the past few days. The stitches where she'd been grazed by the bullet were less inflamed now, but on closer examination it looked like there would always be a scar there. That was the least of her worries. On top of everything else going on around her, she'd got an out-of-the-blue phone call from Freddie Pearson telling her that some Sharon Potter wanted to make contact. Freddie was a go-between, a negotiator for a lot of people, and he was well-respected and trusted, even among rivals who seldom spoke to each other. If he told you something, even if it was to inform you that someone in your circle was betraying you, it was always one hundred per cent true. Sharon was the long-time girlfriend of Knuckles Boyle, so the fact that she was getting in touch with her in the midst of all the turmoil around both their organisations intrigued her. But what if it was some kind of trap, yet another message being sent? That was for another day. She'd been confident and cool with this Sharon when she'd phoned, and agreed to meet her. But it niggled her just the same. Just as she mulled the ideas over, there was a knock on the door of the living room and then it was pushed open. Frankie Martin stood in the doorway, sharp as ever in a dark blue suit with a white shirt, collar open. In the frame of the doorway he looked like a matinee idol, and Kerry had to tear her eyes away from him as he looked right at her.

'Kerry. All right? I'm not late, I hope. I was in the town seeing a couple of people.'

He strode confidently towards her as if he owned the room. She stood up. To her relief, he didn't embrace her, because that would have set a different tone for the meeting. She was in charge here. She was head of the family. He put a hand out and touched her arm, affectionately.

'I'm okay, Frankie.' She pointed to the tray of roast beef sandwiches the housekeeper had made. 'Rosa sorted some lunch for us, if you're hungry. To be honest, I would have taken you out for lunch and a good chat, but I'm not really in the frame of mind to be going out for an afternoon.' She gave him a slightly condescending look. 'So don't be offended.'

Frankie fiddled with the cuffs of his shirt. 'Not at all, Kerry. I know what you mean. I'd love nothing better than to sit with you in a nice restaurant and spend the afternoon eating, drinking some good wine, and talking about the old days.' He shook his head wistfully. 'Jesus, ki—'

Kerry shot him a glance as he almost said 'kid' then went on, 'Jesus, Kerry. Where did all the years go? You know something, when I saw you arriving the other day, when you got in after Mickey, you know, for the funeral, I almost couldn't believe it. The last few times you've been here, I haven't seen you. I've only seen the pictures your ma showed me. But I don't think I've seen you in about eight years.'

'And I'm not getting any younger, Frankie. That's for sure,' Kerry said.

He looked at her, his steely blue eyes more piercing against his lush dark hair, and it was a look that would have seduced most women. And if Kerry wasn't his boss, it might have seduced her too.

'You look ... unbelievable, if I can say that to my boss. Seriously, I don't know how life has been treating you over the years, but you really look ... well, like a film star.'

Kerry waved away the compliment with her hand. Bloody Christ. Frankie Martin, still the charmer who broke hearts all over the city. But not here. Not today. Or any other day, where she was concerned.

'Enough of your charm, sir. Sit down. Let's have some grub. I'm starving.'

She sat on the leather armchair and relaxed into it for a moment, the fire flickering in the hearth, watching as Frankie sat down and leaned forward. He lifted the teapot.

'Will I pour?'

'In the absence of the servants,' Kerry joked.

She picked up a couple of brown bread sandwiches and put them on a tea plate. Frankie did the same, and they ate for a moment in silence.

'So,' Kerry began, placing her teacup on the table. 'I wanted a longer chat with you, Frankie. I need you to give me the lowdown on a few things.' She paused as he watched her. 'I know at the meeting the other day, you told me the way you see things, but—'

Frankie put his hand up. 'Kerry. Look, I need to say this. I'm sorry about the other day. I think I spoke out of turn.

I was wrong. I . . . I was just trying to point out to you that this business is a very different life from the one you've led.'

Kerry tried to keep her patience.

'I take your point, Frankie. That's why I didn't say anything to you at the time. In front of everyone else.' She paused. 'But I need to be clear here.' She fixed him, her eyes cold. 'Don't ever question me like that again around a table with our closest associates. Not ever.'

Frankie went a little red in his neck.

'Understood,' he said, nodding.

But Kerry saw the muscle in his jaw tighten, and the moment or so it took for him to recover and regain his charm.

'Okay,' she said, making sure she looked him in the eye. 'Now that we've got that out of the way, let's talk about the whole situation. The Boyles. How did it come to this? I know we've talked about it before. But I need to know from you. Mickey and you were at the helm, at the centre of everything that goes on here. So I need to know the score. I particularly want the lowdown on the Paradise Club – and the other saunas. Tell me about that.'

Frankie opened his suit jacket, sat back, his legs open, confident, macho. He ran a hand across his chin as he looked straight at Kerry.

'Mickey was some guy,' he said. 'You know what he was like from years ago. He had to be the top man in everything he did. Even fighting in the playground, he had to take the biggest hard-man in the school on to prove a point. And he did. He beat the shit out of Tommy Mason in front of three of his mates, and none of them even moved a muscle to help him. That was Mickey. And that's the way he was in business. Nothing was ever enough for him. He wanted a bigger slice of everything.'

Kerry gave him an understanding look.

'Hence the reason he got us involved in drugs.' She waited a moment before going on. 'Despite my father's wishes. Despite the fact that Dad had always said he would never go down that road. Even when he could see, years ago, how lucrative it was. Dad didn't want that, Frankie – that's what gets me with our Mickey. He had no right to go against my father's wishes and his hopes for this family and everything connected with it.'

Frankie nodded slowly, spreading his hands. 'I hear what you're saying, Kerry. Honest. I really do. But the world has changed – even in the sixteen years since your dad died. Everything out there is very different. It's all drugs now. It's all about cocaine, heroin, cannabis. If you don't operate in the market, then you're out of it. You're weak. What are you left with? A few businesses, saunas, bars and stuff? Then somebody like Mickey comes along from another area and tells you he's taking over your business. These bastards would just trample all over us if we weren't as powerful as them. Drugs are part of the business. It's money, it's power. Nowadays we've got the Russians, the Albanians to contend with, as well as our own. We have to show our muscle. We have to stand up and show that we can work with anyone, in any company, in any stuff they do. Otherwise, we're like the wee corner shop, and nothing. It's all about money and power.'

'You forgot to mention greed, Frankie.'

He shook his head. 'Not greed, Kerry. Not really. We're a big organisation. We're top dog up here. But we have to stay there. So we do what we have to do. Sure, it makes the firm a shedload of money. But it's also about survival.' He seemed a little exasperated. 'I know it's hard for you at this stage, just coming in, and I totally respect how you see it. I do. But we'd be out of the game in months if we weren't prepared to do what the rest of the families from Glasgow to Dublin to London do.'

Kerry listened to him, her face impassive. Money and power. She knew he was right in some of what he said, and that he totally believed it. But no matter what he said, he wouldn't convince her it was the best way. Naive or not, she wanted to fulfil her father's wishes of building an empire, of hotels, restaurants, property. But she wasn't going to win that battle here, so right now she just had to find out a bit more about how things got so out of hand.

'Okay. Right. Leaving that for the moment. Tell me a bit about Knuckles Boyle and his mob. Fill me in on that first. And what our deal was with him. And I want to know about Durkin's and Hill's mobs too. Sure, I can see the big attraction – the money, the drugs, etc. But I need to know more of how you dealt with them. Who do we use to pick up stuff? Give me the actual details. Everything you can.'

Frankie nodded. 'Okay. I'll break it down for you. No problem. And if there's anything I don't tell you today, then we can do it another day, tomorrow or whatever, because it's a lot to take in.' He paused, looked her in the eye. 'But look, believe me, I'm on your side. I really am.'

# CHAPTER ELEVEN

Kerry awoke with the same sinking feeling she'd had all the past week. Every morning, the same crushing heaviness in her chest as soon as she opened her eyes and realised none of this was a nightmare. Her mother was really gone. She'd never see her again, never again feel the softness of her cheek against hers, or enjoy her laughter as much as her indignation when she disagreed with anyone. Today she would say goodbye to her for ever at the funeral. In front of everyone, Kerry knew she was expected to be sorrowful, heartbroken – that was a given, she had lost her mother – but she would also have to be seen to be in control. All she really wanted to do was to bury herself deep under the duvet and weep until she could somehow learn to live with the pain. But there was no time for that. She could never again be the person she had been. All that had changed now. She kicked the duvet back and sat at the edge of the bed, picked up her watch and saw the time. It was seven and still dark outside. The house was a blanket of silence. She pulled on her robe and stood at the window watching the rain drumming on the glass, and the gusts of wind rustling in the trees. Across the driveway in the small gatehouse where the housekeeper and two of the security staff lived, a light was on, and she knew that somewhere out there, the bodyguards would be patrolling the perimeter fence the way they did these days, twenty-four seven. If she dwelt on the security and the lockdown, she'd feel like a prisoner. In reality, she knew that she could walk away any time. Go as far as possible, never come back. She'd allowed herself the thought as she lay in her bath the other night, wondering where she would go. She'd had another life for such a long time. She could go back to London, go to Europe, where she still had friends. But that's not where she wanted to be. She wanted to be here, and over the past days, as she'd scrutinised the business and what they had, the people who surrounded her, she was beginning to feel that she had come home at last. Despite all the times she'd been home for school holidays and visits to her family – even when her mum came to Spain and spent time with her – over the years she had gradually felt that she wasn't who they were. She loved her mother with every fibre of her being, but she didn't want to be in Glasgow, among the people who were part of their lives. But that was changing. And she was changing. She opened her wardrobe and looked at the black clothes she'd worn to Mickey's funeral – little did she know then that she'd be wearing them again so soon. Last night, with the rosary and then the chapel afterwards where her mother's body now lay, she'd seen so many people from her past. Older men, faces she'd vaguely remembered who must have known her family, women she recalled from growing up in the old neighbourhood when they had nothing. All of them now feeling like family. The place was still on lockdown though, and even in the quietness and sorrow at the chapel, the security and the suited-and-booted bodyguards milling around was there for all to see. It would be the same at the funeral. Kerry took a deep breath and let out a sigh. It was going to be a long, tough day. And by the time it was over, if everything went according to plan, she would know what it felt like to have her first taste of revenge. Then she would know if she really belonged here.

Across the city, in Central Station, Jake Cahill stood looking up at the lights on the massive noticeboard. He could have been any other traveller or commuter, watching for their train arriving or the next departure to their destination. But Jake wasn't going anywhere. He'd been watching the skinny, grubby-looking character with greasy hair and a single earring, studying his every move. In fact, he'd followed him from his hotel in Argyle Street nearly an hour ago, and was mildly amused at the way the little bastard kept looking over his shoulder as he walked up to the station, as though he was waiting for someone to pounce. Stupid prick. If he'd any sense, he would have taken a taxi, reducing the amount of time he was walking in the street where he was an easy target for anyone who might want to waste him. Or maybe he was just arrogant enough to think he was untouchable. Jake had done his homework on this little toerag, and he'd found that the shooting at Mickey Casey's funeral wasn't his first hit for the Knuckles Boyle mob. Word was that he'd bumped off a bookie in Salford six months ago, and was now rising through the ranks, cocky enough to leave his calling card – gouging out the bookie's eye, which was obviously more for his own twisted pleasure than anything else, because even someone as warped as Knuckles wouldn't tell him to do anything like that. But that was the trouble with these young pricks. They wanted to be remembered. They fancied themselves as one of the Kray twins, when the reality was they were just some lowlife shitbag with a bloated sense of who they were. Why leave a mark? Jake thought. Just do the job, walk away. He was a master at it – a real pro. None of this leave-your-mark shit for him. Just clean and quick and forget about it. He watched the skinny guy pull his rucksack over his shoulder and make his way to the toilets. Jake followed him. He put his hands in his coat pockets and ran his fingers over his Glock pistol and the silencer. He went into the toilets, glad they were empty, save for his target, already inside. He waited, noiselessly fitted the silencer.

Then as the cubicle door began to open, Jake moved. He pushed the guy back through the door and onto the toilet pan. The element of surprise. As the little shit looked up, Jake made it simple. He fired straight down into his shocked face, the expression of disbelief frozen. He fired again, just for good luck, then he watched as the man slumped back on the toilet seat. Jake took a handkerchief from his pocket and wiped the spatter of blood from his face that had come from firing at such close range. It wouldn't show on his black coat. Then he put his gun back in its holster, flushed the toilet and walked out. It would be a couple of minutes before the next person would come in and see the pool of blood seeping through the cubicle door, but by that time, Jake would be on his way up towards Charing Cross where he knew he could get the best full English breakfast in town.

At St Mary's Church, the mourners gathered outside in the miserable wind that seemed made for a day like this, as Kerry pulled up in the funeral car accompanied by Auntie Pat and Uncle Danny. Pat in her black suit, the beautiful image of her mother, stirred Kerry's heart, because it meant that her mum would never be too far away. Danny was grim faced, eyes scanning the crowd.

'Christ, the place is black with people,' he whispered. 'Your mum was adored. A lot of them will be from years ago; look, there's Nellie Brady. God love her! She never had a thing in her life. Dirt poor, she was. But your ma was good to her.'

'Lot of cops too, I see,' Pat said.

They got out as a trail of Mercs and Jags rolled up, the well-heeled figures climbing out of their motors. Many of them Kerry had seen at Mickey's funeral last week. She nodded to them, and they looked back at her, faces like granite, broken noses, scars, stern and tough as old boots. Then she also noticed some woman close to the entrance of the church, and there was a flash of recognition. It was Maria Ahern. Jesus. They'd been such close friends at school but she hadn't seen her for ages, and they'd lost touch a couple of years after she went to Spain as a teenager. Maria looked cold in the rain and wasn't dressed for the weather. Kerry wondered what life she'd been leading all these years, wishing they could have kept in touch. But clearly their lives had been so different.

Inside, her mother's light oak coffin lay on a pedestal at the front of the chapel. On top of it sat cherished photos of her mum and dad, and of her and Mickey when they were teenagers together. As Kerry sat at the front, flanked by Danny and Pat, the organ struck up and the old hymns suddenly transported her back to a lifetime ago; to the first communion, all the little children traipsing in, hands joined, Kerry in her white dress, her father smiling proudly. She swallowed back tears. The priest, Father Doyle, had been a friend of the family for thirty years, but still looked youthful. He spoke in a soft Irish accent, talking of the years of devotion to the church by her mother, the great family that the Caseys were, and of the tragic taking of lives that had to end, because an eye for an eye brought nothing but more bloodshed. Kerry sat listening, wondering where Jake Cahill was. Even if she'd wanted to, she couldn't stop him now. She paid lip service as they prayed, confessing her sins, forgive us our trespasses as we forgive them that trespass against us. Not a chance, she vowed.

Jake Cahill polished off the remains of his fried breakfast, mopping up the egg yolk and stray beans with a chunk of toast. He waved the waitress over and paid his bill, finishing the last of his mug of tea, then put his jacket on and headed out of the door. The traffic was building up now, snaking up Charing Cross under the bridge heading east. He pulled his coat collar up and made his way over to St George's Cross, where he had watched his next job, Lenny Wright, go into the basement flat last night. Unknown to the thick bastard, Jake had set him up last night with a hooker named Tina. Jake had known her for years, and she was still quite tidy, but most of all, she knew how to roll a punter. Once he'd established where Lenny went at night, these last three nights he paid her to chat him up. He knew she wouldn't mess it up. She would take him back to the flat she used for punters and rented under a false, untraceable name, text him when it was time. Jake's mobile pinged with a text as he crossed the road. He stood outside looking down at the basement where dingy dark curtains were drawn. He waited until the door was clicked open and then he slipped in. Wright was a bit of an unknown quantity to him, so he had to be careful. He'd been part of the Knuckles mob for the past few years and was an enforcer mostly used for bumping off drug dealers who stepped out of line. But if he'd been smart, he would never have ventured into a woman's flat in a strange town. Plenty of time for that when he went back home. But he'd been on his own since he came up here and was probably looking for a quick shag. Jake didn't speak to Tina who was already dressed and ready to make a sharp exit. He looked in, glanced at the jeans on the floor, obviously a rushed job to get her into the sack. Jake leaned over the bed, and just as he put the gun to Wright's chest, the man woke up.

'Morning, old son,' Jake said. 'I'm from the tourist board. I hope you enjoyed your stay in Glasgow.'

Lenny opened his mouth but nothing came out, and he died that way, as the blood spread across his chest and over the grubby bed. Jake heard the door close and he waited a minute, giving Tina a few moments of a head start in case anyone else was up and about. He knew the flat was owned by a fictitious company and couldn't be traced back to Tina once the body was discovered, so she was in the clear. Then he looked at his watch as he stepped out and up the stairs to the street and into the din of traffic. Two down. He was making good time.

To the strains of the final hymn, Kerry braced herself and dabbed her eyes as the pallbearers hitched the coffin onto their shoulders. She walked slowly down the aisle behind her mother's coffin, her chest almost exploding, trying to choke back tears. She could feel them spilling over and could see from the corner of her eye the sympathetic glances and faces of the mourners packed in every seat and right up the stairs in the balcony too. As the congregation sang, she remembered those days so long ago, all singing, the togetherness of a community that had grown older together. This was where *she* belonged. These were her people. And she was now more conscious than ever that she was the only one left in the family. Towards the back, she caught the eye of Maria Ahern, who looked up at her, tears brimming. Then Maria just reached out a moment and touched her arm, and Kerry bit her lip. All those years ago, so many memories flooded back. Why didn't they keep in touch?

Outside, the rain had stopped and the crowds gathered around the hearse, people hugging and tearful. At Mickey's funeral she knew she would be gone by the next day, and all of them, she felt, were just faces from her past. But now she took comfort in them being around her, all of them coming up and hugging her, telling her how sorry they were for her loss. This was her family. And then, Maria. She approached, and automatically they fell into each other's arms, like old friends, like sisters, parted for too long, a childhood friendship that should never have been neglected.

'I'm so sorry, Kerry,' Maria said. 'Really. I loved your mother. She was so beautiful.'

Kerry sniffed, and looked at her pale face, tired eyes, and wondered what life had done to her to make her like this. She saw her shivering.

'Oh, Maria. I'm so sad.' She let the tears roll down her cheeks. 'It's so good to see you. You must come back for something to eat at the pub. I haven't seen you in years. I'd love to talk to you.'

Maria smiled. 'I'm sure you've got plenty of family and stuff to get on with, Kerry. We can meet another time.'

'No,' Kerry insisted, squeezing her arm. 'Please come back. I want to have a chat with you. Jesus, Maria! We had so many laughs and good times as kids. I missed all that when I left. Come on back. Even just for one drink.'

'Okay,' Maria agreed. 'I'll see you there. Thanks, Kerry. It's great to see you. I'm just so sad for you.'

She hugged Kerry and turned away as someone else came up to greet her.

Jake Cahill had got lucky. He had been geared up to go to Belfast to complete the job, when he had got a call late the previous night telling him where to find the final two on his list. Tom McGuinness and Davey Prentice were on the midday ferry from Stranraer. They were meeting their contact in a roadside café near Girvan on the way down, so with a bit of planning he wouldn't have to go all the way across the water. Looking out at the sea as he headed for Troon he was glad, it looked like whipping up a storm and the crossing to Belfast could be a real bastard in high winds. He looked at the clock on his dashboard. It was just after ten, and he was already pulling into the café car park. At this rate, he could be back in Glasgow to share a drink with Kerry and Danny and the family at the wake. An image flashed across his mind of years ago, him and Danny and big Tim Casey, the laughs they'd had as they blagged and robbed. The bank job they did down south that netted each of them two hundred grand was the turning point for Tim and Danny. They took their place at the top table. They'd had money to spend and invest. The three of them promised to stay faithful friends to each other, even though Jake went his own way. They always knew they could call on him if needed. He thought of Danny, how he was as hard as nails, and he had the killer punch too. Tim was hard but fair, and he had his dreams of building his own restaurant and hotel empire. Back then, Jake was clinical about life. He'd learned that from his father. If a job needed doing, he was the man to do it, and he had done hits for the paramilitaries, as well as gangsters. It had made him rich, and yes, it had made him lonely. But he was so used to that now, the loneliness was part of who he was. He glanced around the car park. It was empty so he went in and sat at a table and ordered a coffee. He looked out at the sea, watched the waitress talking to the two other customers, quiet salesman types probably on their way around the countryside. And one guy at a table close to the window on the far side. A few moments later, as he saw a white van coming along the road in the distance, Jake got up and left the café, went to his car and waited. He watched as two men got out, and shook his head as he saw they'd left the doors open. Christ. Where did they get guys like this? They were even stupid enough to park it at the far end of the car park behind the café so nobody would see it from the road. Perfect. Once they were inside the café, Jake slipped into the back of the van. About twenty minutes later he heard them returning, laughing and swearing. He wondered if they had been talking to the man he'd spotted in the café, who had looked like he was waiting for someone. He heard them say 'See you later.' No you won't, Jake thought. Then they got into the van. He heard one of them light up a fag, the other saying when he got back he was going to get a ride first thing as it had been three weeks. They joked. He listened as the key went into the ignition, then he got up. Tom caught his eye in the rear-view mirror, but it was too late. Jake had already fired, and in that second Tom's brain was all over the windscreen. As Davey's hand went to the door, Jake fired through his temple. It was quick. Then he jumped out of the van and walked straight to his own car, and headed up the road. Job done. He'd also taken a bag from the back of the van with all their money in it – just for the sheer hell of it. On the way back he handed it over to an old man on a park bench in Glasgow, whose eyes lit up when he looked inside.

Kerry sat with Maria drinking wine in an alcove a little away from the other mourners. In their turn, everyone had offered their condolences, many of them wanting to tell Kerry stories of the old days, the more drunk they got. This was how it was with family. She could hear the music starting. Soon it would be a full sing-song, and that's what her mother would have wanted.

She looked at Maria, and shook her head sadly as Maria's story of her life unfolded. She had married a local boy when she was a teenager, and he'd joined the army. They'd had a good life, and lived away most of the time, in Germany and in Cyprus with their young daughter and son. But everything had changed after her soldier husband completed two tours of Iraq. He came back a changed man, crippled with stress and depression, and an emotional wreck. Eventually they split up – he disappeared and left her with the two kids, and she hadn't heard from him for nearly nine years. The last she'd heard about him, he was living abroad somewhere. Kerry listened as Maria told her about her daughter, Jennifer, being on heroin, how she was lost to her. Maria said she couldn't make ends meet, no matter how she tried.

'So where is Jennifer now? When do you see her?' Kerry asked.

'I haven't seen her for three weeks. I can't have her in the house. She would steal the eye out of my head. It's just awful. She'll steal anything that isn't nailed down.'

'So where is she living?'

'Christ knows. In some squat down in the Calton. She's on the game and working the drag. I can't even bear to go there and look for her, because I don't know how I could cope if I saw her like that. It's bad enough to see her emaciated.'

'Jesus. That's as bad as it gets, Maria. I'm so sorry. You don't deserve this. Nobody does. What about rehab?'

'Rehab? That's no use. There are more junkies in this city than beds, and you have to wait months to get a place. Most of the time the really bad ones are dead by the time that happens.' She paused, choking. 'I'm just scared that will be Jennifer. Honest to God. I live in dread of the knock on the door some time to tell me they've found her.'

Kerry shook her head. 'This is terrible.'

'And the debts? I've been paying her drug debts until I'm nearly out of the door. I've got some loan shark kicking my door in every week because a few hundred quid I borrowed has now snowballed. Honest, I just wish some days

I'd go to sleep and not wake up. Then I see our Cal. He's the loveliest boy. Clever an' all. He wants to be a lawyer or something. But he's working in a car wash to try to help me.'

Kerry felt angry.

'Loan shark? Christ. You're into debt with those parasites?'

'What could I do? They said they would do Jennifer in if I didn't pay.'

'Christ almighty. What's the loan shark's name?'

Maria gazed at her. 'Kerry, look. I can't do anything that will put Jennifer in any more danger.'

'Tell me his name. Nothing's going to happen to Jennifer. Trust me. What's his name?'

'Tam Dolan. He works out of Maryhill.'

Kerry looked over her shoulder to where Danny had just sat at a table a few feet away. She called over to him and beckoned.

'All right, sweetheart?'

Danny was already well pissed.

'Yeah. I'm okay. You might remember Maria Ahern. We were pals from school.'

'Vaguely. How's it going, darlin'? Thanks for coming and supporting Kerry.'

'Danny. A loan shark by the name of Tam Dolan. Operates out of Maryhill . . . You know him?'

'That fucking scumbag. I know him. I know who he is.'

'Please tell me he doesn't work for us.'

'Fuck! Are you kidding?'

'And we're in no way connected to him?'

'No fucking way! He works out of Maryhill with a mob up there. Ratbag. Why, what's the problem?'

'We'll talk tomorrow. I need something dealt with.'

'No sweat. It will be a pleasure dealing with that wanker.'

He got up and went away. Kerry looked at Maria and shrugged.

'I'm going to fix this. Okay? And I'm not having you living like this. Come and work for me.'

'Kerry, I know you mean well but I can't take charity. My boy would never have it.'

'It's not charity. You'll get a job. We have plenty of places you can work.' She smiled. 'Don't worry. Not the sauna!'

'I'm a bit old for that.'

Kerry was happy to see her smile for the first time today.

'And Jennifer. Find out where she is. We'll get her into rehab.'

Maria suddenly burst out crying.

'Oh, Kerry. I don't know what to say. I'm scared all the time. Honestly. I don't know what to do.'

'Don't do anything. Leave it to me. We'll meet tomorrow. Have lunch or something. Come up to the house.'

Kerry looked up as Danny came over to her table. Behind him was Jake Cahill. Danny leaned down and whispered in her ear.

'It's done.'

She looked up at Jake, his face stern, pale, a drink in his hand.

'Thanks, Jake.'

She looked around the room. She'd expected to feel something, maybe a pang of regret, or even a shade of disgust with herself. But she didn't. She'd dealt with business the way it had to be done, the way it was expected to be done. She wouldn't rake over it in her conscience and fret about what she was becoming. The word would get out across the ranks, and beyond, that this was how the Caseys did business if you hurt them. Whatever happened tomorrow, Kerry Casey was ready.

# CHAPTER TWELVE

Sharon hadn't packed anything more than her small Louis Vuitton hand luggage bag, to avoid suspicion that she was going for good. As far as Knuckles knew, she was off to four nights in her favourite spa retreat on the Costa del Sol with three old schoolfriends for a catch-up. They did it a couple of times a year, so he was well used to her going off on her own. It was the same whenever she decided to take a week out and head for Marbella to chill out with her friends down there. Knuckles had no reason to distrust her. He owned her, as he'd told her many times. And maybe he did, but when he swaggered around talking that kind of shit, it really pissed Sharon off. But she always kept quiet. Because always she was squirrelling away the money she would need whenever this all came to an end. It wasn't something she'd been doing for long, because she would have staked her life on him up until the last couple of years; before he started being so obvious with his women, and it became clear to her that, to him, she was past her sell-by date. That'll be the day, Sharon told herself, as she took every opportunity to stick some more money in the Cayman Islands account she'd set up for herself during a girlie trip there two years ago. But this was it. This was really happening now. It wasn't something she'd done on a whim. She could see the writing on the wall, and she knew it was only a matter of time before Knuckles would make his move. He was smart, and his people knew how to clean up. But Sharon was smarter. In fact, if it hadn't been for her organisational ability and managing so much of his business over the years, he wouldn't be this powerful. None of these bastards who fawned over him like he was some little emperor knew this, except her.

Since yesterday, after Knuckles came home at six in the morning, he'd been quiet, detached. She hadn't berated him or questioned where he had been. She was resigned to it. And even though she wanted to tell him what a bastard he had become, making her feel rejected, humiliating her by shoving this other bird in her face, she bit her lip. Revenge, as they say, is a dish best served cold.

She'd known the moment Knuckles told her Charley would drive her to the airport that her number was up. She always took her own car on the half-hour drive to Manchester Airport and left it in the car park if she was going only for a few days. Knuckles knew that, so when he suddenly told her she was getting a lift, Sharon knew it would be the last lift she would ever get. She'd been preparing since yesterday, carefully concealing things in her hand-bag she knew she would need. As she zipped up her bag and pulled on her leather jacket she saw Charley's car pull into their driveway. She stood back a little so that she could see who was in the passenger seat. Shit! It was that evil little bastard Vic Rennie. Her worst fears were confirmed. The only time she had met Vic was two years ago, and he barely spoke two words to her. But that was his way. He was a ghostly figure who only ever appeared if someone was to be quietly got rid of. She had told Knuckles that he gave her the creeps, and he'd laughed and said Vic was one of his oldest mates, and the guy you'd want in your corner if you needed a hand. She'd never seen him again until now, but she'd heard plenty of stories. There was a knot in her stom-ach and she went to the bathroom and filled a glass of water, noticing the glass tremble when she stuck it under the tap. She looked at herself in the mirror, at the little flush on her neck. 'Calm the fuck down,' she whispered. 'No bas-tard is going to beat you.' She grabbed her bags and headed down the staircase. As she did, she could see Knuckles stand-ing by the kitchen door, gazing out of the window into the middle distance. A sudden pang of hurt or sorrow washed over her and she bit her lip quickly to keep it in check. How could he do this? Knuckles turned around slowly to face her.

'You all sorted then, darlin'?'

'Yep. I'm ready. Don't need much. It's scorching over there.'

Knuckles looked at her and she locked eyes with him, trying to see if there was anything going on behind them. But there was nothing. He was that cold a bastard that there wasn't even a flicker of guilt, or love or anything she had hoped to see, even though he knew this would be the last time he saw her.

'Oh, by the way, Vic's in the car. Him and Charley have got a bit of business to attend to after they drop you at the airport.'

Sharon watched his expression. Nothing. She nodded. 'Okay. It won't exactly be scintillating conversation then if Vic's in the car.'

Knuckles half smiled. 'Yeah. Prince of fucking darkness, that one.' He stepped forward. 'Anyway. You'd best get going if you want a large gin in the departure lounge with your mates before the flight.' He opened his arms and she stepped into them as he embraced her.

She caught a whiff of the freshness of him just out of the shower, and suppressed the urge to put her hand on the back of his head and hold him close. Fuck you, Joe Boyle. Fucking smiling assassin.

'Remember, call me when you get to your hotel or spa or whatever that place is with all them knit-your-own-yoghurt nutters.'

Sharon smiled back.

'They're lovely people. It's all about looking into your soul. Cleansing. It's wonderful.'

Just at that moment, he looked at her and looked away.

'Right. I'm off. Take care of yourself, Joe.' Sharon hoped there wasn't a catch in her voice, because right at this moment the cold anger that had driven her these past few days was replaced with a stab of anguish. She would never see him again. The father of their child. How could he do this? Knuckles' mobile rang on the worktop and he picked it up, blowing her a kiss as he walked from the kitchen down the hall into the living room. Sharon's eyes followed him for a few seconds, but he didn't look back. She headed for the front door, opening it and closing it softly behind her. For ever.

When she got out to the car, Vic jumped out of the passenger seat and made to go in the back. But Sharon was onto that immediately.

'Vic. Why don't you sit in the front? I've got some stuff I want to look over and I've got a bit more room in the back.'

Vic glanced at Charley, and Sharon thought she could see a flicker of disappointment. Whatever plan they'd had involved Vic being in the back. Stuff that. Sharon wanted everyone where she could see them. Vic shrugged and got into the front seat, staring straight ahead as they drove out of the electronic gates and onto the road.

Sharon busied herself with magazines spread over the seat and her mobile, checking messages, trying to look busy and preoccupied. They drove in silence then Charley put on the radio, smooth music – out in the real world people were sitting at home, in their cars, listening to the radio, just like her. But their day was going to be a whole lot different. She wasn't fazed by this. Over the last few months, she had felt herself subconsciously reverting to the tough little cookie she'd been all her life – long before she had set eyes on Knuckles Boyle. Her instinct for survival began growing up in a house where her father beat her mother until she stabbed him, and then authorities moved in. The family was broken up and all the kids placed in various children's homes. They called them a place of safety, but that was the last thing they were. She fought off abusers, bullying teenagers and carers, then ended up out on her own, living on her wits. She wasn't afraid of a fight, and it wouldn't be the first time she'd slashed someone who threatened her. The boyfriend she got in with for a while had been a drug dealer and he taught her how to shoot a gun, so she knew what she was doing.

She was reading the newspaper as the darkness began to fall, when suddenly she looked up and they'd missed the airport slip road. Then they pulled off the motorway and into a quiet road a few miles short of the airport.

'Where you going, Charley? You missed the cut-off for the airport?'

'Yeah, I know, Sharon. Sorry, darlin'. But I know how we can get back on the motorway from here. Don't worry. You'll still make it in plenty of time.'

Sharon's stomach dropped. She knew where this was all

right. About two miles of green fields and back roads leading to farmland and an old quarry, close to the airport, but far enough away. She put her hand into her handbag and ran her fingers over the gun she'd put in there this morning. She'd had it for nearly ten years and nobody had ever seen it. Vic stared straight ahead. Then, Charley faked the car shuddering to a halt. It stopped and he switched the lights off.

'What's up, Charley?' She sat forward, barely breathing.

In one seamless movement, Vic got out of the car.

'Charley, what the fuck is going on?'

Charley looked pale, the betrayal all over his face. He didn't look at her.

'Sharon. I'm sorry about this. I'm only doing what I was told.'

'What?' Sharon faked her surprise. She'd known him for years, trusted him, but she knew he was doing a job. 'What the fuck?'

'Like I say, Sharon. I do what the boss man says.'

'Charley, don't!' Sharon said, as Vic put his hand on the back-door handle.

'I don't make the decisions, Sharon. You know that. It's just business.'

There was a second just as she heard Vic pull on the door handle, but it was enough for her to take out her gun and shoot Charley in the back of the head. She did it without consideration or thought for him or how she'd known him for years. It was purely business. Vic pulled the car door opened and put the gun to her face.

'You shouldn't have done that.'

She ducked in time to hear the gunshot going straight through the window of the rear passenger seat, and as she did she fired a shot off that went straight between Vic's legs. He looked at her with an expression of disbelief as his legs buckled. She immediately let two more shots off into his chest and he collapsed on the ground.

'Fuck you, Joe Boyle. Business. *This* is just business, you cunt.'

She went round to the driver's seat and opened the door. Blood everywhere. She managed to put her arms around Charley and pull him out onto the ground, leaving his head in a puddle of mud, then she jumped into the car and put her foot down. She drove with a burning rage and terror as though she was watching someone else doing this. In about half an hour maximum, Charley's phone would ring and it would be Knuckles. But there would be no answer.

She drove the car towards the edge of the city and pulled into a derelict warehouse car park on an industrial estate, where she abandoned it. The place was deserted. Charley's blood was on her jeans, and there was a smattering of Vic's blood splashed her jumper. She would have to change in the toilet of the airport. Even though she wasn't flying, it was the only place where she felt safe enough to hire a car.

She pulled on her overcoat, buttoned it up and walked a couple of hundred yards before hailing a taxi. She flopped down in the back seat, shaking all over. She was free. Jesus! She was terrified, but she was free.

# CHAPTER THIRTEEN

Cal waited outside the newsagent at Central Station where he'd been instructed to go. The man he would be travelling to Manchester with would meet him there, he was told. He'd get a text message saying 'here' a few seconds before the man arrived. He didn't feel afraid, worried, or even guilty about what he was doing, though he knew deep down he should feel all of those things. He was more buoyed up with the sense of adventure, excited at the prospect of being part of the secret operation. If he could do two or three of these kinds of drops, every couple of months, he'd make decent money. He thought of his mum and felt a twinge of guilt that he'd lied to her this morning on his way out of the flat, saying he was doing a double shift at the car wash and he'd probably not be home till at least ten this evening. He knew she would believe him because she had absolute trust in him, and that was the only part of this that he hated himself for. She'd be devastated if she had the slightest inkling what he was up to. But he told himself there was no choice. It was as simple as that. He could make her life easier by earning real money, and maybe even do something about Jennifer to get her back on track. He missed his sister, missed the person she was when they were growing up. As little kids they'd been inseparable, and Cal had followed her around like a puppy because she was six years older than him and as far as he was concerned she knew everything. It broke his heart to see what she had become, and how she'd pushed him away. He was reduced to the odd contact with her, or watching from a distance as she got picked up and dropped off by punters who'd used her. The thought of it stiffened his resolve, and whatever it took, he was going to get his ma and Jennifer out of this shithole life they were living. If that involved him doing drops or dealing in drugs, then stuff it. Plenty of other people did it and even if you hated them, you couldn't help but notice the money they made and the impact it had on their lives. Sure, he could knuckle down and study, go to university and get a good job. But that would take for ever, and the problems he had were right here and now. Plus, the smell of money that oozed out of the big guy's fancy car when he sat in it last week made him realise that there were easier ways to be successful and make money than slogging your guts out at school. His mobile shuddered with a text and he fished it out of his jeans pocket and saw the word 'here'. He glanced around him, then seconds later a guy carrying a rucksack and a small suitcase on wheels crossed the road looking straight at him. He watched as the guy flicked his cigarette away, then approached him.

'You Cal?'

He nodded. 'Aye.'

'Right. Let's go. Train is in fifteen minutes.'

No name. He fought the urge to ask his name. Keep your mouth shut, he told himself. Speak when you're spoken to and say as little as possible about yourself. You never know who this guy is. As they walked briskly to the platform, the guy handed him the rucksack.

'Here. Keep that on your back. When you're sitting on the train you can keep it on your knee. But it goes everywhere with you. If you go for a pee, the bag's with you. Get that?'

'Yep.'

They went towards the gates, and the guy put his hand into the inside pocket of his wax jacket and handed the tickets to the collector who punched them and motioned them through. As they walked along the platform to their carriage, Cal glanced at the guy's smart light brown leather boots and tight black skinny jeans. He was wearing a cream polo-neck sweater, a bit of designer stubble and slicked back hair. He looked successful, Cal thought. Even though Cal was well dressed, he felt a little shabby alongside him in his faded jeans and Timberland boots with puffa jacket zipped up. On the train, there was nobody sitting within two seats of them, and passengers were beginning to get on, but the carriage they were in wasn't busy so far. Cal sat down and took the rucksack off, placing it in his lap.

'My name's Geo, by the way, son.'

Cal nodded, wondering if he should shake hands but decided he wasn't expected to.

'Cal.'

'Where you from?'

'Cranhill.'

Geo nodded, rolled his eyes upwards.

'Bandit country that. You still in school, I hear?'

'Yeah. Leaving at the summer,' Cal lied.

He knew he was supposed to be going back for sixth year and had hoped to get three more highers. But now he wasn't so sure.

'You got a job lined up?'

Cal looked at him, wondering how he was expected to answer this. Geo didn't look like the kind of guy who would be impressed that he hoped to go to uni.

'Don't know yet for sure.'

Geo sniffed and glanced over his shoulder.

'Well, son. Play your cards right, and you might do all right. If big Jones put you on a job like this, he must see something in you.'

Cal looked at him, but said nothing. Then Geo took off

his jacket, folded it, and placed it on top of the small suitcase at his feet. Cal glanced him up and down.

'You want to dress like me, pal, you just keep your mouth shut, your head down, do the job and get on with it. Know what I mean?'

'Aye. Definitely.'

Geo took a tenner out of his jeans pocket and handed it to him.

'Away up and get us a cup of tea and a bacon roll. One for yourself too. I'm Hank Marvin.'

Cal stood up, picked up the rucksack and slung it on his back. He noticed Geo watching him.

'Don't be long, or I'll be coming looking for you.'

Cal looked at him but didn't answer. Smart dresser and big shot he might be, but he would like to punch him right out. He pushed away the thought and went towards the buffet car.

Three hours later they got off the train and headed for the café Geo pointed out to him where they would meet their man. He told him the drill.

'We go in here, get a cup of coffee and wait. Our man will come in with two small suitcases like the one I've got. He'll sit in a table next to us, and place the cases there. You'll hand me the rucksack and I'll place it where he's sitting, and shove my case over. Five minutes later he'll go, and we'll take the cases he left and fuck off.'

'Sounds fine.'

'Are you scared?'

Cal looked at him, surprised. 'Not at all.'

'Good. Make sure you don't say a fucking word.'

Cal nodded as they went into the café and sat down at the table by the window. The concourse was busy with travellers, many of them families. Cal had his eyes on everyone, wondering what the guy they were meeting would look like – even though he didn't have a clue who he would be – but he'd no idea what they were looking for. The waitress came and Geo ordered a coffee and Cal a black tea. They sat in silence when it arrived, and Cal caught Geo glancing at his watch from time to time. He wanted to ask what time the meet was, but he thought better of it. Geo fidgeted and looked out of the window, and Cal did too but he didn't know what they were looking for. He wanted to ask if the guy was late, but didn't have the courage. But Geo fidgeting like this was making him nervous. Then Geo looked out at the window as a man seemed to look in his direction across the concourse. He thought he saw the man talk into his jacket sleeve, but then decided he'd been watching too many movies. But Geo's face was suddenly white. He leaned across to Cal and whispered.

'Listen, mate. I'm going out for a second to make a phone call. Sit tight. Don't fucking move. Right?'

'Okay.'

Cal sat glancing over his shoulder, then down at the

case. He had the urge to feel the rucksack to see what was in it, but it had to be cash, he'd decided early on. Any of the drops he'd made were drugs, no doubt about that, so they must have been going down here to pick some up. He wondered why they didn't just bring it up by car, but maybe the cops were onto stuff like that now and this was the easiest way. You could certainly disappear into the crowd if you were travelling like a couple of mates as they seemed to be. He looked outside, but suddenly couldn't see Geo anywhere. His stomach dropped, because then the café door opened and in came a guy with two suitcases. He sat on the table next to him, and Cal felt his face go red. The man looked at him square in the eye.

'Where's your mate?'

Cal didn't know what to say. He looked out of the window and to his shock he saw two more men and a uniformed police officer coming towards the café. The officers came in towards the table. Cal stood up on weak legs.

'Sit down, lad.' The guy pulled the rucksack from his lap and grabbed the case. 'You're nicked.'

Cal felt dizzy, and his whole body went so weak he could hardly lift his arms. Bastard Geo! He'd seen the cops and fucked off, leaving him to take the rap, but he didn't even know for sure what was in the cases.

'Where's the man you were with?'

'I . . . I don't know. Look . . . Er . . .'

'Listen, son. I'm DI Birkenshaw of Greater Manchester

Drugs Unit. You're in a lot of trouble. Where's your man? We saw you getting off the train and coming in with him.'

Cal shook his head. 'I don't know. Honest.'

'So what did you think you were doing here?'

'I don't know.'

The officer stood up, sighed, and nodded to the uniformed officer who stepped forward and pulled Cal to his feet. He could see the man behind the counter and the waitress look on, shocked at the scene unfolding.

'Well, you'd better start thinking. And you'd better start talking or you'll not be going back home for a very long time.'

Cal was pulled out and ushered towards the door and as they stepped out, he thought of his mum, and bit back the tears.

# CHAPTER FOURTEEN

Maria was frantic. She paced from the kitchen to the living room window, where for the past two hours she'd watched the darkness creep across the sky, constantly looking down at the car park, waiting for Cal to appear. It was nearly half past ten, and even though he'd told her he was doing double shifts at the car wash over the last couple of weeks, she knew he must be finished by now. Where the hell was he? His mobile had gone straight to voicemail when she'd started worrying about him two hours ago, but now it was switched off. It wasn't like Cal. He would never disappear off the radar like this. Even if he was going to be late in, he'd call her to let her know. He knew how paranoid she was about him. He was everything his sister Jenny wasn't. He was all Maria had. She told herself to calm down. This was madness. He was sixteen years old. He'd probably got a few extra tips at the car wash and gone to a café with his mates. Maybe even for a drink. If he'd done that, she wouldn't go through him, even if she was angry. She walked back to the kitchen, stuck on the kettle, then again crossed to the window. She looked down, and her gut jolted as she saw a black jeep pulling in and two men get out. Again she told herself to calm down. It didn't look like that loan shark bastard, so it could be anyone to see any punter in this building. She watched as the two men seemed to look up, and she shrank back behind the curtain. They disappeared out of view and into the building. The kettle pinged and she went to the cupboard and brought out a mug with shaking hands. She put the cup down as she heard the banging at her front door.

'Oh Christ,' she murmured, holding her breath.

'Open the door, Maria.'

She stepped softly down the hall and to the door, peered out of the spyhole. Two men she didn't recognise, one tall with a couple of days' stubble, the other skinny with hollow cheeks, stared back.

'Open the fucking door.'

'Who is it?'

'If you want to see your son or daughter again, open the door now.'

Maria felt physically sick. She stood rooted, her legs heavy, almost unable to catch a breath. She reached up and managed to open the lock leaving the chain on, so she could see outside. The skinny man looked at her, and she could smell alcohol on his breath.

'Open the fucking door. Are you deaf?'

'Where's Cal? Wh-what's going on?'

The tall man placed his hand on the door and spoke softly.

'Maria. Open the door. We're not going to hurt you. But we need to tell you something about Cal.'

Her fingers shook as she fumbled with the chain and slid it across. She opened the door and they stepped in, the skinny one pushing past her, and shoving her against the wall. She felt light-headed, and her legs buckled a little.

'Easy, Joe. Give the woman a moment. Can you not see she's upset?'

'Where's my Cal? Has something happened to him? Are you police? Wh-what is it? Are you from the car wash?'

The skinny man almost sniggered, the other man looked at her sympathetically.

'No. Listen, Maria—'

She started to whimper. 'What's happened to Cal? Is he hurt?'

'No. Now listen. Calm down and listen. Okay?'

She nodded, her throat tight.

'Right. I'm about to tell you something, and when I do, just take it easy. Stay calm. Do nothing, and Cal will be all right. So will Jennifer.'

'Jenny?' Maria gasped. 'What's happened? Please, tell me.' She could feel a sob fighting its way up to her chest. 'Please.'

'They're both all right. Okay? Cal is in a bit of trouble. The cops have got him in custody.'

'What? Cops? What are you talking about? Where?'

'He's in Manchester at the moment.'

'Manchester? But he was working today. At the car wash. Doing a doubler.'

'No he wasn't. Now, I told you to stay calm. Cal works for us from time to time. And he was in Manchester today doing a bit of business for us.' He paused. 'But it went tits up, and the cops got involved.'

'Business? I don't know what you're talking about. Cal has never been to Manchester in his life. You must have made a mistake.'

'No mistake. All you need to know is that he's with the cops and he's safe.' He paused. 'Well, as long as he keeps his mouth shut.' He drew his hand across his mouth in a zipping gesture. 'Know what I mean?'

Maria put her hands to her mouth and slid down the wall. The skinny man pulled her up roughly and supported her. He walked her through to the living room and sat her on the couch.

'Right. There's no point in getting hysterical. This is important.'

'Okay. I'm all right.' She nodded, her whole body jittery. 'Just tell me what this is about. Please.'

'I told you. Your boy is with the Manchester cops and

he'll probably get moved back up here. Might even get out of custody.'

'But what for? Why is he in custody?'

'As I told you, the operation went tits up. Someone grassed.'

An explosion went off in her head.

'Is it drugs? Not my Cal. No way. This just doesn't make sense.'

'Look, I'm not here to convince you, doll. I'm here to tell you this one thing. The cops will come here soon and tell you what the score is. But you keep your mouth shut. Okay? This little encounter here between us never happened. I'm just here to tell you what will happen if you don't tell Cal to keep it shut.'

Maria said nothing. She nodded. She knew that was all she was expected to do.

'Wh-what about my Jenny? You mentioned Jenny. Where is she?'

He looked at the skinny man who blinked slowly.

'Jenny is all right. Well, as all right as a junkie whore can be.'

Maria burst into tears, her face flushing.

'Stop it,' she managed to croak.

'Fuck's sake, Joe! Shut your fucking rat face! Just shut it!'

She could feel the other man's hand on her shoulder.

'Jenny is all right. She's with some people in our crew. She'll be all right. As long as Cal keeps his mouth firmly

ANNA SMITH | 149

shut. I know you're not daft. I can see that you're understanding me here. So all I need you to do is, when the cops
get here, and when you see your boy, just make sure you
get some time with him on your own to tell him to shut
the fuck up. Got that?'

She nodded vigorously.

They both took a step back.

'Right. We're out of here now. You say nothing about this
or it's all over – for the lot of you. It's not good for us when
things get fucked up like this, but my job is to make sure
the loose ends and loose cannons are all holding up. So you
make sure you do what I ask and this will be over soon.'

Maria didn't know what to say, so she just nodded again.
They turned to go away.

'Now, the cops will be here in the next couple of hours, if
not sooner. So you say fuck all. Act as if this is all news to
you. Pull yourself together, and if they ask you why you're
jangling like this you say you're worried sick about Cal
because it's not like him to stay out late.'

She said nothing.

'We'll be in touch. We'll be watching. We clear here?'

'B-But what am I supposed to do when the cops come?'

'They'll tell you how this works. Our wonderful criminal justice system. They'll get a lawyer for your boy and
take it from there. But until this dies down, you lie low and
say nothing. Jenny is safe. Cal is safe. For the moment.
Don't fuck it up.'

They turned and went down the hall towards the door without looking back. Maria stood watching as the door slammed. She felt her face crumple as she supported herself along the wall until she got to the living room and sat on the couch. She had a few friends here she could tell some of her problems to, but not this. There was only one person in the world she had left that she could talk to. But she didn't even have her phone number. She knew where she lived. She knew that Kerry Casey was the head of a gangster family these days, and she wondered for a moment if this was who Cal was working for, but maybe Kerry wouldn't even know if he was. But Maria had no option. Yesterday at the funeral she'd had a couple of drinks and when she'd confided in her about her Jenny, Kerry was sympathetic. Maria looked at her watch. If what these guys said was true, and it must be, the cops would be here any minute. Then it would be too late. She called a taxi and grabbed her coat.

Kerry turned the fire up, and the coals glowed in the hearth, making the room feel cosy against the howling gale. She sat on the armchair nursing a mug of tea, and flicked on the little stained glass lamp on the table by the fire. The light sent shadows of purple and red and yellow across the framed photographs on the bookshelves. Every image a memory – her mother and father, radiant smiles from their first cruise ship holiday many years ago, when her dad really began to make good money. She recalled her mother raving about the splendour and the rich people swanning around, and them laughing that here they were, part of the jet set. Then another snapshot of herself with her dad, his arm draped over her shoulder on a holiday at her aunt's home in the Costa del Sol, Kerry's face and shoulders suntanned from two weeks on the beach. It was their last holiday before her father died suddenly eight weeks later, and her life changed for ever. Then a photograph of Kerry graduating, in her gown, smiling for the camera, but the radiance was gone from her eyes. The pain still stung her, and reminded her of how sad and forlorn she'd been as a teenager, being sent away like that to a foreign country. Even though her aunt and uncle were there and her mum visited, her joy was gone. She'd lost the carefree little girl she was in the earlier picture. But the truth was that although she lost that little girl, she'd never really left her behind, and in dark days the agony of losing her father so young and then being away from her mother followed her around. She remembered her mother telling her when she was just fourteen years old that she was so precious to them because they had waited such a long time for her. Her mother had three miscarriages before Kerry finally came to complete their family, and she was so cherished that they did everything to protect her. It was hard for her to comprehend why she was being sent away, but she came to understand that they were only doing it for her own protection. Despite that, she had missed so much time with her mother, and now it was too late. She sipped her tea and listened as the rain battered the bay window and the trees thrashed against the wind. So much to be done now, she told herself. She touched her father's picture and murmured, 'Don't worry, Da, I won't let you down.' Her mobile rang and shuddered on the table and she looked at the screen. No name, but she recognised the number. It was Sharon Potter. She pushed the key and put the phone to her ear.

'Hello?'

'Kerry?'

'Sharon. How you doing?' Her voice was deadpan.

'Kerry. I need help. I'm sorry to phone you like this. I'm in big trouble.'

Kerry wasn't sure if she wanted to hear this, but she knew she had to. The moment she'd agreed to meet her, she was already in for whatever was going to happen.

'What's happened?'

'Knuckles. He tried to have me killed. He sent his fucking boys to shoot me.'

'What? Christ!'

'I got away.'

'How did you manage that?' She said it as matter of fact as she could, despite her shock. What the hell had she got herself into?

'Don't ask. But right now, two of that bastard Knuckles'

men are lying in the mud in the middle of a back road near Manchester airport, and I'm heading north.'

'Jesus.' This woman, whoever she was, didn't mess around. 'Seriously?'

'Yeah. Fucking seriously. Look, can you meet me soon? First thing. I'm just south of Glasgow on the motorway. Nobody will look for me up here. But Knuckles will know by now that I got away. Listen, as I told you before, I've got stuff. Information you'll want. I . . . I . . .'

Kerry could hear her voice quiver a little and she knew that whatever she had done was beginning to sink in. She had to think fast.

'Okay. Take it easy. Listen, I'll get you booked into a hotel – One Devonshire Gardens. Okay? Head for Great Western Road, and it's just off that. You'll find it easily. Phone me when you're outside. I'll get someone to look out for you tonight. We'll meet in the morning. Don't worry.' She realised the don't worry bit sounded ridiculous. This wasn't a client she was telling to not worry about a business deal.

'Thanks, Kerry. I . . . I really appreciate that.'

Again, the voice was quivering. Sharon didn't have to say she was terrified. It was coming across loud and clear. They both hung up.

Suddenly there was a knock on the living room door and it opened. Gerry, one of the security men, stepped inside. Kerry looked up, a little impatient at being disturbed.

'Sorry, Kerry. But there's a woman outside banging at the front security entrance. Says she needs to speak to you urgently.'

Kerry looked at him, confused.

'What?'

'Says her name is Maria. She was at the funeral yester-day. She says she talked to you and that she's a pal.'

Kerry stood up, surprised. Something bad must have happened for Maria to come banging on her door. She hadn't given her phone number, which she should have but got caught up, then Maria had disappeared. Kerry went towards the door.

'Let her in, Gerry. I'll come down with you. It's okay. She's an old friend.'

Downstairs, Kerry stood in the kitchen watching out of the window as the steel side door was unlocked by a guard in a raincoat down to his ankles as the rain lashed across the yard. Maria stepped in, soaked, and she was ushered up to the back door. Kerry opened it, and stood looking at her friend, hair soaked, her face flushed and tear-stained.

'Maria. Jesus. You're soaked through. Come in, for God's sake.'

Maria came in, and Kerry nodded to Gerry to go. She closed the door. Maria began to crumple.

'Oh, Kerry! I'm so sorry! I didn't have your number and I knew roughly where the big house was, so I got a taxi but then I didn't know the exact house, and there's nobody in the bloody streets here to ask anything, so I was rapping on doors like a mad woman . . .' She ranted, not stopping for breath.

'Here. Sit down. Don't worry about that. Take your coat off.' Kerry ushered her to a chair at the kitchen table and stuck on the kettle. 'What's happened?'

'Oh, Kerry. It's our Cal. I'm frantic. And Jenny. There's trouble. Cal . . . Our Cal. He's been arrested. Down south.'

'What? How?'

'Christ. I don't know. Drugs or something. All they said was he was dropping something off. Cops have got him.'

For a moment, Kerry thought of their own operations, and hoped that no bastard on the ground who worked for her was doing his own little racket.

'What do you mean? He was working for drug dealers?'

'I don't know. They just came to the flat to warn me that he'd been arrested by the cops and not to open my mouth once they came to tell me. They said they've got Jenny.'

'Who are these guys? Do you know anything about them?'

'No. No idea. They just turned up. Two of them. They said some operation went tits up. I mean, my Cal. He told me he was working a doubler in the car wash. But they said he was in Manchester for them. I'm sick with worry. Cal just wouldn't do that. He's a good boy.' Her face flushed.

'Right. Okay. Just try to take it easy. Listen to me. We'll get this sorted. Where's Jenny?'

'I don't know. They said she's safe as long as Cal keeps his mouth shut.'

Kerry took mugs from the cupboard and placed them on the worktop.

'Right. Let's just sit down and go from the start here, Maria.' She put her hand on her friend's shoulder and felt how skinny she was. 'It'll be all right. We'll sort this. No matter what.'

# CHAPTER FIFTEEN

Kerry had woken early despite another sleepless night. It had been three nights since her mother's funeral and each day she'd thrown herself into work, going over all the businesses they ran, looking at bank accounts and working out where she was going to go from here. It was a long road, but she was on it now. Since Jake Cahill had come over to her at the wake and told her the job was done, Kerry had gone over it again and again in her mind how easily she took the news. She had ordered a hit on four killers, and her instructions were carried out. That part of what she was becoming was not recognisable to her, but it *was* really her. *She* had given the order, and what had caused her the sleepless nights was that she hadn't even flinched. Perhaps she was overthinking it. Nobody else, not Danny, not Marty – though he must have known about it – even discussed it with her afterwards. She hadn't expected Danny to say anything, but she might have expected Marty to mention something, because he saw that she was something more than the head of a gangster family. Perhaps because he saw what her father's hopes had been for them. But if he was affected or disappointed, she didn't know, because he behaved no differently towards her. He was too professional. His job was to look after the legal affairs – as he told her, to keep them all out of jail. She was having breakfast in the study when she heard a knock on the door and Sasha put her head around.

'There's police at the door, Kerry. A DI Burns. He would like to speak with you.'

Kerry frowned. Her first instinct was to phone Marty. For a second it occurred to her that he might be coming to question her over the murders of the hitmen. But she was being ridiculous. Jake Cahill never left any traces that could come back to anyone. She picked up her mobile, scrolled down to Marty's number. Then she changed her mind. There was nothing to be nervous about. Her legal mind told her not to worry.

'Show him in, Sasha. Is he alone?'

'A woman is with him.'

'Fine.'

Kerry stood up and adjusted her skirt and fixed her hair. There was a knock on the door, then it opened and in walked Vinny Burns. He looked at her and she caught him flick a glance up and down her, but his face showed nothing.

'Morning, Kerry. Sorry to disturb you.' He turned to the woman. 'This is DC Galbraith.'

'How you doing, Inspector . . . Constable. What can I do for you?'

'Well. We'd like to ask you about a couple of incidents three days ago. Four men were murdered.'

The words didn't knock Kerry off her feet the way they might have done a few weeks ago. She shot him a give-me-a-break look.

'Four men were murdered? I saw something on the news.' She screwed her eyes up. 'So what's that got to do with me, Inspector? Three days ago. That was the day of my mother's funeral.'

He nodded. 'Yes. It was. Four men were murdered on that day.'

Kerry shrugged and managed a bit of a sigh. 'Well. You'll need to help me out here, Inspector,' she said with more than a hint of sarcasm. 'I would ask you to sit down and have some coffee, and we could chat about the various murders that have happened in Glasgow in recent months.' She raised her eyebrows. 'Or are you going to come here and ask me about everyone who gets bumped off? Because I honestly don't know why you're here.'

She saw Vinny blush slightly and there was a small stab of *serves you right* in her gut. There was history here with this man. He had meant the world to her. Sure, they had only been teenagers, but she could still call up that hurt all these years on.

He looked a little frustrated.

'Look, Kerry, I'm not going to beat about the bush here. I'll just tell you straight. These men, two from Manchester – and two from Belfast. They are known violent criminals. It is our information that they were hired by Joe Knuckles Boyle. That these are the men who came to your brother's funeral – that these are the men who killed your mother, and your brother.'

Kerry let the words hang in the air for as long as she could, feeling the glare of the female detective.

'You mean the hitmen.' She shrugged. 'Well, good riddance to them. Maybe Knuckles Boyle decided to get rid of them in case they talked. I mean, who knows, Inspector? What do you want me to say here?'

She saw Vinny's jaw muscle tighten and she could feel his unease, and sense his defeat.

'Kerry, when I came here last week, after your mother's murder, I said to you that I wanted to help find her killers. I meant that. I wanted to find them and bring them to justice, because that is the way we do business.'

'I appreciate that, Inspector. Thanks. But somebody obviously got there first – because that's how *they* do business.'

She could feel the burst of adrenalin that she was somehow getting her own back on Vinny for the hurt all those years ago, even though she knew that was an irrational notion. But it felt good. In front of this female detective, who probably thought he was some kind of big shot, he was being put in his place by a woman who was having none of his crap.

He said nothing for a long moment, and Kerry stood defiant. Eventually, he gave her a weary look.

'Okay, Kerry. I understand. But these men are suspected of murdering your mother and brother, then they are killed while your mother's funeral is taking place. We don't think that's a coincidence. There is talk that this is a hit by the Casey organisation.'

'Aw, come on, Inspector. Talk? There's always talk. You're coming to me with rumours? Give me a break. We're not the Corleones. Where are you getting this stuff from? I honestly think if you have evidence then you should really take it somewhere and see where you go with it. I have nothing to tell you here.'

Deep down, even though she was winning this encounter, there was still a little part of Kerry that knew he was saying and doing the right thing. That what she had done – ordering the hit – was the wrong thing. What she should be doing was working with him, as he'd suggested a few days ago. But it was all too late for that.

He took a step back.

'Okay. I wanted to give you a heads up about what is being said on the street, and if some nutter like Knuckles Boyle thinks the Casey organisation is behind this, then he will hit back, and he will hit hard. That means you are a target.'

Kerry nodded slowly.

'I think I'm aware I am a target, Inspector. I wish the police had been around when my brother Mickey was gunned down in the street like a dog, or when Knuckles Boyle was planning to come to his funeral and murder my poor mother. I wish the word on the street had come to the police then, and perhaps we could have been prepared so that my mother would still be here.'

The words at the end choked her. Their eyes locked for a moment, then he looked away.

'Fair enough. Fair comment. I'll leave you to it. I'm sorry to have disturbed you. And I'm really sorry for the loss of your mother. It must be so hard to deal with.' He paused. 'But if at any time you want to talk to us, then please call me. I mean any time, day or night.' He turned and left. Kerry stood, feeling her day already ruined.

# CHAPTER SIXTEEN

In the back seat of the Merc, Kerry was on her mobile as the driver approached the boutique hotel. As he swung into the small car park at One Devonshire Gardens, she finished her call with Marty Kane. She'd phoned him last night to ask him to see what he could find out about Cal's arrest. He'd already established that Cal was being held in Manchester by drugs squad detectives but would be getting transferred to Glasgow. It was Marty who suggested he go down and pick him up and see about organising bail for him, rather than have him shunted up to Glasgow in custody.

'Okay. Thanks, Marty. I'll tell Maria. She called this morning to say the police had been at her house last night to inform her he was arrested. She's a bit panicky, as you can imagine, but she'll feel better if she knows you're with him.'

'Don't worry, Kerry.'

'Do you think they'll let the boy out?'

'We'll see. That'll be my plan. I'll do my best.'

'Good. I'm going to meet someone, and will call you later. I want to talk to you about this meeting I'm about to have anyway.'

'See you later.' He hung up.

Good old Marty, Kerry thought. He hadn't even questioned Kerry becoming involved in Maria's problems, despite her being an outsider. It was enough that she'd told him Maria was an old schoolfriend who was struggling and whose kids were in serious trouble. Marty was a family man with two grown-up children and grandkids. She remembered her father telling her years ago that as well as being the best lawyer in the country, he was a man of compassion. She knew he would pull out all the stops to help someone less fortunate than him.

There were two sharp-looking businessmen in the reception area of the hotel when Kerry came through the swing doors and stepped onto the thick, cushioned carpet, into the quiet understated quality of One Devonshire Gardens. It was one of her favourite hotels and oozed discretion and class. The young man on reception glanced up as she came in, but said nothing. He would know who she was. It was the kind of place where the staff didn't approach you unless you came to them – or unless, of course, you looked like you didn't belong there. Kerry knew she belonged here. She'd had dinners and meetings over the years on her visits, and it was the last place she went for dinner with her mother on her most recent visit home before Mickey was killed. She could see pictures of the two of them in her mind as she walked across the lobby, and it brought a lump to her throat that she could never do that again. She swallowed, took a deep breath, and stood for a moment, until the only woman in the room at a table at the far corner below a window looked up. Kerry looked back at the woman, smart, well dressed, dyed hair and suntan, glamorous in a way that was just bordering on being tacky. The woman stood up. Kerry strode confidently across the room. She was in charge here. Sharon Potter knew how powerful she was, and it was she who had made the call asking for help. And the fact that Sharon had more or less told her she'd bumped off her would-be executioners meant Kerry had to stand up to her.

'Sharon,' Kerry said as she got to the table.

'Hello, Kerry. Thanks for coming. I really appreciate it.'

The accent was north of England. Kerry was used to all the different English accents exported to the Costa del Sol, and some of them were rough. Others were posh, old money, ex-pats who opted to live out their lives in the sunshine.

Kerry shook her hand and glanced at the teapot. She turned around where she knew a waiter would be hovering at the door of the lounge. She beckoned him across.

'Some tea for me please.' She looked at Sharon. 'Another pot for you? Food?'

'No. Thanks. Just some water please.'

The waiter almost bowed as he turned and left.

Kerry let out a long sigh, removing her jade green scarf and putting it over the back of the leather armchair. She slipped off her navy coat, put her bag down and sat in the armchair. Only then did she meet Sharon's dark brown eyes, right down to the false eyelashes. Her face was framed by high cheekbones and lush blondish hair. She looked well. No signs of botox or work, unless it was very discreet.

'I'm so glad to see you. I'm glad to be actually alive to see you.' Sharon shook her head, looked a little frustrated. From the brief half-smile, Kerry could see perfect white teeth. So it wasn't all natural – this was at least a four grand job.

'From the sound of you yesterday, Sharon, it was a harrowing day.'

'Not to put too fine a point on it. I'm shattered.'

There was a moment's pause where Kerry felt the need to lay some ground rules. She leaned forward.

'Sharon. I want to be clear about something before we go any further.'

Sharon looked a little surprised; the first few seconds of their meeting had been almost friendly, but now it was being injected with a bit of power.

'Course.'

'Joe Boyle and his mob. I know they sent the squad up to my brother's funeral.'

There was a stony silence.

'In fact, I want to just say this: you've got some brass neck if you knew about that and are now coming to me looking for my help.'

A little colour rose on Sharon's neck.

'Kerry. I swear. I swear on anybody's life that I knew nothing about it. I swear on my own son's life.'

'And Joe's crew killed my brother.'

She looked at the table for a second as though choosing her words, then back at Kerry.

'I'm not going to lie to you. I knew about that. But only after it happened. Knuckles never told me about anything like that. I overheard it. I heard him talking on the phone. Not sure who to. But I heard him say it, but it was after it happened. I swear to God I didn't know about the funeral.'

They sat for a moment saying nothing. Kerry looked at her, waited for her to keep defending herself or see what she would say next. She was squirming a little, and she could see that. Whatever Sharon had expected, she didn't expect to be grilled like this.

'Did you not think I would ask you this, Sharon? Did you think you could come for help and me not ask this? It was your man, your organisation. You're lucky my boys didn't just bag and tag you and send you back Royal Mail to that fucker of a boyfriend.'

Sharon suddenly turned pale.

'Look, Kerry. Please. Christ! I don't know what to say

here. I . . . I just know that I know stuff about him if you want to ruin him. I heard the talk about the funeral and what happened and your mother being killed. Awful. But I know Knuckles is vulnerable. I know every area. If you want revenge I can give you it. But trust me: I came to you for two reasons. Firstly, I knew he was going to do me in and I wanted out. And the second, you seemed to be the perfect person to take him on, from what I've heard them saying about you. I know they are all over the place working out how to deal with you. I liked the sound of who you are and how you are treating people. And I thought – and maybe this was stupid – but I thought, you know something? I can do business with this woman.' She paused for a long moment, then looked Kerry square in the eye, a little defiant. 'But, look, if I got it wrong, then I'll go now. I have money so I can lie low and fuck off. But I'm not going to come here and lie to you. And I don't want to be your whipping boy for what happened. I'm sorry about your mother. Really sorry. I lost my mother when I was a child and spent my life without one. I can only imagine what it must have been like. I hope you can understand that, because if you don't, and want to be mad at me or blame me in any way, then I should just get my coat on and fuck right off.' She swallowed. 'The only thing that keeps me here is my boy. My son. Our Tony. If it wasn't for him, I would just disappear and reinvent myself somewhere far away. But I can't. He doesn't even know I've left yet. He's in boarding school in the Borders.' She blinked, turning away. 'It's only him that's kept me going all these years.'

Kerry said nothing, let her talk. She'd wanted to see what she was made of. If Sharon had come in here and surrendered, ready to take any crap that was dished out to her, then she was not to be trusted. But she could see she was angry and wronged, and fighting back. Kerry liked that. She had the gut feeling that she was telling the truth. She knew that this woman was not naive. She would be well aware that if the Casey family wanted to, her journey would end right here in Glasgow, today. Kerry's instinct was to sit tight and listen. She watched as Sharon fiddled with the gold bracelet encrusted with what looked like real diamonds, matching the bigger rock on her finger. However she had come this far, she looked like she'd been well paid.

Kerry took a breath and let out a sigh. She uncrossed her legs and leaned in a little, fixing Sharon's eyes with hers.

'Fine.' She nodded. 'I didn't invite you here to humiliate you, Sharon, or to give you more grief than you seem to have already had with Knuckles Boyle. I'm sorry about your son. It seems to be a real mess right now, and you know that Knuckles will be all over the shop looking for you. Tell me – would he have any suspicion you'd be heading up here?'

'No.' Sharon shook her head. 'Absolutely not. Knuckles hasn't a good word to say about your family or any of your organisation.'

'Yet he did business with us,' Kerry said quickly.

'Course. Because it suited him.'

'He'll not be doing any more business with us. He'll have got the message by now that the bastards they sent up here to my brother's funeral are never coming back.'

Sharon raised her eyebrows.

'You've already dealt with that.'

Kerry blinked but didn't answer.

'He'll go mental,' Sharon said. 'Honestly. He's a fucking psycho, Kerry. Word will get round that you've had your revenge and he'll have to hit back bigger. He will.'

'I'm not worried about that,' Kerry said, calmly. 'We can deal with him.' She glanced over her shoulder even though they were alone. 'But, listen. Before we go any further, I have some questions to ask you.'

'Sure. Anything I can tell you I will. I can promise you this. I have no loyalty to Knuckles Boyle. Not any more. Not now. He tried to have me murdered. I'm the bloody mother of his child and he tried to get me killed. I'm going to ruin him.'

Kerry nodded. 'Okay. How are you going to do that? What have you got on him?'

Sharon patted her handbag beside her. 'It's me who has moved his money around over the years, set up his accounts so he could launder his dirty money. I have all the inside information, know where the money was being spent, and more. I have it all – the warehouses in Amsterdam: it was me who bought them for him. Knuckles just let me do everything because he trusted me, and he knew I was capable of organising things to make sure he was covered. Well, now I have it all on an external hard drive that can bury him.'

'Good,' Kerry, said, impressed. 'But tell me this. Frankie Martin . . .' She studied Sharon's face, and saw a flicker of recognition. 'You know him, right?'

Sharon nodded. 'I know him. I met him twice. Once when he was down in Manchester with your brother Mickey, and once in Marbella when he came over for a meeting. Maybe I've met him three times – I'm not sure.'

'When was that – the meeting in Marbella? Was that long before Mickey was murdered?'

'Few weeks before it. Maybe a month. I remember him being over. It wouldn't be surprising for the main men from other crews to come over to Marbella and meet up with Knuckles for a bit of golf or something if they were cutting a deal. Mickey and Frankie were here a couple of times over the past two years, when they were making the deals with Knuckles.'

'But Frankie came on his own a few weeks before Mickey got shot. Was that not unusual?'

Sharon shrugged slightly. 'I suppose it was a bit. I mean, it was clear that Mickey was the boss when they were over. But Frankie seemed to get on with Knuckles well, probably better than Mickey. I only met your brother briefly, but he seemed a bit offhand and I suppose kind of brusque.

Frankie was a charmer with everyone he met. I remember a dinner one night in a restaurant in Puerto de la Duquesa and Frankie had everyone in stitches telling stories. Mickey didn't look too happy. But to be honest, all that banter was usually going on with the lads at the other end of the table, and I was with the girls, not really involved in it. I mean, I always had one eye on the game, but I wouldn't be getting told anything Knuckles didn't want me to know. I wouldn't know if anything underhand was going on between Frankie and Knuckles. But I do know they spoke on the phone a couple of days ago, which I thought was strange after what happened at the funeral. I overheard it from my hallway. Knuckles sounded like he was giving Frankie a hard time. I heard Knuckles mention your name, saying that you needed to understand business was business.'

Kerry felt suddenly hot as the truth dawned on her. It was Frankie. It was him all along. And this was as close to confirmation as she could get that he'd betrayed them. She saw Sharon look at her.

'Look, Kerry. All I can tell you is what I saw. I don't know anything between the three of them. They worked together. Mickey was in charge and Frankie was his side-kick. If I knew any more I would tell you.'

Kerry leaned forward and gripped Sharon's wrist.

'I want you to think hard, Sharon. Think. Try to remember everything that was said. Any little reactions or asides. Anything you heard Knuckles talking about during the meetings when Mickey and Frankie were there, and when Frankie came over on his own. I know it was Knuckles who put the hit out on my brother. I know that for sure it was Knuckles who sent the men to his funeral. I need to know more of the betrayal. That's what I need.'

Sharon looked at her.

'You think it was Frankie?'

Kerry nodded slowly.

'Yes. I believe it was Frankie. But I need to be sure.'

# CHAPTER SEVENTEEN

It had taken less than twenty-four hours for Jack Reilly to give Kerry the name of the men who'd visited Maria at her home to issue the threats on Cal and Jenny. When a deal went bad and a fortune was lost in drugs and cash, news tended to spread like wildfire on the streets. There was plenty of gloating when word got around that it was Rab Pollock's deal that had gone tits up in Manchester. He was a dealer from Glasgow's East End who'd got too big for his boots when he broke away from the main unit who ran that side of town. So there was no shortage of people to stick the knife into him. And worse than that, he had sent a daft boy south for the pick-up, and now the lad was in the pokey, probably spilling his guts. But everyone knew the money was the least of Pollock's worries. The man he'd sent with the young boy for the pick-up was nowhere to be found. Denny Thomson had disappeared off the face of the earth, and that could only mean one thing: he'd grassed them up for his own reasons. Kerry had listened as Jack filled her in on all the details, while they worked out where to go from here.

'Cal is on his way up to Glasgow,' Kerry told Jack. 'So we won't know much detail until Marty and his mum get a word with him.'

'Course,' Jack said. 'But we know for sure that it was Pollock's deal, and I know who the thugs were who visited Maria at her house. One of them is a vicious bastard who just likes hurting people. He's not long out of jail. We should hit Pollock's mob sooner rather than later, Kerry. Sending bastards to put the frighteners on an innocent woman isn't on in my book. Plus the fact they're sending a wee laddie on a drop like that. It's fucking outrageous. Amateur night. That's what it is.'

None of this made Kerry feel comfortable. Cal and Maria had never wanted to be part of the Casey outfit, but they were in it now – through no fault of Maria's, but down to the stupidity of her son. Not that she could blame him. She had barely spoken to Cal, but from what Maria had told her of the boy, he would be doing it to help his mother make ends meet. That made her even more guilty. Sure, she was in a position to do something about these bastards who had sent her son down to Manchester, but in reality that didn't make her much better than them. The cycle went on, and she was embroiled in it as much as anyone else. It was people like Maria, like Cal, and his poor drug-addled sister, that were the real victims here. And it was the people at the top who made money from drugs – people like the Caseys – who lived off the victims. That would never sit well with Kerry.

'Okay,' she said eventually. 'I'm going to leave it with you, Jack. Do what you need to do. But my main concern right now is what we do with Maria and Cal. They can't go back to that house. Can you sort out one of our flats for them in the Merchant City or somewhere?'

'No problem. I'll get someone onto it. Once she gets here and you talk to her, you'll get a better idea. But she needs to understand that her life has changed now.'

Kerry nodded in agreement. Nobody had to tell *her* about how life can change in the blink of an eye.


Cal had said very little from the moment the police arrested him in the café at the train station in Manchester, until an officer came into the cell where he was being held and told him he was being released on bail. He had no idea how that happened, but he found himself looking at the officer and muttering 'Thanks, sir.' The officer had looked at him and shook his head as though he couldn't quite comprehend how a boy his age, who was not an obvious toerag, had become so mixed up in a crime like this. One after another, the detectives had come in and questioned him, albeit without much force, to tell them who he was working for. All Cal could say was the truth – that he had no idea of the names. And he hadn't even been told what was in the cases. Whether they believed him or not didn't matter, because at one point the door opened and a lawyer walked in all confident in a smart suit and coat, and told them he was Marty Kane and he was here to bring Cal to Glasgow.

Now, here he was, sinking into the soft leather seats in the back of this big black Mercedes, gazing out of the blacked-out windows, wondering how he was going to calm his mum down when he met her. Mr Kane had told him that he was being released on bail pending further investigations, but may have to go back down to Manchester in a couple of weeks. He told him he was in serious trouble, but they would do their best to keep him from being locked up. The very mention of 'locked up' made his bowels churn, almost as much as they had when the cops picked him up yesterday. He'd felt physically sick all the way to the police station and at one point had to get them to stop the car so he could get out and throw up at the side of the road, with a big cop standing next to him looking disgusted. What a mess, he'd told himself a hundred times over as he lay in the cell overnight at the police station, freezing, angry, depressed and terrified all at the same time. He just wanted to be home with his mum. He was sorry, he would tell her for the rest of his life. There was a big well-built guy sitting on the front seat beside Marty Kane and his name was Jack, and he didn't speak as polite and posh as Mr Kane, but more like himself. But when they'd stopped at a motorway café to get some food and tea, the big man told him in no uncertain terms what a dick he'd been. He'd waited until Mr Kane went to the toilet, then he'd reached across the table and grabbed him by the collar and told him that if he thought he was going to be a hard man then he'd failed big time and he was an idiot.

'Forget about it now and get on with your studies. From what I hear you are a good, bright lad with plenty to get on with, so use your brains,' he told him. Cal wanted to say to him that there was no future in working your balls off to get somewhere when guys like the people he'd worked for over the recent weeks doing drops were driving around in fancy cars and wearing designer clothes. He knew deep down it was all crap, but he wanted a better life right now, not after studying and working like a dog. But he kept it to himself. All he could see now as they were getting into Glasgow city centre was his mother's image in his head and his hands began to sweat. As they drove out of the city and headed up towards Maryhill Road, he wondered where they were taking him. For a split second he thought maybe they were part of the gang he'd been working for and maybe he was getting bumped off.

'Where are you taking me, Mr Kane?'

'To see your mammy, son.'

Cal felt himself blushing, feeling like a stupid child being slapped down.

'But we don't live up here.'

'I know. She's not in her house at the moment.'

'So am I going to your office?' he persisted.

'No. Just sit tight. Stop asking so many questions. If I was you, I'd be preparing for a thick ear and to apologise to your mother. She's been off her head with worry.'

'I'm sorry.' He sank back, looked out of the window as the landscape changed from the tenements to the bigger houses and finally to the great sandstone villas that spoke of wealth and success and everything he dreamed of.

Maria was in the kitchen of Kerry's house, up and down at the window watching for the car bringing Cal up from Manchester.

'He'll be here in the next couple of minutes, Maria,' Kerry said. 'Don't worry.'

Maria turned to her old friend and swallowed the lump in her throat. If it hadn't been for Kerry, she'd probably have been visiting her son in some young offenders' unit down in Manchester. But now he was being driven up the road by Kerry's family lawyer – some guy called Marty Kane, who Maria had only ever heard of in newspaper stories about notorious gangsters, who'd walked free from court because Marty Kane had got them off. She was under no illusion what he was, what all this was, as she'd gazed around the lavish surroundings of Kerry's big stone house up in the posh end of the city. Places like this she would only have ever seen the inside of if she was cleaning them for the well-heeled owners, or one time when she'd worked with a catering company, and they were doing a twenty-first birthday party for the rich couple's daughter. It had always stuck in her mind, the splendour of the place, the clothes people were wearing, the polite, well-mannered guests gathered in the big room, the jazz band playing in the corner. It was a different world, and one she could never be a part of, and yet she didn't feel envious or bitter. The only thing that choked her was the young people, privileged, well dressed and happy, while her Jenny was already a drug addict, living in some squat, using her body to buy heroin, when she wasn't shoplifting to pay for her habit. The one Maria had been in was the home of a wealthy surgeon. But Kerry Casey's home was where the Casey empire had grown up. They were gangsters and everyone knew it. They were feared and respected across the city and beyond. But Kerry had long since been away from all that, living, she'd been told, in Spain or London or somewhere and growing up away from all the trappings of the gangster world. Now here she was, running the show. None of it was lost on Maria. Especially since she knew that it was she who had come to Kerry for help. She did it without really giving it much thought, because she was desperate. But she knew that once you knocked on the door of someone like this and asked for help, then you were for ever in their debt. She would have to find out how to live with that.

Right now, all she wanted was for those big iron electronic gates to open on the driveway and Cal to come walking out of the car. She felt like shaking the life out of him and hugging him at the same time. But this wasn't over yet – not by any means. Because Jenny was still missing. And Kerry had told her that she had people working on that, and not to worry. She had handed herself over to her friend, lock, stock and barrel. And she didn't even care. Because now she felt safe and secure for the first time in many years.

Eventually, she heard a click and the big gate opened slowly, the security guard walking with it until it opened wide. Then the black Mercedes came through and glided into the courtyard, whispering to a halt. She watched as a tall, elegant man in rimless glasses and a blue suit got out of the passenger seat, as the chauffeur came around and opened the door. Then he opened the back door and she could see Cal. He looked small and skinny in the vastness of the car and she watched as he eased himself out, noticing he was dressed completely differently from what he had on when he left the house two days ago to go for a double shift at the car wash. Little bugger must have stashed his good jeans and Timberland boots in a bag somewhere, knowing what he was about to do. But she buried her anger as she caught his eye and he came across the yard and towards the back door.

'Mum,' Cal muttered shamefaced, as he stepped into the kitchen behind Marty. 'I'm so sorry.'

Maria took a step towards him and pulled him into her arms and held him.

'I know you are, son. I know.'

He buried his head in her shoulder.

'I was just trying to get some money for us. I'm sorry. It was stupid.'

'Yes, Cal. It was stupid.' She pulled away from him and wiped the tears off his cheeks with the palms of her hands. 'I hope you've thanked Mr Kane for going all the way to Manchester to bring you home.'

He gave her a sheepish look.

'I have.'

'Thanks, Mr Kane,' Maria said. 'I'm so grateful to you. I'll never forget what you did for us.'

Marty shook his head and smiled. 'No problem, Maria. I'll have a word with both of you once you get settled.'

Maria turned to Kerry. 'Cal, this is Kerry Casey. Remember the funeral I was going to the other day? Her mother? Well, you can thank Kerry for getting you out of this mess – as if she's not got more on her mind.'

Cal looked at Kerry, a little bewildered. He stretched out his hand.

'Thanks, Kerry. I'm really sorry . . . for everything. Really I am. I . . . I can work off whatever it costs for the lawyer and stuff and the journey. I can do loads of things, odd jobs.'

Kerry looked at him and kept her face deadpan.

'I think we know the odd jobs you can do, Cal. That's why you got into this mess.'

Maria looked from Kerry to Cal's blushing cheeks at the rebuke. She knew what Kerry was doing, giving the boy a dig, and she welcomed it, because she knew it had stung Cal. He would know the Casey family by reputation; Maria had mentioned to him that she and Kerry had been old schoolfriends many years ago. But if he thought he was going to get a warm reception then he was wrong. She let him shift awkwardly on his feet.

'I'm sorry,' Cal eventually said. 'I . . . I just meant that I'm grateful, and I can do things, like about the garden or wash the cars or something.'

Kerry's face softened a little. 'Well. We might make good use of you then. Meanwhile, are you hungry after your journey?'

'Starving. I couldn't eat on the way up, I was dead nervous.'

'He's always bloody starving.'

'I'm dying to get home and get a shower, Mum.' He turned to Maria. 'I've been wearing the same stuff since yesterday morning.'

There was a moment's silence.

'We're not going home, Cal,' Maria said sharply. 'We can't go back there.'

Cal glanced from his mum to Kerry.

'It's not safe,' Maria added.

Cal bit his lip.

'Oh, Mum. I'm so sorry.'

'Don't worry,' Kerry said. 'We're sorting some accommo-dation out for you.' She glanced at the table. 'Take a seat and we'll get something fixed up for you to eat. I'll leave the pair of you for a while to get talking.'

# CHAPTER EIGHTEEN

Knuckles Boyle was seriously losing patience. How in the name of Christ could she have escaped, leaving these two dickheads who were supposed to shoot her lying stiff on a country road in a pool of their own blood? Fucking bitch. He should have done it himself weeks ago, once he'd made his mind up she had to be got rid of. Instead of that, he'd left it to two of his trusted boys, and now they were dead, but worse than that, it meant that for the past few weeks Sharon might have been scamming and scheming before she left. He didn't even want to think about what she might have taken with her. She had more information on him and his dealings from here to Morocco to Amsterdam and the Costa than even he did. The only way to make sure all that stayed put was to get rid of her permanently. But now she was out there somewhere. That was his biggest problem. But everywhere he looked, more aggro was coming out of the fucking woodwork. The boys he'd sent up to make some mischief at Mickey Casey's funeral were now history as well. They were supposed to be lying fucking low until it all died down. But their bodies were found all over the place up in Jockland last week. And to top it all, a tidy little sideline he was working with another crew in Glasgow had just fucking gone down the stank. He'd been dealing with some cunt called Rab Pollock from up there, unknown to the Casey crew who would not have allowed it, would have seen it as a conflict of interests. But now that had ended in fucking tears, with the cops busting the whole shooting match at the pick-up point down here, and he'd dropped nearly a hundred fucking grand's worth of heroin in the fucking disaster. Some bastard had grassed, because now the cops were all over the place, sniffing and ripping apart his warehouses, trying to prove it was his heroin. So far, they hadn't got anywhere, and his lawyers were keeping it all at bay. But word was beginning to leak out that Knuckles Boyle's organisation was in trouble, and that was never good. Cunts scenting blood would trample all over you at the first sign of weakness. So he had to start doing something rapid to save face. Frankie Martin had been onto him from Glasgow to say that things were getting rougher up there every day with this Kerry bird throwing her weight around. But first and most important, he had to find that fucker Sharon, before she did any damage. He stood up, paced the length of the table, conscious of his boys watching his every move and wincing at his rant, waiting for the next onslaught.

'Right, Jimbo . . . Talk to me. I mean, there must be some fucking sign of her. She didn't just disappear off the face of the earth. Tell me again, what have you checked?'

Jimbo shifted in his seat.

'Well. You know we found the car and the bodies. And you know we had to torch them before any cops could get a look at anything. But we've had people checking Sharon's credit cards, and taxi firms have been spoken to, as well as car hire firms. We've found every taxi driver that was close by the area where that happened. I mean, she must have got a taxi somewhere – when she got to the end of that road she dumped the car. But nobody is saying a fucking thing. With the cops all over the place on the murders, nobody wants to open their mouths, even if they did see Sharon. Maybe she got picked up by another car or something, just random. Maybe someone gave her a lift and dropped her in town, in which case she'd just be one of hundreds of people who took a taxi that day. It's been impossible.' He paused. 'And yes, we've checked all the hotels in a ten mile radius – but nothing. She's got out of Manchester quickly. Either she hired or borrowed a car. We don't have a clue. Nothing from the car hire places. They don't give any information out on customers.'

Knuckles had been gazing out of the big window into

the city, and the traffic below his office, while Jimbo was reeling off all this non-information that was getting him nowhere. He was still smarting heavily about the loss of his drugs at the train station. He needed to know more on that. Frankie Martin had called him yesterday and told him he thought he'd got some intelligence on who the teenager was that was picked up by cops. The boy had to be shut down smartish in case any of these dicks in Glasgow, who were stupid enough to send him on the job, had told the kid more than he needed to know. Frankie talked to that numpty Rab Pollock whose boy had gone missing, and he was the biggest suspect for grassing them up. But he too had fucked off for the moment, and that was not a good sign.

'Tommy, I want you to get Frankie on the phone again and grill him about this kid that got picked up by the cops and what he knows about him. Get him to talk to Pollock and find what we can. The last thing I need right now is this coming back to me worse than it already is, with cops breathing down my neck. We need to know who grassed us. Maybe it was even Pollock himself. Have you thought about that? Maybe we should just shoot the fucker in case he talks if the cops put him under pressure.'

He came back and sat down at the table, tired, weary and on edge. He looked at Al, a few seats away from him.

'And, Al. I can't believe we have four bastards murdered in Glasgow and we haven't got a single fucking clue as to who did it. Not a fucking clue. I need to know who it was who did the actual hit. Find out who did the shootings and we'll waste him. I don't give a fuck about the boys. They were stupid anyway to do what they did at the funeral. And they paid the price. So fuck them. But somebody from Casey's mob took a bit of revenge out there and sent us back a message, so we need to return that smartish before every cunt starts laughing at us. You got that?'

'Sure, boss. I'm working on it.'

'Good. And don't fucking do anything until you run it past me. Are we clear?'

Frankie Martin was feeling more and more out of the loop. He'd already poured his heart out to Kerry about how loyal he was, and he thought he'd made some inroads there when they met a few days ago. In fact, he thought he'd even caught her stealing little glances at him, and he'd left the room that day with a little inkling in his pants that he could get into hers if he chose the right moment. But in the last few days he couldn't get near her. It was becoming clear that she was distancing herself from him. Frankie was used to having most of it his own way. Especially with women. If he wanted a woman, he snapped his fingers and they were on their knees in no time. He thought about Kerry. She was different. He'd known her all his life. When Mickey died he'd felt that he'd be protective of her, that he'd look after her when she came back. Maybe it would have turned out that way. Things could have been so different if that prick Boyle hadn't fucked it up at the funeral. He was supposed to send a message that would make him look like he was in charge, but the pricks who turned up fucked it up and Kerry's poor ma got caught in the crossfire. He'd never forgive himself for that, because she'd treated him like a second son all her life, and he felt he'd betrayed her. But it shouldn't have happened like that. *He* should be in charge right now. But Kerry was throwing herself about all over the place, stepping on a lot of people. And he was frozen out. He had to find a way to get back in here, or he had to make sure he destroyed her.

Rab Pollock chopped up two lines of coke on the glass coaster on his office table, then leaned down and snorted one, holding his breath till he felt that familiar little bite between his eyes that made everything much clearer, much easier to handle.

'Fucking good gear that. Too good to punt. Get it cut more before you push it out there, mate.'

He pushed the coaster across the table to Tommy McCann, who bent across and snorted the other line, then sat back twisting his face as though he was trying to work the sensation into every nerve end. McCann was enjoying his new role as Pollock's right-hand man, after he'd been bounced out of the Paradise Club by that bitch Kerry Casey, but it had got a little rough in recent days when the Manchester drugs pick-up went tits up.

'Don't worry. It's getting well cut, mate. You'll get a great return on this shit, Rab. Good batch, though. Keep the best for ourselves, eh?'

Rab glared at him, knowing the fat little prick was trying to arse-lick because of the fortune he'd lost him in Manchester. He shouldn't have trusted McCann, when he told him he'd put Denny Thomson on the drop along with some wee guy they'd been using for local drops, who was reliable. It wasn't the wee guy's fault that Denny fucked off and left him. It was McCann who put Thomson on the job, and said he was one of his best men who he could trust. So much for that. Thomson disappeared as soon as the stuff was dropped, and seconds before the cops were all over it. That told you one thing – he had grassed to someone who had grassed up to the cops for their own reasons. Why Thomson did it was a mystery, McCann had said in his defence, but none of that mattered a fuck. As soon as they could find the cunt, he'd be history. But the more pressing problem right now was that Knuckles Boyle had been on the phone to him, shoving a rocket up his arse because he was down nearly a hundred grand of smack that was now in a locked room in a fucking police station in Manchester, while the bizzies were all over his warehouses trying to prove it belonged to him. Knuckles had made it clear to

Rab that he now owned every area of his business until the hundred grand was paid back. Much as it choked him, Rab knew better than to question it. He'd told Knuckles that he had the junkie sister of the boy who'd gone on the drop with Thomson, and as long as he had her, the boy would keep his mouth shut. His boys had paid the mother a visit to make sure she and her son kept it zipped. Knuckles told him he should chop one of her fingers off and get it delivered to the boy's mother to make sure her son kept his mouth shut. But McCann assured him that the boy knew nothing – well, unless Thomson had been running his mouth off during the train journey. So Rab was feeling well fucked.

He and McCann were running a few whores from a house in the East End, but it wasn't big business. McCann had managed to procure a few Eastern European birds, and as long as he had their passports and kept them junked up, they belonged to him. He'd been to the house himself yesterday to see the set-up, and it was busy enough. He'd also seen the room where the Jenny bird McCann had was being held. In fact, she wasn't a bad-looking wee thing, apart from being skinny as a rake. She was spaced out, so she didn't know why she'd been taken there – the stupid bitch must have thought her fairy godmother had come to make sure she'd enough smack to keep her happy. Rab told McCann to put her to work, so she at least earned her keep. He looked across at McCann, whose eyes were coked up bright.

'Listen. We need to find a way to make more money. Everything we're shifting right now is going back down to Knuckles for the smack he lost. I'm going to be in the grubber paying back this cunt.' He sniffed. 'And it's all your fucking fault. I shouldn't have listened to you.'

'Aw, mate. We'll work something out. I've got my ear to the ground. Frankie Martin is still talking to me. I know he doesn't like that Kerry fucker – you know, Mickey's sister, who's running the show now?'

'Oh, you mean the bird who slapped you around your own office, you prick.'

'Aye. Well. That's no' finished yet. She'll pay for that in time. Believe me. Nobody slaps me around like that. Far less a fucking bird. I'm going to fucking torch the Paradise Club. It was *my* place.'

'It wasn't *your* place. You ran it for them. You didn't own it, you dick. Anyway, never mind about that. So what about Frankie?'

'He doesn't like Kerry. Says she's off her head, with a lot of big ideas about moving the business around. He says she's frozen him out and he doesn't have as much clout as he did.'

Rab nodded slowly. 'Interesting. But does he still hear things? I mean, does he know what's going on? If we could get something on her – something we could sell to Knuckles. We all know there's bad blood there. It might be a way to get him out of my hair.'

McCann said nothing, fidgeted in his seat.

'Why don't you have a drink with Frankie? See what's the craic. We could use a guy like Frankie on our side. I reckon this Casey mob are there for the taking, I'm telling you. A fucking woman running the show? I mean, they're a laughing stock.'

Rab went into his drawer and brought out another wrap of cocaine and emptied it onto the coaster.

'Let's think outside the box, man. Know what I mean?'

'Aye. Outside the box,' McCann said, with a slightly bewildered look.

# CHAPTER NINETEEN

Sharon knew the best way to really fuck up Knuckles Boyle was to hit him where it hurt – in his wallet. He'd been obsessed with money from the very first time she met him, when he was a mid-ranking hood, building up a reputation in Manchester as an armed robber, and a trusted enforcer for one of the bigger players. Everything was about money, because money was power. And Knuckles had made plenty of it. He was well established in the north, and very little moved without him knowing it, and because he had made so much money, he was able to deal with the boys in Amsterdam and Spain, organising his shipments. In his warehouse in Amsterdam, shipments of coke and heroin went through in everything from baby food to clothing, and even furniture. His men on the ground there had become expert at concealment, and one of Sharon's jobs had been to set all this up, travelling over there at least a couple of times a year to make sure it was all running like clockwork. She'd been two months ago, to make sure every-thing was straight for the next shipment, and that all the paperwork was ready. If Knuckles had any sense, he would cancel it now that she'd buggered off and couldn't be found. But she knew he was too greedy to do that, and also wouldn't want to lose face. And you couldn't be sitting with a ware-house in Amsterdam packed to the gunnels with drugs. You had to keep stuff moving or someone would get suspi-cious, and the National Crime Agency were everywhere these days. So Sharon had a plan to tell Kerry about it over dinner. She checked herself in the mirror and adjusted her hair a little and went down to the restaurant, once she got the phone call to say that Kerry was in the building. She had barely been out of the hotel room since she arrived three days ago, and Kerry had told her she needed to sit tight while they worked some things out. But she got the impression that she could do business with this woman. Whatever else she was, Kerry was smart and educated. You wouldn't have taken her for a hard bitch by any stretch, but maybe she was learning fast that you don't survive in this game by negotiation. Perhaps Kerry did have the ruth-less streak you needed to get to stay on top in this business. Her swift justice on the boys Knuckles had sent up to her mother's funeral was top drawer, both for how the oper-ation was carried out, and also for the fact that she didn't shy away from it. But Knuckles would be coming after her with all guns blazing now. So it was important to strike again while he was still reeling from the latest blow of losing his heroin to the cops. She knew he would be livid, and, between that and no sign of Sharon anywhere, he needed to be seen to be keeping the ball rolling.

Kerry was waiting for her in the restaurant when she walked in and was shown to the table in the alcove set slightly apart from the restaurant. The place was almost empty anyway, aside for two couples far enough away from them.

'Howsit going?' Kerry said, putting down the menu she'd been reading.

'Good,' Sharon said, easing herself into the leather chair as the waiter hovered, placing a napkin on her lap. 'Well, as good as it can be at the moment.'

'I'm having a gin and tonic.' Kerry raised her glass.

'That'll do for me.' Sharon looked up at the waiter.

Once he was gone, Kerry leaned forward. 'I know it must be hard, Sharon, but we'll get a flat sorted for you, as soon as we've got the right place – somewhere discreet and secure, so that you're safe. By the way, I take it you haven't been able to speak to your son yet?'

Sharon felt a little dig in her heart. She knew Tony would be texting and calling her mobile as well as the house, and she wondered what kind of crap Knuckles was filling his head with. Knowing him, he would be saying she'd run off with another man.

'I haven't, Kerry. And it's breaking my heart. I need to get a word with him. I know there's a big security issue, but he needs to know that I haven't abandoned him. I mean, he's thirteen now, and I don't speak to him every day or anything, but I've not talked to him for nearly a week now. I could email him, but I don't want to commit anything to writing in case Knuckles has people who can monitor the boy's account.'

Kerry nodded. 'I'll find a way to get word to him. We'll get you another mobile purely for talking to him, and get one to him. How will he be with that kind of underhand stuff though? Is he going to freak and talk to his dad?'

Sharon shook her head. 'No. No way. Tony doesn't get on with his dad. Knuckles thinks he's a wee poof because he wants to study and make something of his life. It was a constant source of argument. Knuckles didn't even want him to go away to school. He wanted him by his side, but there isn't a bad bone in the boy's body. He's a gentle lad, and the further he can get away from his dad the better. But I know he'll be suffering. It's five days now since I last talked to him.'

'Okay. Once you get me details of his movements and stuff I'll get the mobile to him. Don't worry.'

'Thanks.'

The waiter came and took their order. Sharon felt more relaxed now than she had in weeks, but there was always the worry that someone could walk in the door of this place any minute and blow them both all over the walls.

Knuckles would have eyes everywhere, and while there was bad blood between him and the Caseys lately, he would still have contacts in Glasgow. Deep down though, he'd be more concerned in looking for her on the Costa del Sol or up in Torrevieja, or even in London. He hadn't the wit to think she'd come to Glasgow.

They ate, talking about growing up, and she was touched at how Kerry spoke easily about missing her family, and confessing she knew how her son must feel being away for long periods. She told her she never took to being away from Glasgow, but eventually it had become clear that her future wasn't here. That all changed after her mother was murdered. They talked about ways to go forward, and Sharon outlined her ideas about money and accounts, and people Knuckles worked with. Kerry arranged with her to meet tomorrow. She'd be picked up and come to Kerry's office to look at the information she had on her jump-drive pen, and explain what everything was.

'That all sounds great,' Sharon said, 'but I've got something more relevant to how we could fuck up Knuckles big time – and soon. In the next week.'

Kerry put down her glass and raised her eyebrows.

'You have?'

'Yes. I didn't want to mention it until we had a longer chat, and I'm glad we did because if you are going to move on it, then we need to act in the next couple of days.'

'Let's hear it then.'

Sharon spread her hands on the table.

'Okay. Just outside of Amsterdam there is a warehouse – I purchased it for Knuckles four years ago. It's where we keep all the drugs smuggled in from various places, and it's where we distribute in lorries to the Costa del Sol and the UK. It's all about moving things quickly in and out. The gear doesn't sit there long – only a few days, maximum a week – before we move it.'

'What kind of gear? Coke?'

'Yes. And smack. Both get moved separately, by different means, and generally to different dealers. But it's all there in the warehouse, for a short period.'

Kerry nodded, stayed silent.

'Okay,' Sharon went on. 'So here's the sketch. There's a big shipment of coke due to come out of there on Tuesday. That is in five days' time. It's for the Costa del Sol and also for Manchester. It's three million pounds' worth of coke, so it's a big do for Knuckles.'

She thought Kerry looked as though she was trying not to show that she was shocked by the figures. This kind of stuff would be all new to her, but she'd have to start learning fast.

'And are you sure Knuckles will go ahead with it, even in the middle of all the stuff that's happening – with you going missing? Will he not think that you're already working on ways to screw this up?'

Sharon shrugged. 'He might be. But his greed will get

the better of him. The stuff has been in the warehouse since the day before I left him, and the people will be set up to move it on. I know that because I made the arrangements myself. I always do. Knuckles left all that up to me. He just wanted to know the bottom line, when it left, when it arrived, did it get there safely. He didn't get involved in the nitty-gritty because he trusted me. In fact he never even went over there himself. He was probably too scared in case he'd get arrested, so he left it up to me to inspect and see stuff. Anyway, he'll be wanting it moved as planned, and I'm confident that it will get the go-ahead.'

Kerry nodded, sipping her wine. 'So what do you want to do about it?'

Sharon paused for a moment and took a breath. Even she wasn't quite sure what to do about it. All she knew was that there was enough drugs in this warehouse to make a significant dent in Knuckles' empire – as well as destabilising him.

'Well, that's what I thought we could talk about. Put it this way: I know that the Durkins down in the Costa del Sol would give their eye teeth for this amount of cocaine at a good price – not that they're short of supply – but they would be doing a fucking Irish jig if they could steal it from Knuckles. They hate him with a passion. So do the Hills in London. Both of them would sell their grannies to get a sniff of this stuff.'

She could see Kerry processing the information in her

head, and she waited, taking a slug of her wine, feeling a tad euphoric that she could almost see Knuckles getting fucked over.

'So,' Kerry eventually said, 'do you propose we sell the tip-off to them? I mean, they would have their own crew to work out how they get a hold of the stuff at the warehouse, which I presume is guarded and secure round the clock?' She looked a little embarrassed. 'Forgive me if I'm not as informed as you on this kind of stuff, but I've led a very different life.'

Sharon waved away her fears.

'No worries. I understand that. Yeah, the place is heavily secured. Big time. But that's up to the Durkins and Hills how they deal with it. They are real players. They have their own people in Amsterdam, or, they leave it until it's in transit, then hit it. On its way down to the Costa del Sol – or the section of it that is going there. Or, you get your people to simply take over the containers and drive them to where you want to take them, then you have them in your possession to control – and to sell to the Durkins and Hills. To me, that's the best bet. I can facilitate all that.'

'But that's risky too, because we'd then have to stash that amount of coke somewhere nobody could find it.'

Sharon shrugged. 'I'm sure the Caseys can handle that.'

Kerry nodded slowly.

'What would you get out of it? Well, I mean, if my organisation tells the Durkins and the Hills that this shipment can be theirs for a price, then that's obviously a big benefit for me in more ways than one. But what about you?'

'Me? I won't be involved in it at all. It'll be up to you to let them know you want to make a deal. The Caseys already work with the Durkins and the Hills – well, I know your brother Mickey did. They'll be well clued up on all the stuff that's going on in the aftermath of Mickey's murder, and your mum's funeral. They'll be expecting you to hit back at Knuckles, but they'll not be expecting you to be this informed, if you know what I mean. And the last thing they'd expect is for you to be able to offer them a shipment of Knuckles' coke.'

She could see that Kerry was a little out of her depth.

'Look. I've been doing this kind of business for a long time, so I'm well versed in how we do people over. The important thing is, first, to make it work, and second, to make sure our information is untraceable. Or if it does get traced back, you'd need to be ready for all-out war.'

'So. What do you mean in terms of money? I know you can see that this is not exactly something I am familiar with. I make no apology for that. My ambition here, Sharon, is to make my entire business legit. It's what my father wanted – it's what Mickey fucked up because of the road he took us down. If I'm honest, I don't know exactly how to handle this. I have people in my organisation who can, but right now it's just me and you, and I have to be able to trust you.'

'Listen. If I wasn't to be trusted you'd know about it by now. I came to you, Kerry. I want to ruin him as much as you. Believe me.'

'So do the Durkins or Hills pay for this?'

'Well, yes, of course. They'll pay top dollar, but less than they would pay elsewhere. But there's more than that. If you deal with them, it will put you in a major position with them. They'll be in your debt for a very long time. So when you go in to try to negotiate yourself out of certain situations with them – like the drugs and the women, which I gather you don't want to be a part of, then they will be more open to listening to you.' She paused. 'And it's not going to be simple for you to tell the Durkins and Hills you don't want to work with them in the future.'

'Meaning what?' Kerry asked.

'Put it this way. You don't just resign from an arrangement with the Durkins or the Hills, who have been punting drugs and women to your organisation for years. You walk away, you get shot. Simple as that. And then they take over your organisation. But this way, by selling them a shipment as big as this, then you are in a good position to tell them where you think the future of your organisation lies. There's a better chance of them respecting that – if this is the way you want to go.'

She waited, watching Kerry, and could see from her eyes that she liked the sound of what she was proposing.

Then Kerry folded her arms and sat back, looking directly at Sharon.

'I like this.' She waved a hand. 'We could take the lot. All three million of it.'

Sharon couldn't help the smile that broke out across her face, and she let out a chuckle.

'Now you're talking my language. Are you serious?'

Kerry smiled and shrugged.

'Why the hell not? What better way to ruin Knuckles Boyle than to do it with his own money? I'm serious, all right. Can it be done?'

'Of course. I've got the connections if you've got the manpower. There are other dealers you could sell it to, not only on the Costa del Sol but also in the north of Spain. Or you could deal with the Durkins and Hills – as it might be wiser to do that for the reasons I've just explained. It's up to you. But once you decide, we could have the stuff out of there so fast Knuckles won't know what's hit him. But it'll cost some money upfront – to pay people off over in Amsterdam.'

'Fine. Then let's talk about it.'

# CHAPTER TWENTY

Frankie lay back on the pillows, his hands behind his head, the white sheet covering the bottom half of his nakedness, as he watched with mild interest the girl getting dressed in the morning light. The sex had been on the wild side, but sometimes he liked it that way. He always felt more relaxed after a hard session – especially with Gina who liked things a bit rough. He hoped she wasn't going to be all over him now, with her stupid suggestions that they make more of the relationship. It was what it was, he'd been clear to her. They were good together in bed, but he had no time for any strings. He hated when birds got all affectionate after sex. For him it was all about the chase, the build up, then the frenzy of passion. But once that was over, he had to restrain himself from kicking them out of bed so he could get some kip. He liked Gina, who he'd met in a club in Glasgow a few months ago, when he'd been holding court with his mates surrounded by the various babes who always hung around them. Gina was all right – discreet as well as being a great shag. But that's as far as it went. He sighed as she came over and sat on the edge of the bed, buttoning her straining blouse over her fake tits. She shoved her hand under the sheet and fondled him. He pulled her hand away.

'You've had your lot, darlin'. I need some sleep.'

He put his hand on the back of her head and pulled her towards him and kissed her on the lips, as though he cared. He was good at that. He stopped when he felt her pushing her tongue into his mouth. 'Go on, nympho.' He smiled. 'Leave a man in peace. I've a lot on my mind.'

Gina stood up, her big blue eyes a little hurt.

'You always kick me out, Frankie. Why can't I stay and make you breakfast – or maybe we could go out for breakfast.'

'Aw Christ, Gina. Give me a break. I'm too busy for all that. You know that.'

'I know. But I mean, it would be good now and again.'

Frankie sighed. 'Right. Okay. I'm busy this week. But I'll sort something out. We'll go for a meal one night. I'll phone you.' He'd no intention of phoning her, but he had to get her off his back.

Gina brightened. 'Great. This week?'

'Christ! I'll phone you, right? Now piss off before you annoy me.'

'Okay. I'm going. But don't forget.'

She pulled on her coat and blew him a kiss as she headed for the door.

Frankie sank back in the pillows and ran a hand across his smooth tanned chest. He worked hard in the gym most days and he was proud of his toned body, hard in all the right places. And his recent tan, topped up over in Marbella a few weeks ago, made him look like a model, compared to the pasty-faced punters he met in bars here, where pulling birds was the easiest thing in the world. But right now there was only one bird he wanted to get in here beside him, and the way things were going it didn't look like it was ever going to happen. His hand automatically moved under the sheet down to his penis as he thought of Kerry. Her tight jeans, everything about her, the lush hair, the way she dressed, her blouses and T-shirts all designed to hug her tits. If only he could get close to her. He assumed she must fancy him – all the birds did – but he knew she wouldn't come anywhere near him because she was the boss. But he fantasised anyway. He had plenty of time to get her into bed, as he'd promised himself. His mobile rang and he picked it up, looked at the screen and saw Rab Pollock's name.

'Rab. All right?'

'Ahm no' disturbing a shag or anything, am I, Frankie boy?'

'Nope. She just left.'

'Listen, mate. Do you fancy coming over for a wee drink

tonight at the Crown? I've a couple of things I want to talk to you about.'

'What like?' Frankie's voice was sarcastic. 'Like have I seen your suitcases of smack you managed to lose at Manchester, you prick?'

Word was everywhere about Rab's loss and people were laughing at him all over the city.

'I heard you sent a wee laddie on the drop. Are you off your fucking head?'

'The boy was all right, Frankie. It was Denny Thomson who did the dirty.'

'Where is the cunt now?'

'Christ knows. But as soon as I find him, I'll cut his fucking throat.'

'I heard you were dealing with Knuckles Boyle.'

Silence for a moment, then Rab spoke. 'Aye, well. Listen, Frankie, I only deal with him now and again. I didn't know it was him behind all that shit with Mickey, and at the funeral. If I'd known that, I wouldn't have dealt with him at all. No way. I'll not be doing it any more.'

Frankie felt himself grin.

'Not much chance of Knuckles Boyle doing any deals with you, mate. Way I hear it is you lost him a hundred grand.'

'Never mind about that. It's done. Nothing I can do about it now. You coming over for a drink later? I want to talk to you about a couple of things. About the future.'

Frankie laughed. 'Future? What future, Rab? You're well fucked, man.'

'Aw, come on, man. I want to talk to you.'

Frankie sighed. 'Right. Okay. Maybe about nine, if I've nothing better to do. I'll see you there.'

The Crown bar was busy and noisy and quite dark when Frankie got there, and at first he couldn't see any sign of Rab Pollock. He went to the bar and ordered himself a large Jack Daniel's and Coke, and took a swig as he gazed around the room at the punters out for a night. It hadn't been a good day. He hadn't been near the big house, where Kerry was spending most of her time, apparently going over all the fine details of the business in documents and meetings with Marty Kane. He knew that sometimes she'd meet with some of the other lads, but they all had their jobs to do and didn't really meet round the table en masse unless there was a crisis – like the first time they talked after Kerry took over. He wished she would confide in him, because he knew more about the movement of drugs and all the players than anyone else. As far as he could see, it was all still running as normal, but he still felt a bit pushed out, and his wrath was building. He heard the odd bit of gossip though, that Kerry was out for dinner at the One Devonshire Gardens hotel, and stuff like that. He had to find a way to get closer to her. He obviously couldn't mention anything about Knuckles, and the further he stayed away from that subject the better. So far, he hadn't had any signs that she suspected him, but it worried him a little that the reason he was out in the cold was because she already knew.

He felt a hand on his shoulder.

'Frankie boy. Howsit hanging?'

'Better than yours, mate.'

He half turned to see the fat, ruddy face of Rab Pollock at his side. Behind him was McCann. Frankie smirked.

'McCann! Fuck me! You're keeping some low company these days since my boss fucked you out of the Paradise Club with a sore face.'

McCann touched the scab on the side of his head where Kerry had hit him. He shifted on his feet and looked away.

'Aye, right, Frankie. Have your fucking fun. Listen, if it wasn't for me, that Paradise Club would have shut years ago. I was making fucking serious money for the Casey cunts.'

'Yeah. You were. And plenty for yourself,' Frankie said. 'But you don't slap the birds, man. That was just bad news.' He grinned at Rab. 'Mind you, I'd love to have had a ringside seat for that moment Kerry Casey walks in and pistol-whips the fuck out of you. Christ, man! That's legend.'

'She's a fucking nutter.'

Frankie said nothing. Rab ordered drinks for all of them and they went across to a table at the far side of the room where it was quieter.

'So, Rab,' Frankie said as he sat down, his legs spread,

leaning back. 'What the fuck happened with the stuff at Manchester? That was some fucking loss.'

'Tell me about it,' Pollock said.

'What happened? I don't know Denny Thomson, but I hear he's a bit of a prick. Why you getting involved with dicks like that? And as for sending a wee laddie! What was that about?'

Frankie listened as Rab told him about the operation and the deal he had made with Knuckles Boyle, and confessed he'd been doing it for months. But he stressed it never interfered with the Casey business, as it was for different turf all together.

'I know it was,' Frankie said. 'That's how we let you do it. But you really fucked off Knuckles. I haven't spoken to him but I understand he is not happy. What about this wee boy that got arrested. Where is he now?'

'Christ knows,' Rab said. 'Up here somewhere. All I heard was that big Marty Kane went down and brought him up from the pokey in Manchester. So I don't know where he is.'

A little explosion went off in Frankie's head. Marty Kane all the way to Manchester on a small matter like this? If it had been something involving the Caseys he'd be sent anywhere in the world, as he was the family lawyer. But what was he doing down in Manchester for a wee toerag? Kerry must be involved in it somewhere.

'Do you not even know who the wee fucker is?'

'Some cunt called Cal. Used to work in the car wash and did drops for us. He was all right. Then we decided to send him down on this, to make it look like a couple of lads just travelling.'

Frankie shook his head. 'Fuck's sake. So where's he from?'

'Cranhill. His ma lives there, but there's been nobody at the house since this happened. So they must have moved in case we get him.'

'You must be shitting it in case he spills his guts to the cops.'

'He doesn't know much. That's how it was. Unless that prick Denny talked about everything on the way down on the train. Maybe he did. We'll never know until we get the fucking knock on the door from the cops.'

'The boy will be crapping himself. I wouldn't worry. If he's already been doing drops for you, he's not about to run in and report it all to the cops.'

'Aye. Well, we've taken a bit of insurance out on that anyway.'

'What do you mean?'

'We've got his sister stashed away, in case he talks. His ma's been told.'

'What? Fucking kidnapping? Christ's sake, man. What age is she?'

'She's no' a kid. She's a fucking junkie whore,' McCann said. 'Heroin addict. We've got her in a flat and told her ma that if the boy opens his gub to the cops then she's getting her throat cut.'

'Christ.'

'So far, so good.'

'How long do you think you can keep a junkie for?'

'She's paying her way. Don't worry about that. We'll keep her till it dies down, then dump her some time, unless we get a smell that the wee fucker is talking to the cops. Then she's getting it, and so is he.'

Frankie smiled. 'You'll need to find him first, will you not?'

Rab shrugged. 'Aye. Well. We'll find him.'

Frankie finished his drink and signalled the waitress to bring the same again. He half listened while Rab and McCann talked to him about how things were changing in the city now, and that the Caseys were ripe for the taking. If Frankie came onto their side, he said, they could make some good business together, especially with Frankie's connections. Frankie nodded at all the right moments, but his mind was on other things. Where was this boy Cal, and why had Marty Kane gone to Manchester to bring him back? He knew there wasn't much point in putting feelers out, because nobody in the organisation would discuss it. But if Marty Kane was involved, then Kerry had to have something to do with it ... The name rang a bell somewhere. Then he remembered. He could recall an old schoolfriend of Kerry's when she was a kid who was called

Maria, but she'd married a soldier and left Glasgow years ago. Then she'd come back and she had a boy called Cal. He'd not seen her for years, until the funeral last week when he'd asked someone who the woman was that was sitting with Kerry.

# CHAPTER TWENTY-ONE

Kerry waited in her study for Frankie to come in for a coffee as they'd arranged. She hadn't seen him since their last meeting, and that was how she wanted to play it. Since talking to Sharon she was more convinced than ever that Frankie was a traitor. She'd felt it from the first time she sat around the table with him and the rest of the boys, but Sharon's information had convinced her – even though there was no clear evidence. He'd been swanning around with Knuckles without Mickey being there, and it was no coincidence that this was weeks before her brother was gunned down. She was braced for her meeting with him, and had wanted to casually grill him over his relationship with Knuckles Boyle. But she decided it was too early yet, and she didn't want to arouse his suspicion that she was onto him. Frankie called her this morning to say he had some information she might be interested in, so she had no option but to agree to meet. She sat in the big armchair and heard a door open and voices coming down the hall. Then the knock at the study door.

'Frankie.' She stood up, smiling. 'How you doing?'

Frankie shrugged, smoothed his tie and his immaculate white shirt then stuck his hands in the pockets of his dark blue jeans.

'Keeping busy, Kerry. You know what it's like. The bookies are doing well. By the way, I was looking at a couple of places – old family betting shops where the owner has died, and was thinking we should buy them over. They're in a good spot. One bang on the Southside and one up at the edge of the city. Rates might be a bit high in the city one, but worth a look.'

'Great. Might be a good idea. Get a costing for me and see what we'd be looking at.' She gestured at the cups on the table. 'Coffee? Tea?'

'Tea would be good. Just black.'

'Sit down, Frankie.'

'How you doing, Kerry, yourself?' He looked concerned. 'I keep thinking about you, about the old days, growing up. Jesus! It all seemed a bit innocent then – even though I suppose it wasn't. We weren't in the middle of a lot of shit though, the way it is these days.'

Kerry looked at him, but kept her expression flat. They were in the middle of a lot of shit that he probably caused, she thought. She half smiled.

'Well, that's the business we are in, Frankie. It wouldn't

have been my choice – or my dad's. But it was Mickey who took us into a lot of the shit we are picking up the pieces for.' She poured tea and handed him a cup. 'But things are going to change. That's for sure.'

Frankie nodded but said nothing and they sat in silence for a moment. Then he ventured, 'I'd be happy to help you any way I can, Kerry. To be honest, I feel as if running the bookies – it's good craic and stuff – but I'm away from the day-to-day things these days. I miss that. You know, being around here. I feel I can be more useful to you.'

'We'll see,' Kerry said flatly. 'Anyway, you wanted to have a chat, so here we are. I've got a meeting in half an hour.'

He looked a little crestfallen with the brush-off, but Kerry didn't care.

'Kerry, I keep my ear to the ground a lot – it's how I've always been. And I picked some information up the other day that you might be interested in.'

'What kind of information?'

'Well, I mean, I'm not really hearing everything that's close to you right now, but a name came up and I kind of made a connection.'

'What name?'

'Cal.'

Kerry knew he was watching her for a reaction. She hoped her expression gave nothing away. What was he playing at?

'Cal?' Kerry said, throwing it right back at him.

'Yeah. Word on the street, well, not exactly on the street, but coming to me is that Cal is the wee guy who was on a drop in Manchester for Rab Pollock's mob. They were buying heroin from Knuckles Boyle, but the whole thing got busted by cops at the meet in the café.'

Kerry raised her eyebrows a little to show interest but said nothing, waited for him to go on. She knew he would. He was bursting to tell her something.

'Did you hear about the cops busting the drop at Manchester?'

'Course I did,' she said. 'Talk of the steamie. Somebody called Denny Thomson appears to have done a runner. Don't know him. Or Pollock.'

'Pollock's an arsehole. It was him who sent the boy down with Denny. And I hear the boy got arrested. This Cal laddie.'

Kerry stayed silent, sipped her tea. Frankie appeared a little uncomfortable with the lack of response he was getting.

'Tell you what, Kerry. I heard that Marty Kane was down and got him in Manchester – brought him back to Glasgow. Then I remembered something. It just came to me. You had a pal called Maria who had a laddie called Cal, did you not? Unusual name.'

Kerry rolled her eyes. 'Frankie, I wish you'd get to the point. This is not a bloody interview.'

He tried to smile, but it was more of a grimace.

'Sorry. Anyway, word is that the boy is in danger, and

that his ma was told. But what I also hear is this mob have got his sister. Jenny. She's a heroin addict.'

Kerry looked at him. 'What do you mean, "got her"? They've kidnapped her or something?'

'Yeah. I know where she is. I thought that might be of interest to you.' He paused. 'Look, Kerry, I'm not trying to get information out of you – I mean, why would I do that? All I'm doing is telling you something, because I get the feeling that Maria, your pal, who was at your ma's funeral last week, is Cal's ma. And I don't want to know what the connection is with him and Rab Pollock, or her and Rab Pollock. But if she's your mate, and she wants to know where her daughter is, then I can help.'

Kerry waited a long moment. 'Okay, Frankie. I appreciate you coming. You're bang on with everything you say. I hope you understand that I haven't been having any kind of group meetings about this. Know what I mean? This is personal and it's about a good friend of mine whose family is in trouble. I'm helping her out. You're right. Cal is her boy. I've taken care of them. But I know they are in danger. Cal isn't talking to cops and he won't be. But Maria is frantic because she can't get Jenny, and these bastards who took her, whoever they are, have told her that her daughter will get her throat cut if Cal speaks. So, if you know where they are, then tell me now.'

'Of course I'm going to tell you. Why did you think I came here?'

'Well, you were being a bit bloody cagey in the beginning, if you don't mind me saying so. Let's hear it. Who's got her?'

'Rab Pollock's mob. Well, not just him. But McCann. The little shit you pistol-whipped.'

'Christ! That little bastard! Where is he?' She found herself on her feet, rage rising in her.

'Let me handle this. Could you just leave it with me? I know how to do this. I can get the girl and bring her to her ma. And I can sort out Pollock and McCann once and for all. They're a couple of wasters anyway.'

Kerry looked down at him, and for a moment she was going to tell him to butt out. But maybe he was being sincere. Perhaps she had got it wrong, freezing him out. Maybe it was time to bring him in, test him out. If he could bring Jenny back to Maria, then that would be a start.

'How will you do it?'

Frankie stood up, and took a step towards her.

'Are you going to leave it to me? If you are, then it's my shout how I do it. But I guarantee no harm will come to Jenny, and McCann will be out of your hair for ever. By the way, he went straight over to Pollock's team when you kicked him out of the Paradise Club, so he will do anything to get back at you. I'm pretty sure neither he nor Pollock know the connection of Maria and Cal to you, and it will stay that way. But I'll bring the girl back to her family.'

'What do you need in the way of back-up?'

He put his hand up. 'I'll sort that, if you just say the word.'

Kerry stood looking at him for a moment.

'Okay. Go ahead.' She paused. 'But do not come back to me and tell me something bad has happened to Jenny because of the way you've handled it.'

Kerry could see by the look in his eye that Frankie was stung by the remark, but he took it well. He gave her a mock salute then turned on his heels and left.

# CHAPTER TWENTY-TWO

Sharon was glad that, as promised, she now had three mobile phones to work with, and a laptop. The mobiles were all untraceable, so she was safe enough to call her contacts in Spain and Amsterdam. She'd had only a few hours' sleep last night, as her mind was buzzing with the plan to get the shipment out of Amsterdam and well away from Knuckles Boyle. This could not go wrong. The consequences of that didn't even bear thinking about. Over the years of going out to Amsterdam, setting the operation up, and looking after everyone who was involved in it, Sharon had built up contacts she could trust. The ones she dealt with were mainly Dutch and ex-pat English, and the fact was that none of them were particularly interested in where the shipment went once it was out of their hands. The plan she and Kerry had drawn up was that it would leave the warehouse as arranged, in three lorries, and head for the various destinations. The risk was that she had to get to the drivers she'd assigned to the job and ask them to stand down and walk away at some stage in the journey, so Kerry could get her own drivers to take over. Sharon knew that by making a call like that to any of these drivers, she could be sealing her fate. If any of them decided not to take her lucrative offer to walk away, then the next call they would make would be to someone in Knuckles Boyle's organisation. Even if they agreed to take her offer, they could still do that, double-cross her, if they wanted. It was a risk she had to take. The drivers either just took the offer and walked away, or Kerry would arrange for the trucks to be hijacked en route, which would present all sorts of problems on any motorway or road that could bring police from all over the place. No. It had to be a deal she made with the drivers, and she just had to pray it would stick. She had considered going over to Amsterdam to make the deal herself, but she'd be too exposed, and if it all went nasty, then she was away from any protection. The main man she dealt with was Jan, the big Dutch driver she'd got to know over the past few years, and who she trusted more than any of them. Whatever set-up they had over there, Jan was at the forefront and organising who would be the best men for certain journeys. She would tell Jan the arrangements, and leave it up to him to inform each of the drivers what was to be done once they left the warehouse. She knew they wouldn't question Jan's authority. All of them had been driving trucks with dodgy cargo, mostly drugs, for years, and they knew it didn't pay to ask questions. Kerry had already sent a team over to Amsterdam, who were in place in a hotel a few miles from the warehouse, and who were ready to track the shipment from the moment it left. Sharon picked up one of the mobile phones and keyed in a number, her stomach knotting as it answered after two rings.

'Jan? It's Sharon. How are you?'

'Ah, Sharon! I'm very well thanks. But no name came up and I don't see a number.'

'I know. It's a different phone, Jan.'

There was a moment's silence, and Sharon knew Jan would be a little suspicious. He'd been smuggling drugs into the UK and all across Europe for more than twelve years, and everything had to be very precise. Any sudden change in phone numbers or arrangements flagged up danger to him.

'Is everything all right, Sharon?'

He sounded guarded.

'Yes. Of course.' She paused. 'I wanted to talk to you about a little change we have to the plan for later this week.'

'I see. Are you coming over to talk?'

'No. I have things to do here, so I need to rearrange matters a little.' Sharon took a breath. 'Jan, I want you and your other drivers to take the trucks as normal at the arranged time, but after that, well, that is where I want to talk to you about the change of plan.'

Again the silence.

'Is the shipment going to another place? Not for the ferry to UK?'

'Yes. Head in that direction, as planned. But then there is a place I want you to pull into. You'll know it.' She reeled off the name of the transport café on the motorway. 'That is when I want you to leave the truck for other drivers to take over.'

'What? Other drivers?'

'Yes. Someone else will take over from there.'

'But I don't understand. Is there something I have done wrong? I work with you for years, Sharon. You can trust me always, you know that, don't you?'

'Of course, Jan. I trust you with my life. I've got to know you very well over the years, that is why I want to make this arrangement with you now. You will be paid a lot of money to do as I ask. More than you would for the journey itself. Almost twice as much.'

She knew the last few words would be uppermost in Jan's mind. He'd made a fortune from moving shipments around for years, but you would never have seen any signs of wealth from him. He lived in a humble apartment and kept a low profile. He'd often told Sharon over drinks and dinners in Amsterdam that when the time came to give all this up and he had made enough money, then he would retire to the Bahamas where he would buy a bar near the beach, and a flat, and live the rest of his life away from all this.

'I see,' Jan said. 'Sharon, you know I am very fond of you,

and if you are in some sort trouble I would help you. Are you sure you are all right? I don't want to ask about the change of plan much, because that is up to you what you want to do. My job is to do what you ask. Always. What happens after I leave the truck is not my business. Always.'

'Jan. I'm fine. Honest. No need to worry. One day soon, we'll have dinner and a bottle of tequila in the Bahamas and we can talk about some good old days. But you're right. We trust each other. And the reason I am asking you to do this for me is that I know I can trust you. You must never speak to anyone about the arrangement we have made. Ever. When you make the handover to the other drivers, they will give you the money, and then it would be best if you disappear for a while. Do you understand?'

'Yes. I understand. I will do as you ask. And please, do not worry about trusting me. You must know that I would never betray you. Whatever your plan is, I know you have a reason. We will talk soon.'

He hung up, and Sharon sat holding the phone, staring at the print on the wall which was of a Glasgow tenement where behind each window there was a little image of a life unfolding. It underlined the desolation she felt, so far away from her son, so far away from the life she had, and now totally alone.

Kerry had kept the fact that she had given refuge to Sharon Potter on a strictly need to know basis. The only people she judged that needed to know were Uncle Danny, Jack Reilly and Marty Kane. As predicted, all three of them were sceptical, raising questions that it may all be a set-up to lob another grenade into their organisation, but Danny did concede that Knuckles Boyle didn't have the wit to do that. Plus, from what he'd heard through the grapevine, Knuckles had another woman on the go, so it looked like Sharon's days were numbered. They were all surprised at the extent to which Sharon organised most of what went on in the drug smuggling, and they were surprised that Knuckles had relied on her so heavily. It just wasn't done. But once Kerry had shown them the evidence of Knuckles' financial dealings and movements on the jump drive Sharon had stolen, they believed it. However, giving Sharon refuge was one thing – stealing a three million pound shipment of the Boyle mob's cocaine was an entirely different matter. Not even Mickey would have the balls to do that, Danny had said. Marty advised against it completely as it had the potential to blow up in their faces. Jack was pragmatic, and said that with the right men on the job and proper planning it could work. Sure, it was risky as hell, but it was a lot of money, and too good an opportunity to miss, was his opinion.

Danny put his pen on the table and sat back.

'So what happens if Knuckles decides to take a trip to Amsterdam in the next couple of days just to see how things are going at the warehouse? I mean, now that Sharon has done a runner, he's bound to be on high alert. And even if he hasn't the nous to think along the lines of her doing the real dirty on him, surely to Christ someone in his organisation has.'

'If he does go there,' Kerry said, 'then everything will look normal. He doesn't even know the drivers. That was always Sharon's job. It's her who got to know them over the years and treated them well, so there is a great level of trust there.'

'There will have to be.'

'So even if he did go, then everything will look as planned. Right until the trucks move out. He could even go and see them doing that if he wanted to, and still he wouldn't see anything untoward. The only way he'd see anything is if he gets the trucks followed to the arranged switch place. And Sharon says that just wouldn't happen. He wouldn't do that.'

'You're putting a lot of trust in this woman, Kerry,' Danny said. 'I'm not saying she would double-cross you, but she's been around the course a lot, and from what you tell us she's probably lived on her wits all her life. She's been looking after herself over the years, squirrelling away Knuckles' money.'

'And quite right, too, Danny. I'd be doing the same myself. But you're right. I have nothing much to base my trust on other than the fact that she took a real risk getting in touch with me. It's just instinct that tells me I can trust her. Boyle tried to have her murdered by his own men, guys she'd known and trusted for years. What kind of asshole does that to the mother of his son? She came to me because she was desperate, and she gauged by some of the stuff she had overheard about him talking about the situation up here that she knew we'd be ripe enough to want to have a go at him. And she's bloody right about that. She's already given me some good information about Frankie and Mickey when they were down there, and how things were with Knuckles and them. Hence the reason Frankie isn't at this meeting, and as far as I'm concerned will never be at any major decision-making meeting here.'

There was a long moment's silence around the table, and Kerry got the impression nobody disagreed with her.

'So,' Jack broke the silence. 'As I said when we first talked about this, I think we should keep most of the shipment in Europe. Bringing it into the UK could present more problems. He won't know the drivers, so it won't matter to him that it's going to be our lads driving. Now, on the Costa del Sol, we've got a couple of places down there we could stash a shipment like that for an indefinite period. Until we decide what we're going to do with it.'

'So where exactly are these places?'

'Down past Estepona. There's a few new developments down there, urbanisations they call them. We own about five or six apartments. Mickey bought them off-plan about five years ago; they're all built now and most of the others in the development are occupied. Ours are still empty. But we have lock-ups attached to them, and underground garages for each apartment. Big areas that we could keep the stuff in.'

'Sounds good. And safe?'

'All the apartments are alarmed up. Mostly professionals or retired businesspeople who live there. Mostly Spanish. It's all gated at the front, so nobody gets in without a key or a code. Once the stuff is there, it's well safe.'

'But with this amount of coke, it's not something we could be running in with lorries.'

'No. We'll put someone in the apartments for the next few months. So they'll look like they're just moving in. Several trips with boxes and suitcases in vans. It'll take a few days, but if it's organised well, then the stuff can all be moved in and locked away securely.'

'Do you have people in mind who could move in now?'

'Yes. I was going to speak to them tonight, but I wanted to run it past you. They're good lads. All from here, and very reliable.'

Kerry wanted to ask what they did on the Costa del Sol but she decided not to. Whatever they did it was illegal and it was being done for her organisation. She mulled over the development Jack had talked about. The fact that Mickey had bought it off-plan was probably the only sound judgement he had made in recent years that would have fulfilled his father's dream. For a moment she entertained the idea of investing the proceeds from the stolen coke on property all along the Costa del Sol. Good property, solid apartments and buildings that would bring them a fortune of legitimate money.

'What do you think, Kerry?' Danny asked.

'Sorry.' She shook herself from her reverie. 'Yes. I like that idea.' She turned to Jack. 'Set it up. Definitely, and let me know a bit more detail of the property and exactly where it is.'

# CHAPTER TWENTY-THREE

Frankie showed up at the bar on the Southside where Rab Pollock had arranged the meeting. The night before, over several drinks, he had listened to Pollock and McCann tell him how much they wanted him to come over to them. Forget the Caseys, Pollock said, they'll be history in a few months now that the boys are taking their orders from a bird. Frankie played along with it, and before they knew it, he'd spun them a story that if he did come on, then he would have to be fifty per cent of the business and the other two could split the difference. The only way he would come was if it was all his show and they were his associates. He even sold them the idea that the Paradise Club was now his, that he'd made arrangements to take over the place from Kerry, who had no interest in it. She'd told him it was his, he lied, as long as he paid her a rent every month. He was going to totally gut the place and turn it into a proper club, right on the edge of the city centre, that would be packed to the rafters every night with good music and DJs and bands. If he went in with Pollock, this was what he was bringing to the table, and this was why he would be the boss. He reeled them in. He told them he wanted to see a couple of the flats they ran the whores out of, as he might be in a position to put them in better, more central flats in the city centre. He already owned three flats in Anderston Quay and rented them out, but he could soon turf out the tenants if he wanted to bring the whores in. So now he was waiting for Pollock to take him to the flat on the Southside, as he insisted he wanted to see the quality of the women. He knew they were taking him to the place where they kept Jenny, because McCann managed to let that slip last night when he was pissed. Frankie waited, knowing his boys were on hand and that once he was in and out, they'd know what to do.

'All right, Frankie?' Pollock came up to the bar. 'McCann's in the motor. We might as well have a look at this place first.'

'Good,' Frankie said, finishing his drink. 'I've got a couple of things on in the afternoon, and I want to take you over to the Paradise Club to look at the plans. It's going to be some place. You'll be well impressed.'

They left the pub and went to the car where McCann was sitting in the driving seat smoking. He drove them half a mile away to the block of flats. It was in a more run-down area of the Southside that hadn't been tarted up yet and was bordering on Govanhill.

'Fuck's sake, boys,' Frankie said. 'This is no place for a

whorehouse. All you're going to get here are all the two-bob wankers of the day. You can't be making much money out of this.'

'We're making a bit,' McCann said as they approached the secured entrance. 'But we do need a better place. It's a bit run-down. But the birds are no' bad.'

They went through the door and climbed the three flights to the flat, Frankie clocking that both McCann and Pollock were puffing and out of breath by the time they got there. McCann unlocked the door and they walked in. The place stank of stale perfume and massage oil. A punter came out of the bedroom slipping on his jacket and stopped, a little startled, when he saw them.

'All right, mate?'

The punter said nothing and sidled past them in the hallway then out of the door as quick as he could. They walked down the hall and into the kitchen where a scantily clad girl of about twenty with legs up to her waist was lighting a cigarette from the cooker. She looked half starved, and she turned to them with the drooping eyelids of a smackhead.

'Fuck me! Are they all smacked out their tits?'

McCann shrugged apologetically. 'Keeps them quiet, Frankie. They're easier to manage. Like having a monkey on a chain.'

'Many punters in just now?'

'Dunno,' McCann said. 'We'll have a look.'

They went along the hall and opened each of the doors, all quiet and darkened, one with a girl giving a blowjob in the dark to some guy. Then they stopped at the last door.

'This is where the bird is,' McCann said. 'That Jenny bird. Remember I told you about the boy who did the drop for us? We got her here.'

He opened the door and Frankie looked in. The girl sat staring into a split in the curtain where some daylight came in. There was an ashtray full of cigarette butts, a syringe and some wraps at the side of a table. She looked up at them and half smiled as though expecting them to be punters. They closed the door again.

'Fuck. What you going to do with her? You can't keep her for ever.'

'Why no'? She's no idea what day it is. She's working for us now. We might sell her on. She's no' bad-looking when she's tarted up a bit.'

Frankie nodded as they walked along to the kitchen. He looked at his watch.

'We need to get moving. I've seen enough here. The place stinks, to put it mildly. It's a shithole. If we're going to do this, then we'll do it right – in a half-decent gaff that doesn't smell of recent shags. Come on. Let's go to the Paradise Club. This will blow your mind.'

They walked behind him, and Frankie could feel the belief on them; part of him wished it was true, that he could run the whole show and have everyone traipse after him the way they did for Mickey Casey. One day, he promised himself.

When McCann pulled up to the Paradise Club and they got out, they stood looking up at the building.

'What?' Frankie said, turning to him and chuckled. 'You're not going to greet, are you, McCann? A bit emotional, eh?'

'Fuck off, mate,' McCann retorted. 'This place was all right. I did well here.'

Frankie went to the padlock on the shuttered doors and opened them, sliding the chains. He looked at his watch. The boys should be doing their bit by now back at the flat. He pulled up the shutters noisily and walked in the door with Pollock and McCann behind him.

'Freezing in here,' Pollock said. 'And stinks of damp too.'

'Aye, well, it's been lying idle for a couple of weeks. Anyway, the whole place is getting gutted inside out. In a few months you'll not recognise it from before. Come on. Along to the office. I'll show you the plans.'

Frankie flicked on lights as they walked along the sticky carpet to the office at the end, and he opened the door. Behind the desk, the tall skinny figure of Jimmy Dick sat grinning. Pollock and McCann looked at Frankie, startled. The penny seemed to drop quicker with McCann, who immediately recognised Dick and turned to the door. But Frankie flicked on the lock.

'You know Jimmy, don't you, lads?'

'What the fuck, Frankie! What's happening?'

Jimmy sat stony-faced behind the desk. He was known as the Grim Reaper, and if you had the unfortunate circumstance to be introduced to him, then your number was well and truly up. Frankie went over and leaned his backside on the desk and addressed the pair.

'This is what happens when you're thick enough to think you can take people on. This is what happens when you realise all you are is a wee prick who got too big for his boots. The two of you. What the fuck did you think you were going to do, taking on the Caseys? It's laughable.'

Pollock's face was chalk-white.

'Frankie. Look, mate. It was all bravado. All shite. We were just going along with it when we were pished. We didn't mean any disrespect. Let's just forget it, man. All right?'

'No, mate. It doesn't work that way. Firstly, you were dealing with that arsehole Knuckles Boyle, when you must have known the bad blood going on with Mickey Casey. You carried on with it for your small-time shite and drops to Manchester. Second, you terrorised some wee guy's ma and kidnapped her daughter who doesn't know what day it is because she's junked up in your fucking whorehouse down the road.'

'Aw, Frankie,' McCann said. 'Listen. I was going to get her back on the street today. Honest. It was a stupid plan in the first place to take her, and we were just going to offload her up to the street tonight. All that crap we were talking to you was just bollocks. Honest, man. Just let us go. You'll not hear from us again. But anything you want us to do we'll do it free. We'll work for you, Frankie – any time.'

Frankie looked at the pair of them. They thought they were hard men, but here they were, shitting their pants because they knew it was over. He would have had more respect for them if they'd put up a fight or pulled a weapon. But they were standing there bricking it, pleading for mercy. He checked his watch. The boys would have been in now and got Jenny. They'd be taking her to the arranged place, and within the next half-hour he'd be phoning Kerry to tell her job done. He'd be a hero, or as close to a hero as Kerry would view him. But it would be a start. And the bonus was he'd get these two pricks off the face of the earth which would also send a message to anyone else out there trying to take them on. Knuckles would get the blame for it anyway, as revenge for losing his smack. He gave them a disgusted look and went to the door.

'Give me a shout when you're sorted, Jimmy.'

He opened the door and walked out, knowing that in the next twenty-four hours an abandoned, burned-out car would be found in the back of Rab Pollock's favourite bar in the East End of Glasgow, with the two charred bodies in it.

# CHAPTER TWENTY-FOUR

Maria had barely slept, but she was full of nervous energy, and was fussing around the kitchen, continually wiping the worktop, polishing the shelves. She'd lain awake most of the night, her ears pricking up at the least sound coming out of the bedroom where Jenny had finally drifted off to sleep. More than anything, she was listening for footsteps in case her daughter had decided to do a runner. She knew Cal too was up and down most of the night, checking on his sister, and she'd heard him in the kitchen a couple of times making tea. Poor Cal. He'd adored Jenny when he was a little boy and followed her around like a puppy when he was a toddler. And she'd been so good with him, fussing around him like the dutiful big sister, helping feed him and playing with him. It broke Maria's heart to see what Jenny had become, but it had been broken a long time ago; Jenny had been so lost to her for the past four years, as she became swallowed up by heroin. The funny, smart-as-a-whip teenager, full of promise, was like a stranger now, her eyes miles away, everything in her day built around getting enough smack to keep going. Maria padded along the hallway and stuck her head around the door of Jenny's bedroom. She could see her sleeping soundly on the double bed, her hollow cheeks like razors, but still with that same pose she'd had as a little girl, her arms stretched back on the pillow. Maria felt her chest tighten with emotion and closed the door, then quietly went back into the kitchen, stuck the kettle on and sat at the table.

She reflected on last night and the phone call she'd been waiting for, to say they were bringing Jenny home. It had been a tearful reunion, with Jenny sobbing and collapsing in her arms, saying she was sorry, but she didn't understand why they took her, or even who took her. Poor Jenny had assumed she'd owed so much money for drugs that her dealer had taken her to use her in the flat where she'd been held. Maria could see that she was in no fit state to be told the truth, so that was for another day. Kerry had arrived along with Frankie Martin, who Maria remembered from years ago as the handsome friend of Mickey Casey. He'd smiled and told her not to worry, that nobody would ever harm Jenny again. Kerry had handed Maria a couple of sedatives she'd been given by a GP the family used, and she told her to give Jenny the pills, because she'd be rattling without the heroin. Then she said she'd made arrangements for Jenny to go into rehab in the morning for the next four months to a private clinic down in the Borders, which she was paying for. When Frankie left the flat to go to the car, Maria had been in tears, thanking Kerry for saving her life. She told her she would repay her, that she would work for free in any area of her organisation. But Kerry had just put her arm around her shoulder and told her not to fret, that she would find a job for her in the next week or so.

Maria got up and gazed out of her kitchen window which looked onto the sloping greens of Kelvingrove Park in the distance. Never in her life would she ever have been able to rent a place like this. The three-bedroom flat in the old tenement building was massive and kitted out tastefully with wooden floors and a fireplace. And instead of looking out of her window twelve floors up, watching nervously for the moneylender to come threatening, she could see people coming to and from their work in their cars, well-dressed ordinary people. It had been so long since she'd lived an ordinary life with the kind of things they had. When she married Tom after he joined the army, her life had been abroad in Cyprus, in Germany, and in north London for a time. They never wanted for anything. Tom was away a lot, so homesickness was something she got used to, and to help this she'd made friends with the other army wives. Then when Jenny arrived, followed a few years later by Cal, and Maria really believed her life was complete. She had everything she ever wanted. But it fell apart after Tom came back from Iraq. Prior to going on his tour of duty, he had been sent on more and more training courses, then Iraq twice. He never spoke about his work out there, but from what other people had told him he was a crack sniper, and was in demand in various provinces where the army was cleaning out rebel dissidents. She often wondered when he was home on leave if he had done something bad out in Iraq that was causing him to wake up with night sweats, when she would find him sitting in the dark of their living room. He wouldn't speak to her about anything. She knew from newspapers that some terrible things happened to innocent people caught in the crossfire in Iraq, and she wondered if Tom had a dark guilty secret that was eating away at him. He became more and more restless and depressed, and within a year he was out of the army and sinking into a deep depression. She just couldn't get through to him. They called it Post Traumatic Stress Disorder, but there was little help for him. He'd felt the army had abandoned him. And then, one day, there was a letter addressed to her on the kitchen table when she came in from the supermarket, and he was gone. He couldn't take it any more, he told her, couldn't live with the depression, and all he was doing was wasting her life. He disappeared and she hadn't heard from him in the past nine years. Once, he did get in touch and they tried again, but it didn't work, and he was off again after a few weeks. There was never a day went by that she didn't think about him, wonder where he was, or if he was even alive. He could be abroad or anywhere. Cal had grown up with the photographs of his dad in uniform but without his arms around him, without the guidance, and despite that he was a strong boy in character, determined to do well. Jenny was another story. She'd become angry and troublesome after her father left and by the time she was a teenager the problems really kicked in. In the run-down council housing scheme, where families tried to live without relying on moneylenders and drug dealers, it was somehow normal for teenage children to be drinking and smoking joints, and she waited up every night for her to come home, drunk or high on drugs. And then one night she didn't. When she found her three days later, she was smacked out of her head, and no matter how hard Maria had tried, Jenny never came back to her.

Now she looked around at everything she had. She knew there would be a price to pay for living in a place like this but she was tired of scratching away to earn a living, tired of being on the scrap heap with every other family in the high flats desperate to get out. She had been given a chance here, and she would grasp it with both hands no matter what it cost. She'd had it with just scraping by and living in fear. Her friend Kerry would look after her, and she would do whatever needed to be done to keep this life.

She heard footsteps in the hall and Cal appeared in the kitchen in his pyjamas.

'All right, Ma?'

He looked tired as he shuffled to the fridge. He sniffed and turned to face her as he brought out some milk and placed it on the worktop, reaching into a cupboard and bringing out a cereal bowl.

'Some gaff this, isn't it? I've got Sky in my bedroom.'

Maria almost smiled. The simple things that could swing a teenager these days.

'Aye. It's a great place to live, son. Different world.'

'Are we going to be able to stay here?'

Maria sighed. 'I don't know. Kerry said we can stay as long as we like. She's getting me a job in her organisation.'

Cal shook cereal into a bowl and poured milk in, then sat down at the table. He looked at his mother.

'They're gangsters, Ma. You know that, don't you? The Caseys. Everyone knows that.'

Maria made a resigned face.

'I know they are. But Kerry has taken over from her brother now, and she wants to make things different.'

'What do you mean, different?' Cal asked.

'She wants to make the firm legitimate. Property and stuff. I don't know. She didn't tell me the details, but only that she hates what her brother did to the organisation.'

Cal said nothing, but shook his head.

'Well. She's done all right by you, Ma. And our Jenny. Is she really going into rehab?'

'Yes. This afternoon. She's being picked up and taken to this posh private place in the Borders.'

'What if she doesn't want to go?'

'She's not getting a choice,' Maria said. 'Listen, Cal. I want you to talk to her when she wakens up. Make her understand that this is the only way.'

Cal nodded. 'She'll be all right with it.' He looked a bit sheepish. 'I didn't tell you this, but I see Jen sometimes in the town and we have a cup of tea together in the café. We've talked about a lot of stuff, like how things were before my da went.' He swallowed. 'I wish I had really known him, you know. I've got some vague memories but I'm not even sure if they're real or if I've just heard you and Jen talking about him when I was growing up. I wish I could see him.' He paused. 'Anyway, Jen's told me loads of time she just wants to stop the drugs but she can't get into rehab as there's no beds. So she'll go. Guaranteed.'

'Jesus, I hope so, Cal. Because if she doesn't, there's no hope for her, the state she's in. If she can go in there and get herself sorted, then she's coming back to a completely different environment, living up in a place like this. Maybe if she does all right, Kerry can give her a job and all. Kerry seems really straight up about that. I know I haven't seen her in years, but we were really close pals growing up since we were wee kids, and it feels like we've never been apart. I know I'm placing a lot of faith in her, and blind faith too, given what their business is. But right now, I don't have a lot of choices.'

Cal nodded. 'I know. They got me out of the shit in

Manchester. But I don't know for how long. I never want to go back into a police cell as long as I live.'

Maria smiled and ruffled his hair.

'Then make sure you don't.' She stood up. 'I'm going to make some bacon. You want some?'

'Aye. Starving.'

Kerry was having breakfast in the kitchen while watching the news, but stopped in her tracks at the footage of men in white boiler suits disappearing into what looked like a police crime scene tent.

*'Breaking news just coming in,'* the presenter said. *'Glasgow police are investigating what is believed to be the charred remains of two bodies in a burned-out car in the city's East End. The wreckage was found at the rear of the Crown pub near Calton. Detectives have set up an incident room on the site, and forensic teams are trying to identify the remains of the dead. The bodies were discovered by a man who saw the wreckage smouldering as he was walking his dog early this morning. Police are treating this as a murder inquiry.'*

Kerry knew even before there was a knock on the kitchen door and Jack appeared.

'You watching this?'

'Yeah. Christ. Is this who I think it is, Jack?'

'I'll be surprised if it's not. Have you heard from Frankie yet?'

'Not since last night when he brought Jenny. He went to

the house with me and we took her back to her mother. I didn't ask him what happened. I decided that since he was so keen the other day that I leave it up to him, I give him the leeway to do that.' She paused. 'But Christ almighty, Jack! I didn't expect this. What do you think?'

Jack seemed unfazed by it.

'I haven't heard anything yet, but the jungle drums will be beating in the next couple of hours. I'm not surprised though. It's how Frankie does things. He doesn't mess about.' He shrugged. 'And to be honest, Kerry, it's a couple of bastards off the face of the earth. No loss to anyone.'

Kerry looked at him but didn't say anything. He nodded and left the room, but she knew he wouldn't be far away.

She dialled Frankie's mobile.

'Frankie. I've been watching the news. Are these bodies in the burned-out car who I think they are?'

There was a short pause and she could hear Frankie breathing.

'Yeah. It's them.'

'Christ, Frankie. I didn't know you were going to do that.'

'What did you think I was going to do, Kerry? Rap their knuckles and negotiate? They're swamp life. You saw that yourself with McCann. Guys like that don't go away if they've been done over. They sit and fester and work out ways to get back at you. And they're the kind of bastards that are so unimportant that people take their eye off them – and that's when you get a knife in your back or a bullet in your head.

They won't harm you or our organisation again.' He paused. 'And it's clean as a whistle. No comeback. I promise you.'

'You should have told me, Frankie.'

There was a moment of silence.

'Kerry, you left it to me. I asked you to let me handle it, and you did. What kind of numpty would I be if I kept running everything past you? I handled it so that *you* wouldn't have to. Don't worry. It's done and dusted. The papers will be all over it. They'll think it was Knuckles because he lost his smack in Manchester.'

She knew he was right about that, but didn't want to agree with him. He was sounding cocky enough without her feeding his ego.

'Okay, let's leave it there for now. I have to go. Talk later.'

# CHAPTER TWENTY-FIVE

Cal had been put to work by Jack at the weekends, who had him valeting the cars in the used-car showroom at the edge of the city, which the Caseys had partly owned for the past two years. They'd bailed out the owner, Dec O'Hara – an old associate of Kerry's dad she remembered from when they were growing up. The company had been about to go under with crippling debts, much of it accrued by Danno, his waster of a son, from gambling and cocaine. Not only did Danno have a gambling and cocaine habit, he had thrown a fortune at the ill-advised investment of a hotel complex on the Costa del Sol, only to discover the consortium behind the project had buggered off with his money. The hotel, which had looked fantastic on the plans, at the edge of an eighteen-hole golf course on the coast, was not even half built, and was now a blot on the landscape of Mijas. After the blow-out, old Dec had cut his son off from the business, and word was that he was last seen somewhere up in Alicante running a bar. Now that Kerry was running the show, she was looking to buy Dec out completely, as he was over seventy and in failing health. But she wasn't that interested in the car showroom, even though it did turn a small profit. She wanted the hotel on the Costa, and the surrounding land, but at this stage nobody was able to tell her how she stood legally, as the consortium had vanished off the face of the earth, and only the foundations were dug. Marty had been trying to talk to Spanish lawyers, but it was a legal minefield of problems and typical Spanish red tape. But meantime, the car showroom had to be kept as a going concern, and Jack oversaw the running of it. He'd told Cal that he was keeping an eye on him, and that if he played his cards right he could make something of himself, as long as he kept away from the toerags at the car wash, who had hooked him into doing drug drops. No fear of that, Cal told him. He liked it here in the showroom. He was drawn there more and more these days, lying to Jack he'd been given a day off school for study leave, but that he would catch up on his books in the evening. Jack suspected he was playing hookie, but he had a soft spot for the kid and took him under his wing. Cal loved polishing the cars till they gleamed, especially the older Jags and Mercs, which he'd sit in, imagining himself cruising through the city. He was doing just that when he saw Jack approaching in the rear-view mirror, shaking him out of his reverie.

'What's this? You slacking in there? Don't even fantasise about taking it for a run.'

Cal knew he was only half serious. He'd fantasised plenty of times about driving the cars, but wouldn't have dared.

'All right, Jack?' Cal said cheerily. 'Aw, man. What I'd give to get a run in that wee Jag sports over there.' He pointed to the old E-type dark green classic. 'I mean, even the smell of the leather inside it is like some kind of drug. Whose was that motor, Jack, do you know?'

'Not sure. I'll ask Dec. Probably some old rich bastard.'

'I see the salesmen turning the engine sometimes. Do you think they'd ever be taking it out for a run? I'd love to be in the passenger seat if they were.'

Jack smiled.

'I suppose so. I'll ask Dec. You had your lunch yet?'

'No. Just about to go down to the bakers. I'm starving.'

'Come on. I'll take you down the café. Seeing it's payday.'

'Thanks, mate.' Cal was out of the car and his jacket on in a minute.

Cal had grown fond of Jack, who was grumpy and funny at the same time. He knew he was some kind of head honcho in the Casey empire, but didn't have the guts to ask any details. He was a big, sturdy guy with a broken nose, and Cal got the impression he was no stranger to violence, if the need arose. He wasn't sure how old Jack was, but guessed he might be around the same age as his father. He'd never known what it was like to have that dad and son kind of thing that most of his mates had, even if they did bitch about their old men drinking or slapping them around. He'd be happy just to see his dad again, even if it was only for a day, just to look at him, ask him why he went away. He seldom allowed thoughts like that to flood into his mind, but when he'd been with Jack, sometimes they did for reasons he couldn't really explain to himself.

The café was on the corner along the road from the showroom and it was busy with lunchtime schoolkids from the nearby private school, queuing up for takeaways, or schoolgirls sitting in the booths. Cal's eye caught a girl who was in his year at school and he kept his head down, surprised that she was sitting with three private-school boys. He wondered what she was up to. He'd only had a couple of conversations with her in the schoolyard and in the dining hall. He'd always fancied her, but hadn't plucked up the courage to ask her out yet. Jack ushered him into a seat opposite them, a few tables away, but Cal could still see them, laughing and joking. The boys were well dressed in their uniforms, and Cal was in his trackies and sweatshirt, and a bit embarrassed because now he caught the girl looking at him. He lifted his chin in acknowledgement as she smiled at him, and the sun caught her bright blue eyes. He felt himself blush.

'What's the matter with you, son? You're all red.'

'Nothing,' Cal mumbled.

Jack turned around and clocked the table, noticing the girl.

'Oh, I see. Fancy that wee lassie, do you?'

'Nah.' Cal shifted awkwardly. 'I just know her from school. She lives up the road from where we used to live, but I don't know her that well.'

'They're High School boys – private, are they not?'

'Aye.' He shrugged. 'Maybe she knows them. Can't imagine why though.'

Jack turned around and looked at them for a longer moment. He bit into his sandwich.

'Something not right there. What are three private-school boys doing with a wee lassie from the schemes?'

Cal didn't answer, but he was watching their every move.

Then, he caught the girl slip something across the table, and one of the boys covered it with his hand. Then with his other hand, he passed something over. Cal felt a little sick and put down his sandwich.

'What's up?' Jack said. 'You look a bit queasy. You really fancy this wee girl? Has she knocked you back?' he joked, sipping his tea.

Cal could feel the rage burning his cheeks and his breath quickened. Before he even knew what he was doing, he was on his feet, out of the booth and going across to the table. His legs felt shaky; he had no idea what he was going to say, but he couldn't help himself.

He stood at the table and looked straight at the girl, who

glanced at him, then down at the table, her face going bright red.

'Mary,' he said. 'You all right?'

She said nothing, her face burning.

'What the fuck do you want, mate?'

The biggest of the three boys looked up at him, contempt all over his privileged face.

'I'm not your fucking mate.' Cal glared at him, then at the girl. 'Mary. What are you doing here, with these pricks?'

As soon as he said it there was a shuffling of feet in the booth as two of the boys made to get up.

'Cal,' Mary said, almost apologetically. 'Look, just leave it.'

'No. I won't leave it. I saw what you just did.'

Mary moved to get up, but the bigger guy grabbed her roughly by the wrist.

'You sit fucking tight, bitch.'

Tears immediately sprang to the girl's eyes.

'Look, Thomas. I need to get back. My sisters are waiting for me.'

'Shut up, slut.'

Cal suddenly grabbed him by throat.

'Don't you ever fucking talk to her like that again, rich boy, or I'll punch the fuck out of you.'

Then it all erupted. The three boys jumped up and they were all on top of Cal in an instant, but he managed to throw a punch squarely at one of the boys and burst his nose. Then as they all grabbed him, throwing him to the ground, he could feel boots laying into his ribs and a foot on his face as he struggled to get up. It all happened so fast, but Jack was on his feet in a second and wading in, lifting boys by the hair and throwing them across the room. The Italian owner came rushing round as people shrank back, cups flying.

'Jack, Jack! What's going on here! Come on! Stop this now! My place is full of customers!'

The boys struggled to their feet, one of them holding his nose, the others more shellshocked than anything. The bigger one got up and had a last kick at Cal as he got to his feet.

'You'll be fucking sorry you ever did this, you shitbag.' Cal struggled to his feet and made to go for him again, but the owner got between them as Jack held the others back.

The boy turned to the girl who was now on her feet in tears.

'And as for your little tramp bird here, she was only good for a handjob. She's good at it – I'll give her that.' He spat, wiping blood from his lips.

The girl stood mortified, as the owner ushered the boys out of the café.

'Fuck's sake, Cal. What do you think you're doing?' the girl said.

Cal looked embarrassed, wiped the blood from his nose. He leaned into her.

'I saw you giving them something, Mary. What the fuck you doing? Pushing drugs to them?'

'What the fuck is it to do with you, Cal Ahern? You think I don't know about you and the drops you made? Don't tell me how to lead my life. I barely fucking know you.'

Jack stood back as the girl made to leave.

'Mary! Wait!' Cal ran after her out of the door. He caught her arm in the street and she started sobbing.

'Fuck's sake, Cal! I just needed the money! My ma's got nothing and my wee sisters have fuck all clothes to wear. What am I supposed to do?'

Cal put his arms around her, feeling her skinny body warm next to his.

'I know. It's okay, Mary.' He held her tight. 'You're all right. Stay away from those guys though. You're better than that.'

She sobbed. 'It's true what they say, Cal. I'm a slut! I don't give a fuck what anybody thinks. I needed the money.'

'No, you don't, Mary. You don't need to do that.'

'I have to go,' she said, pulling his arm away.

He eased his grip and watched as she walked briskly down the street.

On the way back up to the showroom Jack barely spoke, even though Cal was waiting for a stern rebuke from him. Eventually, he put his arm around his shoulders.

'You all right, tiger? I didn't know you packed a punch like that. Might need to take you down to the boxing gym.' He gave him a nudge. 'By the way, I think you should be in school, and you're bullshitting me about study leave.'

Cal's face grew dark.

'I don't want to go to school any more. I've chucked that.'

'Don't be daft. Why? I thought you wanted to go to uni?'

'What's the point? I like working. I want to work for the Caseys.'

Jack stopped in his tracks and looked down at the puny teenager.

'Listen, son. You think because you did some work for the scumbag drug dealers you're a gangster now? You stick to your studies. Believe me – you've a lot more to do than work for the Caseys.'

'But you work for them, and you're doing all right. You said you've always worked for them.'

'That's different,' Jack said. 'My da worked for old Tim Casey and I grew up in the firm. It was different for me. It was what I was expected to do. You've got brains, and more chances than I had.'

'I'm not going back.'

Jack sighed. 'Have you told your mum?'

Cal looked at the ground.

'No. Not yet.' He shuffled his feet, then looked up at Jack. 'Listen, man. I need to ask you something.'

'Sure. What?'

'You know a moneylender called Tam Dolan?'

Jack looked vague.

'I know of him. He's a scumbucket.'

Cal stood for a moment, but he could feel his lip trembling a little.

'I want to do him in. Can you help me?'

Jack looked bewildered.

'What? You think you're in a gangster movie here, son?'

'Jack,' Cal said, on the verge of tears of frustration. 'He's a cunt! I'm going to do him in, whether you help me or not.' He glanced up at Jack and could see him studying his face. 'He raped my mum.'

They stood for a moment in silence, then Jack put his arm around him.

'Come on. Let's get you back to work, son.'

# CHAPTER TWENTY-SIX

Knuckles Boyle was ranting so much while he was guzzling his food that he was spraying it across the table. Three of his boys sat opposite him, one of them discreetly wiping a particle of tomato sauce from his cheek.

'They are fucking winding me up! Every bastard is on the fucking wind up!' He glared at Terry. 'Tell me again what that plonker Denny said before you put a bullet in him.'

Terry was Knuckles' go-to man when he needed information dug out from the streets. He was also good at making people disappear. He sighed and shifted a little in his seat.

'Denny grassed us up, Knuckles. That wanker Nicky Fauldhouse put him up to it, just to make you look like a prick. He was trying to get you back for turfing him out of that pub he ran for you.'

'The cunt had his fingers in my till! That's why I bounced him.'

'I know. But he's still bitter.'

'I'll bitter him when I fucking track him down.'

'Anyway,' Terry went on, 'Denny said he was paid five grand to make the call to the cops. He did it on the train on the way down.'

Knuckles shook his head, incredulous.

'How fucking stupid is that? He must have known he was signing his death warrant the moment he made that call. What is it with these people? Anyway, the cops have got no proof the gear was ours, so we're in the clear – as long as Denny didn't tell that Jock boy who was with him. Did he say anything about that?'

'No,' Terry admitted. 'But he wouldn't have given us the truth anyway. I felt it was important just to get rid of him, and that's what I did.'

'You should have asked him more questions, Tel.'

'He'd have been lying through his teeth, Knuckles. How could we rely on someone who's already grassed us up to the cops on a drop he was getting paid for?'

'Yeah.' Knuckles downed a mouthful of beer from his bottle. 'Suppose you're right. Anyway, what about this fucker Pollock? I spoke to Frankie up there yesterday and he says it was this Kerry bird who ordered the hit. Nothing to do with him.'

'Do you think he's being straight up, Knuckles?'

'Who, Frankie Martin?' He looked surprised. 'He's our inside man, Tel. He's never told us any porkies so far. I believe him.'

'Just thinking. Why hit Pollock, and this other geezer who was with him? They're nobodies.'

'Maybe just in the wrong place at the wrong time. But Frankie told me that Kerry got the word that Pollock was doing business with us and she was having none of that. He says he got done over to send a message to me.' He sat back and snorted. 'Well, who gives a fuck about Pollock anyway. But I'm going to send her a little message to wind her up. We're not doing any business with them now, so we've nothing to lose.'

'What about Frankie? He still works for them.'

'I'm going to leave Frankie where he is. He's useful to us. And once Kerry knows how much out of her depth she is, she'll disappear. Then we'll have it all our own way with Frankie in charge.' He nodded to Terry. 'Put a fucking bomb into one of their businesses just for a laugh. All right?'

Terry nodded.

'What about the shipment coming from Amsterdam, boss?'

With so much shit flying around, the shipment had slipped Knuckles' mind for the last couple of days. It was always Sharon who organised all that like clockwork, and if he was honest he didn't really know where to start. But he couldn't admit that here.

'It's all on course, as far as I know. I usually get a phone call when it's left.'

'You don't think a couple of the boys should go there just to make sure it's all right?'

He shook his head. 'Nah. Well. Maybe. I'll make a couple of phone calls from here, then we'll see. But I'm sure everything's on course.'

Knuckles remembered that some Dutch guy called Jan usually phoned Sharon on the day the lorries were leaving. He didn't even have his fucking number. He hoped that if Jan couldn't get Sharon then he would phone him and let him know. It was either that or send a couple of troops across to Amsterdam where they didn't even know the lay of the land that well. Bastard Sharon. She was out there somewhere. He'd find her, and this time there would be no fucking escape.

As the darkness fell outside, Sharon switched on the lamp. She poured herself a glass of red wine and settled on the sofa, then picked up the piece of paper which had the phone number on it where she could phone her son. Kerry had been good as her word, and had got word to Tony that his mother would be phoning him on this number. Kerry had established that a well-known criminal Marty knew had a son at the boarding school, who could be relied on to get a discreet word to Tony about the call. She drank a mouthful of wine as she wondered what the hell she was going to tell him. For his sake, she'd have to keep it simple. Just tell him she and his dad had split up for the moment. She knew Tony would say nothing about the phone call. She dialled the number and waited. She heard Tony's voice after one ring, and her stomach turned over.

'Mum?'

'Oh, Tony, son! Are you all right?'

'Mum! What's going on? You haven't spoken to me in nearly a week. I've called your mobile a few times and it's not even switched on. And I phoned the house loads, and asked Dad what's happening. I . . . I . . .'

Sharon's heart broke as he sounded choked.

'Aw, Tony, sweetheart, come on now. Don't worry.'

'I . . . I thought something had happened to you.' He sniffed. 'Or . . . that you had just left.'

'Tony, darling! Don't be silly now. You know I would never do that.' She paused, swallowed. 'I will never ever leave you, sweetheart. It'll be me and you against the world for ever. Haven't I always said that, pet?'

'Yeah. But what's wrong? Have you left Dad?'

She listened to him breathing, wished she could put her arms around him and hold him close. He was only thirteen but a young thirteen and, she had to admit, a bit of a mummy's boy. Plus, this was his first term at boarding school, so he was still getting used to being so far away from home. She missed him every day, and had never wanted to send him away in the first place, but there was no option. She couldn't have him in the house in the midst of all they did. Tony would have a different life if she had anything to do with it. If he had been at home, Knuckles would have had him working for him and he'd be ruined by the time he was sixteen. Tony wasn't that kind of boy. He was a sweet, artistic boy, who dreamed of being an actor. That was reason enough in Knuckles' eyes for him to barely speak to him.

Sharon took a breath.

'Tony, listen to me. Okay? I need you to understand things and most of all I need you never to tell anyone that we've had this conversation.' She tried to pick her words to protect him from the truth. 'Yes, I've left your dad. You know how it was. It was coming for a while. I don't want that life for you, and things were getting really messed up.'

'Did he hit you? I'll kill him if he hit you, Mum.'

'No, Tony. No, he didn't,' she said. 'But I've left him for good. I know he will be furious at that, so for me, it's best if he never knows where I am. He never will. I'll never see him again. I'm so sorry to put you through this, as he's your dad and I know nothing can ever change that.'

'He's nothing to me. I hate him. He doesn't even like me.'

'Aw, that's not true, Tony. He's still your dad. He's just a very difficult man. He has a lot of problems.'

'I don't want to see him. I want to be with you. I don't care if I never see him again.'

'Has he been in touch?'

'Yes. He's phoned me twice in the past week to ask if you've been in touch. I told him no. He didn't even ask me how I was doing.'

'Is he coming to see you? Did he say anything like that?'

'No. I don't want to see him. He won't come here. He's never even been here.'

It crossed Sharon's mind that Knuckles was such a bastard she wouldn't put it past him to use the boy as leverage to get to her. He would sink that low if he had to. She had to think of a way to get Tony out of his school and away to somewhere safe without causing a fuss.

'Okay. Well, just keep quiet about our chat. I'm working on a way that we can be together. Away from here. But it's not going to happen right away. It's important that you say nothing and just keep your head down. You know that lad who told you that I was phoning you?'

'Yes. Max. He's a bit of a nutter. But dead smart.'

'Is he all right with you? Not bullying or anything?'

'No. He's in the year above me, but he's really popular and funny. I don't know him apart from to say hello to. He was very cautious when we spoke and told me to keep my mouth zipped. He's all right though. This is his phone he let me use.'

'Good. I'm going to get a mobile down to you so we can keep in touch. It will be one that is untraceable just in case anything happens, and the only person you're to phone on it is me. You got that? I don't want your dad to look at your account and maybe find a way to track me through numbers that have phoned your mobile. You understand?'

'Yeah. But when will I be able to see you?'

'Darling, you just stick into your work. The holidays are coming up soon, so we'll work something out. Meanwhile, are you okay and strong enough to make sure you say nothing if your dad phones you?'

'Of course.' Again the sniffs. 'I love you, Mum. I miss you.'

Sharon bit her lip.

'I know, sweetheart. I love you more. Don't ever forget that. Everything I do, I do it for you. Just keep calm and work hard. I'll see you soon. Don't worry.'

'Okay, Mum.'

'I mean it. Off you go now. Goodnight, my darling.'

'Goodnight, Mum. Love you.'

He hung up, and for the first time since all this happened, the floodgates opened. Sharon could feel her chest heaving and the sob came out like a dam breaking. She wept for the desolation she could hear in Tony's voice, and she wept because it had come to this: that after all these years here she was plotting the downfall of the man she had once loved.

# CHAPTER TWENTY-SEVEN

As Kerry came out of the shower in her white bathrobe and with her hair wrapped in a towel, there was a knock on her bedroom door.

'Kerry?' It was the housekeeper. 'Sorry to disturb you, but there's someone on the house phone wants to speak to you. It's a DI Burns?'

Kerry's ears pricked up. This was never going to be good news, whatever the cops wanted. But she had to take the call.

'Okay, Sasha. If you stick him on the extension here I'll talk to him.'

'Sure.'

Kerry puffed up the pillows on her bed and lay back, splashing some toner on her face, which was flushed from the long hot shower. She'd been looking forward to a quiet afternoon, going over some plans for the business and having a serious look at the documents and legal papers of

Danno O'Hara's failed hotel plan on the Costa del Sol. She patted some face cream on as she lay down and lifted the receiver after two rings.

'Kerry? DI Burns here. Sorry to disturb you.'

Yeah, right, Kerry thought, musing on the determined look he had that day he'd dropped in on her with some vague hope she would divulge all the family secrets. He'd set the parameters of who he was that day, when she almost called him 'Vinny' until she saw how stony-faced he was at her familiarity. But she was curious.

'That's all right, Detective Inspector,' she said with emphasis.

There was a brief silence and she waited.

'Kerry, I was wondering if we could have a chat. If you're free some time.'

'A chat?' Kerry almost smiled, sensing an awkwardness in his voice. 'What about? The good old days when we were all skint?'

'Well. No. Not really. But I wanted to talk to you about a few things. Look, I don't think I handled things very well the other day when we spoke at your house, but I'd really like to talk to further.'

Kerry waited a moment, figuring out how to answer.

'Have you found my brother and mother's killers yet?'

'Actually no. As I said to you, I believe someone got there before us.'

Kerry didn't answer.

'Look, Kerry. Rather than come to the house in a formal way, would you be up for a bit of a chat – maybe some lunch in the city?'

Kerry felt herself smiling.

'Are you asking me out on a date, Inspector?'

She could hear the humour in his voice.

'No. It's not a date, Kerry.'

'Sounds like a date to me.' She played with him, picturing his handsome face.

'Well. Call it whatever you like. But would you be up for an informal chat? Just you and me?'

It crossed Kerry's mind that he might be bent and was organising a cosy lunch with her to put his cards on the table. Wouldn't be the worst thing that could happen. But if this was what it was, she would have to work out how to deal with it.

'Yeah, sure. I can meet you.'

Again, after all these years, the image flashed up of the last day they saw each other, the tears in his eyes. All the promises. It was as though it never even happened. Had he just completely forgotten about it?

'Okay. How about La Lanterna? You know, in Hope Street. Are you free tomorrow?'

'I can make myself free.'

'Good. Thanks. How about one o'clock?'

'Okay. I can do that.' She paused. 'And will a couple of

your flunkies be sitting at the table close by picking up our every word?'

'Nah. That only happens in the movies.'

'Okay. I'll be there. Don't be late. I don't do late.'

'Me neither. See you, Kerry.'

She hung up and closed her eyes, a little unsettled by the phone call. Best not to give it too much thought, she decided, play it by ear. She was smart enough to do a bit of fencing with Vinny Burns. But somehow his call, the sound of his voice, had made her mind drift to places she seldom went these days.

It had been nearly eight months since Kerry had walked out of the relationship with Leo. From the day she'd left the flat in London where they'd lived together for three years, she had pushed all thoughts of him to a place where she could manage them. She was good at that. Building walls was something she'd had to learn very quickly, when she was sent to Spain as a teenager. Back then, as the realisation dawned that this was her life, she'd had to fight hard to put the crippling homesickness and pining for her parents into a place where she could deal with it. And she did. On her visits home, though she loved being back, there was something missing. There was a distance between her and her mother that she had created in order to survive. If her mum noticed it, she never mentioned it, and perhaps she was holding back her own emotions because she knew her daughter's life would have to be away from Glasgow. So Kerry was well versed in zipping up her emotions and putting them in a box, not to be opened again unless she was confident that doing so would not rock her foundations.

It had taken her a long time to come to the conclusion with Leo that whatever they had, it wasn't for ever. However powerful, dynamic, passionate and tumultuous their love was, it was never going to last. He probably knew it as much as she did, but it had become the relationship where they couldn't live with each other and couldn't live without each other. But everything fell apart for her when she lost their baby four months into her pregnancy. The baby hadn't been planned, but somehow it had cemented them. The miscarriage had overwhelmed Kerry, and she'd never known she could feel this much love and loss for a little person she hadn't even met. Leo, no doubt, was going through his own agony, and Kerry knew his pain was genuine, but she couldn't help feeling that there was something of a sense of release for him, because, deep down, he probably hadn't really hankered after the full family-and-settling-down-for-ever picture. So it was Kerry who made the first move and told him it was over. Leo cried and reeled and promised it could be different. But they both knew it wouldn't be. She had never told her mother it was over, even eight months after they broke up, or about losing the baby. She'd planned to tell her while she was home for Mickey's funeral, but that choice was taken from her. She hadn't even thought about it in these past few days – until Vinny Burns walked back into her life.

# CHAPTER TWENTY-EIGHT

Stepping off Hope Street into La Lanterna restaurant was like going back in time, the walls on the way downstairs adorned with old photographs of rural Italy. The family-run restaurant had been an old favourite eating place of her father's in his day, and she remembered happy Sunday afternoons or Saturday evenings in there as a child with Mickey, and their parents, her dad comfortable and enjoying the respect he always got from the old owner. It was a place where rich businessmen, but also rich gangsters, made deals over long afternoons drinking wine and eating perfect food. It was busy enough today, with lunchtime movers and shakers and retired business types out for a treat with their wives or their much younger mistresses. Kerry quickly glanced around the room when she came downstairs, and before she clocked her lunch date in the far corner, she noticed the two younger men Jack Reilly had told her would also be dining in the place. They were there to keep an eye on her from a discreet distance. It was the same everywhere she went these days; someone, often two bodyguards, always shadowing her. After Mickey's shooting, and especially now with the revenge killings from the funeral, Kerry was told she was an even bigger target than before. She understood the need for security, but she didn't always like it. She often yearned for a long afternoon in a restaurant and then going on to a bar just for the sheer hell of it – the way she'd done in Spain or sometimes in London with Leo. But those days were long gone. This was how she lived now. She looked across the restaurant and straight at Vinny Burns who was getting to his feet. Top marks for manners, she smiled to herself, slipping off her coat and making her way across.

'Kerry,' he said as she got to the table. 'Good to see you.'

No handshake, no air kiss. The two of them stood for a moment and studied each other. She couldn't help noticing how impeccably dressed he was: pinstripe suit, white shirt and dark blue striped tie. She wished he wasn't so bloody good-looking, as his cool blue eyes fixed her.

'Inspector,' she said, a sarcastic smile playing on her lips.

'Vinny.' He smiled. 'We can drop the formalities if we're going to sit here in the dark and drink wine.'

She sat down.

'Good to see you too, Vinny.' She bit her bottom lip and glanced around the room. 'Who'd have thought it, eh? After all these years, here we are. Downstairs in La Lanterna, like all the old celebrated hoods of yesteryear.'

He smiled as the waiter came up and stood silently.

'Drink?' Vinny said.

'I'll have wine,' Kerry said. 'Red.'

He looked up at the waiter and ordered a bottle from the menu as though he knew what he was doing.

'You know your Italian wines then?'

'No. Not at all. But I didn't want to just plump for the house wine.'

Kerry watched him as he fiddled with the menu, looking a little uneasy. The Vinny Burns who was sitting opposite her was not the same guy who'd come into her home a few days ago, all poker-faced and full of police business. This was more like an original version of the boy she fell for back in school. And looking at him now, there was a little fleeting wrench of the hurt and pain she'd felt back then – but she pushed it away, as it was silly to even think that way. When her father died, and her mother was sending her to live in Spain, Vinny had promised that this wasn't the end. They would keep in touch, talk on the phone, and write to each other. She'd see him when she came home. But she never did. Why did he simply disappear from her life? She didn't come back to Glasgow for the two months of the summer holidays, and instead her mother came to Spain. By the winter, Vinny was a memory, but still one that could scorch her. Of course it was all ridiculous now when she looked back. Once, almost a year after she'd left, she came back and saw him with another girl, and was surprised how it still stung her. If only he'd told her why, she would have accepted it. It was a lesson that stood her in good stead for her other relationships, where she seldom let down her guard. Really, she should be thanking him, she used to tell herself. And yet, even now, as she saw him, she was dying to ask why. But that was stupid. Don't go there now. Keep it simple, businesslike but friendly.

The waiter appeared at the table, opened a bottle of wine and poured it into her glass to taste.

'That'll do nicely,' Kerry said.

He poured the wine and then stepped back. Vinny raised his glass, leaning forward and clinking hers.

'To . . . What will we drink to, Kerry?'

Suddenly she caught his eyes and for a tiny second she saw herself all those years ago when life seemed uncomplicated, even if it wasn't. She shook herself out of it.

'To . . . to . . . to surviving,' Kerry said. 'Let's drink to that, Vinny. To a couple of kids from the schemes who made it this far.'

'To surviving,' he said, looking at her then beyond her, as though, for a second, he too was somewhere else.

Kerry drank a mouthful of wine, relishing the taste of it and the feeling as it hit her stomach. She had to be careful to go easy on the alcohol as she drank so little now, and the last thing she wanted to do on a day like this was drop any guards. She picked up the menu and ran her eyes down it, although she had made up her mind before she even arrived to ask if they still did the braised beef cooked in Chianti which had been an old speciality. The waiter came across and took their order, unfolding the napkin and placing it on Kerry's lap. Vinny took a drink of wine and put the glass down. He ran a hand across his chin and leaned forward.

'So. How are you? I mean, after your mum. I can't imagine how that must have been that day. And Mickey. That was a shock.'

Kerry sat forward, her elbows on the table so that their heads were close. How was she? It was a tough question. She sighed. She decided to be honest.

'Well, it's hard to say how I am these days, and that's the truth. I guess I'm still numb from my mother's death. I still can't quite believe I'll never see her again. That's the hardest part, suddenly thinking I'll have to tell her something later, and then I remember she's not there.' She paused. 'It's tough. But Mickey? Well, truth is, I didn't get on with him. I don't like the way he ran things.'

'Yeah. I can see why.' He looked at her then down at the table. 'He wasn't the greatest guy, that's for sure.' He half shrugged. 'Anyway, it's all yours now though.'

She nodded slowly. 'Yeah. But it's going to be different.'

They sat for a moment in silence as the waiter brought

the antipasti and she watched as Vinny ate a couple of fork-fuls of meat and poured some olive oil onto a side plate.

'Sure.' He shrugged. 'But how you going to do that, Kerry? I mean, make it different.' He raised his eyebrows. 'It's not as if you can just shut up shop and go into the retail business.'

'I know that.' She didn't need to hear that.

There was a long moment when they said nothing and she felt a little uncomfortable. Eventually, Vinny spoke.

'I'm not trying to wind you up, Kerry. Honestly. But you know what Mickey was into. He surrounded himself with all sorts of bad people. Not just here, but down south as well. Dublin too, and Spain. He had too many fingers in too many pies. That's probably why he got wasted.' He paused. 'Look, all I'm saying to you is it's going to take a bit of doing, getting out of all that – might even be impossible.'

She nodded. 'Yes. I know that.' She felt the need to change the subject for the moment. 'Anyway. Tell me about you, Vinny. How the hell did you become a cop? You kept *that* quiet when we were at school.' She smiled. 'Mind you, com-ing from where we did, that's probably just as well. Not too many cops came out of Maryhill, that's for sure.'

'Just happened after I left. I was in college, and then I saw an advert to join the police force and I thought, what the hell. Decent money, a career. It was either that or go the other way. It was my uncle Harry who came up from London where he was a cop in the Met, and he told me that whatever I did, I had to get out of Maryhill. So I ended up moving down there. It was the Met where I started out.'

'Really? I didn't know that. You were down there all those years?'

'Yep. Did all right. Out of uniform in about three years and into plain clothes. Then the drugs squad. And then promotion to sergeant, and then into the National Crime Agency. That's a different world, Kerry, I can tell you that.'

'Fascinating.' Kerry's alarm bells were ringing. If he was in the NCA he probably knew more about her business than she did.

'Yeah. I could write a book. I was undercover for two years. In Europe and in South America. Mexico, Colombia. Hard graft.'

'Colombia? Not for the faint-hearted.'

'Yeah. Would frighten the shit right out of you, what goes on there. And how far the cartels reach. But it's what they do to people that is sickening. They make people like your Mickey and all the rest of the players in the UK and Europe look like Mother Teresa.'

Kerry watched him swirl his glass and take another swig and she pondered how differently their lives had panned out. Yet here they were, like old friends. She wanted to hear more, her natural curiosity stirred, but her sensible head told her not to ask too many questions. He was telling her this for a reason. He was letting her know that he could buy and sell her when it came to drug dealers.

'So, when did you quit the NCA?'

'I haven't quit – not as such. I'm still with them. Just not living in some backstreet in Amsterdam or Colombia. I'd had enough of that. There was a promotion going in London, and I took it. Then about six months ago, I was seconded up here to the Scottish Drug Enforcement Agency. Drug wars. You know the score.'

Kerry looked at him but said nothing. The main course arrived and as they ate, they got chatting about names of old pals from school and laughing at stories of teachers who used to put them through the wringer. To any of the diners in the restaurant they looked like a couple, or two old mates enjoying a reunion over lunch. When they finished, Vinny poured some more wine into their glasses. He looked straight at her.

'You know you're in a lot of danger,' he said, dabbing his mouth with his napkin. 'You're a number one target. Has anyone told you that?'

Her stomach did lurch a little at how starkly he said it. Hearing it from a cop with the kind of background Vinny had just told her about sent a chill through her. She tried to look impassive.

'It doesn't take any major police investigation to work that out, Vinny. I know I'm a target.'

'That'll be why you're not alone in here, eh?'

She looked at him then at the table. He half smiled.

'The two dudes over there getting into their pasta. If I was to walk over there right now and show them my police badge, then frisk them, my guess is I'd find a couple of Glocks in their back pockets.'

She said nothing.

'Doesn't matter. I know who they are. Look, I'm not interested in them. But at least someone in your organisation is smart enough to make sure people are watching over you.'

She stayed silent a long moment, knowing he was waiting for her to say something.

'So I'm a target. That shouldn't surprise you. It doesn't surprise me.'

He leaned over.

'More so, now, Kerry, after the bodies piling up in the city. You know what I mean. The boys from Manchester who were holed up here for weeks and who killed your mother at the funeral. The revenge attack. We know it was your organisation.'

She said nothing, fidgeted with her glass.

'To be honest,' Vinny said, 'scumbags like that are not a priority for us. We're not even interested.' He paused. 'It's you we're interested in.'

Kerry rolled her eyes to the ceiling.

'Ah, the truth at last. And there was me just thinking you wanted to have a catch-up of the old days,' she said, sarcastic. 'Of course I know you're interested in me.' She smiled. 'Should I be calling my lawyer?'

He shook his head. 'No. Come on. I thought we could meet up and have a chat.'

'What, and maybe I would suddenly just grass everyone up?'

He took a moment before he answered. 'Not grass anyone up. Just consider the spirit of cooperation.'

She smiled and shook her head. 'Yeah, right. Grassing.'

'Kerry. You're from a different world than this lot. Your life has been a world away from this. You can go back to that.'

She sat for a moment, knowing he was watching her.

'Vinny.' She leaned forward, her hand reaching across the table so it was nearly touching his. She saw him flick a glance down at it, but he didn't move. 'You're wrong. I held my mother in my arms as the life ebbed out of her. Everything changed for ever in those final moments. This is who I am now. I wish I could tell you something different, something you want to hear. But this is who I am. The cops? What can they do for me? Nothing, that's what. You think if the names of the people who murdered my mother were handed over to the police they would pull out all the stops to bring them to justice? No way. And even if it did reach court, some smart lawyer would get them off. That's how it goes. You know that as well as I do.' She felt the emotion in her voice and put the glass to her lips and drank the lot.

Suddenly she felt his hand on top of hers and she wanted to pull it away, but somehow she couldn't. Because everything he said was right. She was from a different world. But it was too late now to go back to that.

'Kerry, I understand where you are, what you've been through. But you should know that you can trust me.'

They sat that way in silence, feeling the warmth of his hand over hers for a long, dangerous moment.

# CHAPTER TWENTY-NINE

Cal hadn't been anywhere near the car wash since his disastrous trip to Manchester. It would be asking for trouble. What he did know was that the car wash, like most of the other ones he knew, employed illegal immigrants. In all the times he'd worked there, he was the only non-immigrant, and he was often called upon by some of them to translate for them if a customer was asking questions. One of the lads, Tahir, had become a mate, and on payday sometimes they'd go to the café together. The boy was only two years older than him, but had already been in Glasgow for eighteen months after being smuggled in himself. Cal was fascinated by the story of how he left his war-torn village to make a better life, and how he dreamed of bringing his family over. He'd listen to his dreams, but felt sorry for him because the reality was that none of this was going to happen. Tahir was working illegally for a bunch of gangsters. He could never be legal, and if they wanted to, they could make him disappear any day of the week. Tahir was nobody to them – just a glorified slave in a place where they laundered their drug money. Cal hadn't seen him since the day before Manchester, but he was pleased when he saw his name coming up on his mobile. They arranged to meet at the café, and at first Cal was suspicious. You never knew if someone had got to Tahir, knowing they were friends, and told him to lure Cal to a trap. But he decided he was letting his imagination get carried away with him, so he agreed to meet. He waited for Tahir in the street, close to the café, but far enough away so that if Tahir turned up with anyone he shouldn't, then he could make a run for it. Cal was relieved when Tahir came walking up the road alone and spotted him.

'Hey, man,' Tahir said as he approached, a smile on his thin, pale face. 'How you been? You disappear?' He gave him a playful punch on the shoulder.

Cal smiled. 'Yeah, mate. Had enough of the place. I'm not coming back.'

Tahir looked surprised.

'I asked the boss. He said you didn't call. Just didn't show up no more.'

'I know.' Cal jerked his head to the café door. 'Come on. I'm starving.'

'Me too,' Tahir said.

Cal pushed open the door and they went inside, making their way to a seat in a less crowded section close to the back. They sat opposite each other, immediately scanning the menu on the table, not speaking for a few seconds.

'I need a burger and chips,' Tahir said. 'Had nothing all day.'

'Why not?' Cal said. He noticed his friend's eyes had tired shadows, clocked his greasy hair, and he could see he needed a shower and a change of clothes.

Tahir shrugged, glanced over his shoulder, then leaned a little closer.

'I got not much money right now. I been saving everything I make. I got some plans.'

Cal looked at him and for a moment he wondered if he was going away. He wished they could have been closer friends, and he felt sorry for him because he always seemed alone, and though he must have been made of tough stuff to make it here on his own and survive, there was a kind of darkness about him. He imagined what it would have been like if it was him on his own.

'Really? You going away somewhere?' Cal asked.

Tahir was about to answer when the young waitress came sashaying up, chewing gum, and looked at Cal.

'Can I get you something?'

'Aye. Burger and chips, please. And a Coke.'

She glanced at Tahir with a look of contempt but said nothing. It immediately irked Cal, and he could see that Tahir felt it too.

'I have cheeseburger and chips. And Coke. Please.'

She looked at him and screwed her eyes up.

'Can you repeat that in English?'

Tahir looked away. Cal glared at her.

'Are you deaf?' he said. 'He was speaking perfect English.'

She shrugged, unfazed.

'Didnae hear him right. The accent. Cannae understand these people half the time. They're all over the place.'

Cal felt angrier than he probably should have, and right now he wanted to get up and leave, but he would stand his ground for his friend.

'He said he wants a cheeseburger and chips and a Coke. Now can you write that down and read it back to me? In English.'

'Aye, very funny,' she said. 'You're a comedian, you are.'

'I want to make sure you've got it right. Otherwise I can ask your boss.'

The waitress shot him a furious glare and read the order aloud.

'Great,' Cal said. 'Any time you're ready.'

When she left, Cal winked at Tahir.

'Bitch will probably spit on our burgers now.' He shook his head. 'Arsehole.'

'Never mind,' Tahir said. 'Is not important. I see it many times since I come here. I stopped caring about things like that.' He paused, looked around again. 'Anyway. I have more exciting things to tell you. But first. Why you no come back to car wash?'

Cal sighed. His gut told him he could take Tahir into his confidence, even though they didn't know each other all that well. He knew he was decent and hard-working, and didn't seem like the kind of guy who would betray a friend.

'Long story, mate. I got some trouble, and I have to keep my head down.'

Tahir watched him.

'I thought maybe this is the case. That's why I didn't ask the boss much.'

'Not even sure if he knows about it.'

Tahir narrowed his eyes.

'I see you with the other guys who came up to the car wash that day. The rich guys in the car. They were talking to you. Gangsters, I think.'

'Yeah. You're not wrong.'

'Drug dealers.'

'Look, I don't really want to talk about it, Tahir. Honest. It's not that I don't trust you, man, but I just want to forget it. Less said about it the better. But I've got another part-time job now doing some odd jobs, and I won't be coming back. I got caught up in something I shouldn't have and got my fingers burnt.'

Tahir let out a low whistle and shook his head.

'You must be careful, Cal. If you fucked up on a drug thing, then these guys always look for you.'

'I didn't fuck up. I didn't do anything. But suddenly,

I find myself in trouble. Anyway. It's being dealt with.' He changed the subject. 'So tell me. What's exciting?'

The waitress arrived with the drinks, and set them down noisily on the table.

'Okay. I tell you. My family – well, my brother. He is the only one I have left. He is back in Iraq. But he is coming here. I am helping him. With his wife and their boy and little girl. The boy is three years old now, and the girl two.'

'Really? They're coming here? How?'

Tahir's voice dropped to a whisper. 'The smugglers are bringing them.' He spread his hands. 'Big money, my friend. Cost big money. That is why I am saving all my money.'

'Jesus!' Cal said.

He'd seen stories on the news all the time of smugglers bringing refugees over in boats and containers and cars. Making money from them.

'But that is a fortune, Tahir. How can you pay for that? And it's not even safe. Christ, man! That's well dodgy.'

He nodded. 'I know is dangerous. Yes. I know is a lot of money, but my brother is paying a lot too. He pays the smuggler on the other side and I pay this side.'

'Christ! How much? I mean, who are you paying? How do you know they won't rip you off?'

'I know is a chance to steal my money. But the guy here I was put in touch with through my brother. Is all the same people. I have to pay eighteen hundred pounds, and my brother pays two thousand five hundred. All his money in his life he is paying.'

'Where is your brother now?'

'He is in Turkey. He is staying in a tent there. But is freezing. He is coming soon.'

'But how? On a truck or something?'

He shrugged. 'I don't know the arrangement yet. The guy here says to me, he will tell me when it is ready. I already paid him nearly a thousand pounds.'

'Jesus, mate. Where did you get that kind of money?'

He raised his eyebrows. 'Same as you my friend. From the drug drops.'

Cal's mouth dropped open in surprise. Christ almighty!

The waitress came up and slammed the food down on the table.

'Holy fuck, man. Seriously?'

Tahir shrugged. 'Yes. Has to be done. My brother will be here soon. I am so happy to be seeing him.'

Cal watched him as he stabbed a few chips onto a fork and stuffed them into his mouth, his heart sinking by the minute.

It was getting dark as Cal walked home after saying goodbye to Tahir. When they left the café, they walked together until Tahir took the bus to the digs he shared in Sighthill along with some other immigrants. Cal was angry and scared and depressed for his friend all at the same time. He thought how lucky he was, as he walked up towards Hyndland where the tenement flats had lights and life inside, and people were living privileged lives compared to the one Tahir was living. He was going to a house like this too, but he was far from privileged in the circumstances that led him to be here. But from where he was right now, he felt lucky. His mother would be in the flat, looking better than she had in weeks. His sister was now four days into rehab and they hadn't heard from her, but that's how it had to be for a whole month. At least she wasn't standing shivering in some doorway up the drag. But he couldn't get Tahir out of his mind.

# CHAPTER THIRTY

The day Kerry had walked into the Paradise Club and seen McCann beating up the defenceless girl was the first time she'd seen up close what she had got herself into. That was just how it worked. Girls like the Russian hooker would never have a say in how their lives would turn out, at the mercy of bastards like McCann. He was nobody, yet he had power over the weakest in his own grubby operation. The higher up the food chain, the more power over the weakest. And the ultimate power was with the boss who ran the show – and now that was her. None of this was lost on Kerry in her darker moments, when her conscience plagued her, questioned her, niggled away at her when sleep wouldn't come. Yet it hadn't stopped her stepping in and pistol-whipping McCann on impulse that day, as though she'd been doing it all her life. Maybe the apple didn't fall far from the tree. Maybe she was just as much a criminal as her father and brother were. After all, her conscience hadn't disturbed her at all as she'd grown up in Spain living in comfort on the proceeds of her father's criminal earnings. But now it was different. Her father had been an old-fashioned criminal – a safe-cracker and a robber – and somehow while it was far from respectable, it wasn't something she would hide in shame from. Now it was all drug money. She only had to take a drive back through the old neighbourhood where she grew up to see how heroin and cocaine had swallowed up whole communities. The families who remained untouched by drugs were the lucky ones. She only had to look at her old friend Maria, struggling to cope with how heroin had all but claimed her two children, to feel sickened by what, at the end of the day, she was now a part of. Jenny was in rehab, financed by Kerry, and by all accounts doing well. Cal, according to Jack, was a good lad and shaping up well. Helping Maria went some way to salving Kerry's conscience, because at least she was trying to pull someone out of the mire. Yet despite the jabbing guilt, Kerry was still running the show in this business that was built around drugs. And now, here she was, waiting for Sharon to show up in the restaurant to talk about the shipment of cannabis and cocaine they were about to steal from Knuckles Boyle in Amsterdam.

If ever there was a game of double standards, it was the one Kerry played out in her mind most nights when she lay in bed tossing and turning. But every morning, she pushed her thoughts away, consoling herself with the determination that it wouldn't always be like this. Last night, before she went to bed, she had pored over the plans for the hotel on the Costa del Sol, lying waiting to be built. This would be her first major project. She had already instructed Marty to talk to the old man about selling the car showroom and his entire business. But first, she had to deal with a drug shipment from Amsterdam, as well as her thoughts last night about Vinny Burns. Even after all these years, there had still been a spark as they'd sat together during the long lunch. But it wasn't just that. It was business too. What if the best way to do Knuckles into the ground was to get the cops to clean him out? Maybe Vinny was right, and she should be looking to the cops if she wanted to change things. She'd have to be careful how she broached this with Sharon. Grassing to the cops was how Sharon would no doubt describe it. Kerry preferred to think about it as working with them, a bit of give and take on both sides. She saw it as a possible way out, a means to an end, when she could pursue what she wanted for her organisation.

Sharon appeared at the doorway to the restaurant and Kerry watched as her eyes flicked around the room, empty apart from an old couple and what looked like might be their daughter having afternoon tea. How civilised, she thought, given her own business, as Sharon came striding across to her in tight leather leggings and knee-high flat-heeled black suede boots.

'How you doing?' Kerry said, as Sharon eased herself onto the seat.

'I'm good,' Sharon said. 'Well, as good as it gets right now. Yourself?'

'Much the same. Trying to keep all the balls in the air and watch my back at the same time.'

Kerry was considering telling her about Pollock and McCann's bodies being found in the burnt-out car, but she wasn't sure if she should. Then Sharon beat her to the mark.

'I saw the stuff on the news about that prick Pollock and his mate being found dead in a car. I was wondering if your crew had anything to do with it.'

Kerry looked at her, surprised. 'You know Pollock?'

'I met him once. I know who he is. Knuckles sold to him – heroin, coke. You know that?'

'I do now. Or I found out a few days ago.'

Sharon nodded slowly, as though she approved of the hit, even though Kerry hadn't admitted it was anything to do with her firm. The waitress came and Sharon ordered tea.

'I hear on the grapevine there was some fuck-up with Knuckles' drugs because of Pollock. Heard the dick he sent did a runner. Probably grassed up or something. And some teenage boy was left to carry the can. Arseholes.'

'Yeah. I heard.'

'Knuckles will be looking for that boy. So if you know who he is, you'd do well to warn him.'

Kerry nodded, placing her cup on the table. 'Don't worry about it.' She changed the subject. 'So. The shipment. Anything new?'

Sharon stalled until the waitress had placed her teapot and crockery on the table.

'Not much on the shipment itself. I talked to my man over there and he says it's all on course.' She paused. 'But we need to go over details, routes and stuff.'

'Yeah. We can talk that through today, as far as we can.'

Sharon poured from the teapot and looked up at Kerry.

'By the way, Knuckles is going to Spain in a couple of days, I hear.'

'Really. You know why?'

'Fucker's probably looking for me.' She gave a throaty smoker's chuckle. 'Knowing him, he'll be shelling out money everywhere to try and track me down.' She looked at Kerry, then beyond her. 'We ... I mean he, has a villa down outside Marbs. Close to Puerto Banus. He'll be over there regrouping with his boys. Getting pissed and racking up the lines of coke. Usual shit. Flexing his muscles.'

'I take it he knows about the shipment though. I mean, I know he leaves it all to you, but he must know it'll be on its way to the UK soon.'

Sharon nodded. 'Yeah. He phoned my man out in Amsterdam. Asked if I'd been in touch, and he was told no. But he knows the shipment was planned for the day it is, so he told Jan that I was away on business and that he was just letting him know to go ahead. What a tit. Shows you how stupid he is.'

'It's quite staggering that he hasn't at least sent someone out to Amsterdam to see things before the shipment hits the road. There's a lot of money involved. And especially with him already losing the drugs to Pollock.'

'I know. But he's so arrogant. He'll be thinking that my man out there is too terrified to put a foot wrong, that he will do exactly as he's told. He's expecting the trucks at his warehouse on the due date.' She grinned. 'I wish I could be a fly on the wall for that moment.'

Kerry thought about what she said for a few seconds and still found it hard to believe that Knuckles would just leave it as it is.

'But will he really not be doing anything to watch for the shipment as it leaves – given that two of his men who tried to kill you are dead, and you are out there somewhere?'

Sharon shrugged. 'You never really can be a hundred per cent sure. I'll be honest with you, he might have sent someone in the background to quietly take a look. But, like I said before, when they go to the warehouse in Amsterdam they are not going to find anything untoward. The trucks will be leaving as usual. Unless he has the manpower to follow them, he'll never know. And he won't send someone to track them all the way to the UK.'

Kerry hoped she was right. She waited a moment before she spoke. She hadn't told Sharon of her plans to take some of the shipment to apartments they had on the Costa del Sol and move it on from there. And she also hadn't discussed with Sharon what she wanted from this. Now was the time to do it.

'Sharon.' She sat back, crossed her legs. 'You haven't said yet what you want from the shipment. I presume you're not just going to write it off – like give it away.'

Sharon sat for a moment, studying her.

'What do you mean? Like how much am I looking for?'

'Well. It's Knuckles' shipment. It's not mine.'

Sharon took a breath and let it out slowly.

'What would you propose to do with it? We haven't discussed that yet, Kerry.'

'I know. It's all happening so fast. But what I would do with it, is not bring all of it to the UK, and instead take the bulk of it down to the Costa del Sol. I have places I can store it there.'

'What? Then move it on?'

'I have people who can do that – move it on. And I can use it as a bargaining chip.'

'What do you mean?'

'With the Durkins and the Hills.'

Sharon gave her a wry smile.

'For someone new to the game, you are fast on your feet, Kerry.'

She shrugged. 'Needs must. An opportunity has come my way, through you, and I'd be a poor businesswoman if I didn't look at it and work out what best to do.'

Sharon nodded. 'When you say "bargaining chip", what do you mean?'

Kerry put her head back for a second and tried to pick her words. 'I'll be honest with you. When I agreed to meet you it was only because you came to me offering a way to destroy Knuckles. I admire you for having the backbone to do that. This shipment is one shipment – four trucks – okay, it's worth a substantial amount, but there will be more of that where it came from, and it won't put Knuckles out of business. It'll make a dent. But it won't kill him.'

'And you want to kill him. Of course you do.'

'I want to ruin him. Don't you?'

'You bet I do.'

'Then what if there was a scenario that one of the trucks arrived in the UK at Knuckles' warehouse as arranged, and he was there to greet it.' Kerry paused, choosing her words carefully, but there was no easy way to say it. 'And, say, the cops were there too. And he was caught, bang on, red-handed, up to his arse in a shipment fresh from Europe with his fingerprints all over it.'

Sharon looked at her, a little nonplussed.

'You mean grass him up? Are you serious?'

'It would be a means to an end.'

'It's grassing him up though. I mean, what's the point in even getting cops involved at all? They'll be all over it, and before I know where I am they'll be all over me. Jesus Christ, Kerry!'

Kerry waited a couple of beats. 'Doesn't have to be like that. You don't go anywhere near it – I mean the cops' involvement.'

Sharon looked confused.

'What do you mean? How they going to know?'

'A tip-off. Anonymous.'

'What's the point?'

'Knuckles gets dragged kicking and screaming into custody to await trial. And while he's doing that, the cops uncover all the details of his dealings over the years. Everything. Bank accounts, businesses his name is attached to.'

'Well, who the fuck do you think that's going to come from, apart from me? Are you kidding me?' She glanced over her shoulder, even though there was nobody there.

'No. Not you.'

'What?'

'I'll sort it.'

'What the fuck? *You'll* grass him up?'

'You call it that. I call it working with the cops. I scratch their back, they scratch mine. They get what they want, and you get to disappear off the scene completely so they're not looking for you. Because you can guarantee when they get Knuckles, the first thing he'll do is blame you. But if it's played right, then the cops won't even listen to that. They'll go totally on him.'

They sat in silence for a moment, only the clinks of the cups across the room and the whisper of the quiet family enjoying an afternoon in the comfort of the hotel. Kerry waited while Sharon digested it.

'And what do you get – apart from all Knuckles' drugs haul?'

'I want out of this business – away from the drugs. My father was an old-fashioned criminal. He didn't want to deal drugs – he'll be spinning in his grave because of the road Mickey took us on. I'm going to make that different. I'm going to build a proper, legit, respected business. You name your price what you want from it. Then I do what I want.'

They sat again in silence. Sharon liked this Kerry. From the first moment she met her, and she was coming across all hardass, Sharon could feel her nerves. But she sensed she could punch above her weight all right. Kerry may be new to the game, but it looked like she was learning fast. And above all, she took her in when she was desperate and had nowhere else to go. She owed some loyalty to that, no doubt. But grassing up and getting in bed with the cops? She knew once the accounts and books were out, her own fingerprints would be all over it. Sure, the cops could say they wouldn't pursue her, but how could she trust them? Yet the idea of a fresh start, a way out, that she could begin a new life for her and Tony was tantalising. Finally, Sharon leaned forward and kept her voice a whisper.

'Okay.' She nodded. 'But here's my price.' She looked Kerry in the eye. 'You make me a partner in your business.'

Kerry kept her face impassive. This didn't come as any

real surprise to her, and she had turned over the pitfalls of it in her mind during a sleepless night. Sharon was an unknown quantity who had just bumped off her two would-be assassins and made off with the fate of one of the UK's biggest hoodlums in her handbag. She could do anything she wanted when it came down to it. She was different from Kerry – and yet she could see that they both had something in common. They were driven and determined, and above all, they wanted revenge.

# CHAPTER THIRTY-ONE

Knuckles woke up with Mel gently running her fingertips across his face, then he could feel her hand drift down his stomach and massage between his legs. Christ! Was there no end to this bird's fucking sexual appetite? They'd both been coked out of their heads last night, and he'd banged her all over the place from the kitchen table to the bedroom floor, yet the horny bitch was still shouting for more. Now, as his eyes flickered in the morning light streaming in the bedroom window, he could feel himself getting hard as she climbed on top of him, tossing back her long blonde hair as she sat astride him, her muscular thighs gripping him.

'Jesus, Mel! I'm knackered, babe! You'll need to do all the work, darlin'.'

'Just you lie there and enjoy it, tiger,' Mel cooed as she slipped him inside her.

Knuckles lay back, his eyes closed, enjoying Mel's expert

work. Whatever else she was, this bird was a fucking good shag. He couldn't remember the last time he'd lain in bed like this with Sharon climbing all over his bones. Way back, in the early days, their sex had been explosive, but Sharon was getting older, and there just wasn't the same buzz from her. It was like she accommodated him whenever he asked for sex, unlike this little bitch who was jumping on him at every turn. Sharon just wasn't switched on like this. Sure, she'd supported him over the years, made a home for him and the boy, and looked after a substantial part of his crooked empire on his behalf. But a man is a man, and he has different needs. He needed what Mel was doing right now. And as soon as it was over, she would be getting her butt out of here because he had work to do. She wouldn't even moan about not getting to stay for breakfast. She knew her place.

An hour later, Knuckles was showered and in his office when the boys knocked on the back door. He'd asked Terry and the boys to come in for another brainstorming session, and to see if they had picked up any intel on where the fuck Sharon was. He knew that wherever she was hiding out, this was never going to have a happy ending. She'd be plotting against him big time. In fact, he'd already discovered she must have been, when he'd got Johnny to take a look at the accounts. Something was missing. Like most of his fucking money. It had to be somewhere, Johnny had consoled him. They'd find it. It's not as though she could have spent it all. She'll have put it somewhere, Johnny said, for safekeeping. Hence the meet this morning.

'Fine day out there,' Harry said as he came in the back door. 'It's like spring.'

Knuckles glared at him, then at the others.

'Well, thanks for the fucking weather report, Harry, but I hope you've got more to tell me today than the fact that the sun is fucking shining.'

Harry sniggered. 'Just saying, boss.'

Knuckles motioned all of them to the chairs around the table.

'Sit down, boys.' He sniffed a little and touched his nose. 'I've had a blinder of a night last night, so I'm a bit rough. I really need some good fucking news to cheer me up a bit.' He turned to Johnny. 'So, mate. What's new?'

Johnny cleared his throat, looking a bit edgy.

'Well, Knuckles,' he began, 'I've had someone going through every single email on your computer and business transaction online banking. The boy is a fucking legend when it comes to breaking out information. So . . .' he hesitated. 'I'm afraid what he's found is that she has moved nearly all of your money.'

Knuckles glowered at him. 'What is this, dejà fucking vu? We already know the bitch has moved the cunting money, Johnny. We've been through all this. But where the fuck is it? Christ all-fucking-mighty, man! That's what you were supposed to find out.'

Johnny flushed and put his hands up.

'I'm coming to that, Knuckles. Just let me finish.'

Knuckles shook his head and sighed. Johnny went on. 'So, my boy has found that there is an account in the Cayman Islands with her name on it. And another one in Jersey . . . And one in Liechtenstein.'

'Liechtenstein? Where the fuck is that?' Knuckles asked.

The boys looked from one to the other.

'Deepest Europe,' Harry said. 'It's a tax haven.'

'Right,' Knuckles said, looking at Johnny. 'Go on then. Tell me more.'

'Well, the money. It seems small amounts have been getting transferred there over the past six months – then there was a big transfer recently. The Cayman Islands one has been on the go for years. Same name. But it has a lot of money in it. The Bank of Ireland has a couple of hundred thousand in it as well, and it's a different name. But it all came in over the past eighteen months from your account.'

Knuckles sat staring at the table. Fucking Jesus wept! She'd been siphoning his money all this time. Bitch. Right under his nose. When he tracked her down, he'd fucking hang her by the fingernails over a bonfire. Bastard!

'Right. Good work. Tell the boy he did good. So. How do we get it back?'

Johnny shifted in his seat.

'Well, boss. That's the problem. The big problem. My boy said we can go to your own bank and tell them there's been a major fraud, and that Sharon has moved your money. And they'll be able to see from the accounts where she has made transfers and to where. But the problem is, she's had authority all the time she has been organising the accounts in your name for years. It's not as if they could stop her. She was a signatory to the accounts.'

'Yeah. I know that. Because I fucking gave her the authority. I don't know nothing about this shit. I trusted her.'

There was a stony silence in the room as everyone looked at Knuckles then at the floor.

'Yeah. And I can see that you fuckers are all looking at me like I've got "stupid prick" stamped on my forehead.'

Nobody spoke. Knuckles felt his face redden and he tried to take a breath but couldn't. His mouth was dry. He tried to compose himself.

'What else? How do we get it back?'

'It's a problem. And here's why . . . If you start raising a fraud enquiry with your bank, and making a lot of noise, and then they start asking the other banks where the money has gone to, this will start alarm bells ringing, according to my man. I mean police. The National Crime Agency are all over things like this, and over the years, your accounts have always been organised so they are below the radar. But if you start raising hell, then anything could happen. They could start looking at you seriously. The cops, I mean.'

The room began to swim in front of him, and Knuckles felt a pain in his chest. Probably overdid the coke last night, he told himself. Calm down. You didn't get where you are today by panicking. He saw them look at him.

'You all right, boss?' Harry said. 'You ain't half gone a funny colour. Want a cup of tea or something?'

Knuckles gripped the desk and managed to control his breathing a little.

'Thank you, Nurse fucking Nancy.' He shot Harry an irritated glance. 'No, I don't want tea. I want my fucking money. And I want this bitch found.' He turned to Pete.

'Pete. What about the shipment? Are you sure it's all on course? I talked to that creepy Dutch prick Jan the other day and he said it's all ready to roll in a few days. But keep tabs on him. Give him another call tomorrow, make sure it's all okay. I need to get that shit over here. Especially right now or I'm going to have a serious cash flow problem in the next couple of months.'

'It's all sorted, Knuckles. It won't be a problem.'

'Good. Right. Let's talk about other ideas how to find her. Do you think she might be in Spain?'

Harry shrugged. 'Possibility. But if she is, then she'll not be raising her head above the parapet. We've already made enquiries, but nobody's seen or heard of her over there in a month.'

Knuckles linked his hands together and pressed them tight, feeling the strain.

'Well, we need to keep looking. We need to look further. There's something we're not doing. Maybe it's staring us in the fucking face.' He looked at Harry. 'Go and make that cup of tea, Harry. We need to start thinking hard here.'

# CHAPTER THIRTY-TWO

Kerry had butterflies in her stomach as she got dressed for dinner. Whatever it had been the last time she sat across a table from Vinny Burns, this was definitely a date. It felt like a date. Even when she was choosing the dress she was going to wear, she was thinking how it would look to him. She chastised herself for allowing her mind to indulge in the notion that she could be anything more to Vinny Burns than what she was – an old girlfriend who happened to be in the right place right now. If she struck up a rapport with him, maybe she could be useful to him on his job. But this was a guy whose job was to bring criminal organisations like hers down. It was stupid to think that he had any other designs on her, or that she had any similar thoughts about him. She didn't even know what she was to him, as he'd clearly wiped out of his mind their teenage love story. But *she* knew what *she* was planning to do. Talking to him about his offer that they work together was on the cards, but she wanted to see how the evening went before she would even go down that road. And she had to make sure Sharon was on board with anything that involved bringing in the cops, as she was crucial to it. Danny and Jack had to be convinced too.

It was Kerry who had made the call to him a couple of days ago, suggesting they meet. But what she didn't expect was the little dig of excitement she used to get when she was going out on a date with a man she fancied. But this was *not* what dinner with Vinny was going to be. If she said it enough, she'd convince herself. She checked her dress, her long legs in the full-length mirror, pulled on her cashmere coat and looked out of the window as her driver came in the yard.

She clocked Vinny noticing her when she came in and he stood up, smart in his black jeans and pale blue open-neck shirt. And she saw the look on his face as he stole a glance at her.

'Looking great, Kerry,' he said softly, as his lips brushed her cheek. 'You look like you're going out on a date.'

Kerry smiled as she sat down.

'I don't get out much these days, so it's good to feel as though I'm on a night out. Not sure about the date part though.'

'Well,' Vinny said, shaking the napkin out and placing it on his lap, 'I'm out on a date anyway.' He poured her a glass of wine. 'I took the liberty of getting the best Rioja they had to offer – given your Spanish lifestyle.'

She raised her glass and they clinked, and she took a sip. 'And very good it is too.'

She felt relaxed in his company. There was no awkwardness in their conversation as they waited for the food to arrive; they reminisced about growing up in the housing scheme, of the characters – some who went on to become notorious criminals or the few who made good. Others of their own age had either stayed or got out, and both of them admitted they had lost contact with their old schoolmates. Kerry thought about Maria, and decided there would be no harm in telling him that they were back in touch. When she did, he nodded.

'I wondered about that. I saw she had Marty Kane representing her boy, and thought she might have got him through you.' He paused. 'I'm not fishing, because it's not my case, but did she come to you out of the blue?'

'No,' Kerry said. 'She came up to me at my mum's funeral and it was great to see her. We were such good friends at school, but you know what it's like – you just lose touch. You know, me being away and all that.' She stopped midsentence, as Vinny's eyes met hers and for a moment she thought she saw a little hurt there. She sipped her wine and continued. 'Maria came back to the wake for a drink and we had a good chat. It was then she told me about her daughter, Jennifer, and the heroin. Cal, as far as Maria knew, was a good lad, keeping out of trouble. Then she came to me when Cal got arrested. What else could I do? There's no way I would turn her away. Our lives turned out differently for reasons beyond our control. It's not her fault she's in the mess she is in. That moneylender toerag – Tam Dolan. You know him?'

'Nah.' He shook his head. 'Wouldn't be my concern. He's only one of a dozen scumbags like him who will live off other people's poverty. If I'd my way I'd take them all out and shoot them.'

Kerry smiled. 'And you an officer of the law too.'

He shrugged. 'I know. But it's the truth. Sometimes I don't see it as black and white as I should. I'm a cop, and a good one, I think. I know what has to be done. But working undercover as I did for a long time, I saw such a lot of shit going down that it does make you wonder who has got it right. Sometimes the good people don't get justice when they put their trust in guys like me. The system lets them down. But we can't just abandon the law to let guys like . . .' he hesitated. 'Well, guys like your mob and others run the show.'

Kerry said nothing, taking his words to heart. She knew he was right, but when she heard it said out loud like that, it pulled her up a little. She was part of the 'your mob' he was talking about. But even *he* was admitting the cops were sometimes powerless to do the right thing.

'Sorry, Kerry. I don't mean to offend you, but . . .'

'I'm not offended, Vinny. I know what I am.'

He poured some more wine into their glasses.

'Is it who you are though?'

She waited a moment.

'As I told you before: it is now.'

Kerry was thinking that now would be a good time to sound him out about her proposal. No doubt it would surprise him, but she'd know by the look on his face as soon as she put it to him if he was up for it.

But it was him who suddenly changed the subject.

'So,' he sat back, 'no wedding ring? Hard to believe that a beautiful hotshot lawyer like you didn't have dozens of guys pursuing you. Are you married?'

Kerry looked at him, sarcastic, and leaned forward, lowering her voice.

'Come on, officer. I'm sure you know enough about my history by now to know that I've never married.'

He half smiled.

'Well, yes. I know you didn't marry. But I don't know anything else. Is there a man in your life?'

Kerry fiddled with her glass and looked at the table then at him.

'Not any more.' She took a breath and let it out slowly. 'Not for the past eight months or so. We broke up. After three years.'

'Sorry to hear that.'

She shook her head. 'I'm well out of it. He wasn't the one,

if you get my drift.' She turned the conversation around in case the wine made her reveal any more. 'What about you?'

For a moment he said nothing, as though he was reflecting on an image.

'Widower. My wife died. Cancer. Four years ago.'

'Jesus. I'm sorry, Vinny. That must have been really tough.'

'It was. Thing is, we had split about six months before she was diagnosed. Pressure of work. I was never there, and she was pissed off with that as she wanted to start a family. I was carried away with this job – detective in the drug squad building up contacts. I was so wrapped up. But anyway, we split up. Then she got told she had cancer, and I came back. It was a terrible time. She got no time at all. Eight months and that was it. Gone.'

'Jesus.'

'So that's when I just threw myself into the job big time. Guilt-ridden, heartbroken – all that shit that goes with knowing you didn't try hard enough. That's when I volunteered to go undercover. It got me away, far away from here. Somewhere I could disappear, be anonymous, not be involved in anything except work.' He shrugged, drank his wine. 'And here I am.'

For a while they sat in silence, as she watched Vinny swirl the remains of his wine. Then he looked straight at her.

'Kerry, I want to tell you something. I don't know if you know this. But I need to say it.'

She gave him a bewildered look, but said nothing.

He took a breath. 'Well. You know. All those years ago. When you went away to Spain . . . after your father died.'

Kerry could feel her stomach knot a little.

'Yes. Of course. My heart was broken.' She wanted to say 'leaving you', but it would have sounded silly.

'So was mine.'

The words were like a little explosion and knocked Kerry off balance. She couldn't find any response, so she sat watching him. Eventually she was moved to speak.

'You didn't call me, Vinny. Nothing. I called you so many times. Left you messages. But nothing.' Kerry couldn't believe she had just exposed herself like that in this situation.

Vinny looked at her, then down at the table, his voice low.

'I know. I know you did. I kept all those messages for years.'

'But . . . But why? Why didn't you answer?'

He sat back and shook his head. 'Christ! You don't know, do you? You've never known, have you?'

'Known what? What you talking about?'

His lips tightened.

'It was your Mickey. He got a hold of me in the pool hall the night you left. He told me if I ever got in touch with you again he would cut my throat and he would burn my ma and da's house down.'

'What? Mickey? Are you serious?'

He nodded. 'Oh, you bet I'm serious. I fancied myself as a bit of a player, that I could handle myself, but I knew what

Mickey Casey was. I knew I couldn't afford to take him on at any level. He told me that you were made for better things and you would never come back here, and if I was smart I'd find myself another girl and get over you. So I had to do what I was told. I wish I had been man enough to stand up to him, but I was only fifteen. It broke my heart every time you sent a message and I couldn't answer.'

'Christ almighty, Vinny! I can't believe that. I can't believe our Mickey would actually do that when he knew we were together. The bastard! If only I had known. But even my mum, she didn't say anything.'

Vinny shrugged. 'She probably didn't know. Mickey probably told her we broke up.' He paused. 'Honestly, Kerry, I was miserable. I really was. I didn't want to make any trouble about it because I was worried you might get into trouble as well. So I just left it. But I was heartbroken.'

Kerry shook her head. 'That makes two of us, Vinny. I know we were young, and who knows, maybe it would only have lasted the summer, but I was crazy about you.' She paused. 'You know something? When you walked into my house that first day after all those years, I just about buckled when I saw you. I could never have believed just seeing you would make me feel like that, but it did. Ridiculous, isn't it? After all these years, and all the life we have both lived, I still must have held a bit of a torch for Vinny Burns.'

Vinny finished his drink.

'I'm so sorry. Maybe I should have found a way to let you know, but the truth is I was shit scared of your Mickey, of what he would do.'

'What a bastard he was. You know I never got on with him anyway.'

'I know.'

'But if I had known that during all those months I would have told him to back off.'

'He wouldn't have though. He wanted what's best for you, and you know – you didn't turn out too badly.'

'I can hardly believe all this, Vinny. I'm so sorry it turned out that way too. Who knows what would have happened to us. Our lives could have been so different.'

'Aye. Maybe I'd be working for the Caseys by now.' He smiled.

'Yeah. Instead of trying to jail us.'

Vinny shook his head, and waved the waiter over for the bill.

'Anyway, enough of the maudlin stuff. What do you want to do now? You fancy going for a drink or something?' He looked at his watch. 'I'm enjoying this. I don't want it to end right now.'

Kerry didn't want it to end either. For the first time in months, she felt like a normal woman, enjoying the company out on a date and wondering how the night would end. And now this. At last she knew that Vinny Burns hadn't abandoned her all those years ago. Not that it was going to mean that much now – they'd come so far. But it put an entirely different complexion on the night.

'Sure,' she said, 'but I have to be careful where I go. I don't want to end up in some bar where somebody might point me out as Mickey Casey's sister.'

'Don't worry. I know a place with some music. Good for a last drink.'

The basement bar was noisy, and the live blues band was banging out their version of the Van Morrison song 'Hymns to the Silence'. Kerry and Vinny squeezed through the crowd at the bar. A boozed-up stag do of eight or nine guys had bumped into a drunken hen party, and were getting to know each other on the dance floor as the music slowed. It all felt a little too surreal for Kerry, more used to quiet nights or dinners in Soho or the Costa del Sol, but she was here now, and she was feeling a little euphoric with the information Vinny had just imparted to her.

'You look a bit nonplussed there, Kerry.' She felt Vinny's arm go around her waist for a second. 'Relax. You fancy a couple of fast shots?'

'Sure.' She shrugged. 'Why not? No point in being sober in a place like this. I think I'm still in shock from what you've told me about Mickey all those years ago. I wish I'd had a chance to punch him on the mouth for that before he died.'

Vinny pulled her a little closer to him.

'Don't worry about it. We're here now.'

'Yeah. We are.'

The barman slid the tequila shots across to them and they downed them in one, Kerry feeling it burn all the way to her gut.

'One more?'

'Well . . .' Kerry hesitated.

'Oh, come on. We're out now. One for the road.'

They downed another, laughing as one of the stag party boys fell off his chair.

'Let's dance,' Vinny said. 'I haven't danced with you since I was fifteen.'

Before she could answer, she was allowing herself to be led to the dance floor where a few of the stags and hens were already swallowing each other's faces, bumping into other dancers. Vinny's arms went around her and he pulled her close, and she could feel the muscles of his chest and his hand gently on her back. They shuffled along the floor and she could feel him holding her a little tighter. He eased back a little and looked at her, pushing her hair back from her face. Then he kissed her, softly at first, and then harder, and she responded, allowing herself to be swept away in the moment.

They didn't speak as they left the dance floor, then Vinny turned to her.

'Let's go. I think we've seen it all here.'

He slipped her coat over her shoulders and they walked

out into the night, the cold air after the warmth of the bar making her feel high and excited. Outside, he took her in his arms again and kissed her, his tongue probing. She kissed him back, knowing this was all kinds of wrong, but she didn't want it to stop.

'My house is two minutes from here. Up there.' He pointed to the new block of flats visible across the way. 'Come on back with me, Kerry.'

They crossed the road and up the steps to the secured entrance and in the door. Inside the hall, in the darkness, he pushed her against the wall. She could feel him hard against her, and she wanted him more than she ever imagined.

'Kerry,' he whispered, his breath quickening. 'I want you so much. I've always loved you.'

'Christ, Vinny!' she said, her voice weak. 'Don't say that. This is all wrong.'

'Forget all that.'

He eased his hand up her thigh, caressing between her legs, until she could hear herself moan, and then there was nothing Kerry Casey wanted more than to be like this with Vinny Burns, after all these years.

Joe Molloy had watched them going into the flat from his car across the street. He'd done a good job tonight, and he'd be well paid by Frankie Martin. He'd got a picture through his long lens of Kerry Casey going into a restaurant then coming out with this guy, and then going to the basement bar. He got a bit of a shock, though, when he saw who the guy was. He'd done business with Vinny Burns before, but he knew it wouldn't be good for his health telling Frankie about that area of his life. Joe didn't see himself as a police informer, he just knew that you had to make a few quid wherever you could. He'd no idea why Frankie was asking him to spy on Kerry. It wasn't his job to ask questions. He did the job, supplied the information, and got paid. He looked at the clock on his dashboard. He'd wait till tomorrow to phone Frankie Martin. Right now, he deserved a drink to celebrate a job well done.

# CHAPTER THIRTY-THREE

Cal and Tahir watched from across the street as Tam Dolan went into the café. They'd been clocking his movements for two weeks running now, and at this time of the night he always left his office and went to the café to eat. Cal had looked at this grubby, pot-bellied figure with growing disgust each day. He hadn't ever clapped eyes on him before, except from a distance, that morning when he'd looked out of the window of his bedroom and saw him going back to his car after he'd raped his mother in the hallway. The image was burned in his mind, even though he hadn't witnessed the rape. He'd heard it – the muffled despair of his mum, the grunting and pushing as Dolan shoved her against the wall. He'd never forgiven himself for not going out there and sticking a knife in him. When he'd told big Jack the story that day they'd been in the café after the fight with the posh boys, he could see the disgust in the big man's face. Cal had said he wanted revenge, but Jack had told him all in good time. But now Cal didn't want to wait. Since Tahir had told him that it was Dolan he was paying to smuggle his brother and his family over from Europe, Cal had decided that there was more than one way to skin a cat. He'd do what Jack said, and bide his time to do to Dolan what he'd pictured himself doing night after sleepless night. But right now, there was a chance to rob the bastard blind. So he and Tahir had come up with a plan. They couldn't believe that he didn't have protection all the time. He did have a couple of heavies going in and out most of the day from his portakabin behind the garage workshop, where Dolan dealt with ringed cars that had been stolen and had to be moved on, but at this time of the early evening, his minders seemed to clock off. Cal and Tahir presumed Dolan must have a safe in the office, where he kept the money. So it was a question of getting him to open it.

'I'm nervous, Cal,' Tahir said, hands stuffed in his pockets, jacket pulled up against the biting wind.

Cal looked at his lean, pale face. He should feel nervous himself, he thought, but he didn't. The feeling he had was one of power. At last he was going to start hitting back, and this was only the beginning. Cal put his hand inside his padded bomber jacket and felt the cold steel of the wheel key he'd taken from work earlier.

'Don't be nervous, Tahir. You've seen what he looks like. He's a shitbag. A weak bastard. We can take him, no problem, when he's on his own. Just stay calm.'

Tahir nodded. 'Okay. I'm trying.'

'We'll rob the bastard the way he robs every other person who comes to him for money.' Cal's mouth was tight. 'He's had it his own way for too long.' He nudged Tahir. 'And you'll get back the money you paid him. So we win all round.' Cal stepped into the doorway. 'Quick, in here. He's coming.'

They watched from a doorway further along the street as Dolan came out of the café, lit up a cigarette and crossed the road, the same routine as every night as he headed towards the garage and the portakabin.

'Come on! Let's go!'

They went behind the shop so that they couldn't be seen but would be able to jump out on Dolan as he opened the door to the cabin. They'd run through the drill and planned it over the past few days.

It was getting dark now, as Cal and Tahir pulled ski masks over their faces. Apart from Dolan's jeep, the backyard of the garage was littered with old cars and wrecks, and it looked like part of a breaker's yard. Most of the time they'd seen only one or two people working in it.

Dolan went up the portakabin's wooden stairs and put the key in to open the door. Cal was on him, sticking the wheel key in his back, hoping he'd think it was a gun.

'Open the fucking door and shut your mouth,' Cal spat, hoping his voice was deep and commanding enough.

'What the fuck is this?' Dolan stood rigid, turned his head slightly.

'Open the fucking door and get in.'

To Cal's surprise, Tahir whacked Dolan on the back of the legs with his iron bar. He glanced at him and saw the anger in Tahir's eyes, as Dolan let out an agonised grunt.

'Fuck! You cunts! What the fuck is this? Whoever you are, you know you're dead men as of now.'

Cal said nothing but grabbed the back of Dolan's head and battered it three times as hard as he could on the door. The sound of flesh hitting wood excited and scared him at the same time.

'You'll be a dead man if you don't get in there this fucking minute.'

'Right! Right! Just fucking get a grip, lads!' Dolan, suddenly jittery, pulled open the door and Cal and Tahir bundled him in.

Tahir locked the door behind them. Inside, it smelt of smoke and the stale, stuffy remaining heat of a gas cylinder fire in the corner. Cal glanced around the room at the desk messed up with papers, and the grotty steel three-drawer filing cabinet. He saw the safe in the corner. He pushed Dolan towards the desk.

'The safe! Open it! Now!'

Dolan put his hands up. 'Aw, wait a minute, lads! Listen! Just hold on! What is it you want? A few quid for smack?

Look, I'll sort you out here, no problem. And I promise you. This little stunt will be forgotten about. I know how you boys get when you're desperate, and well done for having the balls. But listen, boys. This isn't happening. I'll give you a few quid and off you go.'

Suddenly Cal pulled out the wheel key and hit him in the face. Dolan stumbled back, his legs buckling. Cal hit him on the back and on his legs and he fell to the floor. Then Tahir stood on his ankle and whacked him again as he screamed out.

'You open the safe now, or you die right here. Your choice. This is fucking easy for me,' Cal said, surprised at his own coldness and strength.

He looked down at Dolan on the floor, blood oozing out of the side of his eye, his cheek beginning to swell. Cal fought to control himself, because all he could see in this fat bastard lying here was him heaving and pushing his mum around, and he wanted to keep beating his face until it was unrecognisable. But that wasn't why he was here. He took a breath. Then he raised the wheel key above his head.

'Wait! Stop, for fuck's sake! I'll open the safe, for Christ's sake! It's only fucking money!'

Dolan struggled onto all fours and fumbled in his jacket pocket for his keys. Tahir stepped in and held his arm, then dipped into Dolan's pocket and brought out his mobile phone. Tahir put it on the desk and smashed it with his iron bar. They watched as Dolan, his hands trembling, groaned in pain as he tried to put the key into the safe.

'Hurry up, you fat prick.'

'I'm going as fast as I can, man. Fuck!'

The safe door clicked and Dolan pulled the heavy iron door open. The boys' eyes widened as they saw piles of money in bundles, some tied in rubber bands, and also canvas bank bags. Tahir looked at Cal in disbelief. Cal kicked Dolan out of the way and he stayed lying on the floor while Tahir knelt down and pulled out the wads of cash. They hadn't even brought bags with them but there were two money bags at the side of the safe that had cash already in them. Tahir stuffed the cash from the safe into each bag until it was full. Cal looked around the room for anything else to put the rest of the money in. He spotted a holdall at the side of the desk, and brought it over to be filled. He had no idea how much was there – he had only ever seen things like this in the movies – but this was the most money he had ever seen in his life. Once they'd filled the bag, Cal looked down at the blood on Dolan's face, and something in him wanted to tell the bastard who he was and why he was doing this, but he knew that was stupid. Let him think he was robbed by thugs. He had the urge to finish him off – that's what he deserved for all the shit he'd dished out to people over the years. But that was for another day. He looked at Tahir and nodded towards the door. But Cal couldn't resist one last hit. He smacked the bar across

Dolan's ribs and thought he heard a crack. Then he sank his boot in between Dolan's legs, making him curl up in agony.

'You're a fucking robbing bastard, Dolan. You rob from poor people. I should fucking kill you right now.'

'No. Please,' Dolan struggled to speak. 'You've got this all wrong. I help people. I get them out of a hole when nobody else will help them.'

'That'll be fucking right. Robbing bastard.' He bent over a little. 'This isn't over yet, prick. You better keep looking over your fucking shoulder for the rest of your life.' Cal lifted the wheel key again.

'Please! No! Don't! No more!'

Cal turned and both went towards the door. They went out, locked the door from the outside, and when they got to the steps, Cal threw the keys as far as he could, over the high wooden fence into the long grass in the garden next door.

'Let's go.'

They ran as fast as their legs could carry them, adrenalin pumping through them as they crossed backstreets and alleys and onto the street that led towards Kelvingrove Park. As they ran and ran, Cal knew that right there and then they had started down a new path – and neither of them knew where it would lead.

In the back of the shed behind Tahir's house, they sat looking at the bags of money, both of them soaked in sweat.

'Fuck, man! That was crazy!' Tahir said, his eyes dancing.

Cal smiled. 'Yeah. Crazy, man! But in a good way. You see the amount of money that was in there? That's all robbed from people like my ma, like you, all the people he robs with his extortion.'

Tahir nodded. 'Many bad people like him,' he said, resigned. 'It's how the world is.'

'Aye,' Cal said, kneeling down and emptying the bags onto the floor. 'But sometimes the bad guys like him get a right kicking when people like us fight back. That happened today, Tahir.'

Tahir smiled. 'What we going to do with all this money?'

Cal rubbed his face, felt the sweat on the back of his neck.

'We'll work that out. We'll give it to people who need it. But we'll get your family here with it as well.'

Cal looked at his friend and could see his eyes glistening a little. Tahir sat down beside him and, in silence, they began unfolding the piles of money and counting it.

# CHAPTER THIRTY-FOUR

Kerry was aware that her absence from the house last night wouldn't have gone unnoticed by the guards working the night shift. They had seen her go out, driven by Eddie the chauffeur and would no doubt have called him when his car didn't return with her, even well into the night. Kerry had made the decision to tell Don not to hang around the restaurant, but that she would call him to let him know her plans. When she phoned him at midnight, to say she would be staying with a friend, she knew that Don would be the soul of discretion. He had simply asked her if she was sure she was all right, and that he would let the staff know. If need be she was to call him in the morning. Kerry had decided to get a taxi back to the house, as she didn't want Don coming to Vinny's flat to pick her up.

She'd smiled to herself when she'd got into the taxi outside Vinny's place in the early morning daylight. There was something of the walk of shame about this that made her feel alive.

Now, as she ate her breakfast of poached eggs, toast, bacon and coffee in her kitchen, she turned on the radio to listen to the news. She heard the newsreader say police were still investigating the murders of the two men in the burnt-out car, and were convinced it was drug-related. Kerry thought of Jenny, and how well she was doing, and was glad she'd been able to help. Maria was enjoying work at the bookies doing the admin and secretarial work, and her boy Cal was doing odd jobs and running errands for Jack. In the couple of times she'd met him, he seemed like a decent enough lad but she'd felt there was a bit of darkness about him, a distance and anger that she could see in him, and she wondered how that would all pan out as he went through life. If it was channelled in the right direction, he could make a success of himself. But from what she heard from Jack, Cal was angry inside. He'd told her about the incident in the café and how Cal had wanted to beat the hell out of the public-school boys. But, more disturbing, was that he had told Jack he wanted revenge for the moneylender Dolan raping his mum. Poor Maria. She had never mentioned the rape, and the fact that her childhood friend was suffering in silence made Kerry feel sick inside. She could understand Cal wanting revenge, and despite her instinct being to tell Maria to report the attack to police, Kerry knew that there was no way that could happen in the world they lived in now. Dolan would get payback for the filthy predatory bastard he was, but it would not be by going to court and making Maria go through the ordeal of a witness box. Kerry left Jack to deal with it, when the time was right.

Kerry hadn't been able to put Vinny Burns out of her mind since she came back this morning. He'd sent her a couple of texts, no name, but she knew it was him, just saying how much he enjoyed last night, and wanted to see her again. She allowed herself to go into a reverie for a moment, remembering the explosive sex between them when they almost hadn't even made it to the bedroom. Then they'd fallen asleep together as though they'd been doing this for years. She shook her head and sighed. The whole point of her going out with Vinny was to sound him out about the setting up of Knuckles for the drug container. But there had never been the right moment, because she wanted to discuss it properly, not after a few drinks, and certainly not in pillow talk as they lay in bed. It would have to wait. But it couldn't wait too long.

She sat back on the sofa and picked up the copy of the plan Marty had given her of the hotel and apartments she had been looking to invest in on the Costa del Sol. It looked fantastic, and she could see that now things were picking up in the Spanish economy, there might just be a future on a big development like this. In the end, they didn't even have to run the hotel or operate it in any way. They could just use Knuckles' money to buy the place, the land, build the apartments and then sell them. They could double the money Knuckles had paid out for the drug shipment that he would never receive. In time, without even a single line of coke being sold, they could make a fortune. It would be payback for her brother's murder, but it would never be enough revenge for killing her mother. That was for another day.

Frankie Martin sat in his car, face like flint, as Joe Molloy opened the envelope and handed him the photographs. Kerry, short tight skirt, boots and blouse, looked even sexier in the black and white images. Molloy had photographed her going into the restaurant at half seven, then back out at ten thirty, this time with a guy. He peered closely at the picture. He didn't think he recognised the man, but from the photos the two of them looked like a couple. Then the penny suddenly dropped. It was that cop who had come to the house just after the funeral to try to get Kerry to talk. He remembered him now. Frankie had been in the kitchen when he saw him coming in, and Danny told him later he was a detective, but that Kerry had sent him packing. Frankie sifted through the rest of the pictures. Well, she hadn't sent him packing last night. He felt himself blush with resentment as he saw the picture of them kissing, then as they went up the steps to the flat. Molloy had been there when she came out at six in the morning. Fuck me, Frankie cursed to himself. Bitch is fucking a cop. But his face showed nothing, and he turned to thank Molloy and handed him the padded envelope with the cash. Molloy nodded, said nothing, and left the car. Frankie hadn't known what to expect when he'd decided to have her followed, but he was suspicious when she'd made a couple of trips to One Devonshire over the past few days. He wondered who she was meeting, hoping he'd find more about what she was up to. But he hadn't expected this. Frankie sat for a couple of minutes, staring out of the windscreen as the rain started to fall. This was it. Fucking Kerry was head of the family, and she was now shagging some detective. This was the kind of shit that could bring them all down. That's what happened when you put a woman in charge of things. But he knew he had to tread carefully. He couldn't take the information to Danny and Jack, not right now anyway. He needed to know a bit more about it. Needed to do a bit more fishing. But he would find a way. What Kerry was doing could ruin all of them.

But, deep down, what really brought the red-mist rage was the fact that she was shagging someone and it wasn't him.

Sharon called Jan using their secret code of three rings then hanging up. He was supposed to answer after two rings. He did. Then she rang again, and he answered straight away.

'So how are things, Jan? Is everything ready to roll? Anything to report?'

There was a moment's pause, and Sharon waited, worried.

'Is everything okay, Jan?'

'Yes,' he said quickly. 'Sorry. I was just lighting a cigarette. Everything is okay as far as I see. But I wanted to tell you that someone was here, yesterday, two men. They were from Knuckles. They wanted to look over the shipment, make sure it was all in order.'

'Really? I don't suppose they gave you their names?'

'No. I don't know if they came from England or were here in Amsterdam or maybe up from Spain. But they came in, and before they come, I get a call from Knuckles to say some of his team were arriving to check things over, because you were away on business. He didn't say their names, or where they came from. Just that they'd be here.'

Prick, Sharon thought. Acting as if he had everything in hand. She almost smiled. He would be in for a shock, if all went according to plan.

'And did it go all right?'

'Sure. They just wanted to see the stuff was packed away. They opened one little package hidden to make sure, but they know it would be stupid to start opening everything as it would just hold the shipment up as it would need to be repacked by the guys. So they just had the check and kind of walked around, then left. That was it.'

'And did Knuckles phone you again?'

'No. Haven't heard anything. Maybe he'll call again before we go.'

'I don't think so. He never gets involved. He always left everything to me to organise, so that his greedy hands weren't in the shit.'

'Yes. I understand.'

'Okay, Jan. I'll talk to you once things are on the road. Don't worry.'

'I am not worried, Sharon. I never worry.'

She could hear the laid-back tone in his voice, the way he always was. Jan was a quiet, dark, humourless figure, but she had no doubt that he could take care of himself. He hadn't survived in this business for all these years and not known how to handle himself if things got difficult. But he wasn't expecting things to get difficult at all on his side of the shipment. By the time the trucks arrived at Knuckles' warehouse, Jan would be long gone. Sharon pictured the chaos and the panic and allowed herself a small smile. She wished she could be there to see the look on Knuckles' face when the cops started swarming.

# CHAPTER THIRTY-FIVE

Kerry's mobile rang and she was glad to see Vinny's name on the screen. There had been a few texts exchanged between them since she slipped out of his flat the other day, but no phone calls. She wasn't disappointed, because his texts had left her in no doubt that he wanted to see her again. He was busy working, and she was too tied up to get involved in anything more than what it was at the moment. Keep it in perspective. She liked Vinny a lot the more she saw of him, but that was it. She wasn't even entertaining the notion that they could take this any further. But she needed him to be able to plant the information that would destroy Knuckles Boyle.

'Vinny,' Kerry said. 'How you doing?'

'Great. Working a lot last night, Kerry. I was going to ask you out for lunch but I'm caught up most of the day.'

Kerry paused for a moment.

'You don't have to make excuses to me. Come on. It's not like that.'

In the silent pause, she could hear Vinny breathe.

'Yeah? What's it like then, Kerry?' he said. 'Look, I really enjoy being with you. I mean . . . everything about it.'

'Me too. But you know, let's just take it easy. There's no rush here.'

'Okay. I suppose you're right. Sorry.' He paused. 'But that's not why I phoned you – even though I did want to hear your voice. There's another reason I called.'

'Yeah? You've got my undivided attention.'

'Ideally, I'd meet you to talk about it, but I've a lot of stuff to do this for a court case that's coming up. So I'm snowed under.'

'Okay. So what's up?'

'Well. It's about the other night. Someone was watching us.'

'What?'

'Someone was following our every move. Taking pictures.'

Kerry felt the colour rise in her cheeks.

'You're joking, Vinny. What do you mean, taking pictures? How? Where?'

'You going into the restaurant, the two of us leaving together, then us going into the bar . . . Me kissing you in the street outside. Then us going into my flat.' He paused. 'And you leaving early in the morning.'

Kerry's mind was such a blur that she couldn't think

straight. Nobody apart from the driver knew where she was going, and he wouldn't have told a soul. So someone was watching her – or were the cops setting her up in some way? She chided herself for being suspicious of Vinny, despite having shared his bed.

'What the Christ! How do you know this? Are you sure?'

'As sure as I have the pictures in my hand, Kerry.'

'Christ almighty! You have the pictures? How?'

'Well, put it this way. It wouldn't be the first time some of the people I know did a bit of double dealing. That's how we get a lot of our information.'

'What do you mean? Someone from my organisation gave you pictures?'

'No. The pictures came from the guy who was hired to take them. As it happens, he does a bit of snitching for us. I mean, he probably wouldn't have let us know about it if it hadn't been me who was with you. I've known the bloke for a long time.'

Kerry was confused.

'Hold on, Vinny, I'm lost here! Tell me what you mean.'

'Well. Here's the sketch. This guy was hired to take pictures of you, see who you were with, basically follow you the other night and report back. That was all. But when it turned out you were with me, then things changed. The guy knows me, and his loyalties are firmly with me and with us, the police, because we've looked after him over the years. He came to me with the pictures because I'm in them.'

It was beginning to sink in now.

'Jesus! So who hired him?'

The silence seemed to go on for ever, then Vinny spoke.

'You're not going to like this, Kerry.'

'Tell me!'

'Frankie Martin. He hired him.'

The red mist rising in her head almost made the room swim, and Kerry couldn't speak. Frankie Martin. She knew she shouldn't have been surprised – she'd suspected he was a weasel from day one. He always had another agenda, and she'd asked Danny to keep an eye on him. But this was treachery.

'You okay, Kerry?'

'Yes. I'm fine. Can I see the pictures?'

'Sure. I'll give you a shout later and arrange for them to be delivered to you. It won't be by me, but you'll get them.'

'Vinny,' Kerry said, 'I wanted to talk to you about another matter. But not on the phone.'

'That's okay. We can do that. Look, Kerry, I don't give a fuck if Frankie Martin wants to come and take pictures of me and you every day. But I care about what it means to you. I mean, it's no problem for people in your position to be seen with coppers – it's always been the case, and I've drunk with plenty of total hoodlums over the years – but this is different. This bastard is doing it for a reason. It's not me he wants to get at, but he's trying to do something to you. And you have to deal with it. But it won't stop me seeing you. I'm dying to see you, and that's the truth.'

Kerry felt relief in there somewhere, amid all the anger and confusion.

'Okay. I'm glad of that, Vinny. And thanks. Look, give me a call later tonight and maybe we can meet tomorrow. But let me know where you can get the pictures to me as soon as possible. Is that okay?'

'Sure. I'll arrange for them to be dropped this afternoon. I'll call you.'

'Thanks.' She hung up.

By the time Danny and Jack arrived at the house, Kerry had gone through the full gamut of emotions. She'd gone into town in the afternoon to the café where Vinny had told her to go, and, good as his word, a young man came in, sat opposite her and waited for the nod. He handed her the photographs, and she finished her coffee and went straight out. She couldn't wait to get home to open the envelope. And when she did, she had to sit down as it dawned on her how serious this was, and how much effort had gone into following her around. At first she was shocked and confused when Vinny told her Frankie had been spying on her. Then it was rage. This bastard was more or less taken in by her mother after his own ma died and his father buggered off. He was treated like one of the family by her dad and by Mickey, and this was how he repaid them. It was Frankie who set up Mickey to be executed by Knuckles' mob, and it was because of *his* recklessness, getting Knuckles to send his thugs up to the funeral, that her poor mum got caught in the crossfire. All of this was why Kerry was here right now, in this house, attempting to run the show, often out of her depth, often wishing she was thousands of miles away. If none of this had happened, she'd have been back in London, or in Spain, or perhaps taking that job she'd been offered in Brussels, working with a corporate law firm. But here she was, wheeling and dealing, thinking like a criminal to keep her empire going. And she would. No matter what bastards like Frankie Martin did to try and destroy her. Because despite the constant conflict of emotions, she felt she was growing into her role here, and she couldn't stop herself. In a moment of paranoia she'd even thought twice about phoning Danny and Jack. What if they had been in on it? What if this was all part of a coup to get rid of her? The thought tore the heart out of her, and she knew, deep down, neither Danny nor Jack would betray her like that. She'd have seen it in their eyes before now. Yet she hadn't seen it coming from Frankie on this scale. She knew he was working behind her back. But this? No. This was unforgivable.

'Sit down, guys,' she said. 'Drink?' She motioned them to the table at the other end of the room with decanters and bottles. 'You might need one for this.'

'Whisky for me, sweetheart,' Danny said. 'Bit of water.'

'Me too,' Jack said.

They both sat across from her on the sofa while she poured their drinks and handed them out. Then she sat on the armchair by the fire.

'Okay. So we're clear here. We talked about my plan to drop some info to the cops on Knuckles Boyle as the shipment gets to his warehouse. So as soon as it arrives, the cops will be all over him. We're all okay with that, aren't we?'

Danny looked into his glass for a second, swirling the whisky around, then he spoke. 'Kerry, we want to nail Knuckles as much as you, believe me, but Jack and me were having a chat, and . . .' He paused. 'Are you really sure you want to bring the cops in on this? I mean, you know we are on the other side of the law, sweetheart. That's how we do things. I've known and been mates with plenty of cops down the years, and sure, you can trust them to an extent. But this is a big deal, and I'll be honest, part of me thinks bringing the cops in could blow up in our faces.'

Kerry hadn't expected this. They hadn't been so vocal when she told them in the first place. 'Well,' she said, 'I haven't told the cops yet. But I'm going to, because we're agreed it's the right thing to do.' She looked from one to the other. In a few moments, she was going to show them compromising photos of her and a top cop, and the fact that they were now backing off from involving police at all was going to make it even more difficult. 'I hear what you're saying. But I think I'm right in this, and I hope you'll bear with me and support me. I've seen the documents and evidence Sharon has on Knuckles, and it can put him away for decades. If I go to them with that material, I feel sure they will play ball with me. So, let's just go with the plan, okay? I need to know you are with me on this.'

'Kerry,' Danny said. 'We're with you. We will always have your back. You don't have to worry about that. We might not always agree, but you're in charge and this is your shout.'

'Thanks,' she said.

She cleared her throat, now feeling a little awkward, knowing she was going to have to admit her dinner date with Vinny Burns and the photos.

'Right. So, DI Vincent Burns – you remember he came here to talk to me in the beginning?' She looked at Danny.

'Yeah. I remember him. He went to school with you, did he not?'

'Yes, he did. Anyway, I've been talking to him a bit, and it was him who approached me and asked if we could help each other.' She felt a little hot. 'Look, guys, I'm going to be honest with you here, as you are my closest confidants, and I know I can trust you. The thing is, I haven't even touched on the subject of collaboration with Vinny yet.' Kerry clocked the pair of them trying to keep their expressions impassive when she mentioned him as Vinny instead of DI. 'But we've been out. We get on well. Old times and all that.' She stopped, swallowed a mouthful of wine, feeling a little embarrassed.

There was an awkward silence. Then Danny gave her a wry smile.

'Listen, darlin'. What are you saying here? You and Vinny are old pals, you've been talking to him. What's the big deal? You got a wee notion of him?' He smiled, Jack half smiled. 'So what! Your business, pet. You don't have to explain that to us.'

Kerry felt a bit silly that she was almost confessing to them. But she was relieved that Danny saw it that way, and by the look on Jack, he was not that interested. She wouldn't be the first head of a criminal family to get pally with the cops. It was all part of the territory. But it was a bit different when you were a woman. They would see that too, but if they did, their faces didn't show it.

'Fair enough. And thanks for that.'

Kerry took the envelope off the bookshelf and opened it. She reached inside and pulled a picture out.

'But the thing is, we went for dinner the other night. We had a night out. And . . . And someone was taking pictures.'

She handed the first photograph of her going into the restaurant to Danny, and he passed it to Jack.

'La Lanterna.' Danny grinned. 'Your dad's old favourite. Many a good night we had in there.'

Kerry nodded. 'And this.' She handed him another picture. 'And this . . .' Another picture of them coming out together. She saw them looking at it. 'And this.' The picture of them kissing.

Danny spread his hands.

'A bit of romance with the other side, Kerry. You're a big girl. You can make your mind up about these things. It's your business. But you know how to be careful.'

'I know that, Danny. That's not the problem.'

She gave the other picture of her going into the flat, and the one of her coming out in the morning.

She looked from one to the other, pushing her hair back, trying her best to look defiant, in control.

'Oh,' Danny said, handing the picture to Jack. 'A bit more of a romance then.' He put his glass down on the table. 'Look. I want to be straight with you, Kerry. It's up to you who you get involved with, but I mean, as I said, you have to be careful. And do you think it's wise to be this much involved with a cop, and talk about us bringing them in on something we are about to do? We are, as I said earlier, on opposite sides here. Do you really want to be sleeping with the cop who you're going to set up Knuckles for?' He looked at Jack who didn't look as though he disagreed.

Kerry's face reddened. Partly from embarrassment that she had to share intimate details of her private life with them, but also because she sensed they were questioning her judgement. She had to stand her ground here.

'Listen, Danny, Jack. I want to be clear here. Spending time with Vinny Burns is my business and I know what I'm doing. I'm not advocating we bring the cops in to nail Knuckles because of my involvement with Vinny. I know you don't think I'm that naive. And I know you have shown me huge respect since I took over, and I appreciate that you have my back at all times, but this is my business. So I'd like you just to put aside my involvement with Vinny for the moment, and consider the bigger situation. The fact that I've spent the night with him might not suit how you view things. But someone taking pictures of me is a totally different ball game. That's what I want to focus on here. Especially when I know who it is.'

They both looked shocked for the first time.

'Really? How do you know? Who the fuck would do that?'

'Frankie.'

Jack and Danny looked at each other.

'Aw, for fuck's sake!' Jack said. 'What the fuck is it with that bastard!'

'Well. You tell me. I take it he hasn't mentioned that these pictures exist?'

'No,' Jack said. 'If he had, we'd have told you straight away. But knowing Frankie, he did it for one reason. To discredit you. To show to us, or to show to other people. He's a fucking arsehole.'

'Bastard!' Danny said. 'This is off the fucking scale.' He looked at Jack. 'We're going to have to deal with him, Danny. He could damage us all if he's in this frame of mind. He's dangerous.'

'I know,' Kerry said. 'What's his game? I mean, what does

he really want? He bumped off Pollock and McCann, and he's come to me a couple of times, telling me he's doing everything for me. He says he wants to be more involved. But I don't trust him as far as I can throw him. He set up Mickey and the funeral hit. I know that for sure. Sharon told me. He's trying to do me in.' She paused, took a breath, then said calmly, 'Well, he's just made the biggest mistake of his life.'

Jack took a swig of his whisky.

'We can just get him taken care of, Kerry. It's maybe time. He's a loose cannon.'

Danny nodded slowly. 'Or we can use him. Find a way to use him to do something he thinks is going to take him on to greater things here. A bigger responsibility. Then he fucks himself up. We just have to think about it. I don't mean we need more proof of what he's done, by the way.' He glanced at the pictures. 'These are proof enough that he's not on our side. Treacherous fucker. Your da would have choked the life out of him for pulling a stunt like that with you, Kerry.'

Kerry sighed, touched by Danny's concern as much as his anger. It would be easier just to have Frankie taken right out of the equation after everything she knew he'd done, but right now she wanted to witness him being found out and made to pay the consequences.

'We can think about it,' she said, looking from Danny to Jack. 'I don't want anything done just now. Nothing changes the way he works, just let him go about as if nothing happened. We'll decide what we do later. But meantime, as I said, I haven't spoken to Vinny yet about how we can throw Knuckles to them. I will though. Very soon. The shipment is going in two days. I'm thinking we should go to Spain once it's in place. How are we doing with the plans for that, Danny?'

'It's all sorted. Our boys are ready to take over the trucks and then it's a matter of getting them down to Estepona safely. The houses and the lock-ups are all sorted. You don't have to worry about that.' He paused. 'But we should think about moving the stuff on as soon as we can. Get the money for it and leave it at that.'

Kerry nodded. 'I agree. I don't want to hold that stuff for any length of time.'

'Then we should set up a meet with Durkin and Hill, as soon as the gear is in place. We'll see what they offer.'

'Great. Can you do that, Danny?'

'Sure.' He drained his drink and stood up. 'And, Kerry, listen to your old uncle, pet. Just be careful on where you meet your mate Vinny. As long as you can trust him, I'm okay with your judgement of that. But rest assured, Frankie will be coming to us in the next couple of days with these pics in his hand.'

'Prick!' Jack said, standing up.

'Well, on that cheery note . . .' Kerry felt relieved the awkward meeting was over. She'd stood up for herself, and she felt she had won with the two people she trusted most in the world. 'We'll call it a day.'

Danny gave her a hug as he was leaving. Once they'd gone she sat down in front of the fire with her glass of wine. They were her family now, they would look after her. She knew they would defend her with their lives, no matter what it took. Yet here, in the quietness of the room, an overwhelming feeling of loneliness washed over her as she sipped her drink.

# CHAPTER THIRTY-SIX

Cal checked his profile in the mirror for the umpteenth time, turning his head a little, narrowing his eyes, raising his chin and glancing into middle distance, like the brooding models or actors he'd see in magazine photo shoots. He ran the brush through his fringe and pushed it backwards, caked with wax, until it sat in the right position. Then he half smiled at himself in the mirror.

'Christ, look at the nick of you, Cal,' he murmured. 'You'd think you'd never been out on a date before.'

And the truth was he hadn't – not a real date anyway. Sure, he'd snogged a few girls at parties once a couple of beers had calmed his nerves and stopped him from being overwhelmed by the unbelievable feeling of a girl pushing himself up against him in a dark room. But at sixteen, Cal was still a virgin. He knew he wasn't the only one in his class, and that some of the eejits who bragged about shagging a different girl every weekend were full of bullshit.

But he also knew a few of them were telling the truth. He wasn't overly anxious about it, as he knew he'd get there some day. He even allowed himself a little fantasy about tonight, and Mary ... But it was only a fantasy. He had no intention of pushing her in any direction at all, and he'd be happy if he got to kiss her. Nonetheless, his stomach was churning with excitement. All the more because he had organised a foursome for Tahir with Mary's best pal, Liz. He'd squared it with Mary that Tahir was a refugee, because some of the Glasgow people were racist and wouldn't want to go near them, but Mary was fine about it, and her pal was a looker too. So both of them were set up, off for a meal and the movies, like proper dudes. They had money in their pockets and were ready to show the girls a good time. It was a celebration, after all – he and Tahir had gone with the money directly to the dealer who would bring his family home. He was some Turk who worked out of the back of a Turkish barber shop in West Nile Street. Cal pulled on his jacket and reflected on the meeting. The Turk had promised them Tahir's family would be here within the month.

The barber shop had only had three people in it when they'd arrived – one on the chair with his face covered in soap, the barber standing over him with an open razor, and a third man, fat, bald and sallow, who eyed them warily from a chair in the corner. The guy with the open razor looked Turkish, and a bit dangerous. The fat man also looked Turkish, but as it turned out he wasn't a customer. More of a bouncer.

'I arranged to speak with Hamid. I phoned last night.'

'Who you?'

'My name is Tahir.'

'Wait.'

The fat guy waddled off through a curtain of coloured mosaic chips hung on strings that rattled as he went through. Cal watched the guy with the razor as he expertly shaved the customer's chin, wiping the soap away. The place was so quiet he could hear the sound of the bristles being scraped off by the razor. He felt a little unnerved. He didn't like the feel of this place at all. But what else could you expect if you were looking to smuggle your family in from Syria? It's not as if you could go to the travel agent. In a few moments, the fat guy appeared through the curtain and nodded him forward. Cal walked behind him. The fat guy put his hand up to stop him.

'Who he?'

'He's my friend. My business partner.'

The fat guy looked at Cal and sneered, as he tried make himself look taller.

'Your business partner?'

He disappeared behind the curtain. Then a moment later he came back.

'Come.'

They went in through the curtains and along the room

full of boxes and crates and bin bags. Then through the mess and another curtain, and into a small untidy office. Behind a desk sat a skinny, lantern-jawed middle-aged man with dark hair and a thin moustache. He looked up at Tahir, then at Cal.

'Who is this guy? You don't have anyone before. What is this?'

'He's my best friend. We work together. We are partners.'

'Doing what?'

Tahir shrugged. 'Whatever we can do. But we make money together and that is why we have good money now. Okay? We have more money now. I gave you already a lot, but now I want it to be quicker. You said last night you could do that if the money is good.'

The man looked sly and let out a slow breath.

'Don't be so hasty, my friend. It is a dangerous thing we do, bringing people into the country. Many borders to cross. Dangerous. And the sea. But your family has made it this far. You know they are in Turkey now.'

'How long till you bring them?'

'When you pay the full amount.'

'You said that last time.'

'But you see now the price goes up. The cops, the authorities are everywhere. More risk for my people. Now is more expensive. You see the news. You see how it is.'

'I can give you money. But I want the guarantees – and this is the most money I can give. How much is the total now?'

'Is four thousand now in total. You gave me . . . let me see . . .' He scanned down a list from a book on the desk. 'You pay already nearly two thousand. So you must come back when you have the full amount.'

'I have it now. But I want guarantee.'

The Turk stood up.

'And what will you do if you don't get a guarantee?' He came across, circling Tahir and then Cal.

Cal didn't know what to do, then he saw Tahir's face going red then pale. The Turk grabbed him and pushed him against the wall.

'You little Kurdish prick. You're nobody.'

Then, from nowhere, Tahir pulled a knife and wriggled in one movement and suddenly the knife was at the Turk's throat.

'I give you the money, but you must phone my brother now and tell him you are doing it, and if you don't and I give you the money I will come back and kill you. You got that, my friend?'

Cal stood there, slack-jawed with shock. His body was shaking but he was ready to leap in if need be.

'Put the knife down, you stupid fuck, and you might live to see the morning – and maybe even your brother again.'

Tahir lowered the knife and the Turk made them sit down. He smiled but it was a cold smile.

'You did a stupid thing just this moment, to threaten me

like that. But you have balls. I give you that. I will get your family here. I promise. Now show me the money.'

Tahir went into his bag and pulled out the wads of notes they had robbed from Dolan. He glanced at Cal, who nodded encouragingly.

'This is everything I have.'

He took the money and counted it. He took his mobile from the desk drawer and punched a key. Then spoke in Turkish and they sat waiting. He hung up.

'My contact will talk to your brother and his family. He can get them in the next wave of people. It will be within a week. You must wait until I call you. That is all. Now get out of here.'

'But can I speak with my brother?'

'No. My contact says he cannot find him, that he is with some people and he will get him tomorrow. He is fixing it. You need to wait. Be patient.'

'Are you sure?'

He glared at him.

'I told you. Get out of here while you can. You little shit, you pulled a knife on me! You should be dead by now but only I have such good nature. Now fuck off out of here, I have things to do.'

Tahir stood up and Cal with him.

'Okay. I will be waiting for your call. I will see you again if I don't get it.'

The Turk reached into his drawer and pulled a gun, pointed it at them. Cal's stomach dropped.

'Are you deaf? Do you really want to die? I told you. They will be here.'

They left the room out into the barber's where the man in the chair was lying with his face covered in a hot towel. The fat man stared at them until they left.

'Jesus, Cal.' His mum made a gesture, fanning the air. 'If you put any more of that aftershave on you're going to have to carry a government health warning. Did you take a bath in the stuff?'

Cal grinned. 'I'm going on a date, Ma. Taking a girl to dinner then the movies. It's important that I smell good.'

'Well, you'll be putting her off her dinner if you don't let that calm down a bit.'

Cal gave her a worried look as he headed for the door.

'Seriously though, Ma. I've not overdone it, have I?'

He was pleased when she smiled and shook her head.

'Go on. You're fine. Your good looks will get you away with it.'

'And my charm.' Cal winked.

It was a long time since he'd seen his ma so happy and carefree. Even though she was always worried about Jenny, who was still in rehab, at least she knew where she was.

She wasn't happy that he'd told her he had ditched his plans to go back to school next year and study for university. He knew she was disappointed, but most of all she was afraid he'd become too impressed with everything the Caseys had. But he'd told her not to worry. All he was doing was washing cars, and maybe he'd get another, better job with them in due course. And anyway, she was also working for them, and the new house and her job had lifted her out of the depression. All he had seen in the past three or four years was his mother sinking further into debt and despair. Now she looked younger and so much happier. Kerry had got Jack to give her a job in the bookies where she worked five days a week. Maria'd told him she was surprised at how quickly she'd picked up the business, but she'd always been good with figures, and this new job was really stretching her. She loved it. Even if she was working for the Caseys, Cal thought, who cares. They're gangsters, and everything they do is dodgy, but if you really wanted to strip down most of the business out there, then they were all the same. Nobody was squeaky clean these days. Cal's view was more and more confirmed as he saw how easy he took to robbing Dolan last week. And the way he saw Tahir dealing with the Turk earlier. You could get yourself killed with people like that if you weren't careful. But Cal was beginning to believe he had the measure of a lot of these guys. And here he was, heading out like a gent, a pocket full of money, and a date with a beautiful girl.

His stomach was doing some butterfly flips at the thought of seeing her.

Cal was surprised to see how well Tahir looked in his leather bomber jacket, black jeans and pale blue shirt. His hair was gelled back and his dark eyes shone with anticipation and excitement.

'You scrub up well,' he said, giving Tahir a playful punch.

Tahir looked a little confused, then he seemed to get the dig.

'New jacket and jeans, man. Like my boots? Thank you, Mr Dolan.'

'Sssh. Don't ever mention that name.' Cal looked in the distance and he could see the girls coming. 'Here they come. Now be on your best behaviour. They're nice girls. You been out with many Glasgow girls?'

Tahir laughed. 'Me? You kidding? I've not even been out anywhere! Most I've done is go to work, go for a burger with you, and go home.'

'Well, this is your big chance. Yours is the redhead, Liz.'

'Wow! She's beautiful. What if she doesn't like me?'

'She'll be crazy about you. Look at the nick of you. You're like something out of a boy band.'

Tahir laughed, his striking white teeth lighting up his face. 'I'm nervous.'

'Me too,' Cal confessed. 'But let's do this. It'll be fine.'

*

It was only four hours later that Cal walked home with Mary, but it felt like they'd been in each other's company for days. He knew Tahir was walking with Liz a little further back as the girls lived in the same street and they were walking them to the bus stop. As they walked, their hands bumped together and Cal took the opportunity to take her hand in his, and she didn't resist. He could feel his heart skip a little. In the cinema earlier they had watched the picture eating popcorn and drinking cola, their knees almost touching. He was dying to put his arm around her shoulder but was too terrified in case she told him to get lost. So this was actually it now. They were holding hands. He wondered if Tahir was doing the same, watching him. They got to the bus stop, chatting and laughing, Cal telling stories about some of the lads at school and the camping trip they'd been on a couple of years ago, which he hated like hell, and twice tried to escape.

'Why did you want to run away, Cal? Did you want your mammy?' Mary prodded him.

'Actually, aye. I probably did. I'm dead close to her. You know all that shit with our Jenny and stuff. Ma's really had a hard time. I try to look after her as much as I can.'

She smiled up to him.

'You're all right, you are, Cal Ahern. You're not the worst of them around here.'

'I hope not.'

They were standing against the wall across from the bus

shelter, and Cal could feel the heat between the two of them, the chill of the evening air on his face, their breath steaming. She was looking up at him, her soft red lips a little open, her thick blonde hair tumbling onto her shoulders. She was beautiful.

'Mary. You're all right too,' he whispered, leaning closer.

Their lips were almost touching, and Cal wished the exhilarating feeling could go on for ever. He had to get this kiss right. He let his lips brush hers and it was like an explosion going off in his head. He could feel his temples pulsating, and her breath on his. Then he kissed her, a long, soft, slow kiss, and he moved a little closer to her so that their bodies were touching. He found himself reaching for her hair, and feeling the softness of it. As she kissed him back eagerly, he felt the touch of her tongue on his lips and he returned his, moving closer, feeling her body pressed against him. He could feel his own jeans bulging, and though he knew this was going no further, the unbelievable feeling that he was actually against her and she was pulling him close made him breathless. Then they came up for air.

'Christ, Mary.' He swallowed. 'I thought I was going to die there!' he joked, kissing her softly again, briefly on her cheeks, on her neck. 'Can I see you again? I want this so much. Being with you like this.' He gently pulled her close to him.

She responded with a soft groan and he thought he was going to explode with excitement.

'I'd like that.' She pulled back. 'But my bus will be here in a moment, so we better stop this. Look, Cal, I'm not the kind of girl who goes jumping around with lots of guys. I mean, what you saw last week in that café? I'm ashamed about that. Really ashamed. I thought you'd never want to go out with me after that – after what they said.'

'Don't be silly. They were just arseholes. I don't care about that. I care about you. That's all. I really like you.'

He went into his jacket pocket. He knew this was risky, but he had his mind made up he was doing it anyway. But he didn't want to offend her.

'Listen, Mary. I know about the problems you have with money, your ma and stuff. I can help. I've got some money. I want you to take it.'

He felt her stiffen a little in his arms.

'What? What do you mean? Pay me for going out with you? Christ, Cal!'

'No, no! Please, don't say that! Of course not! I told you that day I would help you and I will. Even if I never see you again after tonight. I want you to take this money and help your ma and the family.'

'Where are you getting all the money?'

'Never mind that.'

'Are you dealing drugs or something? Because if you are then this stops here. I hate that shit.'

'No. Not drugs. Look. It's not a problem. Let's call it robbing the rich, if you know what I mean. I can't talk about it and I won't, but the money is good. You just don't say where it came from. And I'm not doing it so you will go out with me. You owe me nothing. I know what it's like to be struggling and have your ma upset. Believe me, I do.'

He reached into his jacket again and took out a wad of money. He knew there was four hundred pounds there. And plenty more back in Tahir's bedroom.

'Just take it.'

'I can't.'

'You can.' He pressed it into her hand, and put her hand into her bag. 'Here's your bus. Will you come out with me again? I really like you.'

She smiled, a little bewildered.

'I think you might be a mad bastard, Cal Ahern. But I like you too. Phone me. Maybe we can go to the pictures again and for a meal. That was great tonight. I hope Tahir liked Liz. He's dead handsome.'

'He's a good guy. Like me. We're partners.'

'Aye. Partners in crime, I'd say.'

He grinned. 'But in a good way.'

He gave her one last long kiss as he heard the engine of the bus approach, and when they parted he could taste her even as he watched her get on the bus with her friend. They sat at the window, and he and Tahir watched until the bus went over the hill and disappeared.

# CHAPTER THIRTY-SEVEN

Frankie was less than happy at the way the meeting had gone with Danny and Jack. He'd met with the pair of them at his request in the office at the main bookies, from where they ran the string of betting shops. It was really Danny's territory, but Frankie didn't want to rub any of them up the wrong way by suggesting they meet in a bar or restaurant, which was how he preferred things rather than sitting in an office. In any case, he didn't have a lot to say to them these days. He'd been frozen out in recent weeks and it was becoming more and more obvious to him that they didn't want him at the centre of things. He didn't have so much of a free hand since Kerry took over, and it irked him that she was constantly asking for updates on business and deals. But now that he had the damning pictures of her, he was pretty sure they'd see her for what she was. All that bull about going legit and wanting to be some sort of good gangster was such a crock of shit. She should have been told straight off that business wasn't done that way. That kind of shit got noticed outside by their enemies, by the people like the Durkins and Hills, who would walk all over them if they saw weakness. And especially by Knuckles Boyle. But the pictures he had would do the trick. He knew Danny would be on the defensive, because Kerry was like his own daughter, and he adored her, could see no wrong in her, even though he must know that the decisions she was taking now could put them all out of the game. Jack, he'd noticed, was also too close to Kerry these days, and she seemed to consult him more than anyone. But Jack was pragmatic, and would see how the photographs told exactly what she was up to. So Frankie was surprised at their reaction when he put the pictures on the table in front of them. He saw that while they looked a little stunned, they didn't say much. What were they playing at? Jack did say at one stage that he didn't like it, but they had to handle it discreetly. Frankie had expected them to tell him they'd take it up immediately with Kerry; he'd wanted a result. But Danny told him to keep quiet about it and that he would look into it through his own contacts and deal with it. But what if she's grassing us all up as we sit here on our hands? Frankie had asked. No response that gave him confidence. Danny said to leave it with him, thanked him for his good work and praised him for looking to the future of the firm. All bullshit. But there had been an iciness about the atmosphere – as though they suspected they were suddenly not on the same side. It niggled away at Frankie, but there was no way Danny or Jack or anyone else in the organisation could know for sure that it was him who was behind Mickey's murder, and it was him who sanctioned Knuckles to send a message at the funeral. He felt he was watertight on that. Knuckles had assured him that nobody would ever know that Frankie had been stabbing the Caseys in the back for a long time now.

But Frankie was far from finished. He would keep tabs on Kerry quietly. He couldn't track down his usual contact who had followed her the night she was with the cop, but he was keeping an eye on her. Kerry wasn't out that much, apart from doing business and visiting various places, and always she was with the chauffeur. But he'd followed her himself twice in the past week, and was surprised to see her going to One Devonshire Gardens, the fancy hotel. Unless she was going for a bit of an afternoon shag with that copper, what was she doing there? Who was she meeting? So he followed her again today, keeping at a discreet distance as she went into the hotel. He'd waited in his car and watched from across the street. But she came in and out within an hour. He might have to do a little more detective work himself. But while he was working out his next move, Frankie struck gold.

'Fuck me!' he murmured under his breath as from the corner of his eye, he caught sight of a side door.

At first he only got a short glimpse of her, as she turned

the other way, but it looked like the tall, slender figure of Sharon Potter. He did a double take. It *was* her – definitely. He strained his eyes, wishing he had a camera as he watched her stand there, gaze out to the car park, then light up a cigarette. Fuck. It really was her – no mistake. What the fuck was she doing here? He'd met her on four occasions – twice in Spain and twice in Manchester – in the past eighteen months. He'd noted that she was quite shaggable, knocking on a bit, but still worth a turn. He'd even considered it himself, but didn't want to upset Knuckles' applecart. So this was where Sharon was hiding all this time. And she was meeting with Kerry Casey! Christ! It was dynamite. It was too much of a coincidence for her to be there and for Kerry to happen to go into the same place. He knew Knuckles was tearing his hair out trying to find his bitch, as Sharon was key to a lot of his smuggling operations. But it seemed she'd vanished into thin air, after bumping off two of his men who were supposed to be getting rid of her. Frankie had to smile when he'd heard that one. Fair play to her for having the bollocks to take her assassins out and do a runner. But holed up here in Glasgow and meeting Kerry Casey, the head of the biggest gangster family in Scotland, was a different ball game. He lit a fag and watched as she went back inside. He wasn't sure what he was going to do with this, but given the reception he'd had earlier with Danny and Jack, he'd keep this one to himself for the moment.

\*

Kerry watched out of the window of the café in Woodlands Road as she waited for Vinny to arrive. She sipped an espresso, the strong taste and aroma taking her back to afternoons in pavement cafés in Spain, and breakfasts in the busy, family-owned café where she used to go to people-watch and listen to the chatter. Everyone seemed to go out for breakfast in Spain, cafés bustling in the morning, and she missed all that long after she'd left and gone to live in London. Her ultimate goal had always been to one day go back and live there. She shook her head at the notion of how things change. In her early teenage years she longed to be back in Glasgow, strolling up Buchanan Street or Sauchiehall Street, listening to the buskers, or meeting her friends from school in the evenings. Everything had smelled and tasted so different in Spain, and she was ter-ribly homesick. Then as the years went by she became more and more accustomed to Spain being her home, where she was educated, fluent in Spanish, and even studying in Valencia for a while. London was huge and anony-mous, and despite being the centre of the world to so many people, it had never appealed to her. After her relationship with Leo finished, these past months she had just been going through the motions, thinking of real change. She'd even considered going travelling, losing herself in a far-flung land for a while. Yet here she was, back in the West End, waiting in a café for some old schoolfriend she had a crush on. It made her smile as though she was a teenager again. She saw him at the window and he waved to her and opened the door. He was casually dressed in a polo shirt and pullover, a couple of days' stubble on his handsome face. He leaned over and kissed her on the lips.

'Kissing in public.' She smiled. 'It'll be all over the papers next.'

'Well, the photographs could be out there already.'

'Don't even say that, Vinny.'

'I'm only joking.' He smiled up to the waitress and ordered a black coffee.

'So,' he leaned over, putting his hand on hers, 'great to see you, Kerry. You look lovely – in a Glasgow, London, kind of Spanish way.'

'Oh, yeah,' she joked. 'And you're kind of Mediterranean yourself with that unshaven look. Do they allow that at Pitt Street?'

'They pretty much allow me to do anything, as long as I deliver.' He looked sure of himself. 'Mind you, that doesn't please everyone in the department. A couple of guys would gladly stab me in the back if they got the chance. But they'd better make sure I'm dead if they do. Because if I get up again . . . well, you know how it is.'

'Aye. Proper hard-man you are.'

The coffee arrived and he took a sip, sitting back and stretching out his long legs.

'So, Vinny. I want to talk to you. As I said the other day. About helping each other.'

'Definitely. I want to do that.'

'Knuckles Boyle,' Kerry said. 'You know – the headcase down in Manchester.'

'Too well. A psycho.'

'I can help you put him away.'

His face showed nothing. 'Go on. I'm all ears.'

'I can put your guys right on the spot when his next shipment comes in. Cocaine. A container load. It's in two days though, so you'd have to get your skates on.'

He said nothing for a moment, looked at her long and hard. Kerry wondered if he believed her, and studied his face for clues to what he was thinking.

'You can do that? How?'

'I know where and when. He'll be there to see it in.'

'Where's it coming from?'

Kerry shrugged. 'Abroad?'

He smiled. 'Come on, Kerry. It all comes from abroad – Spain? Amsterdam? Further?'

'Europe. Look, I don't want to say too much right now. But are you into this?'

'Is the Pope a Catholic? But what's in it for you? Well, apart from the obvious revenge for the murder of your brother. It was Boyle's mob who was behind that. And the funeral hit. I'm sure you know that.'

'I know that. But if the police know that, then why haven't they arrested someone?' She knew that he thought the Caseys had already taken their revenge, but she threw it in anyway.

He played it deadpan. 'You know how that goes, Kerry. We need evidence. Bodies. People to talk.'

'I can help you with that. So, with my help, you get Knuckles and his mob on two counts – murder and smuggling. And I mean the full bhuna on the smuggling. I can get you documents, papers, transactions – everything over a number of years.'

He sat back for a moment and clasped his hands together on the table, scanning her face.

'You're serious, aren't you? You think you can get all this?'

'It'll be what it is. I don't know anything about his smuggling racket. But I know someone who does, and all the paperwork is there to be looked at. Well, not paperwork – digitally stored. Enough to put him away for a long time.'

'You know someone . . .' His lip curled in a wry smile. 'That someone can only be Sharon, his woman. She's done a runner. We've long suspected, well, our boys down south have, that she is the brains behind moving the money – but it's always been watertight.'

'What would happen to her if she got caught?'

He looked at her, surprised. 'What do you think? She'd be gone for a long time. But if she got caught, she wouldn't last till the court case. Knuckles has everyone looking for her, and will get her done in. In fact, word is that's why she did a runner. He was sending her to her death with two of his trusted henchmen, when the bold Sharon took them both out.' He shook his head. 'She's some piece of work, and I haven't even met her. But good on her for fighting her way out of her own execution.'

'What if she could provide all the information you need? How would that affect her? Would she be given immunity from prosecution?'

Vinny ran his hand across his chin.

'Jesus, Kerry. Are you her lawyer? Pleading for her freedom? She's in deep shit whatever she does.'

'But if she gives the cops stuff that dismantles his organisation and nails him and others, surely she has to be given some sort of deal. Or does that just happen in the movies?'

'No. It happens. It's possible. All sorts of things are on the table for discussion when someone turns and gives us information that can put bastards like Boyle away. So the answer is we would have to see what she has.'

Kerry waited for a moment, wondering what he was going to ask next. He brushed her hand with his and smiled.

'So. When can I meet this Sharon?'

'One thing at a time, detective.'

Her mobile rang. It was Danny. She looked at Vinny as she took the call and listened, hoping her face showed nothing as Danny told her that Frankie had been to them with the photographs.

'I need to be out of here, Vinny. I want to work with you on this. For all the reasons you talked about. But one thing has to be guaranteed.'

Vinny blinked as though he knew what was coming, but didn't reply.

Kerry looked him in the eye.

'Sharon gets protected. Whatever it takes.'

She stood up.

'I need to move. Call me.'

'Wait. When will I know what's going on?'

'I'll let you know. I promise. I'll make this happen. But you have to make the guarantee.'

He stood up, putting down some coins for their coffees and they walked towards the door together and outside. Kerry waved to the driver across the street.

'I'll talk to some people,' he said. 'See how we can work this.'

She turned and left, knowing he was still watching her as she got into the car and sped off.

# CHAPTER THIRTY-EIGHT

Knuckles was so stunned as he listened to Frankie Martin on the phone that he actually felt dizzy. He had to grip the wall for a second while he steadied himself.

'Hold it a fucking minute, Frankie. Just hold it. I need to sit down here.' He walked out of his office and sat on the sofa in his living room. 'Okay. Start again.'

'You all right, mate?'

'I'm fine. Start again, for fuck's sake!'

'Right. Your Sharon. She's in Glasgow. I've seen her myself.'

'What do you mean, you've seen her? Where? How? You've talked to her? When?'

'Yesterday.'

'Yesterday? And you're only phoning me now, you Jock cunt! Why didn't you phone me immediately?'

Knuckles gnawed the inside of his jaw as he waited for Frankie's response. You couldn't trust this rat's bastard as far as you could throw him. If Frankie really did see Sharon, then the fucker had spent the last twenty-four hours working out how to make the information benefit himself.

'Well ...' Frankie hesitated. 'The truth is, Knuckles, I wanted to work out if I could find a way to get to her. Maybe even deliver her to you. But it's going to be really hard. That hotel is small, and it's used to accommodating rock stars and movie people when they visit Glasgow, so the security is very tight. I don't imagine she'll be booked in under her own name, but whatever, I didn't want to make any enquiries at the hotel that might make her suspicious and run. You know what I mean?'

'Yeah, right,' Knuckles said, not believing him. 'You should still have told me. It's my shit, man, so I should have been told so I can make the decisions. Tell me what you saw.'

'Well,' Frankie said, 'you won't want to hear this, but what I saw before I saw Sharon was that bitch Kerry Casey going into the hotel. I've been watching Kerry for the past few days – you know my view of her. She's just wrong. But that's another story. Thing is, I've seen her going in and out of the hotel twice in about a week. I thought she was meeting some bloke for a shag or something.'

'You think she was meeting Sharon?'

'It's a small hotel. Too much of a coincidence for Kerry Casey to be going there to meet anyone else. I'm pretty sure that's what she's doing. So Kerry is up to something.'

'Yeah. Fucking me right up the arse, no doubt, talking to that bitch who has already robbed me blind, the cunt.'

'What do you mean, robbed you, Knuckles?'

'None of your concern. All I'm saying is she's been helping herself to my money – a lot of my fucking money. Anyway, forget that. How did you see her? You didn't go in, did you?'

'No. Course not. I was sitting in my car and just thought I'd wait and have a fag after Kerry left, then I just about shat myself when the door opened and Sharon appeared.'

'Christ! You're sure it was her?'

'Absolutely no doubt. Sure, I've met her a few times – you know that. We all had dinner in Puerto Banus that night with Mickey. Then I met her twice in Manchester with you. I don't make mistakes like that. She's quite a striking-looking woman.'

'Yeah, was. But fuck her. Look, I need to get my people to Glasgow. In fact I might even come myself and surprise her. Is there anything you can do up there to find out what's going on with her and that Kerry nutter? There must be some way. I mean, you're at the heart of everything, aren't you?'

'Not the same as I was, Knuckles. Not since Kerry took over. She's a bit of a headcase. I think she wants me out.'

'Hmm. Maybe she's figured out you got her brother bumped off,' he said, sarcastic. 'And it was your idea to send a message at the funeral.'

'Aw, hold on, Knuckles! The funeral was your idea, if you remember. I just said it wouldn't do any harm to send a message – I didn't mean for your fucking idiot boys to go up there and start spraying the fucking wake with bullets. That's down to your mob, not mine.'

'Don't get fucking lippy with me, Frankie. If you and I are going to work together, you don't give me any shit, okay? Now listen. I'm not going to fuck this up this time with Sharon. If she's in a hotel in Glasgow, she'll think that's the last place I'll look for her. But the fact that she's talking to Kerry Casey could mean all sorts of shit might be coming my way. I need to get to her pronto before she starts to do any damage – if she's not already done it.'

'Of course.'

'Right, you must know something. What do you think Sharon is cooking up with Kerry? Give me something to think about, for fuck's sake.'

Knuckles waited for a response, gazing through the massive patio glass doors that ran the length of his house and into his manicured garden in the driving rain. An image flashed up to him of lunches at the big stone table out there with Sharon and their son when he was around five or six and life was good. He'd been on the up then, beginning to make serious money through his drug shipments, building his empire in Manchester. He didn't even consider how it had come to this – don't even go there, he told himself. You are where you are, and the woman you fucking gave a movie-star lifestyle to is now working to fuck you up. That's all that matters now.

'I don't know, Knuckles. If I did I would tell you. I'm a bit squeezed out of things these days, so it's hard for me to get anything solid. But I'll see what I can do and come back to you.'

'Listen, Frankie. I don't have a lot of time for this. If I know Sharon, she'll be making plans to fuck right off as far away as she can – and with a shedload of my money. I want to be up there and deal with her right now.'

'I understand that. But you can't just go in there and bump her off.'

'I can put a fucking bomb in the hotel is what I can do. Blow her to fucking smithereens.'

'You don't want to do that until you see what she's been up to, do you?'

'Maybe not. But I don't have time on my hands. And I've got a lot on the go down here. I've got a big shipment about to arrive in the next couple of days so I need to be here to oversee it. Listen, mate. You come up with ideas on how to smoke her out, and you'll be well rewarded – you hear what I'm saying? Those fucking Casey cunts are finished. I'm going to be running the show from here once I get everything sorted. That's always been the plan. That's why Mickey had to go. You know that. You'll be top dog once we get this organised.'

'Sure, mate. I know. I'll do my best.'

'You'll need to do better than that.'

Knuckles hung up and tossed the phone across the sofa. He put his head in his hands and rubbed his face vigorously. Christ almighty! If you didn't do a fucking thing yourself it didn't get done. That had always been the way. The phone rang and he picked it up, and heard his son's voice.

'Hi, Dad. How're things?'

Knuckles had an idea.

Frankie opened the wall safe in his flat where he kept a stash of hard cash in case the time came when he had to run. That time had come. He took out around twenty grand and stuffed it into a small rucksack. He'd decided after his phone call to Knuckles that there was no way back for him. The Caseys were going nowhere in the grand scheme of things, and he was getting out before that bitch Kerry and her lapdogs became a laughing stock among the various crews from Glasgow to London and Dublin. He would do what Knuckles had asked – he'd deliver Sharon to him. And by doing that, he'd stride into Knuckles' backyard as top dog. None of the thick fucks in his mob would mess with him.

He'd spent the day planning and preparing, and he'd known early on he'd have to bring in Joey Tarditti to make it happen. Joey was known as the Fireman, for his unique ability to burn down buildings and premises and leave no trace that it was anything other than an accident. If you needed your garage, restaurant, nightclub or even your house to go up in smoke so you could claim the insurance, Joey was your man. Over the decades, he'd been used by everyone from gangsters to hoteliers who needed a good insurance job. Frankie was lucky that he was in town this week for his grandson's christening. They'd met in a bar in Byres Road earlier that day, and Frankie filled Joey in on the job at One Devonshire Gardens. He told him he didn't want the hotel burned down, but enough of a fire to cause maximum chaos and make sure all the guests got evacuated. He even confided in him that he was looking for one guest in particular, and Frankie's intention was to kidnap her. Joey didn't ask any questions apart from when he wanted it done. Tonight, Frankie told him. Joey left with five grand in his jacket pocket and the promise of another five after it was done.

Now all Frankie had to do was wait. He'd hired a van and stocked it with some simple snack food and water for the journey south. Everything was ready. He looked around his flat one last time and out of the window at the lights of the city twinkling as far as the eye could see. He would probably never see this again. Not that he gave a fuck. There was nothing here for him any more. The only family he'd ever really had were the Caseys, and they didn't want him any more. He tightened his lips. Fuck them! It would be their loss. He crossed the room to the front door and headed out into the night.

'Where are you exactly?'

Joey's voice was almost a whisper as Frankie pressed the phone to his ear.

'I'm directly behind the hotel – where you said I should be. Grey Mercedes van. Where are you?'

Frankie peered out of the windscreen. The street was busy with parked cars, mostly of residents in the nearby flats.

'I see you. I'm across the street to your left and about thirty yards away.'

'Great. So what happens next?'

'In about five minutes I'll detonate the device and the fire will start. I've planted it just inside the back door of the kitchen where they come out to put crap in the bins or for a fly smoke. I managed to do it earlier on while they were busy with meals and stuff. Quite easy really. It's a fairly simple device. It'll ignite and set fire to the nearest material.'

'I don't want the place burning down, Joey, or anyone injured.'

'Don't worry, man. The smoke detectors will see to that. Place will be evacuated before the fire brigade even get here.'

'Okay. This is where it gets a bit tricky, mate,' Frankie said. 'I was thinking after you left that it might be hard for me to be the one to get this bird out of the place once all the guests get evacuated. She knows me. I've met her a few times. I don't want her to start making a scene if she suspects something. So I was thinking of asking you to do it.'

Frankie waited as the line went silent.

'That's not part of the contract, Frankie. I light fires. That's what I do. Kidnapping is different.'

'I'll pay you more.'

Again with the silence.

'It'll cost you another three on top of the five. But all I'll do is bring her to you. Then I'm fucking off. You got that?'

'Yep. That's good by me. I've got the dosh here for you. Have you got a weapon?'

'Of course. But I'm not fucking shooting anyone.'

'No. I don't mean that. Just in case. I want you to go up to this woman and say to her that Kerry sent you, and she's to come with you, that it's not safe here any more. Say to her that Kerry is waiting for her.'

Silence.

'Are we talking Kerry Casey, Frankie? You doing over Kerry Casey? *The* Caseys? Fuck me, man. That's big stuff.'

'Joey. Listen, mate. I don't want to have to explain all this to you. Believe me, you'll see in the next few months how this all goes down, and that I'm right.'

He heard Joey sigh and for a moment he thought he was

going to abandon the job. He knew Joey Tarditti had been thick years ago with Danny and Tim Casey, but as Joey lived abroad most of the time, nobody really got to see him these days. He hoped he didn't feel any dumb sense of fucking loyalty to Danny, or to Tim's daughter. Joey was knocking on a bit, and he might not be in such big demand as the old days, so he was banking on him needing the money enough to agree.

'Look, I'm not asking questions. I've done the job, and I'll do what you ask. Then you won't see me again. You understand that?'

'Course.'

'Okay. Two minutes to go, then I'll go up there, bring her to you. But no rough stuff. I don't rough up women.'

'Of course. But if she protests, then stick your gun at her back. She'll know the score. She's not daft enough to do a runner.'

As Frankie said it, he pictured Sharon shooting her two would-be assassins in the back road to Manchester airport that day and leaving them for dead while she legged it. He braced himself for a bit of a scrap.

# CHAPTER THIRTY-NINE

Sharon's mobile rang and she recognised the number as Tony's secret phone that Kerry had squirrelled down to his school.

'Tony, sweetheart. How you doing, darling?'

'I'm all right, Mum. Just the usual. Not doing much tonight. I thought you were coming down some time. You said . . .'

'I know, pet. I was hoping to come this week, but things are, well, you know how I said to you . . . a bit difficult.'

Sharon sensed by the silence at the other end that something was troubling her son, and her heart ached to be with him. Tony had long given up trying to be a tough guy around his dad, because he just looked inept, but he was a resilient young lad without being a thug. Deep down, though, he was still a boy who wanted to sit down on the sofa with his mam and a pizza and watch television. She missed that quality time with him, and had hated sending him to private school, but it was the only way to get him away from the influence of Knuckles and the mob of hoodlums surrounding him.

'Are you all right, sweetheart? You sound a bit down.'

'Well, I am a bit. It's half-term next week, and I was hoping you'd come down and get me.'

Sharon felt the wrench in her gut. In all this mayhem, she'd completely forgotten about half-term, when Tony would come home, or they would fly off to the villa in Spain. Christ! She missed him so much.

'Oh, I know, Tony, but we'll work something out . . . I—'

'Mum. I was talking to Dad on the phone yesterday and he says he's coming down to get me. Are you two back together again? I thought you'd have phoned me. I don't want to go home with Dad.'

A chill ran through her. Knuckles never went to school to pick Tony up. Ever. Only once since Tony had been there had Knuckles come with her to visit him. They'd stayed in a hotel nearby, and taken Tony out for lunch before driving back down the road on the Sunday. If the bastard was driving all the way to the Borders to bring Tony home with him, then he was plotting. But she couldn't let Tony know her fears.

'You there, Mum?'

'Yes, I'm here. I didn't know your dad was coming down. You know how things are with him and me. He probably just wants to spend some time with you.'

'Yeah. Doing what though? Hanging around those stupid clubs and stuff. I'm not into that, Mum. Can you not come?'

She bit her lip.

'Not right away, son. Leave it with me just now, and I'll make a plan so that we can see each other before you go back.' She swallowed. 'I do miss you so much, my love. I really do.'

'I miss you too, Mum.'

Sharon could hear the crack in his voice and it broke her heart. It always broke her heart that she couldn't see enough of him, but before she'd left Knuckles she'd at least had a level of control. She could drive up there and see him on her own. She hated herself. She should have thought about Tony before she did a runner. But what could she do? It was either stay there and die, or get the hell as far away from Knuckles as she could. Now the scheming bastard was obviously doing something to get her attention. He'd pay for this. She'd bloody make sure of it.

'Look, I'll call you on this phone in the next couple of days. But remember to keep this mobile away from your dad.' She paused, guilty. 'You know I don't like secrets like this, Tony. But things are difficult. I promise I will make it up to you. We've got a lifetime to make this up. This is a hard time for me, sweetheart, but you and me ...' She paused, swallowing hard. 'You and me ... we're buddies for life, aren't we?'

'Always, Mum.'

'Okay. Just go with your dad, and we'll talk as soon as I can. I love you, darling.'

'Love you too, Mum.'

Sharon kept the phone to her ear after he was gone, and could feel her heart thumping in her chest. She had to get out of here. She had to get to Tony before Knuckles did. That fucker was so ruthless anything could happen. She was about to punch in Kerry's number when suddenly the hotel fire alarm went off.

'Fucking Christ!' she murmured, the sound deafening. 'What the fuck is this?'

She could hear doors opening and closing, and activity in the corridor, then suddenly someone knocking on all the bedroom doors. A voice outside was shouting to stay calm and follow the signs for the fire exit. She opened her door and saw various people walking swiftly down the corridor.

'Is there a fire?' she asked the young concierge.

'Yes, madam. You have to leave now. It's all right. Just be calm and follow the signs for the fire exit. Everything's going to be all right.'

'Jesus Christ almighty!' She closed the door and grabbed her coat, phone and handbag.

Everyone moved swiftly along the corridor and down the wide staircase to the main hallway. There was a distinct smell of smoke, but no signs of it coming through from the closed doors off the foyer. Staff and guests bustled around, moving out towards the main door, and when Sharon looked back, she could now see plumes of thin smoke from beneath the door that led towards the dining room and kitchen. The fire alarm was bursting her eardrums and she was glad to be outside despite the chill. Guests were already milling around in the confusion. What the hell was she going to do now? She had to phone Kerry. She took her mobile out of her pocket and punched in her number. She answered after three rings.

'Kerry. It's me. There's a fire at the hotel. We've all been evacuated. Not sure what's happened. But I need to go somewhere. Everyone is just standing around outside. I'm not sure we'll be going back in. I can hear the fire brigade in the distance.'

'Shit,' Kerry said. 'Don't worry. Stay where you are. I'll get someone to pick you up. Just stay put.'

'Kerry, listen. Do you think this is a put-up job? I'm suspicious.'

'I don't know. But I'll get you picked up.'

Suddenly, Sharon was aware of a firm hand gripping her arm. She turned to see a dark, unshaven older man in a woolly hat.

'Come with me,' the man said. 'I've to take you to Kerry.'

Sharon resisted, stood her ground.

'Wait a fucking minute,' she said to the man, then into the phone. 'Kerry. Someone here says they're taking me to you.'

'Oh, Christ!'

Sharon turned to the man and shook his arm off.

'Get your fucking hands off me.'

'Come with me,' he said calmly.

'Kerry! Kerry!'

Sharon felt the hardness of a gun pushed into her back.

'Do as I say and nobody gets hurt,' the man said.

'Kerry. This fucker's got a gun in my back.'

'Oh, Christ, Sharon! I've got someone on their way.'

'Keep walking,' the man said.

Sharon did as he asked and walked as calmly as she could away from the car park and towards the back of the hotel where she could see smoke billowing out of the kitchen and bin area. She saw steps and a small alleyway leading to the street, and the man pushed the gun into her back as she walked. If only she could find a way to get into her handbag and get her own gun, she would waste this bastard right here and now. But where the fuck was he taking her? She walked gingerly down the moss-damp narrow stone steps and into the street filled with parked cars. Then she heard the engine of a van starting up and someone getting out of the driver's side. It was dark and she couldn't make out the face, but as she was pushed closer, she felt it was familiar. But when a shaft of light from the street lamp fell on him, her blood ran cold. It was Frankie fucking Martin. He looked at her, his face pale and his dark eyes full of anger.

'Keep your mouth shut, Sharon, and don't do anything stupid.' He opened the back doors of the van. 'Get in.'

She climbed in, because she had no choice. He climbed in behind her, and made her kneel down while he tied her hands and feet. He held up duct tape in front of her.

'Do I need to put this stuff on, or are you going to keep your mouth shut? Because if you start shouting and fucking around, then I'm going to have to shoot you. Do you understand?'

'You will fucking pay for this, Frankie. You're a fucking dead man walking.'

He stood over her.

'Aye, right. You picked the wrong team, pal. It's you who's going to get it. So keep your mouth fucking shut while I get us out of here.'

Sharon said nothing, watched as he climbed out of the van, slamming and bolting the doors behind him.

# CHAPTER FORTY

'What's wrong, Kerry?' Vinny said. 'You've gone white as a sheet.'

Kerry held the phone in her hand, stunned, her mind racing through a blur of possibilities, none of them good. She had to get Danny and Jack up to the hotel to see what was happening. But it would be too late for Sharon. By the sound of things, she was already being kidnapped.

'Kerry . . . What's happened?'

She put her hand up to silence him as she pressed Danny's number into her phone.

'Danny. You need to get some people up to One Devonshire. The place is on fire. Sharon just called me. It's a set-up. Everyone's been evacuated. But she's been kidnapped.'

She listened as Danny told her he'd get a couple of boys up there straight away. He asked what else Sharon had said.

'Nothing much. Only that she was being taken. We need

to find her. Knuckles must be behind this. He'll kill her if we don't get to her in time. Call me as soon as you get there. I'm going back to the house.'

She hung up and looked at Vinny.

'Christ, I knew this would happen, Vinny.'

'Shit, Kerry! If only I'd known where she was, I'd have kept someone watching her.'

She glared at him.

'That's not helping, for Christ's sake.'

'Sorry,' he said. 'But listen. It's time we got involved in this, Kerry. This is a kidnapping now, organised by a big league gangster. I can't just leave this to you to sort. For Sharon's sake as much as anything.'

Kerry knew he was right. She thought she had Sharon protected in the hotel, discreetly where nobody knew where she was. There had been nothing to indicate that she'd been rumbled. She'd been safe until now. Someone must have found out where she was. It could only be someone from her organisation – only one person. It had to be Frankie. Who else could it be? If it was him, he must have followed her to the hotel. She cursed herself for being careless. Sharon had come to her for help and protection, and to offer her a business deal, and straight away, the first major task since she took over, she'd failed. Now the cops were asking to come in on the operation.

'I need to go, Vinny. I have to get back and speak to the guys to see what we can do.'

'Listen, there's a fire in the hotel, our uniformed boys will be up there anyway as a matter of course. I'll see what we can glean. And I'll get them to ask about guests and if any of the staff or guests saw anything suspicious. Maybe someone saw her being taken into a car or something. I can help get information.'

'But, Vinny, if the police get involved and find Sharon then she could end up in big trouble. We haven't even made an agreement about what we spoke about earlier – about the shipment of drugs and how I could help you nail Knuckles Boyle. You have to give me guarantees that Sharon will be left out of it.'

'I haven't got those guarantees yet, Kerry. It takes time. You don't have time. But if you don't find her soon, then she'll have more to worry about than the cops finding her and looking at her for drug smuggling.'

She didn't reply. She knew he was right. She pulled on her coat and picked up her bag.

'Okay,' she sighed. 'Can you phone me, Vinny – if you get any information?'

'Of course.' He went across and kissed her cheek. 'I'll do what I can.'

Kerry didn't know how far she could take this with the police. She didn't even know if she could trust them. She trusted Vinny, from what she knew of him. They were both on the same side – both trying to nail Knuckles Boyle – but for different reasons. Right now, that paled into insignificance as she thought of Sharon and where she might be headed.

In the darkness of the windowless van, Sharon felt sick with fear. She had no idea where she was going, but she guessed by the speed they were travelling that she was now on a motorway. Probably heading south to be delivered to Knuckles. And that would be the end for her. The thought made her choke with emotion, not for her own safety or whatever may happen to her at the hands of Knuckles, but for Tony, and what this bastard was prepared to put their son through to get to her. And worst of all, she was powerless to fight back. Her entire life was about fighting back, about survival, getting up when you got knocked down and pushing your way to the front. There was always a way to get there, and even when Knuckles had sent her to her death with his thugs, she'd been too clever and too quick for them. But she had nothing to work with here. She peered around the van, looking for something that she could use to loosen the ties around her. She could feel with her hands that it wasn't rope, and it wasn't plastic cable ties, so whatever it was had been done in a hurry. Frankie hadn't planned this kidnapping out, that was for sure. In fact, she could see her handbag slung into the corner. The stupid bastard hadn't even taken her bag off her when he bundled her into the van. That was basic stuff. He was obviously in so much of a hurry he missed simple steps. She had to find a way to capitalise on that. If she could get to her bag, she could get to her phone and contact Kerry. At least she'd be able to say she was in a grey Mercedes van heading south. But what she really needed was to get to her gun. If she could, she'd take real delight in sticking it in Frankie's face and blasting the fucker to death. But with her hands tied behind her back, she was going nowhere. She shuffled across the van until she could feel the moulded edges of the walls, and tried to rub her hands up and down on that to see if it would make any impact on whatever she was tied with. It felt like cloth, so it wasn't that strong, or tight. But it was awkward. She took a breath and tried pulling with all her might to see if she could snap it, but the pressure of pulling with her hands behind her back sent pain shooting up her arms to her shoulders. She sat back in despair. There had to be a way. She thought of Tony, his face miserable as his dad picked him up, and how he wouldn't be saying much all the way home. She felt tears coming to her eyes, but she bit them back. She would get out of this, for Tony and for nobody else. And when she did, she would never let him out of her sight again.

Sharon could feel the van reducing speed and sensed they were coming off the motorway onto a slip road. She steadied herself as it appeared to veer around a long bend and then continued but at a much slower speed. She tried to work out where they could be, figuring she'd now been in the van for almost two hours, so it was possible they were somewhere around the Lake District exit. Perhaps she was being taken there for a face to face with Knuckles. It would be a short handover, she thought. If this van stopped and Knuckles was waiting to greet her, she wouldn't be going any further. Knuckles wasn't the smartest tool in the shed, but by this time he'd have worked out that there was a lot of money missing from his bank accounts. The only way he had a chance to get any of that back was to keep her alive and force her to reveal every secret move she'd been making as she'd plundered his accounts over the years. That was her only hope. She would be shot once he had no use for her, and right now she didn't even care about that. All that mattered was that she could get Tony away from him. She strained again at the ligature on her wrists, but it wasn't moving. And now the van was shuddering to a halt. She sat still, barely breathing, waiting for him to get out of the driver's seat. She heard the door close and footsteps around the van. Then a knock at the door.

'You all right in there?'

'Like you give a fuck!'

'Listen. I'm going to open the door and let you out for a breather. But don't try anything stupid or I'll knock you out.'

'Fat chance of me trying anything with my hands tied behind my back. Christ! Can you hurry up? I need a pee. I feel a bit sick.'

She heard the lock being turned and one of the doors was pulled open. It was pitch black, and she peered out beyond Frankie to get some sense of where she was, but all she could make out were bushes. Then in the distance she could see what must be lights of cars on the motorway.

'Where are we?'

'Down near Kendal.'

'Great. I've always fancied a trip to the Lake District.' She glared at him, eyes blazing.

Frankie drew his lips back. She sat up, grimacing in pain.

'Well? Are you going to untie me so I can get out and have a pee? Unless you're going to help me?'

Frankie stood watching her for a moment as she tried to ease herself to the entrance of the van.

'Look, Sharon, you know the sketch here. I'm taking you to Knuckles. So I'm not about to fuck this up. If I untie you, and you make any stupid fucking move, then I'll be taking Knuckles your body. He's not that bothered how you're delivered, as long as you get there.'

'You're all heart, you treacherous bastard.'

He said nothing for a moment, took a cigarette from his packet and sparked the lighter under it.

'That's good coming from you – cosying up to Kerry fucking Casey. You backed the wrong horse there, pal. She'll be history in the next few months – and so will the whole Casey mob.'

Sharon let her head sink a little to her chest and said nothing for a moment, then she looked up.

'This is not my fault, Frankie. It's not me who started

this, it was Knuckles. He waved goodbye to me in our fucking kitchen, knowing he was sending me to my death. What kind of bastard does that to the mother of his son? I did what I did to survive. I didn't want any of this. We had a life – we were a family. Knuckles wanted me out for some young bird, but he knows I know too much, so he wanted rid of me. Christ!' She sniffed, sensing Frankie was taking it all in. She hoped it was working.

He took a long puff on his cigarette and blew the smoke out into the darkness.

'Not my problem. I'm doing what I've been asked to do.'

'Fine. Can you at least untie me while I go for a pee? I'm bursting here.'

He stepped forward as she eased her way to the edge of the van, so her legs were dangling out. Frankie went behind her and fiddled with the ties on her wrists. She could feel them releasing, then her hands were free. If only she could find a way to reach across and get her bag, but she knew it was hopeless.

'Right. On you go. But don't go far. I'm watching you. It wouldn't be smart to go running off in the middle of nowhere. You'd freeze to death.'

She shot him a glance and shook her head feebly.

'I'm going to die one way or another, so who cares.' She got out and stood up, her legs stiff and her back sore.

Frankie jerked his head behind her to the bushes, and she brushed past him, heading into the darkness.

She walked carefully through the soft earth and stepped into the thicket only a few yards away, straining her eyes to see if she could make out any pathway. But he was right. It was icy cold. They were in the middle of nowhere. It would be madness to make a run for it. From where she squatted in the darkness, she could just make out Frankie standing with his back to her, looking down as though he was scrolling through his mobile. She glanced around the ground and saw a jagged stone a little bigger than her fist. She picked it up and slipped it into her coat pocket. She could feel her heart thumping as she stood up and adjusted her clothing, then padded softly out of the thicket. Frankie still had his back to her, and now she was only a few feet away. She put her hand in her pocket and felt the hardness of the rock. She had one shot at this and it had to be good. If he turned around in the next few seconds, she would leave it. But suddenly his mobile rang, and she caught her breath as he pressed the phone to his ear.

'Aye. I'm on my way, man. Be another hour and a bit . . .'

The force of the rock on the back of Frankie's head stunned him on his feet and he staggered a little. But Sharon was on him again, this time three rapid, frenzied hits, the sound of the rock against his head making a muffled thumping noise in the stillness.

'Fuck!' He dropped the phone.

Before he had a chance to turn around, she hit him one more time, with a force and strength she didn't know she possessed, and he fell to his knees, dazed and confused, blood coming down the side of his neck. In a flash, she was into the back of the van, grabbing her bag, her hands trembling as she thrust them inside and brought out the gun. She pulled back the hammer, ready to shoot if Frankie had moved. But he hadn't. He lay groaning on the ground, his eyes rolling. She pointed the gun at him.

'Fuck!' he muttered. 'Fuck are you doing, Sharon! Stop!'

'Shut the fuck up,' she spat. 'Stay where you are and don't move.'

She slipped past him to the driver's door and could see the keys still in the ignition. She came back and stood over Frankie. She bent down and picked up his mobile phone, and could see the last call he received was from Knuckles. She glanced down at him.

'I should shoot you right now, you bastard. I'd be doing you a favour. Because whoever gets you first – Knuckles or the Caseys – you're a dead man anyway.'

He put his hand up feebly, but she could see he was only semi-conscious. She backed away from him, slammed the back doors of the van, climbed into the driver's seat and started the engine. She switched on the headlights to make out where she was and spotted the narrow track they must have come up. It crossed her mind that this might not have been the first time Frankie Martin or any of his mob had been up here to dispose of someone who had crossed them, and as she put the van into reverse, she wondered how many skeletons were lying in the woods below – food for the vermin as they rotted away. If Frankie was next, she didn't give a damn. It had been his choice. She had run out of choices the moment she realised that Knuckles had no more use for her. It was all about survival now. She'd survived his first attempt to get rid of her, and she'd done it again.

'Fuck you, Knuckles!' she said aloud as she eased the car around past Frankie's body, then sped off down the track where the lights of the M6 were getting closer.

# CHAPTER FORTY-ONE

Kerry sat with Danny and Jack in the kitchen, while a few of the other closest associates came in and out, providing any information they'd picked up. Jack had sent two of his men up to the hotel to make discreet enquiries from staff and guests to find out what happened once guests had been evacuated. They'd established that everyone had been outside and all guests had been evacuated safely. They'd been told to wait in the car park while they organised a roll call to make sure there had been no mistakes. But one of the guests was missing. It was a lady by the name of Marcia Baker – the alias Kerry had booked Sharon under at the hotel. One of the waiters had seen her going away with a man, and didn't think anything of it. He had mentioned it to staff, and they appeared to be satisfied that she had gone away for a while until things were settled at the hotel. She had some clothes in the hotel, but no papers to identify her. Vinny had called Kerry's mobile to say that police were looking at the CCTV footage to see if they could identify who she was seen leaving with. She hadn't heard back from them. And as it was now after eleven, she didn't hold out much hope of getting any closer to finding Sharon tonight.

'I just feel responsible,' Kerry said. 'I should have had someone up there. With it being One Devonshire and stuff, I just didn't think anyone could get past the front door without being a guest, or with a guest.'

'And nobody did, Kerry. So don't blame yourself,' Danny said. 'Whoever kidnapped Sharon must have had someone helping – because the fire is no coincidence. This was all planned. We find out who lit the fire, we might be getting close.'

Kerry's mobile rang and she picked it up. It was Vinny again.

'Kerry, our traffic boys have picked up footage of a silver Merc van leaving the One Devonshire car park just after the drill. They've picked it up again on the M74 and then further down. We're talking to the boys down south to see if they catch any more sightings of it on the M6.'

'Thanks, Vinny. I appreciate that.'

'I'll let you know if we get anything more.'

He hung up. She didn't want to sound ungrateful, but knowing the van was heading towards the M6 didn't make her feel any better. If it was going there, then Sharon was being taken to Knuckles. And that would be the end of it.

'What about Frankie? Anything from his mobile?'

Jack shook his head. 'His mobile is switched off. But if he's taken her – and there's a good chance he has – then he wouldn't be using his own mobile to communicate with Knuckles. He'll have another one. Treacherous fucker.'

'I should have dealt with him earlier too.' She sighed.

'Kerry,' Danny said, 'don't beat yourself up. This isn't over by a long shot.'

Kerry's mobile rang and her eyes almost popped out of her head when she saw Sharon's name come up on the screen. She picked it up.

'Kerry!'

'Sharon!' Kerry glanced wide-eyed at Danny and Jack who looked at each other in disbelief. 'What's happening? Where are you?'

She pressed the phone to her ear as Sharon spoke, and she could hear the tremor in her voice.

'Christ, Kerry! It was Frankie! The bastard kidnapped me from the hotel. I was tied up in this van, but I escaped.'

'You escaped?' Kerry's voice went up an octave. 'How?'

'I'll tell you when I see you. But right now I'm heading somewhere on the fucking M6 in the van and I don't know where I'm going.'

'Hold on a second, Sharon.'

Kerry turned to Danny and Jack.

'It's Sharon. Frankie kidnapped her, but she's escaped and is on the M6 in the van by herself. We need to get to her.'

Jack went to the door and called in two of his men.

'Get into your car and head down the M6, fast as you

can. I'll call you once you're on the road and I have more information.'

The men nodded and left.

Kerry put her phone on loudspeaker so Danny and Jack could hear.

'Sharon. Are you okay?'

'Yeah, I'm fine. Shaken up, but surviving.'

'What about Frankie?'

'Don't know about him. Left the bastard on some hillside near the Lake District.'

'What happened?'

'I twatted him on the head with a brick. I don't think he's dead though.'

Kerry glanced at Danny and Jack and clocked their lips curling in smiles of admiration. She even found herself smiling.

'Christ almighty. Did he hurt you?'

'No. But he was taking me to Knuckles. That's when the really bad stuff would have happened. Listen, Kerry. Knuckles was going to the school tonight to take our Tony out. I talked to Tony earlier on – just before the fire. I don't know what Knuckles' game is. But I'm worried about Tony.'

Kerry looked at Danny and Jack.

'We can get someone down there.'

'I'm worried it might be too late.'

'Listen, Sharon. I've got a couple of guys on the motorway just now and they'll come and meet you. So just see about pulling in somewhere – a motorway café or something. The boys will be with you in a couple of hours. Don't worry.'

'It's tomorrow the shipment arrives, Kerry.'

For a moment, she had almost forgotten about the shipment. The whole day had gone in a blur. She hadn't even sorted the details out with Vinny, if the cops were definitely going to be there or not. But she'd told him enough that they would have already recced the area and would know what to do. It wasn't expected until late in the afternoon or early evening, so there was plenty of time.

'I know. I'm working on that. Don't worry about tomorrow. We'll get that sorted. Just keep out of sight. Our boys will be with you soon.'

'Thanks, Kerry.'

Kerry sighed as she hung up, and looked at Danny and Jack.

'She's got some bollocks, that lady,' Danny said.

Jack smiled. 'Aye. I'd love to be a fly on the wall in Knuckles' house when he gets word that she's fucked him over again. What a prick that guy is.'

'Anyone fancy a drink?' Kerry stood up. 'I could do with one.'

'Definitely,' Danny said. 'Whisky for me. Small one. Could be a busy day tomorrow.'

'Same for me,' Jack said. 'The night's not over yet. When you get a chance for a better talk with Sharon, ask if she's any idea where Frankie turned off the motorway – where he took her. He might still be lying there. I want to find the fucker.'

Kerry nodded, then went to the cupboard and brought out a bottle of whisky and poured them a small one each. Then she uncorked the bottle of red wine she'd opened yesterday and poured herself a small glass. She sat down heavily, thinking of Sharon and the terror she must have been through. Yet she'd survived again. Knuckles Boyle would rue the day he ever took this woman on. And very soon, he would find out that she wasn't alone.

Cal and Tahir were playing pool in the sports centre when Tahir's mobile rang. He watched as his friend's eyes lit up.

'Really? Tomorrow? They should be here tomorrow? When? Where? When can I see them?'

Tahir kept the phone to his ear listening.

'Okay. Call me as soon as you hear anything.'

He put the phone back in his jeans and turned to Cal.

'That was the Turk. Tomorrow my brother and his family will be in the UK. I don't know where or any details, but they are on their way from Europe. He says my brother told him to tell me that he is very happy and excited. His children are too.'

Cal grinned and slapped his mate on the back.

'That's brilliant, man. Fantastic. I'm well pleased for you.'

'Thank you. When he gets to UK, I suppose he will get

some transport here. It was all part of the deal. I pay for the transport to Glasgow and then they tell me where they will be.' A wide grin spread across his face. 'I am so excited, Cal. The last time I saw my brother's youngest child, she was only a year old. Now she is three. Her big brother is almost five, and funny and very cheeky. You'll like them.'

Cal saw Tahir's eyes shine with emotion and he felt a lump in his throat himself.

'Great. We'll be like family, mate.'

'Yes. Thank you. We will be family.'

Cal went to the bar and brought back Cokes for them, but as he stood at the bar watching his friend pot the remainder of the balls on the table, something niggled him. The Turk may be bullshitting now that he had their money. Trouble was, there was nothing they could do but take him at his word. But now he had told them he would deliver Tahir's family tomorrow, Cal could only hope that he did. If he didn't, he couldn't bear to see the disappointment in his friend's face. And if the Turk did fuck them over, Cal resolved that it would be the last time he ever did.

# CHAPTER FORTY-TWO

Sharon began to shake a couple of hundred yards after she drove back onto the motorway in the van. She could feel the panic attack coming from her legs, all the way up her arms to her chest, catching her breath. Her hands trembled uncontrollably on the steering wheel and she gripped harder, willing herself to calm down. Her face was hot and her neck pulsated.

'Come on, Sharon,' she said aloud. 'If you don't get a hold of this you're going to bloody pass out. Just breathe. It'll pass.'

She managed a couple of deep breaths, letting the air out slowly, and could feel the blood pressure around her temples begin to abate. She could do this. She had to. In the distance she saw the next exit was a motorway service station and she knew it was big enough to be anonymous in. Nobody would be looking for her here anyway, not this early on. Frankie, if he ever got up, had to get back to the nearest town or village to make contact, and she decided it was a safe bet that he wouldn't have Knuckles' phone number in his head. She glanced at his mobile on the passenger seat, hoping it wouldn't ring. She picked it up and switched it off. She was tempted to toss it out of the window, but perhaps she'd need it, if only to keep tabs on any messages Knuckles was leaving for Frankie. As she pulled into the massive car park she glanced around and waited a few moments before getting out of the van. Then she stepped out and walked across to the entrance. It was almost eleven at night so the place was fairly quiet, and the customers were mostly truckers and delivery drivers. She bought a sandwich and a cup of tea, put them on a tray and moved to the far corner of the room. She opened the sandwich and nibbled at it, before emptying two sachets of sugar into the tea. It tasted awful, but the sugar was supposed to be good for shock, so she swallowed it down, wincing. She was feeling better already, and was about to phone Kerry to tell her the exact location when her mobile rang. Tony's name came up, from the secret mobile. She snatched it and pressed the phone to her ear. But the voice wasn't Tony's – it was Knuckles'. Her stomach dropped to the floor.

'Teaching our kid your devious ways, you thieving bitch.'

She opened her mouth to speak, but nothing came out.

'Teaching my son to keep secrets from his dad, are you?'

'Knuckles . . . Listen. This has nothing to do with Tony—'

Knuckles burst in. 'Don't you fucking tell me to listen, you robbing cunt.'

'Let me speak to Tony. Please!' Her voice shook with emotion. 'Please, Joe. Please!'

'Shut up. It's not enough that you steal my money and go running to those Casey fuckers, but you try to turn my son against me. You're history, Shaz. History!'

Sharon thought her chest was going to explode, picturing Tony sitting beside his dad, terrified, knowing he'd be worried sick about her. The poor kid must have been panic-stricken when his dad found the secret mobile.

'Knuckles, please listen to me for a second. Let me speak to Tony. Just to make sure he's okay.'

'He's with his father. Of course he's okay,' Knuckles said, his voice thick with sarcasm.

'Mum! Mum!'

Sharon gasped as she heard Tony's voice pleading. Then the sound of a slap and a grunt.

'Mum, tell him! He hit me!'

'Fuck!' Sharon murmured. 'Knuckles. Please. Don't.' Her throat tightened as she fought back tears. 'Please. I'll do anything you want. Anything. I'm sorry for everything I did. I'll give you all the information you need to make things right again. I'm so sorry. Please. Leave Tony alone.'

'Where's Frankie? I'm trying to phone him.'

'I don't know, Knuckles. That's the truth,' she lied. 'I'm in the back of the van and he stopped somewhere. I don't even know where I am. I think he must have fallen asleep.'

'Arsehole that he is. Do you know where you are?'

'No. I'm still in Scotland, I think. Frankie just put me in the van and drove away. I don't know where we went. Then the van stopped. I thought I heard him get out, but I don't know.'

Sharon held her breath in the silence, praying that he was believing her.

'If you're lying to me . . .'

'I'm not. I'm locked in the van. I can't even get out.'

'Why don't you phone your pal Kerry Casey?'

'I don't want anything to do with that mob. I made a mistake even contacting them. I want to come home. I'm so sorry.'

'You fucking shot two of my best men.'

'You sent them to execute me, Knuckles.'

Her voice shook. Even after everything he did and everything he was doing now, the torture, the pain, it still hurt her to the core that he was actually going to have her murdered. She could never forgive him for that, and she would kill him with her bare hands if she got the chance, but it still tore the heart from her that he wanted her dead. She waited for what seemed like an age as she listened hard for any signs of whimpering or pain from her son. Then she heard his voice.

'Mum,' Tony sniffed. 'Are you all right? Where are you?'

'I'm okay, son. Listen. Don't you worry. Everything's going to be all right. Just do what your dad tells you and be a good boy.' She paused, swallowed her tears.

'But, Mum! I need to see you. When can I see you?'

Sharon bit her lip. Bastard Knuckles was using Tony to lure her to him. She knew what would happen as soon as she showed up within ten feet of Tony. Knuckles would be waiting for her with a gun.

'Soon, pet. I'll see you soon. Now be strong. Be a good lad. I . . . I'm proud of you, I really am.'

She heard him sniffing and sobbing and she covered her mouth with her hand.

'You see how you've upset the lad, you fucker? Right. You listen to me. Get banging on that door of the van until someone comes to help you. I know you're not daft enough to go to the police. So as soon as you get out of there, let me know where you are and get your fucking arse down here. I have to go. I've got a big shipment coming tomorrow and I want you there for it. And I'll tell you this, Sharon. You'd better be here or you'll never see your boy again. You got that?'

'Knuckles. I'll get out of here. I promise. And I'll make this all up to you. I'm sorry for everything. We can be good again. I want that so much. Please believe me. Don't take this out on Tony. He's just an innocent lad.'

He hung up and she sat with the phone in her hand, staring at it. Then she called Kerry.

'Kerry. It's me.'

'Are you all right? Where are you?'

'I'm in the Tebay service station, just off the M6. Please come. I've had Knuckles on the phone. He's got our Tony and he's found the secret mobile. Oh, Kerry, I heard him slapping the kid. Our Tony is such a gentle boy. I'm terrified he's going to do something to him.'

'Okay. Don't worry. He won't harm his own son. He's not that much of a bastard. He's just using the boy to get to you.'

'I know he is. But you don't know Knuckles, Kerry. He'll stop at nothing. He thinks I'm still with Frankie, and I told him the van was locked and I was somewhere in Scotland. He's never going to come looking for me. But he wants me down there. The shipment is coming tomorrow and he wants me there. He wants me there, so he can kill me. He's got Tony and he's luring me down to my death.'

'That's not going to happen. Just sit tight. We'll be with you in the next couple of hours.'

She hung up, and Sharon sank back in her seat. For the first time in her life she felt she had no control over what was going to happen next. Even the day she was being driven to her execution, she had still known that with a gun in her handbag she had a fighting chance of survival. And she'd won. Right now, she was at the mercy of other people. Her son was at the mercy of a father who didn't even like him because he had shown no appetite for the thuggery that had made him a fortune. But she could do nothing but wait.

Kerry called Vinny's mobile number.

'Vinny. Sharon's been in touch. I'm going to see her.'

'Is she in Glasgow?'

'No. Somewhere in the north of England – and I'm not bullshitting. But if you want to talk to her ahead of this shipment arriving tomorrow, then now would be a good time. I'm going to get her a hotel for the night, and I'll be there in a couple of hours.'

'Fine. I'll follow you. Let me know where, and I'll meet you.'

'Totally unofficially though.'

'Of course. But if we're going to be involved in an operation tomorrow then I have to get people organised and in place.'

'Sure. But just don't turn up mob-handed to meet Sharon.'

'I won't.'

# CHAPTER FORTY-THREE

Kerry was tired by the time they got to the hotel outside Manchester. They'd agreed they would hole up for the night, and be in place for the next day. She'd been relieved to see that Sharon was waiting for her inside the Merc van, as arranged, in the car park of the motorway service station. She and Jack had come down in the Jag with the chauffeur, and Danny and a couple of his men travelled in a 4 × 4. She still had no idea how things would pan out tomorrow, but she'd told Vinny all the details of when the shipment was coming in and exactly where. This was their chance to nail Knuckles – as long as he was in the warehouse when it arrived. And even if he wasn't, it was still a shipment of drugs being delivered to a premises he owned and used. After Sharon's call, she was sure that Knuckles would be there in person to oversee the shipment's arrival. But she knew the shipment was only part of his agenda. As soon as Sharon showed up anywhere close to the warehouse, all hell could break loose. They'd have to wait and see. She poured Sharon a cup of coffee as they sat at the table in the suite she'd booked for the night. Sharon's eyes looked puffy from tiredness and perhaps crying. She couldn't blame her.

'You must be shattered, Sharon.'

'I passed shattered about three hours ago. I'm wired to the moon now,' she said, lifting the cup to her lips. 'I just want to get this over with.' She shook her head. 'To be honest, I'm weary, Kerry. When I heard my Tony crying tonight, I nearly lost it. All I want is for him to be safe and happy. Not with that bloody thug for a father. He deserves better. Even if I get myself shot tomorrow, I just need my son to be safe.'

'Don't even think that way.'

They sat in silence for a moment, Kerry watching as Sharon stared at the table, biting her lip.

'Kerry. Listen. If anything happens to me ... I mean, I don't even really know you, but I trust you, from what I've seen. You've taken me at face value, so, whatever happens tomorrow, I appreciate you taking me in when I was desperate. I hope I get out of this and we can work together. But ... but if I don't, if something happens to me, and if Knuckles gets done by the cops, then he's facing life in jail. My Tony will have nobody.' She swallowed. 'I shouldn't even ask you this, but I have nobody else I can ask. If something happens to me, will you please see that Tony gets looked after?'

Kerry reached across and touched her wrist.

'Sharon. Nothing's going to happen. Of course I will make sure your son is looked after. But I won't need to. You'll be there for him. His dad will be in jail, and you and Tony can have your own life together. Don't worry.'

It sounded convincing. But Kerry knew that anything could go wrong tomorrow. All she had done was pass on the information to the police – how they handled the operation was up to them. She knew the officers would be armed and in position wherever they were, so if it came to a shoot-out, anything could happen. It didn't bear thinking about. She would be far enough away until it was over, but Sharon had to be at the heart of it. That was the only way to do it.

There was a gentle knock on the door, and Jack got up and answered it. He turned and made eyes at Kerry, and she knew it would be Vinny. Jack wasn't that comfortable with this entire cooperation situation with the cops, as it went against the grain of everything he'd done all his life, but he knew this was the only way to take Knuckles Boyle down. And in the end, everyone would benefit. Vinny came in, looking pale, his face showing nothing as he glanced around the room. He nodded to Kerry, then looked at Sharon. Kerry gestured for him to sit down next to her.

'Sharon, I'm DI Vincent Burns.' He put his hand out and she shook it briefly, nodding. 'Okay, Sharon.' He glanced at everyone. 'Right now we are completely unofficial, off the record, you understand? Nothing is going to happen to you here as a result of this meeting. But I want to say thanks for your help, and what I hope will be your continued cooperation.'

Sharon said nothing. Kerry watched Vinny. He'd already seemed to take some of the heat out from Sharon just by his approach. At the end of the day he was a cop first. But having worked undercover over the years bringing down drug barons, he was obviously good at getting people onside.

'So. When was the last contact you had with Knuckles Boyle?'

'Tonight. He called me on the secret mobile my son uses to talk to me. He must have found it. He took my boy from his school, and I really fear for his safety more than anything, Inspector. More than my own. That's all I care about.'

Vinny nodded. 'I can understand your fears. And we'll be well aware that your son's safety is paramount. Now. Tomorrow. Have you made any firm arrangements with him?'

'No. But he's going to be phoning me back, no doubt soon, because when I talked to him, I said I was still in the back of the van, that I didn't know where Frankie Martin was.'

Sharon looked at Kerry, not quite sure if she was saying the right thing.

'It's okay,' Kerry said. 'I've told the DI everything that happened. He had people up at the hotel within minutes of you being taken, making enquiries. You were clocked on CCTV leaving the car park with a man.'

'Yeah. That wasn't Frankie though. That was some other guy.'

Vinny pulled a photograph out of the folder he carried, and then another one. He put them on the table.

'Is this guy the one who took you out of the car park?'

Sharon leaned over and had a closer look.

'Yeah. Same guy. Older man. He stuck a gun in my back. You know who he is?'

Vinny nodded and looked at both of them, then at Jack.

'Joey Tarditti. Known as the Fireman. He's the go-to man for insurance jobs or general destruction of property, or anything really. He sets fires. It would be him who set the fire. Started in the kitchen.'

Sharon nodded but didn't say anything.

'Have you found him yet?' Kerry asked.

'No. His grandkid is being christened on Sunday, so he's here for that, but he's lying low after tonight. But we'll get him. Frankie will have hired him.'

They sat in silence for a moment. Sharon spoke first.

'So what happens tomorrow? I mean, if he phones me? He's already told me I have to be at the warehouse. The shipment is coming in – usually late afternoon or early evening. He gets them all the time, and the place is totally watertight. Lots of security even down the road a bit. I don't know how this is going to pan out.'

'We're on that,' Vinny reassured her. 'Don't worry about that. You just be as natural as you can. You're obviously distraught after your ordeal today and in recent weeks, but it's important that you are able to stay calm. Do you think you can do this? We would want to wire you up. How do you feel about that?'

Sharon sighed.

'If I get found with a wire, I'll be dead before I take a step forward. No two ways about it.'

'Do you think they'll search you?'

'For a weapon they will.'

'That's okay. Our equipment is very, very discreet.'

Sharon shrugged. 'Yeah. Okay. I'll wear a wire. I'll do whatever it takes.'

'Good.'

Sharon looked at Kerry.

'Then I walk away, right? With my son.'

Kerry and Sharon both looked at Vinny, who said nothing for a long moment. Kerry glanced at Jack, whose face was stern.

'Yes,' Vinny eventually said. 'But we're a long way from that. It's a big operation tomorrow.' He stood up. 'So let's try and can get some sleep.'

He stood up and went towards the door, then turned.

'I'll see you in the morning.'

Knuckles sat opposite Tony at their kitchen table, trying not to look at his son's surly face. How the hell could a guy like him produce a wimpy kid like this? He shook his head as he flicked off the cap from a beer bottle. He handed Tony a can of Coke. The big pizza box that had just been delivered sat in the middle of the table, like a peace offering.

'Well. Go on then, kid. Get stuck in before it gets cold.'

He watched as the boy didn't reply, but gently opened the box and pulled out a slice of pizza. He looked at his father and put his hand out for Knuckles' plate.

'Oh, right,' Knuckles said, chuckling. 'Manners and everything. At least I'm not wasting my money up in that Jock private school to turn out a boy with no manners. Here you are.'

Knuckles handed him the plate and Tony didn't answer, but placed the slice of pizza on it and handed it back to him. Then he put a slice on his own plate, lifted it to his mouth and tore a piece off. Knuckles watched him, glad that at least the little bugger had stopped crying and looked like he was enjoying his scran. He took a chunk out of his own pizza and watched Tony as he chewed. And somewhere inside there was a little twist of pain or regret or something he didn't recognise, but he hadn't felt it before. This little nipper across the table from him, with his baby-bum pink cheeks and big blue eyes, was his own flesh and blood. Yet, in all the time he'd been around, they'd never spent any time together – just the two of them. That was partly his fault, he knew that, because he was always busy and he left Sharon to do all that baby and toddler shit, as well as running after him when he was a little boy. But as he'd grown older, Knuckles had somehow missed it. The boy scarcely looked at him or gave him the time of day. He was a mummy's boy, always hanging around her in the kitchen or out in the car, and if he was in the house, then he was either on his computer or had his head buried in a book. I should be proud of that, Knuckles chastised himself, but he hadn't been. He'd chosen to ignore the boy because he didn't want to be part of his world. But now there was only the two of them. And after tomorrow that's how it would always be. So the pair of them better start getting used to it.

After they devoured the pizza, Knuckles brought ice cream out of the freezer and spooned a few dollops into bowls for them. He watched, impressed, as the boy polished it off.

'You were hungry, kid, weren't you?'

'Yeah. Starving.' He sat back and yawned. 'I'm tired now, Dad. Do you mind if I go to bed?'

'No. Course not, lad. You get some sleep. It's been a long day.'

Deep down, Knuckles wished he would stay around a little longer, maybe even have a conversation. But maybe it was too late for that. Maybe it had been too late a long time ago.

The boy stood up and pushed his chair in.

'Listen, son,' Knuckles said, awkward. 'Look. I'm sorry I hit you earlier.'

Tony glanced at him and his face reddened, then his eyes went to the floor. He didn't answer.

'Really. I'm sorry. Things just got a bit out of hand. I've had a lot on my mind of late. And things ... Well, things with your mam and me, they're not great.'

Tony nodded his head slowly.

'Is Mum coming back tomorrow?'

'We'll see, kid. On you go to your kip now. Get some sleep.'

He watched his son go out of the room and could see him in the hall as he padded slowly up the stairs to his bedroom. Knuckles sat back and sighed.

'What a right fucking mess.'

# CHAPTER FORTY-FOUR

Kerry and Jack were in the hotel room as the female detective fitted Sharon with the wire device in the loo. Vinny had let them see it before they put it in. It was no bigger than a watch battery, and sealed with some special tape onto the front of her bra. They'd told her it was completely undetectable even by electronic equipment, but Vinny didn't expect Knuckles to have any sophisticated searching device other than one of his thugs patting Sharon down. Sharon looked tired and drawn, the last couple of days had taken their toll, Kerry thought, as she emerged from the bathroom.

'You all set?' Kerry asked.

'As much as I can be.' She sat down, poured herself a glass of water. 'Knuckles phoned me this morning. On my own phone this time. And he put Tony on to talk to me.' She screwed up her face. 'It was a bit weird, in that Knuckles wasn't angry and threatening. He said he had a pizza with

Tony last night in the kitchen and that it was good spending time with him.' She puffed. 'That's a first, I'll tell you that. He never spends any bloody time with the boy. They have no relationship whatsoever. So I'm not sure what his game is. But it feels a bit like I'm being lulled into some kind of sense of security so that I turn up as arranged and hand over everything I have. But I don't bloody trust him. As soon as he gets what he wants, I'm history. I'm not daft. But I played along with his Mr Nice Guy routine anyway. I've seen it before.'

'How was Tony?' Kerry asked.

'He was fine. Seemed more relaxed than yesterday. Not as scared. But he kept asking when he'll see me.' She swallowed and turned away from them, standing up and going across to the large window. 'Can see the whole city from here. I can almost see pictures of myself across the place from when I was a little kid out with my mam, until all the mad stuff took over.' She shook her head. 'Christ. My whole life is out there.'

Kerry exchanged glances with Vinny and the detective. Jack's face was impassive. They stayed that way in silence for a long moment, each with their thoughts. Kerry knew Jack had made his own arrangements for bodies to be posted in strategic spots near the warehouse, and there were already two of their cars on the tail of the truck carrying the container of cocaine since it left Southampton an hour ago. She hadn't shared this information with

Vinny, but then he hadn't shared any of his plan with her either. He had simply informed them that this was a big operation involving Glasgow and Manchester armed police as well as officers from the National Crime Agency.

Vinny's mobile rang and he put the phone to his ear, then nodded to the constable and they both left the room. Jack stood up.

'Kerry, I'm going to make some calls. See where the boys are and check things are going okay.'

'I hope your boys know that Knuckles will have everything covered around that area. It's a private road up to the warehouse, so he'll have someone on the bottom of that to check the truck in.'

'We're all right,' Jack said.

Kerry said nothing. Before she'd decided to bring in the cops, the plan had been to use the shipment arrival to wipe out Knuckles and any of his mob who were present. They'd talked about planting their own men in the truck, so that when it arrived all hell would be unleashed on Knuckles. Everyone would know in time how the Caseys dealt out the final revenge for the killing of Mickey and for the stunt at his funeral that left her mother dead. Danny and Jack had been against getting into bed with the cops from the start, but Kerry had convinced them that getting him nailed by the cops with a drugs haul like this would mean he wouldn't see the outside of a prison cell for a very long time. If it all went wrong in the police operation, and

Knuckles was killed in the crossfire, then so be it. That would be an even better result. She had left the logistics up to Danny and Jack. If they had a plan to take Knuckles right out of the game in the middle of the chaos, she didn't want to know.

Frankie Martin was so cold, he thought he must have died. It was the chill through his bones that finally made him stir and he began to feel his eyes flickering. Where the fuck was he? One of his eyes began to open and he could see greyness above, and feel cold rain on his cheeks. He was outside somewhere, and as he attempted to move his legs, he could feel the dampness and icy cold on his back. He dug his heels into what felt like soft earth. He blinked his eyes open, but when he moved them from side to side, a searing pain shot through his head. Then he remembered. Fuck! The bitch had hit him with something. He slowly moved his hand up to touch the source of the pain with his freezing fingers. His hair felt solid, and when he pulled his hand away there was congealed blood. Bitch! How the fuck had it happened so quickly? Slowly he began to move his legs and his arms, and eventually was able to half sit up, leaning on his elbow. He peered at his watch. It was eight o'clock. He must have been lying here all night. How the fuck was he still alive? He forced himself further up and got to his knees and then his feet, his head pounding. He felt dizzy and staggered for a second before taking a breath and steadying himself. In front of him was a narrow path down through woodland leading Christ knows where. He turned slowly around, and he saw the path going the opposite way to the motorway. What the fuck! He'd been in this spot a couple of years ago, along with Mickey and a couple of the lads disposing of the body of Tim Duffy, a fuckwit dealer who'd tried to muscle in on their turf, and who had had the cheek to pull a gun on Mickey in a nightclub weeks earlier. Frankie looked down the narrow path. His body, or, more likely, his bones would be down there somewhere, given the length of time that had passed.

Now Frankie's head was beginning to clear, he remembered everything. Of course, he'd brought that bitch Sharon here, because he knew the landscape well, and how easily accessible it was from the M6. But when he'd woken a few moments ago, he hadn't a clue where he was or how he got there. That was scary. He felt in his pocket for his mobile. But it was gone. Along with the van. No gun in his jacket pocket either. He pulled out a packet of cigarettes and lit one, his hands trembling with cold and shock. He looked at the road down the motorway. He couldn't go there, because as sure as shit some cop car on routine patrol would stop and pick him up. He took a long drag of his cigarette, feeling it burn all the way to his lungs. He looked at the path towards the thicket, and slowly picked his way, heading down to wherever it led.

*

Cal and Tahir sat in a café across from the Turkish barber shop, watching the people going in and out. It was Cal's idea to keep a discreet eye on the place, because so far the Turk hadn't called Tahir to say exactly what time his brother and his family would arrive, and he knew Tahir was getting more and more edgy, the longer he waited with no word. Cal had wanted to go right back in and rattle the Turk's cage and ask what his game was, but Tahir was afraid to get his back up in case he pulled the plug on the operation. Tahir said that the Turk's sidekick had told him that people-smuggling was a major business, and that his family weren't the only people who were down on the list to be shipped out this week. There were people going all over the place, he was told. Some could end up anywhere – from France, to Italy, to Greece. It just depended on the circumstances. If it was people who had families paying for them on the other side, then they almost always got priority and were sent to where their families were. But other people – many from North Africa and the Middle East – had no family abroad and a lot of them were young men looking for a better life. As long as they had enough money to pay for their passage, they could be dropped anywhere. It didn't matter to them, as long as they were in Europe. They could then disappear into the black economy once they linked up with a gangmaster who could make them invisible, as they worked illegally in the various restaurants or labouring jobs. Tahir was told his family would be protected, because he had paid up front, and the people on the other side knew he had to come to Scotland. So why hadn't the Turk got in touch to say they were on their way? Cal had insisted, as the time went on, that they should just be close by the Turk's place and wait out the rest of the day, and perhaps then Tahir should call into the shop and ask if there was any update.

'Seems to be more activity there than we saw the last time we were in,' Cal said. 'But from what I see, there is no queue of people waiting for a shave or a haircut. I can see people going in and then disappearing behind the curtain.'

'I know. Maybe the Turk does a lot of other business. I wouldn't be surprised.'

'Are you kidding?' Cal looked at him. 'You don't think for a moment he's just some Turkish barber who decided to do a wee sideline of smuggling illegal immigrants, do you?'

Tahir didn't answer, but Cal could see he looked a bit hurt. He gave him a playful nudge.

'Sorry, mate. I'm not trying to be a smart-arse. I know you've not been in the country all that long, but anything I ever heard from people is that so many of these Turkish barber shops are a front for drug dealers. Same as the tanning salons and stuff. All drugs. Dirty money being cleaned up.'

Tahir shrugged. 'I suppose you are right. I am maybe a bit stupid for not knowing things like that. I know there are lots of gangsters in this city and drug dealers, but

I don't know how it works. Well, apart from doing the drops that I have to do, like you did.' He sighed. 'I'm not going to do any more of them though, once my family arrive. We are going to look for serious work. I know it won't be easy. But there are labouring jobs in the fruit farms and factories. We will get something in time. My brother will have some money saved. We are getting a new start. There is always jobs for cleaning and stuff like that. But no more drops for me. I just want my family here so we can start again.' He smiled. 'I am very excited to see them.' He looked across the road to the barber's again.

Cal watched as three men went in.

'Look,' he said. 'These guys who just went in. They're locals. They're not in for a haircut. I can see them go right through the back. They could be cops. Or criminals. Hard to know. But most of the people we've seen going in there in the last two hours, and before when we came here, they were all foreigners – probably people paying to get relatives across. But these guys, they look different.'

Cal wished there was a way he could get more information. But there wasn't. They had to sit tight. The guys who'd just walked in looked to him more like gangsters than cops, so that told him that Glasgow mobsters were also somehow behind the trafficking. He couldn't help feeling sorry for his friend who had thrown in all his hopes and his money with this mob, because he had nowhere else to go. He was alone in a foreign land with nobody, and all he

wanted to do was bring his family over. Cal's compassion
was slowly turning to anger when he thought about the
heavies who had just gone in and were still inside the shop.
People like Tahir would never be able to take guys like this
on, ask questions, make demands. Perhaps his imagination
was running riot, but it seemed to him that the Turk was
nothing but a go-between for the gangsters here who traf-
ficked people and the foreign traffickers who picked
people up and took their money off them, leaving them for
weeks in ports and towns from Syria across Turkey while
they waited for promised transport into places like France
and the UK. Everyone was making money out of these poor
people, and maybe the gangsters in Glasgow were the ones
who made the most money. He wondered if the Casey
organisation was involved in trafficking. He didn't think
so, because big Jack and any of the men he'd come across
did not seem the kind of guys who'd be involved in something
as low as that. Sure, he knew they dealt in drugs – large
amounts of heroin and coke came through them and onto
the street. But that's what gangsters did. He had only met
this Kerry Casey woman once, when he'd been brought
home by the lawyer after that shit happened in Manchester. His mother had told him later that Kerry was not like
the other mobsters he may have seen or heard of around
Glasgow. She told him Kerry was cleaning things up, that
in a few years' time they would be a legitimate big business, and all the drugs and shit would be behind them.

How the Caseys had made their fortune hadn't mattered to him – he was just impressed by where they sat now, top of the heap. Kerry had stepped in and saved his mum and also saved his sister Jenny, who would be out of rehab in the next week and be back in her family. Since all this had happened, he had looked at the Casey family, listened to big Jack during their chats over cups of tea, and he knew where he wanted to go in life. He would work for them. They would see in time what he was capable of, and that he was loyal and fearless.

After their third cup of tea, Cal checked his mobile.

'It's nearly five o'clock, Tahir. I think we should pay the Turk a visit.'

Tahir looked worried.

'I don't know, Cal.'

'Listen. We can just go over there, and you can be all trusting and nice to him, and say you are just a bit concerned that you haven't heard anything. It'll be fine.'

'Okay.'

Cal stood up and went to the counter to pay the bill. He came back as Tahir was pulling on his jacket.

'Let's go,' Cal said, and they walked out of the door and crossed the street.

They pushed open the door and the bell pinged, heralding their arrival. The barber, who was working a clipper on the back of some guy's neckline, turned towards them. He raised his chin, but didn't speak.

'I'd like to speak with Hamid,' Tahir said, a little sheepish.

The barber put the clipper down and went across and stuck his head through the curtains and said something in Turkish. He came back out and jerked his head for them to go in. Cal was surprised, as he hadn't seen the other men come out, so the Turk had company. Tahir went in first and Cal behind him. Inside, the Turk sat behind his desk as two of the men sat opposite him. The third, the same fat, shaven-headed guy with a thick neck, sat on a chair at the side with his back to the wall. Cal stayed a step behind Tahir and watched. The Turk looked pale and was smoking furiously. The other men looked irritated at the interruption.

'What do you want, boy?' the Turk said. 'I told you I would phone you when things move.'

'Sorry,' Tahir said. 'It's . . . You said they would be here in a couple days, but I have heard nothing. I am worried.'

The Turk glanced at the two men in front of him, and Cal watched as the guys sitting on the seat stared straight ahead. Cal recognised him from one of the drugs drops he'd done a while ago. He was almost certain the fat guy had been in the back of the car when the package was handed to him for delivery. He made a mental note to talk to big Jack about it. These guys were in here either to launder drug money or because they were part of the smuggling racket. Or maybe both.

The Turk stubbed out his cigarette and Cal could see his hand tremble.

'I will call you when I am ready. Now go away. Don't come here again.'

'But I am worried.'

One of the guys turned around with a bored look on his face.

'Look, son. Fuck off. You've been told. Don't want my boy having to throw the pair of you out of here. You heard the man, now fuck off before you get hurt.' He was well dressed, but his accent was rough Glasgow.

Cal saw Tahir's shoulders slump, and when he turned around there were tears in his eyes. Before Cal could stop himself he squared up.

'You fucking took his money. So can you not give him some solid information? It's his family.'

Before the Turk got a chance to answer, the Glasgow guy glanced at the fat man. He was on his feet and across to Cal in an instant. And now he had him by the throat and slapped his face so hard Cal could feel his cheekbone bruise almost immediately. Then he slapped him again, and this time Cal's legs buckled a little and the fat guy let go of his neck. He dropped to the floor but got up immediately.

'Get to fuck out of here. Before you get hurt,' the well-dressed man said. 'And who are you anyway, you little cunt?'

Cal's legs shook as Tahir grabbed his arm and pulled

him towards the curtain. But before he left he looked at the fat guy, his face burning with rage and resentment.

'You'll be fucking sorry you did that, you fat bastard.'

Tahir dragged him out, and by the time they were at the door they could hear the bastards guffawing behind the curtain.

# CHAPTER FORTY-FIVE

Kerry was driven out towards the area of Manchester where Knuckles' warehouse was, and where the truck carrying the shipment of drugs would arrive. She would be well out of the way. Danny had done a thorough recce of the area earlier, and told her if things worked out, Sharon could be brought to her and the two of them would get away safely. This was the closest Kerry had been to any serious action since she took over. Sure, she'd pored over documents and papers and accounts and planned for the future. She'd dealt with that bastard at the sauna straight off, and she'd ordered the hits on her brother's killers and the gunmen at his funeral. But she had never been right on top of the action. She was surprised by how unfazed she was. Part of her wanted to be with Danny and the boys, wherever they were. She knew they'd be planning to take Knuckles out of the game, and deep down, she wanted to be the one who pulled the trigger. That wasn't a new feeling for Kerry. Since her mother died in her arms, an anger and a ruthlessness had come over her. She had told herself that never again would she be under threat from people like Knuckles Boyle – or any of the rest of the big shots, from London to Dublin. She didn't want to go to war with them right now, but if it came to it in time, then she wouldn't shy away from that. She knew that on the outside her family may have looked weak because they had lost Mickey, and he'd been replaced by his sister, but nobody was going to mess with the Caseys ever again. Her mobile rang and she saw it was Danny.

'Danny,' she said. 'How are things?'

'We've clocked the truck. It's about four miles away from its destination. Our boys are following it, but they'll pull back once it gets off the main road and onto the backroad.'

'Okay. Be careful,' Kerry said.

Danny didn't answer and the line went dead.

She looked at Eddie, her driver.

'Shouldn't be long now. One way or another, we'll know what's happened within the next hour, I think.'

The driver nodded. 'Are you okay, Kerry?'

'Yeah. Sure I am. I could have left it all to the cops, I suppose. But Danny wanted to be there. I can see why, and I let him have his head on this. I think it's what my father would have wanted.'

He nodded slowly, looking reflective.

'I think so. Your father was not a violent man, Kerry. I mean, he took care of things, and he wasn't a stranger to violence – that's the world we lived in and that's how it was. But anything he did was done for the right reasons and to protect the people around him. But he believed in an eye for an eye. Danny is right. Knuckles can get fifteen years in jail and that's good, but it's not enough for what he did. For what happened to your mother.'

Kerry didn't answer. She pictured her mother the night before the funeral, the quiet time they had had in the house, drinking tea and talking. Her words rang in her ears, and not for the first time.

*I wish you weren't going away tomorrow . . . Could you not stay a while longer?*

Kerry swallowed hard and stared out of the windscreen.

In her earpiece, Sharon caught Vinny's voice.

'Can you hear me okay, Sharon? Are you all right?'

'Yes,' she said. 'I can hear you.'

'Okay, as we went over in the drill. You won't be speaking at any time once you go into the situation at the yard, but we will be able to hear everything that is going on. So if you do say anything to Knuckles or anyone else, just be careful that you are not conscious that you know we are listening to it. Sometimes people's conversation is guarded or different when they know they're wired up, so you must try to forget you're wearing a wire. I don't want him to be suspicious of anything, and I don't think he will be. Just stay calm.'

'Okay. I'm trying.'

'Good. Now I can tell you that the truck is only a few minutes away. Have you heard anything from Knuckles yet?'

'No. Not so far. I told him I was in my hired car and I would head to the yard. But I'm waiting for his call.'

'Okay. But just remember when you get in there, we are with you all the way. I have people close by. I know you are worried and I know it is dangerous. But we will have your back at all times. Trust me, Sharon.'

'Okay,' Sharon said, knowing her voice was trembling a little.

Then her spare mobile rang.

'My phone is going now. I have to go.'

'Okay.'

He hung up and she pressed the answer key on the mobile. She heard Tony's voice.

'Mum. Are you okay?'

Sharon took a breath and swallowed hard.

'Of course I am, darling. Are you okay?'

'Yes. Are you coming home?'

'Yes. I'm coming to see you soon. Is Dad there?'

'Yes. He's here. He just wanted me to get you on the phone. I'm out at the yard. I'll see you soon.'

Her stomach lurched. Bastard Knuckles had brought Tony to the yard as insurance that she'd turn up. He was obviously suspicious of something, maybe he even already knew she was in with the cops. Surely to Christ he wouldn't do anything to her in front of their son. Then she heard Knuckles.

'Sharon. Sweetheart. Where have you been?'

She felt sick. His voice was like a snake wrapping itself around her, strangling her. She tried to speak but her mouth was dry as a stick.

'Joe. Please. Is Tony all right?'

'Of course, pet. We had some good father and son time last night. There's a lot this lad could learn from his old dad.'

'Joe, send him home to the house, please. Don't have him in the yard when you've got a shipment coming in. I don't want him to see that. Get him out of there, please.'

His tone was cold, rasping, whispering. 'Listen, you thieving fucking bitch. You don't tell me what to do with my son. I'm bringing him up my way now. So you get over here and get things sorted out. You have a lot of explaining to do.'

She felt her throat tighten.

'Joe. I never wanted this—'

'Shut up and get here. Where are you?'

'I'm about five minutes away.'

'So get moving. The shipment is due here any minute.'

'I'll be there. But you don't need me there for that.'

'Just get here. You want to see your son again, don't you?'

'Joe, stop that. Don't speak like that. I'm on my way.'

He hung up, and immediately Sharon could hear Vinny's voice in her ear.

'Stay calm, Sharon.'

She put her car into gear and drove off.

'How can I stay calm? That bastard's got my son. I was afraid he would pull a stunt like this.'

'Don't worry. We're on it.'

'Get my son out of there before you do anything else.' Her voice croaked. 'I don't care what happens to me. Just get my son out of there safely. Please. I'm driving there now.'

'Stay calm. Don't speak to me any more. We're listening to everything you are doing, and we're with you.'

She heard nothing else and could feel her head pounding and the blood pumping in her neck as she drove out of the car park and down to the main road towards the back road that would lead to Knuckles' yard. She had been here so many times over the years for various reasons, mostly to check over the staff and security. She had never really gone into the shipments to check things physically, Knuckles had staff to do that, but she had always been impressed with the different ways the dealers and smugglers came up with to camouflage the cargo. Sometimes it was hidden in plastic or metal tubing, others inside the lining of mattresses, and the last time it was in containers of powdered baby milk.

She could see the cut-off on the road coming up and felt sweat sting under her arms. She'd escaped her own execution once, and got away from Frankie Martin. But now, she had nothing except the promise of the police. If they screwed up and got rumbled, she'd be the first to go. If that was to happen, she had no control over it now, but all she prayed for was that Tony didn't witness her death. She felt cold clamminess in her hands on the steering wheel and gripped it as hard as she could, feeling herself start to panic. Calm down, she told herself. Breathe. You can do this. You have to.

# CHAPTER FORTY-SIX

Knuckles Boyle went into the office at the back of the warehouse, where Tony was playing a game on his mobile.

'You're never off that bloody thing,' Knuckles said. 'Shouldn't you be reading or studying or something?'

Tony looked at him, bemused, and he realised that the boy was probably surprised to hear him say that, because he'd never encouraged him to study or even taken an interest in his schoolwork. But something had changed in Knuckles over the last day, and despite his fury over Sharon's humiliation of him as she'd robbed him over the years, something niggled in his gut now at what he was about to do. Christ almighty! He didn't have time for a crisis of conscience, he'd told himself as he'd talked to his men, making sure the shipment was on its way without any problems. At the end of the day, Sharon had robbed him. She'd been plotting to get away from him for a while, judging by the amount of money she'd squirrelled away, so she was going anyway – whether he'd decided to bump her off a month ago or not. Today was the first time he'd actually questioned himself about that, and he'd come to the conclusion that he'd been right. She had to go because she knew too much. It would have been impossible to just pay her off and tell her to move out, because she was in a position to bring them all down. The problem is she still was. As long as she lived and breathed, she could ruin him and his organisation. So he told himself that whatever twinge he was having in his conscience now, it had to be shoved to the side. Business was business. She had to go. Nothing had changed. And maybe, realistically, he should look at getting out himself before it was too late. He had pots of money, even without the fortune Sharon had stolen, though he was still determined to get all of that back before he disposed of her. He looked at Tony, Sharon's voice from their earlier conversation ringing in his ears. He didn't want his son around to witness any of this.

'Right, Tony,' he said. 'Get your coat. Jimbo will take you back to the house. No point in you hanging around here doing bugger all.'

Tony looked up at him.

'Will Mum be there?'

Knuckles glanced at him, and then busied himself with his mobile.

'Not at the moment. You know what she's like. You just

get back there, and Jimbo will order you a takeaway for your dinner. I'll be home later.'

From the side of his eye, as he scrolled down his phone trying to look busy, Knuckles could see Tony giving him a long look that said he didn't believe him, or that he wanted to know more. But there was no room for this shit.

'Come on then, lad! Chop, chop!'

Tony stood up and took his jacket from behind the chair and put it on as he walked to the door. Knuckles went behind him and crossed the warehouse to speak to Jimbo quietly. Then he beckoned Tony over.

'Off you go now. I'll talk to you later.'

He watched as Tony looked a bit surly, then walked off behind Jimbo towards the car.

As Sharon drove up the deserted country road, she could see the long low sprawl of the warehouse in the distance. She hadn't passed any cars on the road, and that freaked her out a bit. She'd been hoping to see some sign of under-cover cops or anything that would give her the comfort of knowing they were close by. Her gaze travelled the breadth of the landscape, but she could see nothing. There was a derelict farmhouse and outhouses a couple of hundred yards away, so maybe they were in there. But it looked too far away to give her any faith that they could spring into action and help her once Knuckles decided what he would do. As she got closer to the gates she could see a couple of Knuckles' thugs on patrol.

'I'm only about fifty yards away from the entrance now. Can you hear me?'

She was relieved when Vinny's voice came back.

'Yeah. We hear you. And we've got your exact location. Don't speak any more now.'

'Okay.'

She didn't want to say she was crapping herself because she couldn't see any sign of them, as it was all a bit late for that. She took a sip from a bottle of water and drove towards the entrance. The boys recognised her and one of them spoke on a walkie-talkie, then he and his mate pulled open the big steel wire gates. As she drove through, she could see in her rear-view mirror that they didn't close them again. The shipment must be coming at any minute. She drove up to the entrance and parked the car, and as she was switching off the ignition she spotted Knuckles coming out of the warehouse into the fading late-afternoon light. She saw him looking straight at her, his eyes dark and his forehead knitted in a frown. She took a breath, steadied herself and got out of the car. She glanced around, wondering if anyone was going to approach her and frisk her. She stood at the car, about thirty feet away from Knuckles, and said nothing. Then Jamie came out of the warehouse and looked at Knuckles, who nodded him to go towards her. This was it. If he found anything, there would be no discussion, no last-minute blaming of each other, no rows. She'd be shot dead on the spot. She braced herself. Jamie motioned her to raise her arms. She did. She could feel him frisk along her arms, then her waist, and then he caught her eye as he made her turn around and felt around her waistline and the top of her thighs back and front. He turned to Knuckles and shook his head. She let out a breath. Knuckles walked slowly towards her until he was standing a few feet away. As he walked, she could see the outline of his revolver shoved into the waist of his trousers.

'So. You're not a ghost then, Shaz?' he snarled.

'That's no thanks to you,' she snapped back, sticking out her chin, defiant. She knew Knuckles wouldn't expect anything else.

He glared at her without speaking, then she saw him look her up and down.

'You stole my fucking money.'

Sharon raised her eyebrows. 'You tried to have me murdered by your thugs.'

He puffed. 'You think that makes us even?'

Sharon looked at the ground, feeling the adrenalin pumping through her body, trying her best to buy time, because this could blow up at any minute. She knew the short fuse Knuckles had if he was under threat.

'You know something, Joe,' she said, trying to sound

calm and hurt at the same time, 'we'll never be even. No matter what. *You tried to have me murdered.* We have a son together. We had a life, a family. And you sent me out of our house that day to my death. We will never be even.'

Knuckles said nothing, but she could see the red rise in his neck.

'You were nothing when I met you. I gave you a fucking life you'd never have had.'

'Don't give me that shit, Joe. I had your back every bloody day and night. I took our son to visit you in bloody jail when he was a little boy, and spent the rest of the week explaining to him that you were on a fucking business course and would be away for a while. I protected you. I hid your money, everything you did.'

For a long moment he stood there and said nothing.

'Yeah, you hid my fucking money all right.' He shook his head. 'So cut all this crap and hand over all the information you took so I can get my money back. Every last fucking penny of it.'

'Where's Tony? I want to see him.'

'I sent him home. He's fine.'

'I want to talk to him.'

'No. You've already talked to him. The talking is over.' He put his hand out. 'Give me the USB drive with all the shit on it that I need. Hand it over.'

She stood looking straight at him but said nothing. Then they both heard the sound of the truck coming in towards the gate. He looked over her shoulder and she turned her head to see it.

'My shipment.'

'I know,' she replied. 'It was me who organised it. It was always me who organised it, went to Amsterdam, did all the work so you wouldn't get your hands dirty.'

'Shut it. Stay where you are. Don't move.'

As the truck pulled up, Knuckles walked across to it and Sharon watched as the driver jumped down from the cabin and came to the back of the truck. He shook Knuckles' hand, and two more men appeared from the warehouse and approached the truck. Sharon watched, wondering what was going to happen next. Was he going to unload the gear and then bump her off? Where were the bloody cops? She tried not to look away from the truck in case she aroused any suspicion. The driver talked away to Knuckles as he undid the bolts and locks and bashed a couple of levers so he could slide the locks down and release the doors. Sharon could see the doors begin to open. Then, as the other two men from the warehouse dragged the doors fully open, they stepped back coughing. She took a couple of steps towards where everyone was standing, then she saw Knuckles in front of the wide open doors, his face drained of colour.

'Fucking hell!' she heard him shout. 'Fucking hell!'

He covered his nose with his hands. And as the foul, sickly stench came towards her, she put her hand to her face as she took a step closer. She was only a few feet away now, and in the darkness of the truck she could see it was full of various boxes and furniture. But as she strained her eyes, she gasped when she saw the body of a pale little boy lying still on the floor in the arms of a young woman. Beside him lay a little girl held by a young man, all of their faces white with the pallor of death.

'For fuck's sake!' Knuckles screamed. 'How the fuck did they get in there! Jesus fucking wept! Fucking refugees! Get them out of here!'

His words were barely out when suddenly a battery of lights blazed and sirens blared as cars and vans sped up towards them through the gates and screeched to a halt. Knuckles and his cohorts had no chance to see what was happening; they stood, dazed and confused, looking from the corpses in the truck to the armed police now piling out of their vehicles and racing towards them pointing their rifles. Sharon looked on, shocked, rooted to the spot as she saw the cops roughly take the men and make them kneel on the ground. Then Knuckles turned around and looked straight at her, his eyes full of menace and rage. She stared him down, defiant. And just as she did, he staggered back as a bullet hit him square in his head and he crumpled to the ground. All the officers dropped to the ground, screaming, 'Get down, get down!' their weapons raised. Sharon dropped to the ground. This wasn't mean to happen. Or if it was, nobody told her. She could hear an officer radioing for an ambulance, as she saw Knuckles lying on his back, blood seeping out of his head and running down his face, his eyes wide open in shock. Somewhere inside her, she wanted to go over and kneel beside him, to speak to him one last time. But she couldn't. He was gone.

# CHAPTER FORTY-SEVEN

Kerry watched as the car that had picked up Sharon from the warehouse came speeding towards her. At that moment, her mobile rang, and she saw Danny's name.

'Danny. How did it go?'

'It's done. Jake dropped him. I let him do it. He wanted it as much as any of us. Single bullet in the head. Perfect.'

For a second, Kerry didn't answer. Her first instinct was happiness; Knuckles Boyle, the bastard who had her brother executed, who sent gunmen to his funeral where her mother died in a hail of bullets, was dead. She hadn't fired the gun, but she felt as though she had. She hadn't told Vinny it would happen, and she hadn't told Sharon. She hadn't issued the order to kill, but she knew that unless she'd told Danny not to, then it would go ahead. And now, she saw the pale, shocked face of Sharon as she got out of her car. Kerry had stood by and allowed the father of her child to be gunned down. She braced herself.

'Good job, Danny. I have to go. I'll see you later. Tell Jake well done.'

She put the phone on the dashboard as Sharon came around the front and threw herself into the passenger seat.

'Jesus Christ, Kerry!' Her voice quivered. 'You could have told me.'

Kerry's face was impassive, her voice controlled.

'No I couldn't, Sharon. That's not how it works.'

'But we're supposed to be partners.'

Kerry was silent for a moment, then she looked at Sharon and could see her face was about to crumple.

'We're partners now, Sharon. But what happened to Knuckles was personal. I couldn't let that go. My mother died in my arms because of him. He was never going anywhere but straight to hell. And if the cops hadn't weighed in when they did, you'd probably be dead by now. You must know that yourself.'

Sharon said nothing, sniffed and wiped the tears from her cheeks. She nodded.

'I know. It was . . . It was just something about him today. He was still the same angry, vicious bastard with that look in his eyes, but it was as if he had softened when he talked about Tony. Maybe I was just imagining it, but part of me – and I hate myself for this – part of me wanted him to say he was sorry for trying to get me murdered and ask me to go back to him, to be a family again. Somehow I thought maybe he was ready to change.' She shook her head. 'I know he wasn't. But I . . . I just feel awful.'

Kerry squeezed her arm.

'You'll be fine. Come on. Let's take you to your son.' She tapped the driver on the shoulder. 'Give Eddie directions from here. It's over now, Sharon. This is a new beginning.'

They drove out of the car park and onto the main road in silence, then Sharon spoke.

'There were dead people in the back of the truck when it arrived. Christ! It was awful. The smell. Two little kids . . .'

'What? What you talking about?' Kerry said, bewildered. 'Dead people?'

'Yes. Refugees, they must have been.'

'Christ almighty! How did that happen?'

'It happens, I suppose. You see it on the news. They must have stowed away when the driver wasn't looking. But they must have suffocated. Jesus! There was a wee boy in a woman's arms, and a little girl held by her father, probably. All of them dead. And the stench of death . . . Jesus!'

'What did the cops say?'

'I don't know. It all happened so quickly. The doors were pulled open and I saw the shock on Knuckles' and the guys' faces. Then suddenly the cop cars come racing up with guns pointing, and then, before anyone knew what was happening, Knuckles got hit. Then the car came for me.'

'Did you see Vinny?'

'I don't know. They all had ski masks on. Like a SWAT team or something.'

Kerry nodded slowly and looked out of the window at the landscape as they headed along the motorway.

Cal and Tahir waited with Jack in the hall of the Casey house. He had gone to Jack after the news emerged on TV about the dead refugees in the back of a truck from Europe believed to be carrying a shipment of smuggled cocaine. He'd been with Tahir when the news had come on, and although they didn't see pictures of the perished family, Tahir had become hysterical. It took Cal all the strength he could muster to control him and stop him from going to the barber shop to kill the Turk. Cal had pleaded with him to wait until he spoke to big Jack, that he would know what to do next. And anyway, they had to wait to have the names of the refugees or anything that would identify them. He was heartbroken as he watched Tahir go to pieces. Now they sat outside after talking to Jack who had promised them a meeting with Kerry Casey. Cal wasn't sure what she would say, but if she fobbed them off then he would take things into his own hands.

Tahir and Cal sat in the study and looked up as Kerry came in. She nodded to Cal, and glanced at Tahir, giving him a sympathetic look. She went around the table and put her hand on his shoulder. Then she stretched her hand out and he stood up.

'Tahir. I'm Kerry Casey. I'm so sorry for your loss.'

Tahir's eyes filled with tears and he wiped them with his sleeve as she motioned him to sit down. She sat opposite him and Cal, then glanced from one to the other.

'Jack has told me everything you told him, so we are trying to run down who exactly is behind the smuggling and how this happened. We'll find out.'

'I want to kill the Turk,' Tahir said, sniffing. 'He is like a murderer. He took my money and told me he would bring my family safely – a safe passage, he said. And now this. I will never see them again. I tried phoning the Turk but he won't take my calls. Bastard.'

'Okay,' Kerry said, calmly. 'I understand how angry you must be. But if you go into things in a fit of blind rage, you will get yourself killed. Both of you. So listen to me. I will have my own people look at this, and we'll see where we go. The Turk at this end – of course he's partly guilty, but the people who put or helped put your brother onto the truck are the people we want to get. They are taking people's money, so they should know that a truck like that is not safe. Let me see what I can find out first.' She looked from one to the other. 'Now, it's important that neither of the two of you do anything at the moment.' She glanced at Jack. 'Jack will take you out for a bite to eat, then take you home. We'll be in touch.'

It was just after five in the morning when Frankie Martin got off the bus at Buchanan Street station, his head thumping. He buttoned up his Crombie coat against the biting wind and kept his head down as he walked quickly through the concourse and into a taxi. He could see the driver glancing suspiciously at him in his rear-view mirror, and he wasn't surprised. He looked like shit. Unshaven, and still with some congealed blood in his hair, and his trousers and shoes muddy from traipsing through the field until he got to a village where he could get transport to the nearest place that would take him back to Glasgow. The closest was a bus station in Kendal where the city link buses stopped en route from Manchester to Glasgow. He'd sat at the back of the bus, shivering and exhausted, but with a feeling of dread in his gut. He had to get to his flat as quick as possible, get some more money, his passport and some clothes and get out of town. Kerry Casey would know by now that it was him who kidnapped Sharon, and she'd have worked out that he was spying on her. There was nothing left for him here except a bullet in the head. And he wasn't going to allow that to happen. He'd be in Spain by tonight. He still had friends there. He could lie low, until this all blew over. Give Kerry Casey enough time to fuck up the business, then he would come back and take over. Frankie Martin wasn't finished yet. Not by a long shot.

# CHAPTER FORTY-EIGHT

Danny had set up the meeting with Pat Durkin and Billy Hill, but Kerry would be running the show. She knew she didn't have to spell that out to Danny. She could sense he had been impressed by how she was growing into her role as head of the family. But she'd left the arrangements and venue up to him. And the security. Given that Knuckles Boyle had already sent his thugs to Glasgow to murder not once but twice, Danny said you couldn't be too careful. Durkin and Hill might say they come in peace, looking to do business, but the Caseys had to be prepared in case the bastards came out shooting. Pat Durkin Junior was a loose cannon, by all accounts, and anything could happen. He had initially invited Kerry to the Shelbourne Hotel in Dublin for the meet, and though it was a swish venue in the middle of the city, Danny had said the Irish mob would have no qualms about causing mayhem there. In the past few months, in an ongoing war between two rival families, there had been at least four very public and bloody assassinations. Durkin and Hill were told the meet would be in Glasgow – take it or leave it.

Kerry stood scrutinising her image in her bedroom's full-length mirror. In her black slim-fitting suit, tight blue blouse and ankle boots, she looked as slick as she would if she were walking into any corporate meeting as the high-powered lawyer she was. But that was not who she was any more. Her cornflower blue eyes looked back at her. She was a gangster now, and about to go into a summit to offload three container-loads of cocaine to a couple of Europe's most wanted drug kings. She was okay with that, though. She'd done her soul-searching. From her window she saw the Mercedes pull into her backyard, and Danny and Jack get out. It was time.

They drove into the car park of One Devonshire Gardens. Danny had chosen there because he knew the place back to front, and the staff knew who he was, so they'd be discreet and accommodating. Plus, it was better than any kind of city centre location where someone could walk into the foyer and shoot you. The meeting would be in a boardroom at the back, and Danny had armed men posted discreetly all over the car park and inside the hotel. They got out of the car, and one of his security men came forward.

'They're already here,' he told Danny as they climbed the

steps, pointing across the car park. 'Three cars over there. The Range Rover and the two Mercs. Four of them have gone inside. Durkin, Hill, and two others. Not sure who they are. They're waiting in the lounge. I've got two of our guys on the roof, guns pointing at the cars in case they start any stupid shit. We're well covered here.'

Kerry waited outside as Danny went in first. She could see them all through the stained glass window of the lounge, Danny greeting the men as they stood up. Then they came out to the foyer, and headed towards the room at the end of the corridor. Kerry was waiting until they were in the boardroom, and then she would make her entrance. She stiffened her shoulders, strode up the steps into the hotel and down the corridor, her guard at her back, and turned the handle. As she walked in, all four of them stood up: Pat Durkin, thick-set, his ruddy complexion and podgy face giving him the look of an overgrown baby with bright smiling blue eyes. Billy Hill, older, sophisticated, with a shock of unkempt blond hair and a suntan that had been built up over months spent soaking up the proceeds of crime far away from his London empire. He flashed a six-grand smile, and Kerry raised her eyebrows in acknowledgement. But she was most conscious of the man on Durkin's right, eyeing her up. A tall, lean, handsome man with a Mediterranean look about him with his designer stubble and lush black hair. A small, squat, sallow, low-browed man with blank dead eyes stood by his side. Kerry eyed Jack who stood against the wall, arms folded. He gave a slight shrug.

'Kerry, this is Pat Durkin and Billy Hill,' Danny said.

'How you doing,' Kerry said, reaching out to give a firm handshake.

'A pleasure to meet you, Kerry,' Hill said. 'I've been looking forward to meeting the woman who brought down that fat fucker Knuckles Boyle.' Hill's cockney accent could have cut glass.

Kerry's face showed nothing.

'How you doing, Kerry.' Pat Durkin's hand was soft and fleshy, and a little sweaty.

'I'm good,' Kerry said, without a smile.

She looked in the direction of the dark-haired man. Durkin stretched his hand in an introductory gesture towards him.

'And this is Pepe Rodriguez,' he said. 'He's an associate of mine, and we work together in Spain. He's from Colombia. We do a lot of business with the Colombians these days – supply and transport.'

Kerry didn't shake his hand. She could sense Danny watching her as she glared at Durkin.

'I don't do business with the Colombians,' she said. 'I came here to meet you two. That's all.' She glared from Durkin and Hill.

The Irish man's baby face fell as though someone had pulled the toy out of his hand. Hill looked surprised.

The Colombian's eyes darkened. He turned to his friend and said something in Spanish, which Kerry immediately understood.

'*La dama es un tigre – exactamente como me gustan mis mujeres*' – 'The lady is a tiger, just the way I like my women.'

Kerry immediately snapped back in Spanish.

'*Hablo español con fluidez. No seas sabihondilla.*' – 'I speak fluent Spanish. Don't be a smart-arse.'

The Colombian drew his lips back in a smile that was more of a warning that he wouldn't forget this moment. Kerry could feel her heart beating hard in her chest, but she wasn't afraid.

Durkin stepped in.

'Okay, guys, listen. We're not coming here to fuck about. Let's just sit down and talk.' He turned to Kerry. 'You don't have to work with the Colombians. What you are here to do is to sell your gear to us. And we're willing to buy. Is that the set-up? Anything that happens after that, and believe me we would love to work with you, will be for later. Let's not fall out, Kerry. We're all reasonable people.'

Kerry moved towards the table. From the corner of her eye she could see Danny, looking a little amused. They all sat down.

'So,' Hill began, 'anyway, as I said, we're all grateful to have Knuckles out of the way. And by the way, Kerry, condolences for your mother's death, sweetheart. That was a fucking scandal, that was. But it just shows you the measure of that Knuckles prick. And of course Mickey's death. Well, that was one of those things. Mickey was a difficult man to work with, Kerry, I'm not going to lie to you. He was storing up trouble for himself all the time.'

'Mickey was nothing like me,' Kerry said quickly. 'Not in any way. Things in our organisation are going to be done differently now.'

'Yes,' Durkin enthused. 'I hear you're going into the hotel business. In the Costa del Sol?'

Kerry nodded. 'Yes. Work is about to get under way.'

Durkin shook his head and looked wistful.

'Bastard of a place to work in, Spain, with the officials and red tape. The Spaniards are as slow as fucking treacle, and they create problems all the time. You'll need some help to get round that. I have a lot of friends on the inside down there, Kerry, I'll be happy to smooth the way for you.'

Kerry looked at him, deadpan.

'Yeah? In return for what?' she said.

'Christ, you're direct, aren't you?' Durkin made a surprised face at Hill.

'Yes, I am.'

'Well, me and Billy here, we have a lot of property interests in the Costa – all over Spain, and Portugal actually. Few problems after the timeshare business went tits up and some of our lads got banged up. We lost some money, but we're coming back big time over there. We've got apartments, bars, restaurant interests. But a big fuck-off hotel ... now that would really be something.'

'Yeah. It is. And it's something for me. It's exclusive. I'm doing it for my organisation. Alongside other property interests I'm pursuing.'

'Just saying, sweetheart,' Hill piped up. 'If you want any investors as your costs mount up.'

'That's taken care of. And please don't keep calling me sweetheart.'

Hill grinned at Danny, who remained poker-faced.

'Oh, sorry ... swee ...' His voice trailed off.

Durkin was quiet but Kerry could tell he was irritated. He wouldn't be used to this kind of blatant arrogance from a woman.

'Well,' Durkin said. 'Security. You'll want to watch the security down there. Lot of real thugs and villains, from the thieving Moroccans to the Albanians.'

Kerry was conscious that Rodriguez had been staring at her and sensed his simmering wrath.

'And Colombians,' he sneered. 'But we always come in peace. To begin with.'

Stony silence. Kerry stared him out until he looked away. She could feel sweat trickle down her back.

'Anyway,' Durkin said. 'That aside. You've got these truckloads of stuff you want off your hands pronto, Kerry. So let's talk.'

'It's quite straightforward. Three containers, all offloaded and in a safe place. Here's my price. Two million. Pounds, not euros. It's below the market and you're getting a good deal – given that you didn't have to bring it in yourselves.'

Durkin looked at Hill, whose mouth turned down a little.

'That's a bit steep, Kerry,' Hill said. 'Especially if you're keen to offload it quickly.'

Kerry clasped her hands together and sat forward.

'You don't want it, I can move it elsewhere.'

'Where? I thought you wanted out of this business?'

'As I told you,' Kerry said, 'my business is going to be different in future. But that doesn't have to be today or tomorrow. It's a plan I have. I want to move this gear on, but if you don't want what I've got at this price, then I will move it elsewhere. That won't be a problem.'

'You know, Kerry,' Hill said, twirling the heavy diamond ring on his finger, 'you should take things a little easier here. I know you're young, and you're nothing like Mickey. He was impetuous and impatient, and quick to anger. And it didn't make him friends. You need friends in this business. I think you could make friends if you just comply a bit.'

'I don't like where Mickey took my family,' she replied. 'I wouldn't even be sitting here if it wasn't for him. This is not what my father wanted.'

'Ah, come on now,' Hill said. 'That's the world we live in. Everything is business. You think all these hotels and restaurants just got there by themselves? It's all money-laundering. We have so much money and so much flow and so much demand, you'd be a fool to turn your back on what we could do together.'

'Spot on, Billy,' Durkin said.

'I hear what you're saying, Billy, Pat. But that's what I'm doing.'

'It's not just as easy as that,' Durkin said, shifting in his seat. 'Mickey dealt with a lot of people, and there are a great many tentacles to the organisations he was involved in. You need to be aware of that.' He paused for effect. 'And, also, there are debts too.'

Kerry's gut stirred.

'What do you mean, debts?'

'Well, for a start, he was director in a few of our business interests. We still have an interest in your organisation.'

'Not on any papers I've seen.'

'Precisely,' Hill said. 'But they are on our papers.'

Kerry could feel rage inside, but she had to control it. She caught the Colombian staring at her as though she was prey.

'Tell me about it,' she said.

'Your casino, saunas, your apartments in Edinburgh, and three quayside penthouses in Liverpool. They're all part of our organisation. We have to think about that.'

'Well then, first, I need to see these papers. Then I'll have my lawyers look at it and we'll work something out. But the deal will be done with the money from the cocaine sale – nothing more. Once you pay for that at a price we agree, you have no more interest in any part of my organisation. Understood?'

'Yeah, sure. But we are interested in your hotel. We could make some job of that if we worked together.'

'That's not up for discussion.' She could feel her face burning.

Silence.

'Well,' Hill said. 'Not yet. Let's go back to your lawyers and see how we go. I'm sure we can work something out in your businesses if you want to buy us out of them. And the coke. Sure. We'll take that.' He glanced at the Colombian. 'You can take care of that.'

'I told you, I don't work with the Colombians,' Kerry snapped.

'Then you should be very careful, *querida*.' The Colombian's tone was cold and threatening.

Kerry glared at him. Darling. Bastard's calling me darling. '*¡Que te jodan!*' she snapped – 'Go fuck yourself!'

A few minutes later, they were coming out of the building, shaking hands. This time Kerry did shake the Colombian's hand, and when he held it too firmly, she pulled away and glared at him.

'I hope to see you again, Kerry.' He bared his teeth like a smiling assassin.

She didn't answer, but she had a feeling she hadn't seen the last of Pepe Rodriguez.

# CHAPTER FORTY-NINE

Kerry saw Vinny at the corner table in La Lanterna where they'd sat the first time they'd had lunch together. He looked up as the waiter led her over, then stood, a smile spreading across his handsome face. For a moment, as he kissed her lightly on the cheek, Kerry felt a twinge of regret that their lives were so different that nothing real and wholesome or even normal could ever come of the relationship they had embarked on over the past few weeks. She had known from the start, even before they fell into bed together for the first time, that it could never really go anywhere. But somehow the reality had got lost in all the activity going on, between her helping him nail a massive drugs bust, turn a blind eye while Sharon disappeared, then all the various mopping up Kerry's own organisation had to do. Knuckles Boyle was gone now and his operation in the north of England was in tatters. Already the hoodlums were circling the spoils like hyenas, fighting over turf, but they would never be a match for the Durkins or the London mob who were picking them off one by one. Kerry didn't want to tell him that she'd had a meet with the Durkin and Hill mobs on her own turf. She was still smarting from that, and the menacing way they slipped in the line that they still had business tied up with the Casey empire. She hadn't expected that, and Marty was already going over the papers they had made available. At the moment, the deal with the coke was still on the table, but she hated the idea that the Colombian was anywhere near it. Pepe Rodriguez gave her the creeps, and she'd be glad when this deal was done and she was well rid of all of them. The cocaine sale would bring in a fortune, and Kerry promised herself it would be the last drug deal the Caseys would ever do. They'd made it clear they were keen for a piece of the action in her hotel plans, and the talk of security being a problem was a veiled threat from them. But she vowed they would never get their grubby hands on her hotel. However, she had to play it vague, promising to meet them on the Costa del Sol some time, once things looked like getting off the ground. But she would never be their puppet.

She was leaving tomorrow for Spain, and it was time to tell Vinny.

'You look fantastic, Kerry,' he said, sitting down, pouring them wine. 'When I saw you a week ago, I thought you were tired-looking, drained.'

'I was,' she replied. 'And you looked a bit knackered yourself.' She raised her glass. 'But it's all over now.'

He raised his glass. 'What will we drink to?'

'A lot to celebrate, Vinny. For one thing, you'll be getting promoted with your big drugs bust. You'll end up running the show.'

'Aye, stuff that. I like doing what I do – organising, getting my hands dirty, taking down arseholes like Knuckles Boyle.'

They looked at each other and the irony wasn't lost on either of them – what Vinny did was take down gangsters, sure, like Knuckles Boyle. But her family had supped from the same trough.

'Well, we can drink to better days. The Casey organisation has big plans,' she said.

'Yeah?'

'Yep. We're moving into property. Restaurants, hotels, building houses. I'm cashing it all in, Vinny. I'm investing a lot in Spain. Building a hotel there. All in the planning, but the deal has been done.'

He looked crestfallen.

'You're moving to Spain?'

'Not permanently. But I'll be back and forth. Sharon will run things a lot over there. And we'll have trusted staff from here as well as locals on the ground.'

He sighed. 'You know what these things are like, Kerry. Every gangster from Murcia to Marbella will be crawling all over it, wanting a piece of the action.'

She shook her head.

'They won't be getting it. This will be a high-end hotel, no riff-raff, and certainly none of the thick-neck thugs in suits you see all over the Costas. I'm building apartments too – in Spain and here.' She watched as he went quiet, sipped his drink. 'I know what you're thinking. That it's all dirty money anyway.'

'I didn't say that.'

'But you're thinking it. And who cares. I work with what I have, with what I was left with. It's not about the past now, Vinny. It's about the future.'

He looked down at the table then straight at her, his eyes piercing.

'What about us?'

Kerry said nothing, but she knew he could see it in her face.

'What can we do, Vinny? We came from the same street almost, but we live in different worlds. It's . . . It's . . .' She sighed. 'I don't know. It seems impossible. Where can we go with this, with what we have? You know the answer as well as I do.'

He nodded slowly. 'I know. But it doesn't make it any easier.' He frowned and reached across the table. 'This wasn't just a fling for me, Kerry. It wasn't just something for old times' sake. I . . . I have feelings for you. I want you to know that. I always did. I should have fought for you all these years ago. I should have fought Mickey for you.'

Kerry swallowed hard.

'Jesus, Vinny. Don't make this worse. I know that. And I feel the same way. But we have to be realistic.'

'So,' he said. 'After tonight. I won't see you any more?'

'I'm going to Spain tomorrow. For a little while. Not sure how long. I'll be back though. But . . .'

'This is the part where you say, but we can still be friends.'

She half smiled, but inside she was gutted.

'We'll always be friends.'

The waiter came up and stood at the table to take their order.

'I haven't even looked at the menu yet,' she said. 'But tell you what. Let's have what we had that first time in here. It was great. And the same wine.'

'My thoughts exactly.' Vinny ordered and when the waiter left them he reached across and put his hand in hers. 'This is not goodbye, Kerry. I'm not saying goodbye.'

She looked at him and he held her gaze and she wished he was right, but tomorrow afternoon she would be in another country, wrapped up in another life, where there was no room for a man like Vinny Burns.

Sharon slipped into the bedroom and stood in the darkness watching Tony as he slept. She listened to his gentle, rhythmic breathing, remembering how she used to do this when he was a baby, when she would gaze lovingly at him and wonder what his life would be, where all of them would be in years to come. Now there was just the two of them. When she'd broken the news about his father's death, Tony had said nothing for a few moments, then he'd started to cry. She'd held him, and between sobs, he told her that the last day with his father had been the happiest he'd ever been with him. I know, Sharon told him, but he would want you to be a strong boy, and be the best you can. She would never tell him that his father had tried to have her murdered. When Tony eventually went to bed, Sharon had sat in the darkness of their living room, nursing a mug of tea. Tomorrow, she would tell Tony that they were moving to Spain, for the next few months at least. It would be a new life, a new beginning. She had enough money to last her for a long time, but she would work with Kerry Casey, and together they would build their own empire. But it would not be built on fear or murder or smuggled drugs. It would not be run by the hard men like Knuckles Boyle who trampled their way to a fortune. But first, they had to make sure that the gangsters who were already sniffing around were left in no doubt that they were no longer running the show.

Cal was with Jack and Tahir as they were driven towards the barber shop. They pulled in behind the tenement into a back court, where Jack had told them to wait. They knew the Turk and his sidekicks came out at eight in the evening as they'd recced over several days. Tahir had tried to get in touch with him to ask what happened, he'd even left messages, but the Turk never answered. Jack had already had his men find out more about who was responsible at the Istanbul connection, and they had the names of two individuals. He already had Jake Cahill on it, and they'd be gone in the next few hours.

Cal wasn't nervous or scared when Jack handed him the gun. It had felt heavy the first time he'd held it a couple of weeks ago, when Jack told them he was giving them the chance of revenge. Tahir took it in his hand and examined it, and Cal noticed that he seemed to know his way around a gun. Now, as they waited, the Turk came out, along with two heavy-set men, who glanced at the car. Jack opened his driver's door and stepped out, then went towards the boot as though he was getting something out of it. Cal could see in the wing mirror that the men were watching them. Then Jack tapped the boot – the signal they'd agreed. Cal and Tahir got out of the car. Tahir pointed the gun at the Turk.

'Don't be stupid, son,' one of the men said.

'Shut up. Get out of the way. It's not you I want, it's him. Move.'

The guy stepped to the side a little and the Turk looked nervous. But swiftly, the minder went into his pocket and brought out a gun. Tahir was startled enough to take his eye off the Turk, when suddenly there was a crack and he was hit. Cal saw him drop, and automatically he turned his gun and shot one of the henchmen in the leg. He dropped to the ground, then Cal shot the second man. Then the Turk came towards him, and held the gun to Tahir's head. Cal stood, stunned for a second, then he almost instinctively fired straight at the Turk, who staggered back. Cal fired again, this time in the chest, and watched as blood pumped out, and the Turk's legs buckled as he keeled over. Jack came across as all three lay on the ground.

'Come on, Cal. Pick Tahir up. He's bleeding heavily.'

Cal and Jack picked him up and carried him to the car.

'You're okay, Tahir. You'll be fine.'

'We got him, Cal, didn't we? You got him, my friend.' Tahir clutched his hand.

'We did,' Cal said, feeling the cold clammy hand in his.

'Am I going to die?' Tahir asked.

'No. You're not going to die, man.'

Jack started the engine.

'Don't worry,' he turned to Tahir, 'we'll get you fixed up, son.'

'What we going to do?' Cal said. 'We can't take him to a hospital.'

'It's okay. I know where to take him. We have people who deal with this kind of stuff. You'll learn as you go along.'

The car sped out and into the main road and up the road out of the city.

'You did well, there, kid.'

Cal nodded. He did well. He wasn't even scared. Nothing would ever make him scared again.

# CHAPTER FIFTY

The dinner at Kerry's house was the first time she had sat around a table like this as head of the family. Looking at Marty, Danny and Auntie Pat, she remembered the old days when they'd been here with her father and mother, sitting long into the night while she listened to their laughter from the top of the stairs. Jack was here too tonight, a measure of how he had become one of her most trusted friends. John O'Driscoll had been sent to the Costa del Sol to keep an eye on things. The only one missing was the traitor Frankie Martin, but wherever he was, he would never sit with them again. At the end of the table sat Jake Cahill, nursing a whisky, chipping in now and again with stories of the old days. To look at him, Kerry thought, you would never know the dark world he inhabited. The fact that she knew it first-hand should make her shiver, but it didn't. She was glad Danny had suggested inviting him. She needed him on her side. This was as much a gathering to celebrate the future as the past. And Sharon, sitting across from Kerry, was going to be part of their plans to take the Casey empire to greater things. Now that they would soon get the green light from Spanish planning authorities, Sharon would be spending a lot of time on the Costa del Sol, to oversee the building of the new hotel complex and property deals. And Kerry was glad that Sharon had gained the respect from the others, as she'd been crucial to bringing Knuckles down. It took guts to do what she did, and loyalty.

Kerry had felt exhausted by the time she got there – a combination of the last few days, plus there was a pang of something like regret for the way it had ended with Vinny earlier in the afternoon. She pushed away the image of Vinny's expression as she told him there was nowhere for them to take the relationship. And really there wasn't. These days they were both in different worlds. They would have to live with that. And whatever pain came along with it would fade in time.

'I want to propose a toast,' Marty said, swirling his brandy glass.

All eyes turned to him, and Kerry enjoyed seeing him a little tipsy and relaxed, as he looked at her, his eyes twinkling. Earlier, he'd been proudly showing photographs of his six-year-old grandson, Finbar, who was appearing in his primary school play. It was good to see Marty relishing his own family, even if she'd always felt he was part of hers.

'To the Caseys.' He stood up. 'To my old friend Tim Casey who had dreams for his children and his family, as he'd every right to have. I think he will sleep easily now knowing that his beautiful, capable daughter has taken the reins.' He paused, swallowing. 'We've come a long way, Kerry – all of us around this table. And we know that not all of it has been easy or pretty. But the future is all yours, and I think your father, and of course your dear, beautiful mother, will be smiling down on you tonight, knowing the family is in safe hands. Here's to you, Kerry; to all that you are, and all that you will be.'

Kerry felt choked as everyone raised their glasses.

'To us.' Kerry raised her own glass. 'To the great things we will achieve in the memory of my father and mother.'

She swallowed as she saw Auntie Pat brushing away a tear.

The shrill ring of a mobile across the table broke the silence, and she saw Danny fish the phone out of his pocket and put it to his ear. From the corner of his eye, as everyone began to chatter, she noticed Danny's expression change. He covered one ear with his hand, his brows knitted in concentration, then he stood up and walked to the other side of the room, waving a hand to excuse himself. For a moment everyone looked at each other, not sure what was happening. The chatter stopped. They could hear Danny's muffled tones on the phone, and all eyes were on the door as it opened and he came back in, his face grey. He looked at Kerry, then Jake Cahill.

'Kerry. That was John on the phone. We have a problem. In Estepona. At the apartments where the gear is. There's been a shooting.'

'What? How? Nobody knew where we were,' Kerry said.

Danny shook his head.

'Somebody found out. Not from my boys. They're solid. But some bastards have tried to get in there tonight, and the boys shot two of them dead. They phoned John as soon as it happened. Colombian fuckers, two of them were. They said they were taking the gear. Just like that. Bastards. Tooled up, and shot one of our boys on the leg. But we took care of them.'

Kerry felt her stomach drop.

'Colombians? But how? I mean how could they know?'

'I don't know, Kerry, but we're on it. I've got the stuff on the move right now, and more lads with it.' He ran a hand over his face. 'But we have a problem down there and we're going to have to deal with it. John is pulling in some more people. But they'll be good lads. I want you to go down there, Jake.'

Kerry saw him flick a glance at Jake Cahill, whose face was impassive.

'We'll know more in the morning,' Danny said.

'Whose men were the Colombians? Have we got anything from the guys before they were shot?' As she said it, she knew deep down what the answer would be.

Danny's expression was grave.

'Aye. One of them, the driver, was Irish – Pat Durkin's mob. So we can guess whose men they are.'

'Pepe Rodriguez,' Kerry said.

The room fell silent.

# ACKNOWLEDGEMENTS

Switching to a new character is big challenge for me, so I've dug in, and hopefully created something readers will enjoy. But when I come out of the bunker after slogging away, I have a huge support network to keep me sane. Here are a few of them:

My sister Sadie who has always been there through the laughter and sometimes the tears. Matt, Katrina, and Christopher, who inspire and enthuse about everything I write. And Paul, who keeps my techno stuff right – and is off to begin his own new chapter in Australia. My brother Des, who always finds time to ask me about my novels and takes a great interest in my work. My cousins, the Motherwell Smiths, and the Timmonses, as well as Alice and Debbie and all their family in London. My cousins Ann Marie and Anne, Helen and Irene.

I am lucky to have so many close friends: Mags, Eileen, Liz, Annie, Mary, Phil, Francie, and journalists Simon, Lynn, Mark, Maureen, Keith, and Thomas in Australia. Also Helen and Bruce, Marie, Barbara, Jan, Donna, Louise, Gordon and Janetta, Brian and Jimmy, Ian, David, Ronnie, Ramsay, and globetrotter Brian Steel.

In Ireland, I am grateful to Mary and Paud, for their support, as well as Sioban and Sean Brendain. And in La Cala, Yvonne, Mara, Wendy, Jean, Maggie, Sarah and Fran – all of them who help promote my books on the Costa del Sol.

Thanks also to my editor Jane Wood for encouraging me to write this book, and to her assistant Therese Keating for her hard work. Also to Olivia Mead in publicity, and all the team at Quercus, who are the best.

And not least, the growing army of readers I'm so lucky to have. If it wasn't for them, I wouldn't be writing this.